Made To Be Yours

Yours In Seattle Book Two

Eve Sterling

ISBN-13: 979-8-88796-184-2

Cover design by: Eve Sterling
Photo: Canva Pro
Edited By:
Dee's Notes: Editing & Proofreading Services
Corbeaux Editorial Services

Printed in the United States of America

To all the Violets that still dream of getting their Dante.

TRIGGER WARNING

This book contains scenes with explicit sex, implied stalking, and violence against women.

This book may not be suitable for all readers.

PLAYLIST

"Crush" by Tessa Violet
"Treat You Better" by Shawn Mendes
"Please Notice" by Christian Leave
"Can't Fight This Feeling" by Bastille
"Clarity - Acoustic" by Foxes
"Treacherous (Taylor's Version)" by Taylor Swift
"Once in a Lifetime" by Landon Austin
"I Guess I'm In Love" by Clinton Kane
"When It Ends" by Avery Lynch, JORDY
"Goodbye My Lover" by Gabriella
"You Are The Reason" by Calum Scott
"You Set My World On Fire" by Loving Caliber, Selestine
"New Year's Day" by Taylor Swift
"I Was Made For Loving You" by Tori Kelly, Ed Sheeran

PROLOGUE

4 Years Ago . . .

Deep breath, Violet.

You can do this.

Deep, cleansing breath.

The brown door in front of me is plain and nondescript, exactly like every other door lining this long hallway, except for the numbers 2-1-2 stenciled in black, smack dab in the center. I check the number again on my room assignment just to be sure I'm in the right place. The only thing scarier than walking into this room and meeting the girl who will be my roommate for the next year would be walking into the wrong dorm room altogether. The embarrassment would be beyond painful.

I tuck the paper with my room assignment and class schedule back into my pocket and grip the handle of the suitcase at my side. Placing my other hand on the doorknob, I take one more deep breath to steady my frayed nerves and then push the door open.

The room in front of me is almost painfully empty with its white cinderblock walls, plain pine furniture, and bare mattresses. The only thing with any color at all is the girl at the far end, pulling bright yellow sheets from a box labeled bedding.

Her head jerks up at my arrival and her deep brown eyes grow large. My first thought is that this girl is tall. At least taller than my five feet, two inches, she must have a good six inches on me at least. Her skin is tinted a light brown that's leaning toward olive and looks absolutely flawless, which just makes me that much more aware of the pimple that popped up on my chin this morning. I fight the urge to lift my hand to hide the glaring red blemish. I knew I should have thrown some makeup on this morning, but I just figured I would sweat it off with all the boxes I'm going to have to haul up the stairs to get unpacked.

A smile stretches across the girl's face as she drops the sheet she was untangling back into the box and moves toward me.

"Hi, I'm Bianca Moreno but my friend's all call me B. You must be my new roommate?"

"Y-yes, hi. I'm Violet Daniels. It's nice to meet you." I extend my hand to her but before I can blink, she has me swept up in a bear hug causing me to let out a little squeak.

"It's so good to meet you. We're going to have so much fun this year." Thankfully, she lets me out of her embrace before her enthusiasm cracks one of my ribs. "I'm so excited! So, tell me about yourself. Where are you from? What's your major? Have you gotten your classes yet? I hope you don't mind; I was going to take the bed next to the window, but we can totally switch if you want."

The questions are being lobbed at me so quickly I can't keep track. "Um, there's not much to tell. I'm from Seattle,

I'll probably major in some kind of English specialty, yes, I got my classes with my room assignment, and um, no problem, I don't care which bed is mine. The one against the wall is great."

Bianca lets out a loud laugh. "Okay, you're good. If you can keep up with me, we're definitely going to have fun this year."

I shoot her a smile and pull my suitcase over to the bed that's not currently housing Bianca's boxes and set it down. Just as I'm about to head back downstairs to my car to get another box, I hear the door behind me crash open, causing me to swing around in fright.

Standing in the doorway is a large man holding onto a bulging cardboard box that looks like the bottom's about to fall out. I'm not quite sure how he fit through the door with it. His shoulders are so wide it seems like he has to squeeze them through the frame. I stand there, still as a statue, in my shock and mild panic that a man's just walked into our room without so much as a knock.

"What do you have in this box? Rocks?" His voice comes out in a low gravelly tone that I find unexpectedly pleasing. I wonder if I handed him one of my books if he would read out loud to me. I shake my head to clear myself of that silly idea as he continues, "Where do you want this, pumpkin?"

"Those are just art supplies," she answers before indicating that he should put the box down in the corner. He grunts while settling it into its new home, and I realize that this must be Bianca's father. They have the same coloring, same rich-brown hair and eyes. Eyes that are suddenly studying me when he turns back around.

"Hi, I'm Bianca's dad, Dante Moreno." He sticks out his hand and I hesitantly shake it, hoping he can't tell my palms have been nervously sweating since I pulled my car into the parking lot downstairs. This man looks nothing like my own father. Dante Moreno has to be at least fifteen years younger than Robert Daniels and let's face it, a whole lot better looking. His jaw is squared with just a hint of stubble on his chin and cheeks. There's not even a hint of gray in his short-trimmed hair to give away his age. How old could he possibly be?

"Hi, I'm Violet. It's nice to meet you." The presence of these two attractive people in the small dorm room is enough to make it painfully obvious that I'm, well . . . not. My skin is so fair that it feels like it burns the moment I step out into the sun. You can forget about laying out and getting a tan. My black hair is long and pin straight. No matter how much product I use or how long I spend with the curling iron, any volume I achieve falls right out within the hour. I would say I was mousy if it wasn't for my large blue eyes that I got from my father. I've been told on more than one occasion that they're my best feature.

Before my thoughts can make me feel any more insecure than I already do, I decide I better get a move on if I'm going to be done unpacking before nightfall. "I'm just going to head downstairs and grab some more of my stuff, I'll be right back."

"Are your parents here?" Mr. Moreno asks me, looking over my shoulder to the door of our room.

"Nope, it's just me. They had a previous engagement." I try to brush off the fact that they aren't here by telling myself it's for the best, and truthfully, it probably is. No matter how much I'd love to have parents here to help me move in, with mine, it would most likely have been a disaster. They would be nothing but critical and would probably say something to offend my new roommate and her father. The Danielses tend to look down on anyone that doesn't run in their same social circle and I really don't need to start off on the wrong foot with Bianca. She's stuck with me for the entire year after all.

"There's no one here to help you?" Mr. Moreno presses. There's a little frown of concern on his face and a crease in his brow that's more attractive than it should be.

"My dad had a business commitment and needed my mom with him. It's fine, I'm used to doing things on my own." I paste a smile on my face to show him I really don't mind but that only seems to make the little crease on his forehead deepen. If I'm being completely truthful, my dad knew about move-in day months ago and could have avoided scheduling anything today but something like this just doesn't rank high on his list of priorities against his high-paying clients. My father is a well-known corporate attorney and my mom is the socialite he married who seems to have a martini surgically affixed to her right hand. I rarely see her without it nowadays. I doubt she would even be able to set it down to help me lift a box.

"I'll go down with you and help," he says.

"You really don't need to do that." I hate causing other people trouble but I have a feeling that he won't let this go.

"If you do it by yourself it's going to take you all night, besides I really don't mind. I'm sure I can do with the exercise." He gives me a gentle, reassuring smile like he can sense that I don't want to put him out.

"That would be great, Dad, thank you so much," Bianca chimes in. Holy hell, I had forgotten she was even in the room with us for a second. "The faster Violet's stuff gets up here, the faster we can arrange our room and then find out where the parties are tonight."

Mr. Moreno lets out a groan that I'm pretty sure matches my own. Partying is not exactly on the top of my priority list. Sure, I want to have fun and experience all that college has to offer but my shyness and anxiety usually keeps me from most social activities. I can't seem to relax around strangers. But just like her dad, I have a feeling that Bianca isn't going to take no for an answer.

"Can you two not party the first night you're here? And if you do, don't talk about it in the presence of your old man."

"You're not old." The words slip out of my mouth before I even fully form the thought and I immediately slam my mouth shut, sure that I'm turning the color of bright-red embarrassment.

Great. Just great, Violet. Now he's going to think you have a crush on him. Which you totally do *not*.

Bianca just lets out a laugh and links her arm through my own like we've been best friends for years, not that we just met ten minutes ago. "Well, he's got seventeen years on us." She shoots a saucy look back at her father. "Don't worry Dad, we won't do anything you didn't do at our age."

He lets out another groan and shakes his head before his eyes settle on me. "Come on, kid, let's go get your stuff."

Him calling me a kid makes me frown a little but I shake it off and dutifully follow him out into the hallway and down to the parking lot, just grateful that I have someone that cares enough to help me at all.

Two Years Ago . . .

"Whose is this?"

I jerk my head up from where I'm setting the dining room table. Dante is standing across the small room holding up a copy of *The Count of Monte Cristo*. My copy.

"That's mine, actually, you can move it if it's in the way."

"Not at all, I was just curious. Are you enjoying it?"

"Yeah," I answer, continuing to lay the silverware around the small table, my eyes dutifully fixed to the task at hand. "It's actually the third time I've read it. This time it's for one of my classes."

"It's a great story."

I bring my eyes up to his oversized frame that's leaning against the sideboard. "You've read it?" I ask.

"What? You think just because I'm in construction that I don't read?" His face is stony as he looks at me, and I start internally freaking out. That's not at all what I meant. First, I would never judge who reads and who doesn't based on occupation. I've just never seen him with a book or heard him mention anything that he's read before. Second, I think he's playing down owning his own growing construction company plus the fact that he owns a dozen rental properties in the Seattle area. Including this one.

"No!" I practically shout in my panic to correct his misconception. "Not at all! I would never think that. I—"

He lets out a laugh, cutting off my desperate apology. "Relax, Violet, I'm just messing with you. I've got to keep you on your toes." He shoots me a wink that makes the butterflies that have taken up residence in my stomach flutter. I silently tell them to get it together. The butterflies and I are supposed to be working on getting rid of our teeny, tiny crush on Dante Moreno, not melting into a pile of goo at his feet.

"That wasn't very nice of you," I say, shooting him a glare that I'm sure I don't pull off.

"Sorry," he says while still chuckling, which certainly takes away from his apology. "I enjoy reading in my downtime, I find it relaxing to not have to think about work all the time. *The Count of Monte Cristo* has actually been one of my favorites since I was a kid, but I'm surprised you don't have an eReader," he says before joining me at the table. He grabs the remaining silverware out of my hand, his fingers brushing across mine, and I try to suppress the shiver that wants to run through my body. How am I supposed to move on from this stupid crush I've had for the past two years if when he touches me my body reacts that way?

"Oh, I do. I love my eReader. It's perfect for something like the latest thriller or romance but, I don't know, there's just something about the classics. I like being able to hold them in my hands and turn the pages. It's silly," I say, slightly embarrassed.

He shoots a smile my way as he finishes setting the table. "It's not silly. I get it. There's something about reading the classics as an actual book. It's how they were meant to be read."

Before I can respond, Bianca comes into the room carrying an enormous bowl of spaghetti and meatballs while Hollie follows behind her with a platter of garlic bread and a bowl of salad.

After we're all settled into our seats, plates piled high with carbs, Bianca taps her spoon against her glass, bringing us all to attention.

"Since this is our first night in our new house, I think it's only appropriate that we have a toast." We all raise our glasses, dutifully following her lead. "To the three of us, for kicking college's ass. We've made it halfway through ladies and I couldn't have found a better group of friends to join me on this journey." She bequeaths us all with a wide smile that's filled with warmth, and I can't help but think of how lucky I was to be matched with her as my roommate that first day. I don't know how school would have played out for me, but without a doubt, it would have only been a shadow of what I've experienced without her and Hollie at my side. "And to my dad. I can't thank you enough. Not only for letting us stay in this beautiful house while we finish up school but for all the love and support you've given me over the years. So many people in my art classes complain about their parents pushing them to change their majors and how jealous they are when I tell them how you've always supported me and how you're convinced that I'll be a success."

"I'm going to buy your first piece, it'll be priceless some-day," Dante interrupts, and I wonder, not for the first time, what it would be like to have someone that supportive in my life.

"To us!" Bianca finishes her toast with a flourish and we all clink glasses with a chorus of *here here*s and *love you*s.

We're just starting to dig into our meals when Hollie pipes in with, "This place is amazing, Mr. Moreno. And I really do appreciate you letting us move in here but I don't feel right not paying some kind of rent. You could make a mint on renting out this house in this neighborhood. I wish you would let me pay something for letting me stay here."

I'm not surprised she's brought this up, it's been a point of contention for her since Bianca suggested we move in with her. Bianca and I met Hollie our second day at Branson, she was assigned to the room two doors down from our own and helped us figure out the washer and dryer. It was embarrassing being an eighteen-year-old that couldn't wash her own clothes but we always had housekeepers to do that sort of thing at home. However, Hollie didn't make me feel bad about it, just matter-of-factly showed me how it worked, and since that day, the three of us have been inseparable.

Since day one, it's been obvious that Hollie doesn't like to take anything she perceives as a handout. She works hard in her classes and at her variety of part-time jobs to support herself. I've offered her money repeatedly but she's always refused.

I know that she's uncomfortable with Dante's generosity in giving us all a place to stay. Frankly, I wasn't exactly one hundred percent on board with allowing him to cover my rent either but the alternative was moving home or having my parents pay for a place and honestly, living here rent free would come with fewer strings attached than taking a handout from them. Besides, I really wanted to live with Bianca and Hollie.

"How many times have I asked you to call me Dante, Hollie?" He places his fork back down to the table and leans onto his forearms, his expression one of determination. I haven't spent a lot of time with Dante Moreno over the past few years but it's enough to recognize the fact that you're better off arguing with a brick wall than with him over this. "Bianca wouldn't be paying me any rent so what difference does it make if it's just her staying here or the three of you? Besides, you're actually doing me a favor, Hollie. Without you and Violet, Bianca would be living here all alone, and I want to make sure that she's safe. Sure, I'm only a few blocks away but that's not the same as having more than one person in the house. It just makes sense for the three of you to stay here together."

Hollie seems slightly appeased but still skeptical of this explanation. However, her practical side soon wins out and she flashes him a smile. "Well, when you put it like that, how can I refuse?"

"You really can't." He laughs. The conversation glides easily into less tense topics as I sip on my wine, enjoying the quiet evening with my friends and the man I've been secretly crushing on for two years. Hollie and Bianca are discussing one of Bianca's latest pieces for her advanced painting class when Dante draws my attention back to him. Doesn't he realize I've been trying to avoid him as much as possible? Every time I look at him, I'm sure he can see my feelings written all over my face.

"So, is *Count of Monte Cristo* your favorite book? You said you've read it three times."

"It's an amazing book and I love it but no, it's not my favorite." I take another sip from my glass, hoping to distract myself from his steady gaze.

"Let me guess, all you English Lit majors are the same, your favorite must be *Pride and Prejudice*."

A giggle bursts forth from my lips. "Why Mr. Moreno, are you stereotyping? I thought you were above such things." I raise my eyebrow up at him in a silent challenge.

He lets out a laugh. "You're absolutely right Miss Daniels, please forgive me."

"I guess I can't be too hard on you because you were close. My favorite isn't *Pride and Prejudice* but it is an Austen novel, *Persuasion*."

"I've never read it. I'll have to check it out."

"Sure," I say, barely suppressing an eye roll. I don't think there's any way in hell Dante Moreno, mans-man, is going to pick up and read a Jane Austen deep cut in his free time. "I'm not really surprised. It's not her most popular novel, obviously, but I think it might be her most romantic."

"Are you trying to tell me you're a romantic, Violet?" he asks teasingly. I'd love to admit that I'm a romantic at heart but I don't think with my parents' beliefs that I'm going to end up with the epic love story of my dreams.

"I'm not sure that's in the cards for me," I say, shrugging off his question.

"You're too young, you can't be this cynical already."

"My parents aren't exactly the type to let me have some kind of grand, romantic love affair. If my mother has her way, I'll be married off to one of their friends the day I graduate." He jerks his head back slightly, obviously surprised by my response. Neither Bianca nor Hollie are paying us any mind so I try to steer our conversation to topics that are safer than my parents' expectations. "So, tell me, what advice would you give a young cynic with all this time ahead of her?"

"Wait and hope."

Wait and hope? Did he just . . .

"'All human wisdom is contained in these two words: Wait and Hope.' Did you just quote *The Count of Monte Cristo* to me?" I can't help but grin at him. How does he remember that line?

"I told you it was one of my favorites. Just wait and hope, Violet. Things will work themselves out for the best." He shoots me a smile that riles up those butterflies again and leaves me desperately wanting to believe that he's right.

Three months ago . . .

I really hate this dress. It's like my mother sees something that she knows will be uncomfortable and automatically buys it to torture me. Normally I would just thank her for the dress and relegate it to the back of my closet, but I couldn't do that today since she's actually deigned to grace us with her presence. I should have just told her that the draped silk fabric was too heavy for an outdoor summer party but most of the time, it's easier to just do what she says than to argue with her. I tug at the high neckline again, trying to will some air circulation to run through this silver monstrosity.

I glance around the crowded backyard trying to spot someone to speak to while simultaneously avoiding my parents. I never would have invited them to this graduation party but Dante insisted we include all of our parents as well as any friends we wanted to invite. Hollie's mom isn't here and, in unkind moments, I wish my mother had stayed away as well.

My eyes inadvertently land on Dante as he stands chatting in a group of people that includes his ex-wife Amanda, and Bianca's boss from the gallery. It's a little unnerving to find his eyes already focused on me. It feels like every time I've caught sight of him today, he's been looking at me and it's making me feel self-conscious. I know the dress isn't great, but I didn't think it was *that* bad. I hope he thinks it's the warm weather that's causing my cheeks to flush and not his attention.

Before I can look away, he lifts his beer to me in a small toast and I raise the cup in my hand back at him before continuing my hunt for my friends.

"Violet, stop slouching it makes you look like a slob." I close my eyes for just a moment, steeling myself for the coming confrontation. I turn and open my eyes, facing the storm to come.

"Hello, Mother, I'm happy you could make it." I shouldn't be surprised that she's standing in front of me in a short cocktail dress wholly inappropriate for the setting, but somehow, I still am. She has one hand looped through the arm of my father who's dressed in a black bespoke suit and has his gaze glued to the phone in his hand. Her other arm is clutching her signature martini glass. I don't even know where she got that thing. The only drinks you can get here are in beer bottles or plastic cups. Could she have actually brought that with her?

Instead of responding to my greeting she continues on as if I haven't said a word, which is par for the course with her. "And couldn't you have made some kind of effort with your hair? Thank God I got you that dress or who knows what you would have shown up in. Frankly, I don't even know what we're doing here. Why have a graduation party when you're still going to school?"

I force myself not to sigh audibly. We've gone over this so many times. "I'm going to graduate school for my Master's, Mother. It's not the same thing."

"I just don't understand why you won't meet some of the perfectly acceptable young men I have lined up for you. You really should be concentrating on getting married and not wasting more of your time holed up with dusty books. All that reading is going to give you crow's feet and then you'll need Botox before you're thirty!"

"I know, Mother, I'm sure you've picked out some wonderful men, but I want to concentrate on my studies right now. We've talked about this."

"Robert, you try talking some sense into your daughter, this rebellious phase of hers is getting out of hand."

My father doesn't even bother looking up from where he's furiously typing away on his phone before answering, "Violet, don't argue with your mother."

"But Dad—"

"Mr. And Mrs. Daniels, it's so nice to finally meet you." I'm so caught up with my parents I didn't even notice Dante's imposing figure sidling up to our little group. I should feel relieved that he's taking the attention off of me but instead my stomach sinks. It's not a good idea to put yourself in the sights of Vivian Daniels.

"And you would be?" my mother rudely asks. I can physically see her nose raising into the air in disdain.

"Dante Moreno, Bianca's dad. I've heard so much about you both from Violet." I almost choke on that lie. Talking about my parents is not something I make a habit of doing. Even if I hadn't spent the past few years trying to avoid Dante to shake my crush, I would never volunteer information on the people who happened to birth me and not much else.

"Well, she hasn't said a word about you."

Instead of being offended, Dante just shakes it off, deflecting the obvious jab. "That's probably because she's much too busy to hang out with her friend's dad. I'm sure you're both proud of her for graduating Summa Cum Laude. I only wish my daughter had that kind of drive," he says while shooting them a kind smile.

How did he know I graduated with honors? Bianca must have told him because I know that I never mentioned it. I also know for a fact he's extremely proud of his daughter so he's obviously saying these things solely for my benefit.

"Yes, well what she'll do with a degree in English Literature, I don't know. At least if she had majored in something practical like business she could have gone to work for her father. Can you please explain to me what you plan on doing with your life, Violet?"

"I-I haven't decided, Mom. I might try to work for a publishing house or maybe I'll teach—"

"Teach?!" she practicality shrieks. I can feel eyes around the backyard turn our way, and I suddenly wonder if Dante has been keeping up his backyard. If not, maybe there's a sinkhole he hasn't found that will open up and plummet me to the sweet relief of death. Anything to get out of this situation.

Before my mother can cause more of a scene by going off on a tangent about how Danielses are made for more important things than teaching, Dante jumps in. "Mrs. Daniels, it looks like you could use a refill. If you head on over to the bar, they'll fix you up with another martini."

"It appears you're right, I could use another drink, especially in this heat. I'm not sure why this entire thing isn't inside," she says as she moves away from us toward her next drink, dragging my barely present father along behind her. The weight that's been sitting on my chest lightens slightly when they're no longer in sight.

"So, those were your parents." It's not a question but a statement of a sad fact. I want to apologize for their behavior. I want to tell him he didn't need to jump in and rescue me the way he did but the fact of the matter is, I'm glad he inserted himself. If Dante hadn't stepped in, I'm sure I would be in the middle of a scene right now, with every eye in the place staring at me, either feeling sorry for me or wondering what kind of idiot I am.

I should really thank him but instead I just answer lamely with, "Yeah."

"Come on, I have something for you." He grabs my elbow and starts steering me inside the house. It takes all my self-control to stop myself from wrenching my arm from his gentle grasp. The simple act of placing his hand on my body does things to me I don't want to analyze too closely. I've worked so hard to not think about Dante Moreno but it sometimes feels like a hopeless endeavor. With no effort at all, the man has lodged himself firmly into my head and every single interaction we have seems to embed him there more deeply.

We stop in front of a bookshelf in his living room with three small boxes wrapped in ribbon sitting on one shelf. He grabs one of the small squares and hands it over to me without a word.

"You got me a present?"

His body seems to freeze up for just a moment before he starts to fidget, placing his hands in the front pockets of his pants, then pulling them out again. Is he nervous about something?

"Those other two are for Bianca and Hollie. I got gifts for all three of you. It's nothing, really. Just something to celebrate your accomplishment. It's a big deal, graduating from college, I mean, I never did it. I was going to give them to you all later, but I thought you could use a little pick me up after what happened outside." He's rambling now and I wonder what has him so nervous.

I start to unwrap the box and notice that the ribbon is a light purple color. "A little on the nose with the ribbon, isn't it?" I ask jokingly.

He just gives me a shy smile. "I had to tell the boxes apart somehow, a violet ribbon for Violet seemed to make sense." I pull the top off the box and nestled inside the velvet-lined box is a delicate silver chain. Attached to the necklace is a closed silver book pendent with a large V etched into the cover.

I nearly let out a gasp, this isn't some generic present. He certainly didn't get the same thing for Bianca or Hollie. It's so personal and thoughtful, and just so . . . me. I look up from the necklace to see Dante studying my face intently, like he's worried that I might not like it.

"It's beautiful, Dante. It's perfect. Would you . . ." I hand the necklace over to him so that he can put it on me.

"Of course." He takes the delicate chain from my hand and moves behind me, brushing my hair off my neck and to the side. The moment feels private, almost intimate, as he draws the necklace around my neck and fumbles a little with the clasp before securing it. His hands rest on my shoulders for just a moment while I finger the charm that signifies that this man understands me more than my own parents.

I close my eyes, letting myself savor this one moment in time. It's one I know I'll both cherish and resent. The moment that showed me what being with Dante Moreno could feel like and reminding me it's something I'll never have. I know that I'm young enough to be his daughter and I've never forgotten the first day we met when he called me "*kid.*" I know that's all he'll ever see when he looks at me. A kid.

"What are you two doing in here?" My shoulders immediately stiffen and Dante's hands fall away from me. I can feel a coldness at my back, telling me he's taken a step away, removing himself from my orbit.

"I was just giving Violet her graduation gift, pumpkin. Why don't you go grab Hollie and you guys can have yours too." She lets out a high-pitched squeal and I can't help but laugh. No one loves surprises more than Bianca.

"Why don't I go get Hollie so your dad can give you yours now?" I head to the French doors that lead to the backyard and the rest of the guests. I need to get out of here, my emotions are a mess. How many times have I told myself that I had to get over this silly schoolgirl crush on Dante Moreno to no avail? It's painfully apparent now that if I don't make a genuine effort, I'm going to be hung up on this unattainable man forever. The time's come to walk the walk and move on. It won't be easy but there's nothing else for me to do.

ONE

VIOLET

"Hey, Violet! Wait up!"

At the sound of my name, I step out of the stream of students flooding the hallway and press my back against the wall, hugging my messenger bag of books and laptop against my body. I glance at where the voice came from and spy Tyler Crosson fighting the flow of pedestrian traffic to get to me.

Like myself, Tyler was an English major before graduate school, and we've shared a few of the same classes over the years. We've spoken sporadically and have always been friendly with one another, happy to share notes and study guides. This year we're both in the same Theory and Practice of Literary Criticism seminar. Believe me, the class is as boring as it sounds and that's coming from a literature nerd.

"Hey, Tyler, how are you?" He finally makes it to where I'm leaning against the wall and stops in front of me, a wide smile on his face, while the rest of the students of Branson College go about their business.

"I'm great, thanks. How are you liking Dr. Muzio's class so far?"

"Well, he's certainly . . . thorough."

Tyler lets out a laugh. "Yeah, I think he's boring as hell too. I was hoping that we could exchange notes, maybe get together and study. You know, join forces."

"Sounds like a good idea," I say.

"And maybe we could hang out sometime? You know, not just to study?"

Oh god, is he asking me out? Or is he just trying to find a study partner for this class? I'm so bad at this. Tyler Crosson is exactly the type of guy I should be going for. He's attractive enough in that boy-next-door type of way. With sandy blond hair, blue eyes, and that tall-but-not-too-tall height. I'm sure there are plenty of girls on campus that would be happy to go out with him. He's always been nice enough to me but unfortunately, I've never felt even the slightest twinge of attraction toward him.

I've dated here and there during my four years at Branson, but it's always been with guys that perused me and it's never lead to anything more than a few lackluster dates and some awkward fooling around. To be honest, there's really been nothing wrong with any of the guys I've dated. It's just that when I'm sitting there across the table from them at dinner, talking about getting drunk or where the big party is going to be that weekend, all I can think, besides how boring that all sounds, is they're not *him*.

I'm not naïve enough to believe that I'm actually in love with Dante Moreno. I don't know him well enough for that. This entire crush started with an intense attraction to an admittedly gorgeous man that showed me kindness on a day I was anxious and in need of help. Over the years, each little interaction I've had with him has deepened that attraction until I've placed him up on a pedestal as my perfect man. To be honest, it's a fantasy I'm sure not even Dante himself could live up to.

I've been telling myself that I need to move on for years but after the graduation party he threw a couple months ago, I decided to really make an effort to move on from the fantasy of Dante Moreno. Being hung up on him has been holding me back from maybe finding someone of my own and I really do want that for myself. I've started pulling back, not joining Bianca so often on outings with her dad, which she always invites me to. I've been concocting excuse after excuse the past few months, and frankly, I'm surprised she hasn't called me out on it yet.

Now that I've managed to put a little space between us, phase two of my plan is to get myself out there and start dating. There has to be someone out there for me who isn't my best friend's dad who will never see me as anything more than a child.

I've never been the type of person that needs to surround herself with tons of people. The small group of close friends that I keep have kept me happy over the years, but recently I've started craving more, the kind of emotional and physical intimacy that you can only share with a romantic partner. I want what I've only read about in romance novels. I'm twenty-three years old and have never had an actual relationship.

My mother has been trying to set me up for years with a long parade of my father's business associates and her friends' sons. She has them just waiting in the wings for when I finally cave to her constant nagging. Going out with one of her "socially acceptable" picks would certainly get her off my back but I'm afraid if I give her that inch, she'll have me sold to one for four goats and a blanket before the end of the night.

I suppose going out with Tyler would kill two birds with one stone. I can get my mother off my back and maybe find someone to help me move on from my little infatuation. What better way to put my plan into action than by agreeing to go out with Tyler? I mean attraction doesn't have to always be immediate, sometimes it can grow. At least, that's what I've read.

"That actually sounds great, Tyler, I'd like that."

"Yeah? Really?"

"You seem surprised," I say.

"Well, I feel like I've been dropping hints about asking you out for years and you've never seemed very interested. I figured I should finally bite the bullet and just ask or give it up once and for all."

"You have?" I ask in surprise. "I honestly had no idea. To be honest, I'm terrible with this kind of thing so you might have to be a little patient with me."

He shoots me a grin and runs his fingers through his messy blond hair. "I can do that. Is your number still the same from when we had Comp Lit last year?" I give him a nod and a smile. "Great. I'll text you so we can set something up." He reaches forward and I force myself to not flinch as he brushes away a strand of my hair that's fallen forward into my face. What can I say? I'm not used to people touching me.

My heart starts beating a little faster than it was before. Someone likes me! Someone nice who has the same interests as me. Well, reading at the very least. This could be the start of something. I told myself I was going to move on and I'm doing it. *Go me!*

"Listen, I've got to run to my next class but I'll text you soon."

"Okay, thanks," I answer, pulling the strap of my bag up higher onto my shoulder.

"Soon, Violet," he reiterates before turning and hustling down the hallway that's emptied of harried students.

Since that was my last class for the day and my adviser rescheduled our meeting I head home, stopping at the grocery store first. I want to celebrate this little step forward by doing some baking.

When I make it back to the house, I lay out all the ingredients that I'm going to need on our marble countertop before getting started. There's something that's so soothing about baking. With every step, every measurement, I can always feel my stress and anxiety washing away.

Admittedly, not all my forays into the baked arts have been unmitigated successes. I've made the occasional miscalculation or unfortunate substitution. Plus, I like to experiment with new flavors or with things we have on hand and those haven't always been . . . edible. I think that Bianca once renamed a batch of my triple chocolate chip cookies "Mini Salt Licks of Doom." To be fair, I did accidentally mix up the salt and sugar on that one but they *looked* delicious.

Just as I'm taking the golden-brown loaf of bread out of the oven, I hear the front door open and close. A few seconds later both Hollie and Bianca come into the kitchen, setting down their own bags of groceries.

"Oh no." Bianca lets out a groan. "She's baking. What have we done to deserve this?"

"Did we do something to upset you, Vi? Is this our punishment?" Hollie teases.

I can't help but laugh, from anyone else it might have hurt my feelings but I know that these two women have nothing but love for me. Besides, I can't deny that some—okay most—of my baking experiments have turned out badly and they are usually my unfortunate test subjects.

"You two better be nice to me, or I won't share," I say, eyeing the loaf of bread that's currently on the cooling rack. It really does look tasty if I do say so myself.

"Oh no, say it's not so," Bianca says in the most deadpan, sarcastic voice I have ever heard.

I answer by simply throwing the kitchen towel at her and laugh when it gets stuck on top of her head.

"Hey, did you guys see that they finally sold the house next door?" Hollie asks, drawing Bianca's attention from me before we can engage in a full-on towel throwing match. "There's a sign up."

Bianca makes her way to the kitchen window, presumably so she can see the proof for herself. "That place has been on the market for months. I'm surprised it didn't get snatched up immediately. It's not like this is a terrible neighborhood."

"I wonder who's going to move in," I say.

"With any luck, it will be three hot guys. One for each of us. We could use some eye candy in this neighborhood. If it's another family with a boatload of noisy kids, I'm going to scream," Bianca says.

I can see Hollie roll her eyes behind Bianca's back. We both know she has no tolerance for children. "I, for one, really don't care who moves in," she says.

"Of course not, now that you've got a sexy as hell boss waiting for you every day at the office why care about the lack of single men around here? But think of Violet and me. Don't we deserve something pretty to look at?"

Hollie just started working for the CEO of Clarke Hotels and even though she adamantly denies it, both Bianca and

I know she's got the hots for her billionaire boss. Honestly, I've seen the pictures. Who wouldn't?

"How many times do I have to tell you? I'm not attracted to Mr. Clarke. If you knew how much of an asshole he was, you wouldn't be either."

"Hey, sometimes I like my guys a little mean, it's hotter."

"Jesus, Bianca, you need to get laid." I laugh.

She grabs a bottle of white wine from the fridge and pours herself a generous glass. "Girl, look who's talking. I don't know how you've survived to the age of twenty-three without some dick."

My cheeks heat just a touch. "Hey, I've got my *friends* in my drawer and an entire internet's worth of porn. I don't see the need to complicate my life with some man-child that will only annoy me and waste my time. Besides," I continue before Bianca can interrupt, telling me how wrong I am, "I got asked out after class today."

Both Hollie and Bianca freeze in their tracks. It looks like they're doing the statue challenge, and it sends me into a fit of giggles. "Well?" Hollie asks. "What did you say to him?"

"I told him yes," I say and turn my back to them both so I don't have to look at them while they holler and whoop like I just scored the winning touchdown. They've always been my biggest supporters in anything I do.

I slice the now cooler bread and plate it before setting it onto the kitchen island in the middle of the three of us.

"Who's the lucky guy? When are you going out?" Bianca asks.

"It's this guy, Tyler, from one of my classes. We've known each other for years and I guess he's been dropping hints that he's wanted to go out for a long time but I've just never caught on."

"Not surprising," Bianca mumbles which I choose to ignore.

"Anyway, he's going to text me to set something up."

Hollie rounds the island and envelops me into her arms, giving me a warm hug. "I'm so happy for you. I mean, this is good, right?"

I sigh a little as she lets go. "I mean, yeah, it's good. It's just that I'm not super attracted to him. I mean, objectively, he's a cute guy but I've never really looked at him *that* way."

"Well, attraction can be an intellectual thing for some people. Maybe you're one of them and after your date, you'll have so much fun that the attraction will just grow," she offers.

"That's what I've been telling myself." I smile. "It's time for me to really put myself out there before my mom makes the decision for me and just starts sending eligible bachelors to wait on our doorstep."

"Wait, that was an option?" Bianca asks, suddenly intrigued. "We could have been getting hot guys on demand over here?"

"I never said that they would be hot, just eligible."

"True." Bianca has her phone out and is pulling up her social media apps. "What's his name again?"

I groan but give her his name anyway. I should have known I wouldn't escape without a thorough dissection of all things Tyler Crosson.

"Found him," she exclaims while scrolling through his feed of pictures. "Some selfies, pictures of him with friends, not too many with random girls. He's definitely cute. Congrats, Violet, it looks like you might have bagged a good one."

"Let me see." Hollie reaches over and plucks the phone from Bianca's hand so that she can scroll through herself.

"Oh yeah, he's totally cute in that normal-college-guy type of way and there aren't a ton of pictures of him getting drunk at frat parties. I approve," she says with a smile.

"Gee thanks, guys, I've just been sitting here all afternoon, on pins and needles, hoping that the two of you would approve of my date."

"Hey, the friend stamp of approval is important," Bianca protests. "Besides, this is just the tentative approval. We have to meet him before he gets a full endorsement."

I grab the bottle on the counter and pour myself a glass of wine. By the looks of how my bread turned out, I deserve it. "Well, I think we have a few steps between him asking me out and introducing him to my friends."

"That's true. So, when is this big date?"

"Who knows." I sigh, the weight of responsibility beginning to level on me. "I've got to start looking for a part-time job so I can actually afford to eat. That's certainly going to limit my dating availability."

"I know you don't want to hear this," Bianca says gently, "but I'm sure your parents would give you money if you asked."

I let out a groan; I know that she's right, it's not like they can't afford it. "You know that taking money from my parents always comes with strings attached. It's bad enough that I'm having to rely on them for tuition. I think it's just best for me to get a job and do this on my own."

"Well, let us know if you need anything. Now that I'm a personal assistant to one of the most influential CEOs in Seattle, I have a feeling that my reference might hold a little more weight than when I was a lowly college student." I knew Hollie would wholeheartedly support me in my quest for financial independence. It's always been very important for her to have the ability to take care of herself as well as her little sister that still lives with her deadbeat mom.

"Of course, Vi. Whatever you need. If this is important to you, then it's important to me too, you know that." Bianca rounds the kitchen and pulls me in for one of her bear hugs. I hug her back with all my strength, hoping that she can feel how grateful I am for her constant support. "Oh! Not to change the subject from Violet's awesome news but do you guys think you can come to brunch with Dad and me this weekend?"

My head jerks up and my heart starts beating a staccato rhythm in my chest, forcing me try to play it cool. "He just took us to brunch last weekend to celebrate Hollie's new job. Are you sure he wants to see us again already? Doesn't he want to spend some time with you alone?"

"Please, you know he loves the two of you just like you're his own daughters." *Ouch.* I try not to wince at the sting of that one but it's a fitting reminder of where I stand and why I agreed to go out with Tyler in the first place. "Plus, we wouldn't be alone anyway. My mom is going to be in town. She's finally single and thinking about moving to Seattle to be closer to me. If you two come to brunch with us, it won't be as easy for him to just bail when he sees her."

"Wait, you're inviting her to brunch and not telling him?" Hollie asks.

"You know if I tell him she's coming there's no way he'll go. He's always been cordial with her but never spends any real time with her unless he has to. He wouldn't have even invited her to our graduation party if I hadn't insisted. It's the first time she's been single in forever and if she moves up here . . . maybe they can get to know each other again and they'll realize how perfect they are for each other."

My heart stutters in my chest. She wants her parents to get back together? Is that something he wants? I've only met Amanda Moreno a few times over the years but she honestly doesn't seem like someone who would be "perfect" for him. I know I should say something instead of just standing here in the middle of the kitchen like an idiot but all I can manage is to bring my hand up and absentmindedly stroke the small book pendent that's resting against my chest.

Hollie, my hero, saves me from having to add anything intelligent to this conversation. "B, didn't your parents get divorced when you were like two? You are way too old to be parent trapping them."

"It's not parent trapping if we're all going to be there. I just want them to spend a little time together. Mom always has the worst taste in men, and I haven't seen Dad go on a date in ages. I think he may have given up." She frowns like the thought makes her truly sad and, not for the first time, I envy the father-daughter bond the two of them share. "There's nothing wrong with giving the two people I love most in the world just a little nudge toward each other."

"He might date and just not tell you about it. I'm sure he doesn't share every hookup with you," Hollie interjects, and I'm pretty sure both Bianca and I turn a little green at that thought.

"Gross, Hollie, I don't need to think about my dad's one-night stands. And if there was anyone significant, he definitely would have introduced her to me. This is all beside the point, I just need the two of you to go to brunch with us on Sunday. Pleeease." She gives us her best puppy-dog face, and even though the thought of being in the middle of a romantic setup for Dante makes my stomach turn, I know I can't deny Bianca. She would do it for me if I asked her. Besides, this is just the kind of thing I need to see to help me move on. If Dante and Amanda hit it off, maybe seeing that will finally break the hold he has on me.

"Fine, I'll go. But you need to admit I'm the best friend you'll ever have," I say.

"Same," Hollie pipes in.

"You both are the best friends a girl could ask for; I would be nothing without you. You're the best." She makes her way around the kitchen, giving each of us a hug, and I desperately try to change the subject.

"So, who wants a piece of bread?" They both eye my offering dubiously, like it might come off the plate and attack them.

"What kind of bread is it?" Hollie asks cautiously.

"It's like zucchini bread," I answer.

"Well, that can't be too bad."

They both reach for a slice and take a bite, chewing a few moments before stilling and looking at me with wide eyes. It's Bianca that rushes to the trash can first, spitting the chunk of bread out with a *ptui* noise. Hollie expels the offending bread slightly more discreetly into her hand.

"What the hell, Vi?" Bianca asks. "You said this was zucchini bread. Did you use thousand-year-old zucchinis or something?"

"No. I said it was *like* zucchini bread. It's pickle bread."

"Holy shit, Vi. That's not *like* zucchini bread," Hollie says while chugging her glass of wine. "That was the most sour piece of bread I've ever eaten."

"It can't be that bad, you guys. Just look at it, it's perfect." I grab a slice and take a healthy bite.

Okay, so it's just the tiniest bit sour. As my saliva glands start to work overtime, I have to admit it might be more than just a little sour. Maybe I shouldn't have added the juice to it as well as the pickles. I try to swallow but decide I can't do it and spit it right into the trash next to Hollie's and Bianca's.

"I think with a little tweaking this could be delicious. Maybe I just added a little too much of the juice. I mean, there's hardly a difference between pickles and zucchini, it should taste great."

"Violet, honey," Hollie says in a soothing voice like she's worried I might explode if she says the wrong thing. "You realize that just because zucchinis and pickles are both long and green it doesn't mean that there's hardly a difference between the two."

"She's right, Vi. Not all phallic vegetables are created equal," Bianca adds.

I let out a laugh and slide the rest of my pickle bread into the trash, right where it belongs.

TWO

DANTE

Amanda Calling . . .

I throw my head back against the leather headrest of my office chair and let out a groan. What could my ex-wife possibly want now? With Bianca finally graduating college I figured that most of our communication would die out. Sadly, that hasn't seemed to be the case. If anything, the frequency of her calls has been ratcheting up the past few months.

I look back down at the phone that's happily buzzing away on my desk and quickly hit the decline button. I'm too busy to deal with whatever drama Amanda Moreno is trying to drag into my life.

I would feel worse about dodging her calls if we were ever really in love but we weren't. We were two stupid kids in high school that fooled around and ended up pregnant. Amanda isn't a horrible person, we were just never right for each other. When we found out about Bianca, we did what we thought was best for her and got married. The signs that we weren't going to make it were apparent before our daughter was even born but being young and optimistic, we carried on anyway.

The years we spent together weren't unhappy ones. Though, the two of us never really connected, we had our daughter, and she brought enough joy into my life to keep me there. It wasn't until I found out that Amanda had been cheating on me and spending his money all over town that I finally threw in the towel on our relationship.

I'm a man that values honesty and loyalty. We may not have been in love but we made a commitment to each other and to our family. The moment she stepped out of our relationship, it was over between us.

It devastated me. Not so much the losing of my wife but that I had to split the time with my daughter who I was accustomed to seeing every day. She was so young back then, growing and changing every day. It felt like my heart was being ripped in two when I was away from her. Moving three hours away to Seattle had been the toughest choice I ever had to make, but it afforded me a job that I could eventually catapult into my own business and gave me the means to support Bianca in anything and everything that she's wanted to do in her life.

Bianca has dreams, big ones, and I work hard every day so that she can reach for her dreams and not have to worry so much about finances.

Thoughts of my daughter are put on hold when I hear my front door slam downstairs. It's either Bianca or Jake, one of my foremen. No one else has a key to my house.

"I'm in the office!" I shout to whoever is currently climbing my stairs. The heavy footsteps let me know that it's Jake before his frame fills my doorway. His utilitarian tee shirt, jeans, and work boots are covered from head to toe in dust, letting me know he came here straight from the job site. Even his short brown hair has streaks of cement particles running through it, making it look almost silver.

"Hey, boss, how's it going?"

I take a moment to look pointedly around my home office, taking in the desk filled with Post-its and the stacks of paperwork on every open surface that isn't the filing cabinet where they belong. "Just great, can't you tell?"

He lets out a laugh and grabs a stack of what I'm pretty sure are lumber receipts from the chair in front of my desk and unceremoniously shoves them onto the bookcase before taking the seat the paperwork previously occupied.

"Do you think maybe it's time to move to an actual office?" Jake asks.

I let out a sigh and rub the bridge of my nose, hoping to stave off the headache that's been lurking at the edges of my consciousness all day. "I don't think I'm ready for that yet. We're only running two crews right now, but between that and keeping up with all of my rental properties, the paperwork is just getting a little . . . out of hand."

"You don't say?" He laughs, stretching his long legs out in front of him and leaning back in his chair. I'm not a huge guy but with both of us in my home office it makes the place feel positively claustrophobic.

Jake came to work for me when I was getting my own firm off the ground. He was just out of high school and had a work ethic of someone twice his age. Ten years later and he's not only my most trusted employee but one of my closest friends. He's asked me about Bianca a few times but I know him well enough to keep him far, far away from my daughter. He's a good-looking kid and when we go out to the bar together, he rarely goes home alone. I've never seen him with the same woman twice, so he can stay far away from my girl.

"What are you doing here anyway? Shouldn't you be at the Kamber Street job?"

"That would be correct. Except, the shipment of tile for the kitchen and bathrooms didn't show up this morning. I called Dimitri and he said that he emailed you."

"Fuck," I mutter before pulling up my emails. We have a tight timeline on that job and can't afford any delays. "I don't remember seeing anything from Dimitri," I say just as I spot the email that came in two days ago. "Fuck."

"Yeah, that's pretty much the general sentiment." Jake laughs.

I scan the email quickly before slamming the laptop closed a little harder than necessary and wince. I hope I didn't break it.

"He says that the shipment won't be here until Monday. Considering it's Friday, that means we're fucked for the weekend. I was hoping on getting in there and doing some work tomorrow to get us ahead. Now I'll have to do it just to keep us on track."

"Boss, you've got to stop working on the weekends so much."

"With all of this shit"—I wave my hand, indicating the mess that is my office—"I'm hardly ever out on the job site anymore. I miss it."

"You miss being hot and dirty all day? Why don't you go out and have some fun for once instead?"

"I have fun," I say defensively.

"All right, let me clarify. Meet someone. Girl, guy, whatever your preference. In all the time I've known you I've never seen you date anyone."

He's right, he hasn't seen me date anyone. I realized years ago that casual dating wasn't for me. I'm an all-or-nothing kind of guy and simply not built for the culture of dating multiple people at once and one-night stands. After a while, I just gave up. It has always been easier to focus on my career and my daughter. That focus hasn't been misplaced. Moreno Construction has been growing by leaps and bounds the past few years, I have over a dozen properties that I own and rent out, and my daughter has graduated from college with zero debt, ready to take the art world by storm. If all of that comes at the sacrifice of my romantic life, then so be it.

"You worry about your own love life, Jake. I'm just fine."

"Yeah, yeah. Well, just remember, if you change your mind, I'm sure I can find someone to set you up with. We could even go out and find you some fun for just an evening."

"Not interested, but thanks anyway."

"Okay, I'm dropping it." He holds his hands up to me in surrender. "So since we don't have the tile, I figured we'd start working on installing the cabinets in the kitchen."

"I guess that's all we can do. I can't believe I missed that email."

"Are you really surprised?" he asks looking around the chaos in the room again.

I let out a sigh and go back to rubbing the bridge of my nose. "Maybe it's time to get some help. Just with some light filing and organization. Maybe someone to go through emails so that this shit doesn't happen again."

"It's about time."

"And *you* should get back to work before I fire your ass."

Jake just laughs and pulls his oversized frame up out of my guest chair and heads toward the door. "You got it, boss." We both know there's no way I'm firing him. I have a great team of guys working for me but none I trust more than Jake. With him running one of my crews and another trusted team member running the other, there really isn't much reason for me to be on-site and not right here trying to manage the minutia that comes with running my own business.

Jake's departure leaves me in silence once again, and I decide that it's best to start combing through the two hundred emails in my inbox so I don't miss anything else important. Ten minutes in and I'm bored to tears. I'm just not cut out for office work. It's one of the reasons I got into construction. Not only do I love getting to work at different sites and getting to do different things every day, but I can't deny the physical perks as well. As a young man I never stepped foot in a gym and regardless, I was always in great shape. No, I never had a six-pack, but I was definitely a solid wall of muscle. I may not have dated many women but they certainly noticed me. I got my fair share of phone numbers and salacious offers.

However, I've been spending less and less time in the field the past few years and it's showing. Don't get me wrong, I'm still in pretty good shape for a man about to hit forty but there's a softness to my middle that I don't remember being there before. Maybe it's time to actually make use of that home gym that's just been gathering dust.

My phone buzzes once again but this time I smile and hit accept before bringing the device up to my ear.

"Hey, pumpkin. How's it going?"

"Hi, Daddy! What are you up to?" Talking to my little girl always puts a smile on my face but I know she's up to something any time she calls me Daddy. She officially grew out of that at about ten years old. Now, any time I hear it, I know that I'm about to get rolled.

"What do you need, Bianca?" I ask with amusement coloring my voice.

"Hey, that's not fair. Why do you think I need something?"

"Well, first of all, you rarely call me in the middle of the day. And second, I'm not giving away your tell."

She lets out a *hmph* that I can hear over the line, and I laugh at the image in my head of her as a little girl with her lower lip stuck out and pouting. "What's up, pumpkin?"

"I just wanted to make sure that we were still on for brunch on Sunday."

"Of course. Unless you need to cancel that is." I always give her an out. I'm a lucky father in that my daughter actually seems to enjoy spending time with me and our regular Sunday brunches are my favorite part of the week. But I'm not so naïve to think that there won't be times when something or some*one* might take precedence to our standing date.

"Nope, just the opposite actually. I was hoping it would be okay if I bring Hollie and Violet along this week."

I can feel my heartbeat pick up and my palms start to sweat.

"They're both coming?" I ask with a mixture of what I could only describe as ridiculous hope and abject dread.

"They're both confirmed. If that's okay with you, that is."

I let out the breath that I had apparently been holding, lean back in my chair, and cast my eyes to the ceiling.

Violet.

Violet is the one complication in my simple, almost boring life. If you could even consider her actually *in* my life. We have zero personal relationship. All our interactions are predicated upon the fact that Bianca is my daughter and Violet is her best friend. We've spent no significant time alone together. That hasn't stopped me from becoming fascinated with her.

When we first met, she was nothing but a tiny little thing that very much looked like the child she was trying to leave behind as she entered college. I didn't give her much thought at all honestly. She was my daughter's roommate and best friend. Someone I cared about in only the most general of terms and who was on the periphery of my life. But that changed about a year ago. I remember the exact moment, clear as day, when I began to *see* Violet Daniels.

It was Bianca's twenty-first birthday, and she graciously allowed me to take her and her friends out to lunch before spending the evening doing things I'm sure I don't want to know about. I entered the restaurant, eyes on the lookout for my daughter and her group of friends. As I scanned the crowd, my eyes caught on a beautiful woman sitting at the bar, her back to me. All I could make out was the miles of glossy black hair falling down her back and over her shoulders, a glimpse of delicate porcelain skin on her neck that proved she obviously didn't spend her days out baking in the sun like me.

My feet swiftly moved toward her with no conscious direction from me. As I approached from behind, I took in her petite stature. She was just a little slip of a thing, easy to tuck into my side or carry in my arms. My eyes traveled down her back, skimming the gentle swell of her hips, her tight rounded ass that looked like it was begging to be cradled in my hands, on down to her short but shapely legs that I wanted wrapped around me.

My thoughts somewhat shocked me; it had been a very long time since I'd had such an immediate attraction to a woman. I'd certainly never felt a pull like that before. My eyes were drawn back up her body as she tossed her head back and laughed at something one of her companions said. Her laughter hit my ears, sounding both melodic and familiar at the same time. Kind of like an old favorite song that I couldn't quite place. I took a deep breath as I reached her and just as I was about to tap on her shoulder and introduce myself, she must have sensed my presence because her head whipped around and suddenly we were face to face.

I was stunned. And not only because the woman whom I had noticed across the room was my daughter's best friend, no it was the look that I saw on her face. For just a moment her face looked open and unguarded, her eyes filled with yearning and affection. The way I always dreamed that a woman would look at me.

Now, I'm not so far gone that I don't realize that wasn't how she was really looking at me. Violet has always been a little shy and guarded around me. Hell, I'm pretty sure she's like that around most people that aren't my daughter and their mutual friend Hollie. No, I realize I was just projecting all my hopes and dreams onto the first female that I had felt an attraction to in years. In no time at all, I saw that guarded look back on her face and the moment I had created was gone. That didn't stop from opening my eyes to the woman that Violet Daniels had become.

For months after that I tried to purge her from my mind, but it was of no use. Violet had been firmly inserted into my head and she was living there rent free whether I liked it or not.

It's bad enough for a thirty-nine-year-old man to have a crush. It's downright embarrassing for it to be on a twenty-three-year-old girl. Not that I can ever see her as just a girl again.

Ever since that moment, I've lived in some kind of torturous limbo. Both eager for and dreading the next time that I would see her. What's made matters worse—or better, depending on how you look at it—is that for the past few months, she's barely shown her face when I've been around.

If I'm ever at their house, she's not home or seems to have something pressing to do in her bedroom. Whenever Bianca invites her roommates to one of our outings, Hollie will frequently show up, but Violet has been noticeably absent. Well, noticeable to me anyway.

I've begun to worry that maybe she's been able to pick up on my attraction to her and is trying to distance herself from me. Not that I would blame her. If I was a young, attractive, college student I certainly wouldn't want some creepy middle-aged man mooning over me.

"Dad?"

My attention is drawn out of my head and back to the phone in my hand. "Of course, sweetie. You know Hollie and Violet are always welcome."

"That's what I told them. Thanks, Dad. You know." I can hear the tone of her voice shift to one I can't quite put my finger on. "If you're dating someone, you could bring them along to brunch one week. I wouldn't mind."

I try hard not to choke on my saliva and lean forward in my chair. "Dating someone? Where is this coming from?"

"Well, I was just thinking that I've never really met any of your girlfriends or whatever. You don't have to hide them from me, okay?"

I let out a laugh. "Oh really? Thanks, I'll keep that in mind."

"I just want you to be happy, Dad. That's all. You know that, right?"

"Of course, pumpkin. If there's ever anyone significant in my life, you'll be the first to meet her. I promise."

"I better be. Listen, I've got to head over to the gallery before I'm late, but I'll see you Sunday, okay?"

Before I can answer, the line has already gone dead. A sigh escapes my chest. I know my daughter is a grown woman but I still really miss the little girl that would hang onto my leg when I had to leave the house. I know I should consider myself lucky and I do. At least she likes spending time with me. Most people her age are out making a life for themselves and feel like cutting off their parents is the place to start. Both Amanda and I raised her to be a strong independent woman and I couldn't be more proud of her.

I put down my phone and turn back to my dreaded emails, trying to concentrate on them instead of the fact that I get to see Violet on Sunday.

THREE

VIOLET

"So, you all come here every Sunday for brunch?"

I take a sip of the ice water in front of me and opt to let Bianca answer her mother's question.

"Dad and I do this most Sundays and Hollie and Violet come sometimes. I thought it would be nice, since you're in town, that we all got together today." Bianca smiles at her mom and turns back to her menu, avoiding eye contact. I wonder if Amanda knows that this is all some kind of setup put together by her well intentioned, but meddling, daughter. I don't really know the details of her divorce from Dante. Maybe she's enthusiastically hoping to get back together with him. She could be in on this plot just as much as Bianca is. The thought makes my stomach turn slightly but I remain quietly seated at our round, white-clothed table and take another sip.

"What a treat that you ladies could join us." Amanda's voice doesn't quite convey the same appreciative sentiment that she's touting. When she reaches for her water and elbows me without apology, it's clear she wishes that Hollie and I would disappear from the table. Either she wants some alone time with Dante and Bianca or she just really doesn't like Hollie and me. Since we've only met a handful of times over the years, I'm going with the former.

"When Bianca asked us to join you, we couldn't refuse. We'd love to get to know you better, especially if you're going to be moving here and brunch at the Singing Lark is always a treat," Hollie adds diplomatically. Her eyes slide to mine and widen ever so slightly, letting me know she's also picking up Amanda's displeasure at our presence.

I jump when the waitress suddenly appears at my side, notepad in hand. "Can I get you ladies anything to drink while you wait on the rest of your party?" Before I have time to answer, Hollie rushes out her order.

"Mimosa. Please." I almost laugh at her slightly desperate need for alcohol but decide that I'm also going to need something to help me get through this meal and quickly add another mimosa to the order.

After the waitress leaves to retrieve our three mimosas and one Bloody Mary—for Amanda—we settle in to wait on Dante. I can't keep my eyes from darting to the door every time someone walks in, seeking him out. While I know that this meal is going to be a little rough, and most likely awkward, I can't help the excitement I feel at the prospect of seeing the object of my forbidden crush. I just hope he doesn't fawn all over Amanda in front of me. That's really not something high on the list of experiences I'd like today.

With another whoosh of the front door, my eyes divert back to the entrance and my heart skips a beat at the sight of Dante walking in. He's wearing a pair of jeans that are snug enough to show off his powerful thighs but not so tight as to be uncomfortable. They're slightly worn at the knees showing that these pants aren't for fashion, they're for working. An opened button-down flannel covers his gray tee shirt. Perhaps it's a nod to the Seattle grunge fashion scene of his youth. His head turns left to right, searching, until his chocolate-brown eyes catch my own.

A smile lights his face when he sees me, and I pause to mentally capture this moment. The most handsome man I've ever seen is smiling a genuine smile of warmth and welcome at me.

Then his eyes move to my left.

He stops mid-stride and the smile drops from his face the moment he spots Amanda sitting beside me.

"Dad! Over here!" Bianca jumps out of her chair and waves to him enthusiastically. I can see him mentally shake off his surprise at coming face to face with his ex-wife at Sunday brunch and head toward his daughter, wrapping her in a hug.

Beside me, Amanda has also arisen from her chair and made her way around the table to the embracing duo. "Dante," she says while pulling on his shoulder, effectively removing him from Bianca, "it's so nice to see you." She wraps him in a hug that he seems to return reluctantly. I glance over to Hollie and see she hasn't missed the awkward exchange either. We seem to be the only two picking up on how uncomfortable Dante is in this moment. While I desperately hope that means he doesn't want her here, I'm not naïve enough to discount the fact that he could just be surprised that she's here. I'm sure seeing your ex can bring up all sorts of emotions.

"Amanda," he says, "I didn't know you were going to be joining us today." He looks over at his daughter with narrowed eyes, and I can't blame him for his annoyance. I definitely wouldn't want to be setup like this either.

"Well, she was in town and I thought it would be fun if we all got together. Isn't this great?" Bianca interjects, her voice wavering just slightly.

Dante is quick to reassure his daughter. "Absolutely. It's nice to see you, Amanda. What brings you to our neck of the woods?" he asks while taking the only empty seat at the table. The one that just so happens to be right next to his ex.

She angles her body toward him and leans forward slightly, giving him a glimpse of the cleavage down her shirt.

"I was actually thinking about making a move to Seattle. I thought it might be nice to spend some more time with Bianca . . . and you too, of course." Her tone has turned sickeningly sweet, and I get the feeling she wants to move here less for her daughter's sake and more for her ex-husband's. It appears Bianca wasn't totally off base with wanting to orchestrate the reunion of her parents. It's pretty obvious that her mom is thinking along the same lines. Not that I blame her, I'd be kicking myself for the rest of my life if I was married to Dante Moreno and then let him go. I can understand her wanting to get him back, but I really don't want to be here for the rekindling of their romance.

"What about your job?" he asks while studying the menu he's seen a hundred times in the past four years. "I thought things were going well at the office."

"I've been bored lately so I sent out my resume to a few places near downtown. I have an offer to run a doctor's office here starting next month."

"Yes, I remember boredom being a problem for you," he grumbles, almost under his breath, just as the waitress arrives and hands out the much-appreciated alcohol. She takes our food orders, then hurries away to attend to her other tables.

I grab my mimosa and down the entire glass in two gulps. The liquid burns my throat and forces out a sputtering cough.

Dante leans toward me, his forehead furrowed, a look of concern in his eyes. "Be careful, Violet, are you okay?"

Great, now he thinks I'm a kid that can't handle a single mimosa. This is perfect.

"I'm fine," I say, careful to mask the embarrassment and irritation in my voice.

"So, Dad," Bianca interjects, thankfully pulling his attention from me, "I was telling Mom about all the rental properties you have now, and I thought maybe she could rent out one of your places."

Now, it's his turn to choke on his drink. "One of my places?" he sputters.

"Oh, Dante that would be so great, it would really help me out. When you rent a place, you never know how your landlord is going to be. At least I know what I'm getting with you." She sets her hand down on his forearm, squeezing it familiarly, like she's done it a hundred times before and I have to look away before the jealousy shows on my face.

"Um, that's a nice idea but I don't actually have any properties available right now. The only vacancy I have is in the middle of renovations."

"You don't have anything at all for me?" Amanda practically coos at him.

"Like I said, there's nothing available." She snatches her hand back from its resting place on his arm and turns to give Bianca a steely look. The awkwardness sits heavy over the table and I can't help but try to clear it.

"I'm sure there are plenty of vacancies in the city right now," I interject. "We could keep an eye out for you. Maybe check around and see if we know of any places? I'm sure we can find you something near Bianca."

Both Bianca and Dante shoot me appreciative looks while Amanda doesn't bother sparing me a glance before muttering, "Sure."

The rest of the meal is dotted with Amanda's attempts to engage Dante in conversation with his not-so-subtle re-buffs, while Bianca tries to play peacekeeper, with Hollie and I interjecting when we can. I haven't enjoyed a meal less since the last time I went home for Christmas.

We're nearing the end of our entrées when Bianca gives her plan one more shot. "Dad, Mom and I were planning on doing at little sightseeing and shopping after brunch. Do you want to come with us?"

"I'd really love to, pumpkin, but I have a ton of work I need to catch up on."

Bianca gives a tiny pout but continues to push, "You can't have that much to do. C'mon, it will just be for a couple of hours."

"It's okay, darling. We're used to hanging out on our own without your Dad," Amanda says with barely contained disdain dripping from her words.

Dante ignores the jab from his ex and looks genuinely regretful, he never could resist a pout from Bianca. "I really can't, honey, I'm sorry. The office is covered in paperwork that needs to be sorted and I missed an important email last week that's set us behind. Things are such a disaster I'm actually thinking of hiring someone part time to help with some of the admin stuff."

Bianca's face lights up and a smile forms on her lips. "That's perfect!" She claps her hands together in excitement.

"It is?" Dante asks, obviously confused by his daughter's sudden enthusiasm.

"Absolutely." She nods. "Violet was going to look for a part-time job but if you have one available, she can just work for you. Two birds, one stone, and all that." She leans back in her chair looking quite pleased with herself.

My head jerks up from the empty plate I was studying, and I can feel my eyes go wide. "Excuse me?"

Dante makes a little choked sound and I'm pretty sure his eyes are as round as my own when he asks, "Violet?"

"She's right, it is kind of perfect," Hollie adds. "Working for Dante would be infinitely better than being stuck with an ass of a boss like mine."

Well, she's not wrong. A part-time job working for Dante would be great *if* I wasn't pretty sure there were hearts in my eyes every time I looked at him. But if the expression on Dante's face is anything to go by, it doesn't seem like I'm his ideal candidate.

"I don't really think it's up Violet's alley. It's just some filing, sorting emails, maybe making a few calls. I'm sure she's not interested."

I absolutely do not want the job. Having to work for Dante would be a special kind of torture. Torture that I have been doing an excellent job of avoiding the past few months. I should be thankful to him for immediately putting down Bianca's idea. But . . . something about him not even considering me has my ire up. Does he think I can't handle it? Or does he think that I'm too stuck-up to lower myself to office work? Not to mention the fact that he told Bianca I wouldn't be interested without even asking me. All of a sudden I can't stop thinking about how my parents have been telling me what I can and can't do my entire life with not a single concern for what I want.

"What are the hours?" *Did I just ask that?*

Dante jerks his head toward me, eyes wide with something that looks suspiciously like panic. *What the holy hell am I doing?*

"Well, I hadn't really thought about it. I would only need someone for about ten hours a week so I guess the hours could be flexible . . ."

"Perfect," I find myself saying. Dammit, did I just talk myself into working for Dante?

Apparently I'm not the only one surprised that I just weaseled my way into a job. Dante is looking around the table with a bit of a stunned expression on his face. Well, he might not think I can handle working for him but that just makes me determined to be the best admin he's ever seen.

"So, when would you like to start?" he asks without looking me in the eye.

"Is tomorrow good for you?" I ask with much more confidence than I'm currently feeling.

"Uh, great. Do you want to come to the house at nine tomorrow morning and I'll show you the ropes?"

"That would be perfect." I give a determined nod and look back down at my plate. There will be time to freak out about this later. Right now, I just need this brunch to be over so I can make a tactical retreat from this situation. As if answering my silent plea, the waitress shows up with our check, sending everyone at the table reaching for their wallet. Everyone except Amanda.

"You've got this, right, honey?" She smiles at her daughter. Bianca opens her mouth to respond right before Dante jumps in and says he can cover the three of them. Yeah, I'm definitely not getting motherly vibes from her, and I just hope that this move doesn't leave my best friend broken in its wake.

"You know, you don't have to take the job if you don't want it." I turn to look at Hollie, who's relaxing on the couch digging into a pint of Ben and Jerry's next to me while Bianca is still out with her mom. Just another ten hours until I have to be at Dante's place for work. Not that I'm counting.

"What do you mean?" I ask.

"I saw your face, Vi. I know you. When Bianca brought it up it looked like you would rather walk on hot coals. It totally threw me when you said you were interested." I should have known Hollie would pick up on my discomfort. She can be annoyingly perceptive like that. While I might notice things and keep them to myself, Hollie has no problem bringing what she's observed to the forefront and talking about it. Talking about things is not my specialty.

"I just wasn't really thinking about a regular office job, that's all. I thought I could find something that was connected to my degree but maybe this is a good thing. You said it yourself, at least I know who my boss is. I won't end up with a jerk that's awful or takes advantage of me."

"Yeah, but what about the thing?"

"What thing?"

"The thing where you're totally crushing on Dante." I can feel my mouth hanging open but I can't seem to close it. Over the past four years, I have done everything I can to keep my attraction to Dante out of the public eye. I thought I had done a good job of it until now. "Don't act so shocked. I told you I know you, Vi."

MADE TO BE YOURS

"You can't tell B," I rush out. Oh god, if she finds out, she'll kill me. This is her dad. Her dad that she's trying to push back together with her mom. She can never know, she'll hate me.

"First, you know I would never tell your secret to anyone. Not even B. Second, I really don't think she would care, I mean, it's just a harmless crush, right?"

"Of course it's just a crush! It's not like I want anything to happen between us." *Lies.* "I could never be with someone as old as him." *Lies.* "And I'm really excited to be going out with Tyler." *More lies.* "Plus, I could never do that to Bianca, and could you just imagine what my parents would say?" *Truth.*

"Hey, no need to tell me, I believe you." She laughs. "I just want to make sure you're all right with this and we didn't push you into anything."

I let out a sigh and settle back into the couch. Even though I'm embarrassed, it's nice to have someone to talk to about this for once.

"It's fine. Actually, it's better than fine, it's great. A job that won't be too taxing while I concentrate on grad school with a boss I already know *and* has flexible hours. The likelihood of me finding something that's a better fit than this is pretty slim. I've been working on getting rid of this stupid crush anyway. What better way than having him boss me around. I'm sure that will take this from crush to annoyance in no time."

"That's probably true." She says while pointing the spoon she's using to devour her ice cream at me. "Take it from me, the girl with the most infuriating boss in the world, a few times of him ordering you around without saying thank you will get rid of that crush real quick."

"Uh-huh." I'm not so sure about that. She won't admit it, but Hollie is crushing hard on her aloof rich boss. But who am I to point that out to her?

Just as I'm about to turn my attention back to the television that's been droning on in the background of our conversation my phone buzzes on the coffee table. I pick it up and the corners of my mouth turn up when I see who it's from. "Speak of the devil."

"Is that Dante?"

"Nope, Tyler." I swipe open my messaging app to see what he's said. "He wants to go out on Friday."

"That's a good thing, right?"

"Absolutely," I say with more conviction than I'm feeling at the moment. "This is just the thing I need to help me get over my Dante thing."

"And Tyler seems nice," Hollie adds encouragingly.

"He really is," I say, forcing a smile. This is a good thing for me and I'm starting to look forward to going out with Tyler. I quickly type out a reply letting him know that Friday sounds great and that I'm looking forward to it.

Tyler: Not as much as me.

With a genuine smile on my face this time, I place my phone back down and pretend to go back to watching the television. Maybe this will all work out. I have a job that will potentially help me get over my impossible crush and I have a date with a genuinely nice guy. For once, maybe things are starting to go my way.

FOUR

DANTE

What the fuck was I thinking? Oh, right, I wasn't. This is all my overly helpful daughter's fault. Who raised that girl anyway?

I'm pacing the length of my kitchen—back and forth, back and forth—trying to work off my nervous energy. I check the clock on the microwave for the one hundredth time. It's still 8:43 a.m. The damn thing must be broken. I take a large gulp of my second cup of coffee which was probably a mistake. It's doing nothing for my nerves.

The last thing I want is to have Violet working for me. While having her in my space does hold a certain appeal, I can't act on my feelings and that makes this entire thing a nightmare. It's not like I could turn her down for the job while sitting there in front of everyone. What would my excuse have been? This job is certainly nothing that any college graduate couldn't handle. She's perfectly qualified and since my office is in my house, it's not like I'd rather have a stranger coming in and out of here. No, on the outside it's the perfect situation. I get someone that I know and trust to help out with office tasks and she gets a flexible part-time job she can work at around her school schedule. *Perfect.*

Once I started to *see* Violet, I started noticing things. Collecting little pieces of information about her. I know it's ridiculous but everything about her seems to fascinate me. I know that, contrary to her name, her favorite color is green. I know that when she's out into the sun for even a few minutes, she gets the lightest smattering of freckles across her nose and cheeks. And I know that given the choice between drawing attention to herself and sitting in a corner she'd choose the corner every time. Maybe if I'm lucky, I'll barely notice that she's here. We'll both just quietly get our work done and then she'll walk out the door to live her life, leaving me here alone, just as it should be.

The doorbell finally rings and I set down my mug. Taking a deep breath, I admonish myself for acting like some teen getting to spend time alone in an empty house with his crush. I can only hope that I don't do anything to give away my feelings. How embarrassing would it be if she actually knew I wanted to follow her around like a puppy?

I open the door to find the woman of both my daydreams and nighttime fantasies. She's wearing shorts and a simple v-neck tee shirt but she might as well be wearing the latest designer dress for all I care, she looks stunning. The shy smile on her face does something to warm my insides that I don't want to examine too closely.

It takes a moment before I realize I'm just standing here, blocking the doorway. I step back so she can enter, and I mean to say hello but it comes out as more of an unintelligible grunt. I head to the kitchen and start rummaging through the junk drawer, trying to find the spare key to the front door when a gentle throat clearing from behind me forces me to turn around.

"So, I know you were kind of ambushed yesterday," she starts out. She looks almost as nervous as I feel. She's standing in front of me, her arms crossed in front of her in a protective gesture and she's bouncing back and forth from foot to foot. "I totally understand if you don't want me to have the job. I know you couldn't say no in front of Bianca, but I get it if you want someone with experience working for you. This whole thing is probably a bad idea."

Even though, just moments before, I was lamenting having to have Violet work for me, a thread of panic runs through me at the thought that she might walk out the door. I've barely seen her in months. If she leaves now, when will I see her again? I shouldn't care. I know I shouldn't. But that doesn't seem to matter because I do care.

"Not at all Violet." I give her a smile hoping to ease her nerves. I guess I can understand how she would be nervous. It's a new job and she thinks I probably don't even want her here. I need to push away my feelings for her, concentrate on the work, and making her feel welcome. "I'm glad that Bianca said something. Of course I'd rather have you than a stranger. I'm just sorry because the work isn't anything special, I know you're going to be bored."

"If you're sure . . ." she says, tilting her head to the side and taking me in.

I wonder what she sees when she looks at me. Instead of letting those thoughts run away from me, I hand her the key, making sure that our fingers don't touch. "I'm sure. Here's the key to the house, since your hours are flexible I may not be here when you want to work so go ahead and just let yourself in." She tucks the key away into the pocket of her shorts, then follows me up the stairs to the bedroom I've converted into a home office.

The moment we step inside, I'm reminded, again, of how much of a bad idea this is. All thoughts of being able to ignore her while I work are thrown out the proverbial window. This room is way too small for the two of us to work together. Well, too small for us to work together at the distance apart that I need to be able to function. As she scoots by me to enter the room, I catch the floral scent of her shampoo—I think it might be jasmine—and barely resist the urge to lean forward and take in another lungful of the tempting aroma.

I take a step back and head over to my desk, too late realizing that I haven't thought this through. I was so worried about having Violet in my space that I failed to account for the fact that there's nowhere for us to work together in this room. I guess one of us could sit on my small loveseat that's pushed into the corner but that doesn't seem very practical. For now, I pull out my chair, indicating that she should sit.

She hesitates for just a moment before asking, "But isn't this your desk?" She scans the room seeing that there really isn't anywhere else practical for her to sit.

"Yeah," I say while rubbing the back of my neck, trying to ease some of the tension in my body. "I wasn't expecting to hire someone so quickly so I don't really have a setup for you yet. Why don't I show you the ropes today and then tomorrow we can go out and get you everything you'll need for your own workspace."

She looks up at me with those big blue eyes that have been floating around in my mind. "I don't want you to go through any trouble. I could sit over there on the couch and bring my laptop from home—"

I'm already shaking my head before she can finish her sentence. "Nuh uh, no way. You're not going to make me into a terrible boss before we even get started. As your employer it's my job to get you anything you may need to do the job. As you can see"—I gesture around to the stacks

MADE TO BE YOURS

of papers precariously perched on nearly every available surface—"I need all the help I can get getting organized."

She lets out a laugh, one that I've missed hearing these past few months and finally agrees to let me get her a full workstation set up. We spend about twenty minutes going over how I'd like emails sorted and paperwork filed. She picks up my processes immediately and even offers some suggestions for improvements.

"Honestly, whatever you can do to get this stuff under control, I'm all for. As you can see, office work isn't really my forte."

"I can't imagine it's your favorite thing to do. I worked in my dad's office a couple summers in high school so at least I know the basics of a smooth working system. Do you miss doing the actual construction work?"

"I never would have thought baking in the sun and throwing out my back carrying supplies would be something that I'd miss but I actually do. That's one of the reason's I wanted to hire someone to help with all of this office stuff. I'd like to get back out on the job sites occasionally. Right now, I'm almost never out there and when I am, I feel like there's something important I should be doing here."

She reaches up and pushes strands of long black hair out of her face and tucks it behind her ear. "Well, now you have me. Hopefully, after a while you'll trust me enough to get back out there with your guys. I'll hold down the fort, I promise."

Suddenly, I'm acutely aware that I'm leaning forward, hand braced on the back of the chair she's sitting in, my face close to hers. Too close. Especially when she's telling me that I have her now. Because I don't have her and I never will.

I straighten up and take a step back, noticing a small frown on her lips before she schools her face back to its normal serene expression. She must think I'm acting crazy today, and she's not wrong. I really need to get out of here before I make a fool out of myself.

"Actually, I'm going to go down to the site on Kamber and check in with my guys. We had a shipment that was delayed last week, and I want to make sure they delivered everything this morning and that we're on track. I think you have a handle on things here. If you want to work on getting things organized, that would be great. Just keep track of your hours and lock up when you leave."

I'm already heading toward the door when her soft voice reaches my ears. "Don't worry about a thing, if anything important comes up, I'll call."

"Thanks, Violet," I say over my shoulder as I escape the room. This is going to be more difficult than I thought.

"Hey Boss, I wasn't expecting to see you today," Jake says as I walk up next to where he's standing in the house's kitchen that's undergoing massive renovations. The owners bought the house but are having the entire thing torn down to the studs and rebuilt before they plan on moving in. I thought that the shipment delay from last week would have really set us back but looking around, it seems Jake has it under control.

"Yeah, well, I wanted to make sure we were on schedule. We can't afford to get too far behind on this project since I've got another one lined up for your team immediately after."

"You know I've got this," he says.

"I can't let you have all the fun, can I? Maybe I should start on that bathroom," I say, eyeing the pallet of expensive tile they've parked in the backyard.

"George is going to start on that as soon as he's back from lunch. I told you I had it under control. Shouldn't you be back in your office making sure we're running like a well-oiled machine or something?"

I let out a sigh as Jake goes back to measuring for the countertops. "I hired someone. She's back at the house right now working on getting that mess organized."

"She?" I can practically see his ears perk up at the mere mention of a female. Jake may have a way with the ladies but I'll be damned if he or anyone else that works for me gets anywhere near Violet.

"You don't need to worry about her," I practically growl at him.

Instead of warning him off, this seems to spur him on-ward. There's a glint of mischief in his eye when he continues with, "I wouldn't say I'm worried about her. I just think it's only polite if I go and introduce myself since we're coworkers and all."

I know just how he'd like to introduce himself to Violet. "You don't need to know her, she'll be working exclusively in the office. Besides, she's too young for you."

"She eighteen?"

"Of course," I snap at him. He just smiles in response and goes back to measuring. I know I should just leave it. The more I talk about her, the more he'll realize she's a sensitive subject for me and the more he'll push my buttons. He's the kid brother I never had or wanted. "You don't even know who she is or what she looks like." I cross my arms over my chest, and I know I look defensive but fuck it, Jake needs to understand that she's off-limits.

"I'll know exactly who she is and what she looks like when I go introduce myself. C'mon boss, you know it would be nice to have something to look at besides dirty sweaty dudes all day. You don't get to keep her cooped up in your house and have her all for yourself."

"Keep your eyes to yourself, you don't need to be looking at her. This discussion is over." He just laughs and I stomp out to the yard where I start carrying in heavy packages of tile so that they're ready to go.

Just as I'm headed back for the second load, I can feel my phone buzzing in my pocket. I quickly reach in and pull it out, realizing with nervous anticipation that it could be Violet with a problem in the office. Instead, all I see is *Amanda Calling*. Fucking spectacular.

I'd normally send her call straight to voicemail and go on with my day but I need to find out what she's up to. What with hiring Violet yesterday I haven't had time to think about her decision to move to Seattle. Amanda's always been a decent mother to Bianca. Maybe not as warm and fuzzy as I would want for her but Bianca's managed to grow into a strong, confident, and talented young woman. I'm not stupid enough to credit myself with all of that. Still, in the four years that Bianca has been living in Seattle she's never once expressed an interest in moving here.

Amanda has always seemed content living back in South Hill. Her family and all her friends live there and she also has a stable and well-paying job running the office of the most popular OBGYN in town. She says that she wants to move here for Bianca but she's never been one to be overly attached. I'm worried she has an ulterior motive.

I immediately shake my head at myself in admonishment. That's not fair to Amanda. Maybe she really does miss Bianca and wants to be here. I know that I've been far happier having her in the same city as me than not. I quickly answer the phone before it can roll over to voicemail.

"Hey, Amanda."

"Hey, yourself. What are you up to?"

"I'm working right now, is there something that I can do for you?"

"Geez, is there anything wrong with me wanting to have a friendly conversation with my ex-husband?"

"There is when we never have friendly conversations and I'm in the middle of a construction site. If there isn't anything you need, I'm going to have to go."

"Wait," she says before I can hang up the phone. "So what do you think of me moving to Seattle? It's great, right?"

"You know me, as long as Bianca is happy, I'm happy. It sounds like you'll get to spend a lot of time with her so that's nice."

"Of course! I'm really looking forward to it. Maybe the three of us could do some stuff together. You know, like a family."

"Amanda, we are a family in the loosest sense of the word. If you move here, I'm sure we'll cross paths but I don't want you to think that things are going to happen here that won't."

She lets out a *harrumph* and quickly moves on to another topic that I don't really want to talk about. "Are you sure you don't have anything that I can rent? That would really help me out. I don't want to go searching for something and money is a little tight right now . . ."

Ahhh, so that's why she wanted to move into one of my properties, so she could stiff me on the rent. She doesn't think I'll throw the mother of my child out on the street . . . and she's probably right. That makes me doubly grateful that I have nothing for her right now.

"Look, Amanda, I really don't have anything available right now. Most of my places are filled with long-term tenants and like I told you yesterday, the only place that's unoccupied right now is being worked on. The girls said that they would keep their eyes out for you, but I just really don't have anything."

"You could at least try to be helpful, Dante," she says letting the annoyance creep into her carefully cultivated calm demeanor.

"You know what, I have to go. I'll talk to you later, Amanda. Have a nice day."

"Dante Moreno, don't you dare—"

I save myself from hearing the end of that sentence by hanging up the phone and shoving it back into my pocket. I feel a little bad for not being more supportive of the move but I have my own problems to handle. Amanda and I were never really friends, even when we were together. We were just kids filled with lust and hormones. When she cheated and our marriage ended, it had been hard but only because of Bianca. If I didn't have my daughter, I would have been perfectly fine with never seeing Amanda again for the rest of my life. I can only hope that her presence here doesn't overly complicate things for me.

FIVE

Violet

After Dante left yesterday to head to one of his job sites, I couldn't help but feel a little lost. It wasn't the work. No, that was relatively easy. The job isn't complicated, in fact, once I get the backlog of work organized it should be pretty easy to keep him on track. I've only been in Dante's house a handful of times before and I've certainly never been here alone. I'd like to say that my curiosity didn't get the better of me but that would be a lie.

I've never been overly nosy. With parents like mine, that just wasn't allowed. My childhood fell more into the category of children should be seen and not heard, and if they could get rid of the seen part too, they would. I resigned myself to sitting in corners quietly reading whenever we would go out or they would entertain at home. I've always been the consummate good girl who does what she's told. But yesterday all that went out the window when I was left alone in Dante Moreno's house. I filed most of the stacks of paperwork away before heading to the bathroom where I might have taken a quick peek in the medicine cabinet. As expected, there wasn't much there besides a first aid kit and some aspirin since this seems to be a guest restroom.

When I exited the bathroom, instead of turning left to head back to the office, I went right. The first door I came to opened to a guest bedroom that was mostly filled with stacked cardboard boxes. I hoped that those weren't more paperwork that needed to be filed that he just shoved in there. Forgoing the boxes, I continued down the hallway to the door at the end. By the process of elimination, I figured that this was Dante's bedroom. I just wanted a quick peek. I slowly opened the door like I was afraid something might jump out at me and call me out on my snooping.

The room was dark, too dark. There were heavy drapes covering the windows, but I was afraid to turn on the lights, like somehow if I did, Dante would know that I had been in here. I took a few tentative steps farther into the room before turning in a circle and taking in my surroundings.

The room was filled with dark wooden furniture that included a king-size bed against the far wall that was draped in dark blues and grays. There were no feminine touches anywhere, which made me feel ridiculously good. The room was comforting yet masculine. All Dante. Before I could give in to the temptation to sit down and see how soft the bed he slept in every night felt, I made my way out of the room, firmly closing the door behind me.

Now I'm standing outside his front door the next morning in the light drizzle that is Seattle's signature weather. I debate whether or not to use the key he gave me and decide to knock. I'm not comfortable enough to just walk in yet. Hell, I'm not sure I'll ever be that comfortable with Dante.

"There you are," he says, pushing open the door after I ring to bell. "Didn't I give you a key?"

"You did, but I wasn't sure if I should use it when I know you're home. I don't want to just walk into your house, I want to respect your privacy."

He waves away my concern and instead of ushering me inside, he slips out the door to join me on the stoop and uses his own key to lock the door.

"Are we going somewhere?"

"Yup, we've got to get you someplace to work. The two of us sharing a desk doesn't seem like it's going to work." At the mention of the two of us and a desk, an image fills my mind of me sitting on the edge of the desk with him between my legs, kissing me senseless. I quickly shake my head to disperse the image. How Hollie manages to work for her crush every day I'll never know.

"I feel bad," I say as we make our way to his truck that's parked in the driveway.

"Why would you feel bad?"

"I don't want you to have to spend money on me. You're already paying me; I really don't need anything fancy."

"Violet, of course I'm going to pay for it. We need it. I'm still getting the better end of the deal here. Yesterday was the first time in months I've been able to get out to a job site. I saw what you did when I got home and you're almost done getting the backlog of filing put away. I couldn't be happier. Besides, once you get bored of the monotony and quit on me, I'll still have the setup for the next person."

"I won't quit." He opens the door to the massive truck for me. "I really enjoyed yesterday." I actually did enjoy the work yesterday. He's right, it's not super interesting or exciting but I liked the monotony of it. It was soothing finding a place for everything. He lets out a little laugh under his breath while I examine the best way to climb up into this behemoth while still maintaining some dignity. If I had realized I'd have to scale his truck today, I wouldn't have worn my favorite skirt.

Just as I'm about to make a jump for it I feel two hands firmly gripping my hips and lifting me into the air. I'm so surprised by the sudden move that I let out a little squeal, but before I know it, I'm settled into the big passenger seat and he's swinging the door closed, securing me in the cab.

Once he's in and we're on our way, I try to think of something to say to break the silence that hangs heavy in the cab but talking never was my strong suit. Instead, I sit with my hands primly in my lap and watch Dante out of the corner of my eye, trying to ignore that I can still feel where his hands held my hips. He has a death grip on the wheel, if the whiteness of his knuckles is any indication. He's clenching and unclenching his jaw, making it obvious that despite what he says, this is the absolute last thing he wants to be doing right now. I make a promise to myself that I'll make this as fast and pain-free as possible so we can get back to the house and he can get back to work.

We pull up to the small parking lot of a commercial-looking building that doesn't resemble the office supply super-stores I've seen at all. "Is this the place?" I ask.

"Yup," he says, hopping out of the truck. Before he has time to make it around to my side, I open my door, take a deep breath, and make the jump down to the pavement below. I take a small stumble but am otherwise none the worse for wear.

"Violet," he barks and sounds angry. I freeze in my tracks. Dante has never used that tone of voice with me before. It shoots a bolt of lust through me and I almost take another stumble. "Don't do that again. You could get hurt. You need to wait for me next time, understand?"

Between the scolding and the desire, I can't do much more than nod at him. He gets closer to me and puts a finger under my chin, tilting it up so that I'm looking him in the eyes. If he knew what his touch was doing to my body, he certainly wouldn't have his hands on me. "Say it," he says gruffly.

"I-I won't jump out of the truck again." My voice is breathless even to my own ears.

"Good girl." *Gulp.* He pulls his hand away from me and I almost fall forward. Why is it that I'm always on unsteady footing in his presence?

Without another word, he turns and starts heading into the squat gray commercial building and I dutifully follow behind. When we step inside, he warmly greets a man named Ray. I take in the interior and am surprised by how large it seems on the inside. They lined the walls with large shelving units filled with everything from cases of paper to filing cabinets. The center of the room is crammed with different pieces of office furniture in every style you could imagine. We start making our way through the throngs of desks pushed together on the floor.

"This isn't what I expected," I say.

"No? What did you expect?"

"I just figured we'd be going to one of those chain stores."

He glances at me over his shoulder while making his way deeper into the building. "Nah, I try to buy from local small businesses whenever possible. I'm a small business so I know how much it means to be supported. A purchase from me can make Ray's day, where it's not even a drop in the bucket to a big box store. It may be a little more expensive sometimes but it's worth it."

"I like that." And I really do. I've never thought about the consequences of where I purchase things before. When I was with my parents, I never bought anything. Everything was purchased for me either by them or our housekeeper

Martha. When I moved out on my own, there was never really much that I needed anyway.

"Why don't you go ahead and pick out whatever you want. We'll get a desk and chair here and then we'll go down the street and get a laptop."

I glance around the room again, taking in all the choices. "Don't you want to choose? It's going to be in your house after all."

"You're the one that's going to be sitting there, whatever you want will be fine."

Not knowing where to start, I walk ahead of him and run my hand over the smooth surfaces of the desks. I can feel Dante's eyes on me and I wonder what he's thinking. I spot a desk to my left that looks like it would match the furniture he currently has in his office and point to it. "How about that one?" He looks the desk over and frowns, and I get a sinking feeling in my stomach. "What's wrong with it?"

"You want this one?" He stands beside me and eyes the large, boxy, dark wooden desk that I've pointed out.

"Don't you like it?" I ask, suddenly unsure. I really wish he had just picked out what he wanted himself.

"Well, I like it but it doesn't seem like your style. Did you pick this just to match my other pieces?" I know that I'm blushing at getting called out. I really don't like being put on the spot like this. I thought the desk would make him happy and now I'm just confused.

"Isn't that a good thing?"

"I want you to pick out what *you* want, Violet. Not what you think I'll like."

I look away from him when I say, "I don't really know what I like. I've never picked out my own furniture before."

"What are you talking about? Never?" He comes closer to me, filling my vision, ensuring I can't look away. "How is that possible?"

"When I lived at home either my parents or the house-keeper picked out everything for my room. After that, I went to the dorm and they already had furniture. When we moved into the house, I just picked up whatever I could afford from garage sales or thrift stores for my bedroom."

His frown deepens like he's troubled by what I'm telling him. "Bianca must have redecorated her room twenty times as a teenager. I have the credit card bills to prove it." It doesn't seem like that big of a deal but suddenly I'm embarrassed by the fact that I've never done that myself. Life would have been so different if I had someone in my life like Dante. Not for the first time, I feel a little jealous of Bianca's upbringing. "Well, now's your chance. Whatever you want, it's yours. Go ahead."

He spends the next thirty minutes dutifully following me around the packed warehouse and chatting while I examine one desk after another. I think I sit in every chair they have, testing it for comfort. One chair seems to swallow my slight frame whole and Dante just laughs and gives the chair a spin, causing me to burst out into laughter and hold on for dear life. I'm having more fun just hanging out here with Dante than I've had in months.

Once I've picked a delicate writing desk with cabriole legs that I know for a fact they wouldn't have in a big box store and what has to be the most comfortable chair I've ever sat in, Dante pays but won't let me see the total. I start to get nervous thinking maybe I've picked things that were too expensive but he sees the look on my face and tells me to cut it out and meet him outside. I'm happy to oblige. I could use a few minutes away from him.

Once I'm outside on my own, it feels like I have a moment to breathe. Spending so much time alone with Dante is a heady thing. I'm supposed to be getting rid of my crush, not feeding into it. As if to remind me just how off-limits he is to me my phone buzzes with a text from Bianca in our group chat.

Bianca: I've decided I want a birthday party ladies!
Hollie: Isn't your birthday like, soon?
Bianca: Yup so we better get planning.
Hollie: How big are you expecting this thing to be, you know we don't have a lot of room . . .
Bianca: Don't worry, I've got it covered. I'm pretty sure Dad will let me have it at his place.

Well, it's true, there may be three of us living there but Dante's house is much larger than ours.

Me: Does he know that he's throwing this party yet?
Bianca: Not yet but he will. It won't be a problem. You know he can't say no to me. I'm bringing wine home tonight and we can plan!

Just as I'm about to reply to Bianca, letting her know when I'll be home, Dante exits the warehouse. "They're going to deliver the furniture later this afternoon. Who's that you're talking to?" he asks, trying to peek over my shoulder.

"Just your daughter. Looks like you have a party to throw."

"I what?" He looks taken aback by my declaration.

"Yup, she's decided that she wants a birthday party and since your place is bigger than ours, I guess you're the venue."

He lets out a groan and tilts his head back like he's looking to the sky for guidance. "Didn't I just throw a graduation party?" At the mention of the graduation party, I reach up and lightly finger the book charm around my neck, quickly snatching my hand away when he brings his eyes back to me so that he doesn't see. If he's ever noticed that I always wear the necklace he gave me, he's never mentioned it. "Well, if I have to throw a party, you're helping this time."

"I am?"

"Oh yeah," he says with a laugh before helping me back into the truck, leaving me breathless once again. "That's the beauty of being my employee now. You have to do what I say." He shoots me a wink through the window before climbing into the driver's seat and taking off out of the parking lot. The thought of Dante bossing me around, particularly without any clothes on, has my heart rate picking up and I shift in my seat.

After stopping off at another mom-and-pop shop for a laptop, we're finally ready to head back to the office. Unlike yesterday, he doesn't leave. I sit on the loveseat that's pushed into the corner of the room and sort through the remaining piles of paperwork while Dante works on his computer and makes several calls to clients and suppliers.

When he first offered me the job, my greatest fear was the awkwardness that I knew would surround us as we sat in a room together and worked. However, it seems like our outing today has washed that away. In fact, I feel a sort of contentment sitting in the same room with him, not interacting, but just being near him. I've never had the opportunity to spend time with him alone before. I love hearing his gruff voice on the phone, the hard clacking of his keyboard keys, the muttering under his breath while he reads emails. It's all a symphony of sound that is putting me at ease. It's gentle background noise that's perfect for working, and I would get a lot more work done if I wasn't sneaking peaks at him every few minutes. Luckily, he hasn't seemed to notice.

My phone buzzes in my purse again and I reach for it, assuming it's Bianca with more details on her upcoming birthday party. Instead, I'm surprised to find a message from Tyler.

Tyler: Can't wait to see you in class tomorrow gorgeous and looking forward to Friday!

A feeling of guilt immediately washes over me because I haven't actually thought about Tyler in days. I've been so caught up in my new job working for Dante that Tyler hasn't really factored into my thoughts. I know I should be looking forward to our date but I'm really not. Especially after I spent the day with Dante today. My plan to get rid of my crush is definitely backfiring. If anything, my attraction to my best friend's father seems to be growing the more time I spend with him. This job was a terrible idea. I need to be getting over him, not leaning into my attraction.

I glance back up to where Dante is sitting at his desk and find his deep-brown eyes already on me. I immediately feel guilty for being on the phone when I'm being paid to work. "Sorry," I say while shoving my phone back into my bag. "I won't let it happen again."

"Violet." Every time he says my name it's like a tingle shoots up and down my spine. The sound of my name on his tongue shouldn't do these kinds of things to my body but here we are. "You can use your phone. I'm not some slave driver." He looks like he's about to say something else but instead goes back to his emails.

I figure that now is as good a time as any to work out my schedule with him. "I just wanted to let you know that I have class most of the day tomorrow so I won't be in. I hope that's works for you."

"No problem, you don't have to be here every day. This is only supposed to be a part-time gig for you, remember?"

"Great, thanks." I look back to where my purse is resting next to me on the couch and decide I might as well make my Friday arrangements as well. "And on Friday, do you think it's okay if I come in early and leave around three? I have something in the evening I need to get ready for."

He doesn't bother looking up from his computer. "Of course, I told you that your hours were flexible. Why? You girls have something fun going on Friday night?"

I don't know why, but I really don't want to tell him I have a date. For some reason it feels like a betrayal to him, which is insane. Dante and I are nothing to each other. Until two days ago he wasn't even my boss, just my best friend's dad that I would see occasionally. I don't owe him anything so why do I feel so guilty?

"Actually, I have a date that I want to get ready for." I hear a *thump* and look over to see that Dante has dropped his phone on his desk, but instead of picking it back up, he seems focused solely on me.

"A date?" His voice is gruff and his eyes are boring into mine, making me squirm in my seat. "Who are you going on a date with?"

I don't know if it's the guilt or the prying question but I can feel my defenses going up. "Does it matter?" I ask with probably more attitude than he deserves.

His chocolate-brown eyes darken and there's a crease in his brow that I don't quite understand. He probably didn't appreciate my tone. "I just didn't know that you were dating anyone."

"There are a lot of things you don't know about me." I'm looking him straight into his eyes, unflinching, practically daring him to ask me more questions that are frankly none of his business.

"I guess so," he says before physically turning away from me and focusing back in on his work. "I hope you have fun." Something about his tone tells me he wishes I would have anything but.

"Thank you, I will." The awkward silence is back and feels suffocating. I know he says my hours are flexible but he apparently doesn't like me taking off early to go out. I told him I would come in early so I don't understand what his problem is. I'm also aware enough to realize that my defensive answers didn't do the situation any favors. I don't know why I reacted that way to him. I don't give anyone attitude . . . ever. It's not my style. I always do as I'm told, speak when spoken to, never let my emotions bubble to the surface. That was bred into me at an early age as a Daniels.

I can only take it for a few more minutes before sighing and grabbing my bag. I'm almost done here and have some work to do before class. "I'll see you Thursday?"

He grunts out an unintelligible response and doesn't even bother looking up from his computer screen at me, so I just place the pile of receipts on top of the filing cabinet and walk out of the office, not bothering to spare a glance behind me, even though I can feel his eyes boring into my back.

I'm glad this happened. It just reminded me that, no matter what happened on our shopping excursion today, we're not friends. He's my employer and my best friend's dad and I'd do best to remember that. His hot-and-cold attitude today is enough to show me it would never work between us even if by some miracle he was interested in me. We're just too different. It's time for me to look to the future and that starts with my date with Tyler.

SIX

DANTE

She has a fucking date?

There are certain things you can count on when it comes to Violet. She never passes a child without giving them a smile and a wave. She can't resist kettle corn. And she definitely doesn't fucking date. Or at least she hasn't since I've been keeping a close eye on her.

Up until that point, I had really been enjoying our time together. I've always liked Violet. She's a beautiful and intelligent woman. I just didn't know that I could have so much fun with her. The fact that we were doing nothing put picking out some office equipment pretty much floored me. I can't remember the last time I enjoyed myself so much in the company of a woman. Then she had to tell me about her stupid fucking date.

I don't know why her mentioning it to me has sent me into such a spiral but it has. Of course she's going to date. She's young, beautiful, smart, and caring. Hell, she has everything in the world going for her. I'm surprised that there aren't guys lining up around the block for just the chance to be with her. But apparently, for all I know, they are.

I go to the kitchen and grab a beer from the refrigerator, quickly popping off the top and downing the beverage in just a few gulps before I grab another and head to the couch.

The fact that I couldn't get any information out of her about it was almost as bad as hearing about the date itself. Who is it with? Has she been out with him before? Is it getting serious? This is all information that I have absolutely no right to. That doesn't mean that I don't want it. If I stopped a moment to analyze my behavior, I'd realize that I was acting like a jealous teen, but frankly, I couldn't give a fuck. Instead, I make the split-second decision to check in on my daughter, for totally innocent, fatherly reasons. That's my story and I'm sticking to it.

"Hey, Dad!" my daughter exclaims when she picks up my call.

"Hey, pumpkin. So, I hear that I'm throwing a party now?"

"How did you—Oh, right. Violet. You don't mind do you, Daddy?"

"Well, since I told Violet she was going to have to help me now that she's my employee I guess it should be okay. But you have to help. I don't want to be stuck doing everything myself."

"No worries, the girls and I are going to work out all the details tonight. How about you and Violet handle the food?"

"How many people are you expecting at this thing?"

"Oh, I don't know." I can tell by the tone of her voice she wants to ignore the question but if she wants me to provide food and drinks, she better come clean.

"Bianca." I know she can hear the warning tone in my voice.

"Okay, fine. Maybe fifty? I'm not positive yet. I'll work that out in the next few days."

I let out a groan. No one has ever accused me of being a skilled cook before so I guess we're going with catering. That should cost a nice chunk of change.

"Just . . . try to keep it under control Bianca."

"C'mon, Dad, you know me."

"Exactly, I know you." Before I can think better of it, I blurt, "Violet told me she's going on a date Friday." There's a pause at the other end of the line and I let my head fall forward into my palm.

Smooth Dante, real smooth.

"Oh . . . she told you about that? I'm surprised," she says hesitantly.

I hurry to cover up my snafu. "Well, she just mentioned it so she could get some time off. I want to make sure she'll have time to help with the party. If she's dating someone, she might not be around."

"Don't worry about it. It's just a first date, she's not even sure she likes the guy. Besides, you know Violet. She always puts her friends first. I just can't believe she mentioned it to you because she seems kind of nervous about it, but Hollie and I told her she should absolutely go. It's time for her to get out there, you know?"

"Yeah, sure," I say begrudgingly. Is it bad that I want to reach through the phone and strangle my daughter for pushing Violet to go out on a date she's not sure about? You would think since it's a first date, and that she doesn't really seem into the guy, it would ease this tension that I've been holding in my body since I've heard about it, but it doesn't. "Well, it will be a great party. My daughter only turns twenty-three once."

"Hell yeah, it will. I've got to run, I'm meeting Hollie and Violet soon to party plan. Thanks, Dad! I love you!"

"Love you too, honey."

I wasn't expecting to feel this lonely. I've only worked in the office with Violet for a day and already the room feels empty without her. The freshly delivered desk and chair are sitting off to the side of mine, and they seem bare without her sitting there, filling the office with her own personal brand of sunshine and light.

Am I being ridiculous? Absolutely. I just don't know how to stop.

I hear the key in the lock downstairs and suddenly perk up. Maybe her classes let out early and she's here to get in a few hours of work. I sit waiting at my desk with bated breath until Jake comes sauntering in like he owns the place. My entire being deflates a little and I try to shake myself out of it. I've got to stop this shit or her working for me will never work out.

"What can I do for you Jake?"

He takes his usual seat in the chair in front of my desk and leans back, legs outstretched in front of him, arms resting behind his head. If I didn't like the kid so much I'd chastise him for treating this place like some lounge instead of a place of work.

He looks around the room before completely ignoring my question. "So, where's the new girl?" Ahhh, so that's why he's here.

I straighten up in my chair and practically growl at him, "I told you she is off-limits."

He looks at me with surprise on his face. "Well, that's what you said, but I didn't think you were serious."

"Deadly serious." I hold his gaze while he seems to search mine. After a moment he breaks out into an enormous grin.

"So, it's like that, huh?" he says with a chuckle.

"I don't know what you're talking about, just stay away from Violet."

"Violet." He says the name like he's rolling it over his tongue testing out the feel of it in his mouth, and I almost come out of my chair. Instead, I take a few deep breaths and count to ten. I know he's just trying to push my buttons at this point. Unfortunately, he's succeeding.

"Was there something that you needed?" I glance down at my watch. "You guys should be wrapping up for the day, I'm surprised you're not headed home."

"I am, I just wanted to stop by and talk to you about something real quick. Jose's wife went into labor early so he's going to be out for a few days. I can get one of my on-call guys to come out on Friday but tomorrow is going to be a problem. Without him we'll be a man down and I don't want to get behind."

"Everything okay with his wife?" I ask. Even though I haven't spent much time with Jose since he was hired after I'd been mostly relegated to office work, I make it a point to keep up with my guys.

"I think so, she's only a few weeks early. He's going to let me know when the baby is born. He was worried before he left for the hospital about leaving us a man short but I told him we'd take care of it."

That's another reason I like having Jake as one of my second in commands. Not only do I trust him implicitly, but for the most part, he handles situations the way I would handle them myself. I believe in family first. If his wife needs him, then Jose needs to be there for her. It's our job to make sure that things keep running smoothly, not his.

"Thanks, Jake. Let me see if I have anyone available for tomorrow." I start going through my list of backup guys until the empty desk and chair catches the corner of my eye. Maybe it's best if I'm not here when she's working to-morrow. I feel like I'm getting way too attached too quickly. Yesterday was a great day but I don't want to trick myself into thinking she has any kind of feelings for me. Hell, she has a date with another man in just a few days. Maybe it's best if I give myself some space.

"You know what, I'll take his place tomorrow. You said you have someone for Friday, right?" He nods at me. "Great." This is half the reason that I hired someone to work in the office anyway, to give me time to get back out there on the job sites.

"I don't know, old man. Are you sure you're up for a full day of physical labor? You haven't gone too soft sitting here in your cushy office?"

"Shut up, Jake. I can still work circles around you."

He lets out a laugh before rising out of his chair. "I'm looking forward to it, boss-man."

Early mornings are kind of a requirement in my line of work but the next morning I get myself out of bed espe-cially early. After a quick shower and pulling on my work clothes, which consists of a well-worn pair of jeans and a Henley, I make myself a quick cup of coffee and I'm out the door before Violet has time to arrive.

I spend the day sweating and cursing as I try to get the tiled backsplash for the kitchen counters just right. I may have been exaggerating just a little when I told Jake I would work circles around him. He's spent the past hour hauling bags of cement into the backyard for the new patio we'll be laying. Just watching him makes the muscles in my back twitch. Oh, to be that young again. A tiny voice in the back of my head whispers, *if you were that young maybe Violet would be interested in you.* I push the foolish thought out of my mind and try to concentrate on what I'm doing.

By the time the day is over I'm covered in dust, dirt, sweat, and can't wait to get home and veg out in front of the television or with the new mystery novel that's been sitting on my nightstand.

When I pull into my driveway, I don't see Violet's car at the curb in front, so I can only assume she's left for the day. Upon entering the house, my suspicions are confirmed. The place feels cold and empty.

Before heading to take a shower, I stop in the office and look around. The place looks better than it has in years, if it's ever looked this good. As soon as I step in, I'm hit in the face by the scent of her floral shampoo and I take just a moment of indulgence to inhale the aroma, wishing my nose was buried in her hair.

There are no signs of the piles of paperwork that once littered every open surface, and it looks like she may have dusted the shelves and vacuumed. I'll have to talk to her about that, it's not something that I expect of her, though, it is nice.

I move over to her desk and see a variety of colored Post-it notes laid out neatly on the surface. Some have notes regarding the filing system and others look like reminders for things she wants to tackle tomorrow. I'm a little blown away by what she's managed to accomplish in such a short time. I head over to my own desk and see she's left some papers for me along with a note. Her handwriting is neat and feminine with round, looping letters.

It appears while filing she took a look at my phone and Internet billing and decided that I was paying too much. She called the carrier and switched us to a business package that's going to give us faster Internet while lowering the price. It's something I never even would've thought of and here she is, already making changes to make the company more productive and cost efficient. For a moment I regret not being here to see her at work but let the thought go. It was for the best, the team needed me and there's no reason for me to spend any more time with Violet than I need to.

Just as I'm stepping out of the shower, I hear the front door slam downstairs. This place has been like Grand Central Station lately. I check the clock on my nightstand and see that it's 6:30 p.m. so I know it isn't Jake or Violet coming in. That just leaves one person.

"Daaaaad!" I hear from downstairs. I smile before throwing on some sweats and a tee shirt and head down to greet Bianca.

"What are you doing here, pumpkin?" I ask her back as she rummages through my fridge, knowing she's going to be sorely disappointed by what she finds in there.

"Where's all the food?" She grabs a beer and closes the fridge before taking a seat at the kitchen table. I snag my own beer before joining her.

"When do I have time to do shopping? I just ran through a drive-thru on my way home today."

She shoots me a frown. "That stuff isn't good for you, Dad. You need to take better care of yourself. You're getting up there."

It's nice to know I'll always have my daughter to make me feel old. "Hey, I'm not even forty yet. Besides, I ate a salad earlier this week." Bianca just stares at me without saying a word in a silent challenge. "Okay, fine, it was macaroni salad and it came as a side to the corn beef on rye I was eating. Are you here for a reason or just to bust my chops and make me feel old?"

"I just really wanted to thank you for letting me have the party here. I know it's not how you'd like to spend an evening but it means a lot to me." That's where she's wrong. I'm happy to spend any time I can get with my daughter. From the day she was born, Bianca's been the best thing that's ever happened to me. I kept waiting for her to go through that phase where she doesn't want me around anymore, that old dad would cramp her style, but that just never seemed to happen. Sure, she does most things with her friends and coworkers but she never hesitates to spend time with me or invite me to something that she's going to be doing. From the horror stories I hear from some of my friends with teenagers, I consider myself very lucky.

"You know I would do anything for you, pumpkin. But just know that you're going to have to do the cleanup. There's no way I'm cleaning this house by myself after fifty of your friends have been running through here."

She picks at the label on her beer bottle. "No problem. Hollie and Violet already said that they would help with the setup and cleanup. Plus, you said that Violet was going to help you get the food?" I just nod my head, keeping my eyes locked on the bottle in front of me. I'm afraid that if I look her in the eyes she'll somehow be able to get a glimpse of how I feel about her best friend. And I'm worried that they are starting to develop into true feelings now after spending time with her alone. I thought my crush was bad before but it's nothing compared to the thoughts that have been rattling around in my brain the past few days. I'm an old fool. "Just make sure that Violet doesn't bake anything, okay?"

"What?" My head jerks up and I look at my daughter who is giving me a nervous smile.

"You know I love Violet, she's my best friend." I nod my head so she continues, "It's just that she loves to bake. I mean, she like really loves it."

"Okay, so what's the problem?"

"The problem is that she's terrible at it. Horrible."

I give her a reproachful look. "That's not a very nice thing to say about your best friend."

"You're right but it's true. Even she knows how bad she is at it. You want to know how great of a friend I am? I still try anything she asks me to, it just usually ends up in the trash can instead of my stomach. I'm telling you, Dad, just promise me you won't let her bake a cake or something. The last thing I want to do is send my friends home with food poisoning."

I roll my eyes at my daughter. There's no way that Violet's baking is that bad. Of course, I've never tried it myself but how hard can it be to follow a recipe? "Okay," I say, humoring her. "I promise I won't let her bake anything. I'll also be sure to make myself scarce during the party so you can have fun with your friends."

Her expression turns a little more guarded now and I wonder what she's up to. "Actually," she says, "I was thinking about inviting Mom if that's okay with you. Then maybe you two could hang out together and you'll have someone to talk to."

I suppress the groan that wants to escape my lips. Hanging out with Amanda in the middle of a party is not my idea of a good time. In fact, I would absolutely rather be holed up in my bedroom reading a book or watching something on the TV.

"Of course you can invite your mom, honey. It's your party, but I doubt that the two of us will spend much time together. Honestly, we haven't had anything in common for years now. Nothing except you of course."

"Well, you guys hardly ever talk. Maybe you have more in common than you think. And since she's planning on moving here, maybe it would be good to get on more friendly terms with her, you know, so the three of us can hang out together sometimes."

I shake my head before she even finishes her sentence. "You're the only twenty-three-year-old that I know who enjoys spending time with your parents. Is there something wrong with you?" I ask in jest.

She just laughs. "What can I say, I've got two pretty cool parents."

"Can I get that in writing somewhere? Someday I'm going to have to convince you I'm cool and I want the written proof."

"Whatever, Dad, you can be such a weirdo."

"Ah, that feels better. I've lost my cool badge already and I'm back to weirdo." She just rolls her eyes at me and continues drinking her beer.

Not too long later Bianca takes off, leaving me alone in my big empty house. I've never really felt lonely before. I was always working, first as a foreman for someone else and then tirelessly building my own business from scratch. When I wasn't working, I was spending as much time with Bianca as I could since I didn't get to see her every day like her mother did. Now this place feels too big for just me. Not for the first time in the past year, I wonder what it would feel like to share it with someone. Have them waiting for me, book in hand, in our bed. Happy to see me home. Maybe we could actually cook something together instead of constantly getting takeout, that seems like it would make my daughter happy.

I would be lying if I said that the *someone* I'm picturing in my bed and in my house, making it feel like a home, wasn't Violet.

SEVEN

VIOLET

"Do you have the Kamber Street file?"

I look up from my computer screen in the corner and look over to where Dante is searching through the old beat-up filing cabinet.

My first week working for Moreno Construction has flown by and with the flexible hours Dante has allowed me, it's fit in well with the rest of my schedule. The more time I spend here, the luckier I realize I am. No other boss would be so accommodating about school and studying. Not to mention the pay is more than I could hope for from any other part-time gig.

He tried to give me a check this morning to cover this week, and I balked at the total. There was no way he owed me that much. He just told me it's what the standard was for people in the industry. I'm not sure I believe him but beggars can't be choosers. I reluctantly took the check, thanking him profusely and promising him I'd be the best office admin he'll ever have. He just smiled at me and said that there was no doubt that would be true, which made me feel uncomfortably warm inside.

I spent about five hours in the office yesterday and didn't catch a single glimpse of Dante. I was somehow both extremely relieved and deeply disappointed. Is there a word for that? I feel like I should know that, being an English major and all. However, without his hulking presence there to distract me, I achieved an unbelievable amount and was even able to brainstorm some improvement processes to add to the office.

"Violet?" he calls out to me again, making me realize I haven't answered him.

"Uh, yes, of course. The Kamber project." I pull a file from the stack on my desk. "I've been working on digitizing these. You should actually be able to pull most of the information up on our shared drive right now, I only have a few more things to add to it."

"All of this is in the computer?" He holds up the thick file like he's not sure he believes me. I just give him a smile and approach his desk, motioning to his computer with a silent request to control it. He gives his assent with a nod. As I lean forward across his chair, I can hear him take a quick inhale, like I've somehow surprised him. Choosing to ignore it, I carry on, showing him how I set up a shared drive between our two computers and where he can access the client files that I'm digitizing and adding to the system.

"Everything should be in here. I've also downloaded some project management software so that we can use it to track what needs to be ordered for each job, what orders have been placed, when shipments are scheduled to arrive, and to make sure projects are running on time."

He's looking at me with an expression on his face that I can't quite figure out and I immediately feel like I've messed this up. God, I've overstepped my bounds. He just wanted someone to file paperwork and sort emails and here I am, barging in and taking over. "I'm sorry, should I not have done that? I just thought it would be helpful after you told me about that late shipment last week. We don't have to use it, it's not a big deal. I'm really sorry," I rush out.

He holds his hands up to stop my rambling. "Slow down, Violet, it's a great idea. I feel kind of stupid, I could never figure something like that out myself. I've always known that office work wasn't for me." He chuckles under his breath. "I'm just a little stunned that you've managed to set something like that up already."

"Well, it's not totally done yet. Kamber is going to be my trial run and I'm still entering everything into the system for them." I'm still leaning over his chair and navigating the computer. I'm so close to him I get a whiff of the spice from his soap along with something else, an underlying masculine scent that I presume is just him. I look up and his face is mere inches from mine. If I had any amount of courage at all, I would lean forward a few centimeters and brush my lips against his. His eyes are burning into mine and I haven't seen them this color before. They've gone from a rich chocolate brown to an almost black. I suck in air since I apparently haven't been breathing and quickly jump back from him, heading straight to my desk. I stare at my screen, refusing to look in his direction, knowing that I'm doing nothing but making a fool out of myself by mooning over him.

As I'm working on the Kamber project, I notice we were due a delivery of sinks and fixtures for the kitchen and bathrooms. I scan my notes and see that Jake Aguilar is the foreman at the site but I don't see any contact information listed for him. "Dante, do you know where I can find the number for Jake Aguilar?"

His eyes quickly leave the screen and home in on me, piercing right through me. His body seems to tense right before my eyes. "Why?" he asks rather gruffly.

"I wanted to call him and make sure the shipment that was due today got delivered so that I can mark it off."

"I'll call him," he says, grabbing the phone off his desk and placing it to his ear. *Okaaaay, so he thinks I'm not ready to speak to his employees?* I'm more than just a little insulted so I sit back and listen to his one-sided conversation.

He doesn't even bother with a greeting before barking out, "Jake, did the sinks and fixtures get there this morning? . . . Why didn't you tell me? . . . No, forget it, I'll take care of it." He lets out a weary sigh. "Yeah well, let me call them. You know, this is probably something that you should have told me *this morning* . . . We're going to start tracking it now so if something doesn't arrive, just let me know, okay? . . . Yeah, all right. I'm calling the supplier now." He hangs up the phone and starts rifling through the thick file he took from me that's now covering his desk. I know he's trying to find the phone number but I have it right here on my screen. "Fuck, fuck, fuck," he mutters under his breath.

It's obvious the supplies haven't reached the site yet, so this time, instead of asking for permission, I pick up my phone and dial the contact listed in the file. He obviously doesn't think I can handle dealing with the actual people in this business so I'm going to prove him otherwise.

I flip on the speakerphone so Dante can be in on the conversation before the call is answered on the second ring. "Build Warehouse, this is Dimitri."

"Yes, hi, Dimitri. This is Violet Daniels over at Moreno Construction." Out of the corner of my eye I see Dante's head whip in my direction but I keep my eyes locked on the screen in front of me, refusing to look at him. I need all the confidence I can muster for this call. I'm not usually a pushy person but I need to show Dante what I can do.

"Well, hello there, little lady. What can I do for you today?" I don't bother to conceal my eye roll at his condescending nickname.

"Quite a lot actually. You were supposed to have a shipment of fixtures out to our site this morning but it's now three p.m. and it hasn't arrived."

"Let me check," he says. I can hear rummaging on the other side of the line and figure he's scrambling to find the paperwork for the load I'm talking about. "Uh yeah, honey, it looks like that won't make it until tomorrow."

Out of the corner of my eye I can see Dante lifting himself out of his chair, ready to take over the conversation. Before he can make it two steps, I hold up my hand, effectively freezing him in place. He reluctantly sits back down and silently waits to see what I'll do next. I'm thankful that he's giving me the leeway to prove myself.

"Actually, Dimitri, that's not going to work for us," I say, keeping my voice strong and steady. Calling me an aggressive person would be the understatement of the century. However, I can't tell you how many hours I've spent listening to my lawyer father on the phone coaching clients, playing hardball with other attorneys, and just generally dominating every conversation and negotiation that he's ever been a part of. Robert Daniels may not have given me attention, but he certainly gave me the tools to deal with a guy like Dimitri.

I can hear him laugh over the line. "Unfortunately honey, that's just the way it's got to be. My delivery truck got delayed but they'll be there tomorrow." I glance over at Dante just to make sure that he's with me and he gives a gentle nod of encouragement.

"Like I said, that's not going to work. It's my under-standing that you were late with our materials last week as well, correct?"

"Well, yeah but—"

"Then it seems to me you're in breach of contract."

"Now wait just a second—"

"I've reviewed all of our recent orders with your company and they all have a delivery guarantee on them. Now it doesn't say here what we get when you're in breach of contract but I'm going to assume that last week wasn't the first time you've been late with our shipments." There's silence on the other end of the line which I take as an affirmation so I continue. "Industry standards dictate when you aren't able to deliver according to the contract we're entitled to compensation." That certainly gets a reaction out of him. All I can hear on the other end of the line is flustered sputtering and I catch Dante looking at me with what I can only describe as a mischievous sparkle in his eye.

"Now, if our shipment doesn't get delivered today, we'll be paying your invoice less any delivery charges along with a five percent discount on the materials."

"You can't do that!" His voice is laced with anger that he seems to be trying to hold back rather unsuccessfully.

I forge ahead. "Actually, we can and we will. Then we'll start looking for other suppliers. I think you'll agree that this is a rather large city and there are plenty of other peo-ple that can make good on their delivery date guarantees."

There's silence on the line and for a second I worry that I've pushed too hard. I don't know Dante's relationship with this man, maybe he needs to use Dimitri for some rea-son I'm not aware of. But the fact is, Moreno Construction can't do their job if they don't have the supplies and it seems like Dimitri has been taking advantage of the somewhat "disorganized" office procedures before I got here.

Finally, he returns to the line. "The shipment will be there by four. Just make sure that Jake's there to sign off on it." I can hear his barely controlled anger over the line and I can tell he's holding onto the mask of civility with a tight grip.

Since I definitely won this round, I sweeten my voice as much as possible, "Thank you so much, Dimitri, we'll let Jake know. I look forward to working with you in the future." Unsurprising, he grumbles something unintelligible at me and hangs up. I take a deep breath trying to damp down the adrenaline the call shot through me. I've never stood up to someone like that before, it felt amazing.

Before I even know what's happening Dante is pulling me out of my chair into a big hug and laughing. "That was amazing, Vi. You're amazing." I can feel my breasts pressing against his solid chest, his arms circled around me. I know my face is flushed as I feel my heart rate start to accelerate and the telltale tingle of arousal between my legs. Dante has never hugged me before and I'm a little shocked that I feel more from this one platonic embrace than I have from any of the kissing or fooling around I've done with any guy in the past. My nipples harden under my blouse and I really hope he can't feel them.

Suddenly, his arms drop away and he turns from me. I have just a second to spot his flushed face. Maybe he's embarrassed by his sudden display of exuberance or, worse, maybe he noticed my body's reaction to him. Where is God with a lightning strike when you need him?

"How did you learn how to do that?" he asks me while busying himself at the filing cabinet across the room which suddenly feels much smaller than it did just moments ago.

I shrug. "I guess I have my dad to thank for that one. We don't talk much but every time we're together he's on the phone negotiating something or other. I must have just picked it up over the years. I hope I didn't overstep."

"Not at all. I wish I'd dealt with Dimitri like that years ago. I've just been so busy keeping our heads above water that I've never had the time or inclination to get into it with him. Even if I did, I don't think I could have done better. Did you really look up industry standards for deliveries?" he questions.

I let out a laugh. "Are you kidding me? When would I have had the time to do that? No, I just did a little bluffing."

"Damn, I don't think I'd want to go up against you in a game of poker."

"You'd have to teach me the rules first."

"Maybe I will he," he says with a grin.

As if to remind me that I shouldn't be playfully bantering with Dante, the alarm on my phone goes off, letting me know that it's time to leave so that I have plenty of time to get ready for my date with Tyler tonight. I reluctantly switch off the alarm and look over at my boss, my best friend's dad, my unattainable crush. "I guess it's time for me to head out. Will you call Jake and let him know about the shipment?"

His face sobers up immediately. "Okay, yeah, no problem. Thanks for all your hard work today."

"Of course, it's been fun." And truthfully it has been. The work isn't taxing but I'm really enjoying coming up with solutions to make the office more efficient and putting Dimitri in his place was a thrill I haven't experienced before. Getting to spend time with Dante is the icing on the cake. Okay, honestly, spending time with him might be the entire cake.

While I'm closing down my computer and straightening my desk Dante saunters over to my side, hands shoved down deep into his pockets, looking slightly nervous. "The big date is tonight, right?"

I'm a little surprised that he remembered. "Yup, got to go home and get ready."

"You'll tell Bianca where you're going right?" He looks away from me and seems to be staring at the wall, his brow has a little furrow in it I'd like to reach up and smooth out.

"Always. Safety first and all that." He just nods and keeps his eyes on the wall.

"You be careful, all right?"

"Of course, this isn't my first date after all." I try to laugh off his seemingly parental concern but I can see him flinch slightly at my words.

I grab my purse from underneath my desk and sling it over my shoulder just as he turns to me. "Just . . . if there's a problem. If you need help or a ride, or anything . . . you can call me. You know that right?" My head jerks back in surprise. Of all the things I thought he might say, I wasn't expecting that. I don't want him to worry about me.

"Dante, honestly, you don't need to worry. Bianca and Hollie know where I'm going and who I'm going with. I'll be fine."

He's nodding his head at me. I can see concern in his face along with something else that I can't quite place. "Just promise me, okay? If you need me, you'll call me?"

I feel like this is completely unnecessary. I'm a grown woman, more than capable of handling a date on my own. Still, he seems genuinely concerned and I decide to appease him. "Sure, I promise. If something happens, I'll call you, okay?"

He just nods and moves back to his desk across the room. With the conversation apparently over, I grab my keys from the bag slung over my shoulder and head out of the office, down the stairs, and out of his house, reminding myself that this date is a good thing. It's a necessary thing. That's becoming more and more apparent the more time I spend with Dante.

When I arrive back at home it looks like I'm the only one here. I know Hollie is working but Bianca's schedule at the gallery is sporadic and you never know when she'll be home. I have just over three hours to get ready. That's way more time than I'll need. I'm not usually one for primping and preening but if I want to give this date a real shot, I'm going to have to make myself look as good as possible. Still, three hours is a little excessive.

I decide to pour myself a glass of wine and sit on the couch with the romance novel I purchased earlier this week to wind down from the day. Maybe this will get me in the mood for my date tonight. I want to make sure that I'm concentrated on Tyler and not Dante. It's only fair to him.

I try to focus on the eReader in my hand but I keep replaying that last conversation I had with Dante repeatedly in my head. The more I think about him questioning my safety and making me promise to call him if I have a problem, the more I realize that he still sees me as the same kid he saw four years ago, the day Bianca and I moved into our dorm. It doesn't make me angry as much as it makes me sad. I've always known that I never had a shot with him but if he can't think of me as a woman after all these years, even now that I work for him, then there really is no hope. It's time to lean heavily into this date with Tyler.

Just as I finish my glass of wine and am about to hop into the shower the front door bursts open and an enraged Bianca comes storming through, slamming it behind her.

"Our new neighbor is a total asshole!" Her volume raises on the word asshole and I know she hopes said new neighbor can hear her from inside. I glance out the window and spot a tall, imposing figure glaring in our direction.

"Is that him?" I ask.

Bianca leans across me so that she can look out the window as well and instead of ducking back instantly like I would do, she instead gives the man a smile and wave. He doesn't look impressed. In fact, he spins on his heel and starts stomping toward the house next door. It isn't until then that I notice the boxes lining his porch.

"Did he just move in today?"

"With any luck, he'll move out today too," she huffs. I'm surprised by her reaction to our new neighbor. Bianca doesn't normally let much bother her. He really must have gotten under her skin.

"What happened?"

"He practically tried to arrest me," she says throwing her hands up into the air.

"What are you talking about? What could he possibly have you arrested for?"

"So, I parked my car the teensiest bit over into his driveway. You know how parking is on this street, it's impossible to find a spot and I'm used to that house being empty."

"Okay, so he asked you to move it?"

"Ha!" she says without any humor. "He didn't ask a damn thing. He demanded I move it. I mean seriously, Vi. It's like an inch into his driveway." My eyebrow raises in a silent challenge. I don't think either of them would be worked up over an inch. "Okay, so maybe it was more like a foot . . . or two. It doesn't matter! He can totally get his car in and out of the driveway. And you know me, Vi. I would have moved it if it was a real problem." I just nod my head along, waiting for her to get out the entire story. Bianca's always been a bit dramatic, I just figure it's the artist in her. "He just kept demanding I move it so I told him if he was that worried about it he could call the cops."

I suck in a breath, that seemed to have escalated quickly. "He's going to call the cops on you?"

"No! That's when he told me he *was* a cop."

"And that's when he threatened to arrest you?"

"Well, he didn't expressly threaten to arrest me . . . but it was implied! So instead of giving him another moment of my time I just took off and came home. I mean can you believe that? We're going to have to live next door to this guy? What an asshole!"

I take a moment to weigh my words, trying to be diplomatic. "At least you know now that parking there is a bad idea. Next time you can find somewhere else." Bianca lets out a groan and flops down onto the couch beside me. "At least he's kinda cute. Hey, you wanted a hot guy to move in, remember?"

"I didn't want one that was an asshole *and* a cop. God, what a nightmare." She sits up suddenly and turns to face me. "I know! You should totally bake him something!" She's got a grin on her face that stretches from ear to ear and looks only mildly terrifying.

I know I should feel insulted at the devious glee she has at the thought of me giving our new neighbor one of my creations but instead I find it almost as amusing as she does. Hey, I know where my talents lie and even though I love it, baking is not high on my skill set. "Are you trying to poison our neighbor with my innocent baked goods?"

"I'm just saying, he deserves a friendly wel-come-to-the-neighborhood present, that's all." She leans over and gives me a tight squeeze before releasing me. "Hey, don't you have your date tonight?" I feel bad that she's asking with more excitement than I'm actually feeling so I once again try to get in the right headspace to have a good date with Tyler.

"Yup, I sure do. I was just about to start getting ready."

She checks her watch and looks at me with wide eyes. "You better get a move on. I would be doing my makeup by now if it were me." Oh, I have no doubt about that. Bianca's beauty routine probably has about twenty more steps than my own. Every time she walks out of the house she looks like she's ready to hit the runway. I have neither the time nor inclination.

"Do you want to help me with mine? You know I suck at blending and all that stuff."

She claps her hands together. "I would love to. This is so exciting, Vi!"

"Before I forget, let me text you where I'm meeting him and his full name. You know, all that good stuff, just in case."

"Perfect, and if you need an urgent call to get you out of it, I'm your girl."

"I'll keep that in mind." I laugh nervously, hoping I won't need it.

"But in all seriousness," she says, her tone matching her words, "if you need me, call me. I'll be there in a flash. Say the word and I will kick his ass from here to the Space Needle."

I want to roll my eyes. What is it with the Morenos being so overprotective today? Instead, I just give her another hug. "You know, your dad told me the same thing today."

"Well, I'm not surprised." We both make our way to my bedroom so she can sort through my limited makeup supply and I can get ready for my shower. "You're just like another daughter to him. Of course he's going to worry about you."

The comment makes me flinch, and I hope Bianca hasn't noticed.

Okay, universe, I get it, no need to send any more signs. I'm moving on.

EIGHT

VIOLET

I pull into the packed parking lot of the sports bar near campus that Tyler has chosen for our date and squeeze my car into a space near the back. Before I get out, I check my makeup one last time in the mirror. I'll always believe Bianca is a miracle worker when it comes to makeup. Her own always reflects her personality, colorful and bold. However, she took a much lighter hand to mine tonight. She has my makeup looking soft and enhances my natural features. She's done something to my blue eyes to make them look twice as large as normal and the subtle sheen of nude gloss makes my normally anemic looking lips slightly poutier. Even if Tyler doesn't like the look, I certainly do.

Getting out of the car, I take a moment to smooth down my dress. It's nothing flashy, just a simple black with white polka dot dress that falls a few inches above my knees—one of my favorites—coupled with a pair of black low-heeled booties. I figure if I'm walking into a potentially awkward situation I might as well be comfortable.

I know that if Bianca could, she would have tried to get me into one of her flashier outfits but luckily, she knows that anything she owns would be swimming on me. Bianca is a statuesque beauty, a Botticelli babe. And I'm, well, not. If I put enough product and effort into my hair, I just kiss the five-foot, two-inch mark. My breasts are a comfortable B cup that look good on my compact frame but my curves aren't anything like those of my two beautiful roommates. Don't get me wrong, I'm happy with the way that I am but I know I don't necessarily fit the tits and ass requirements that a lot of guys my age look for.

Deciding that I've had enough of analyzing my date-night look, I head toward the main door of the bar. It's well-lit and there are people milling around outside. The hour is too early for many people to be stumbling around the parking lot drunk just yet.

Tyler offered to pick me up, but I declined, figuring it was better to have my car with me just in case. Once I get to the front of the bar, I shoot Tyler a text letting him know that I'm here. It takes a few minutes for him to respond but he lets me know that he's already inside sitting at a table near the back.

I push inside and weave through the Friday-night crowd. The place is filled to the brim with a combination of students that are here for the baseball game that's lighting up the TV screens or for general shenanigans which seem to be taking place around the pool tables and dart boards. I scan the room and finally spot Tyler sitting at a table near the back, staring up at a television screen.

It takes a few moments for him to notice my approach but when he does, he jumps up and gives me a hug, then grabs the single red rose I hadn't noticed sitting on the table and hands it to me. "A beautiful rose for a beautiful lady," he says with a smile. I know that I'm blushing; I'm not really used to compliments, especially those from attractive men.

"Thank you." He pulls out the seat for me and it's then that I notice there are several empty beer bottles on the table. "Am I late?" I ask, worried that I got the time wrong and that he's been here awhile.

"You're right on time." He gestures to the bottles in question. "I got here a little early to catch some of the game. Do you mind if I sit on this side of the table so I can catch the score?"

The question seems pretty moot at this point since he's already seated me in the chair that's facing away from the television and settling back into his own. "Uh, sure. No problem."

"I'm so glad we're finally doing this," he says.

"Yeah, me too." I give him a gentle smile. We make awkward small talk until the waitress comes around.

"Oh, great," Tyler says when the harried looking waitress approaches our table. "We'll have two more beers and a shot of Patron each." I know Tyler is just trying to be nice but I don't really care for beer and I definitely don't want a shot. Not when I have to drive home. But I don't want to embarrass him in front of the waitress. Instead, I just ask her to include a water for myself. "Did you want any food? I already ate." I just shake my head. I'm not going to be the only one of the two of us eating. It's a good thing I had a snack before I left the house.

After the waitress takes our order, she heads off presumably to get us our drinks. "I love this place." Tyler has to raise his voice to be heard over the din of customers. "I found it sophomore year and I've been coming here ever since."

I don't mind going to a sports bar occasionally but it's not really my scene. I'd much rather go somewhere quiet where we can talk, maybe take a walk together or do an activity but he told me he would handle planning the date so I figured that was nice of him. "Yeah, it's busy in here," I say with a smile.

We fall into the comfortable topic of classes and professors that we've shared over the years. He has me laughing at the impression he does of our third year Comparative Lit professor who could never seem to find his notes. It's . . . nice. Comfortable.

I'm slowly sipping on the beer that the waitress delivered to us, trying not to grimace at the taste. I'm a wine or fruity drink girl all the way but I can handle a beer for the evening. Tyler grabs his tequila shot and holds it up in the air, waiting for me to do the same. I eye the tiny glass of clear liquid skeptically. I surreptitiously check the time on one of the enormous TV screens and figure I have enough time to get it out of my system, so I join him in raising my own tiny glass of liquid hangover.

"To our first date," he says clinking his shot against mine.

"To our first date," I repeat.

"And to date number two." He smiles before downing the shot in one go.

I smile and pour the small amount of liquid into my mouth but only manage half of it before I'm coughing and sputtering. Tyler laughs and reaches around to pat me on the back while I try to get my throat and lungs under control. I can't even remember the last time I took a shot. It was probably at some party with Bianca and Hollie early on in our college careers.

"You okay there?" he asks with a smile.

"Yeah, I'm just not used to shots. I'm more of a lemon drop kind of girl."

"Don't worry, hang out with me some more and I'll have you downing those shots like they're nothing in no time." I have absolutely no intention of becoming a skilled shot taker but I figure now's not the time to tell him that. Instead of waiting for my response, he goes into an in-depth story about some shot contest he entered at a frat party. He doesn't seem to need much input from me so I just sit quietly and nod, eventually letting my mind drift. And of course, it drifts exactly where I don't want it to go.

I wonder what Dante is doing right now?

My mind falls into its familiar pattern of fantasizing about Dante. If I called him and told him I needed him would he show up right now? Would he storm into the bar worried about me? The thought sends a chill up and down my spine. I try to surreptitiously glance at my notifications just to see if maybe he's texted me to check in. He hasn't. There's no reason that he would. He's never texted me before. In fact, I'm not sure he even has my phone number.

I give myself a mental shake and try to concentrate on Tyler who has now moved onto a story about him and his brothers pranking their high school principal by TP-ing his house. I continue with my painted-on smile and try to look engaged. It's not fair to Tyler to be thinking of someone else while I'm here with him. Sure, this hasn't been the best date I've ever been on but it certainly hasn't been the worst. I can't help but remember the guy freshman year that brought his mother along to dinner. That's a story I'll tell my kids someday.

Tyler suggests another round of drinks but I decline, letting him know I need to head home. I make sure to grab the rose that he brought me and gather up my purse while he pays the tab before we make our way through the crowd that seems far drunker now than when I first arrived. He's placed his hand on my back in a protective gesture and is guiding me through, making sure that no one bumps into me. It only serves to remind me of how it felt when

Dante's hands were on my waist lifting me into and out of his big truck. My entire body came alive from his touch. Unfortunately, I feel nothing like that from Tyler's hand on my back.

Once we make it outside, I show him where my car is, and he walks me over. We're both standing a little awkwardly in the darkened corner of the parking lot and I'm not sure if I should just bolt for my car door and go or what.

"I had a good time tonight, Violet."

"Me too, Tyler. Thank you for the drinks. I would have been happy to split the tab with you."

"No way, Vi. When you're with me, you're going to be treated like the lady you are. You can expect more of that in the future." I don't know how to feel about his statements regarding another date. I did have a nice time but I'm just not feeling a romantic connection with him. It definitely wouldn't hurt my crush situation to go on another date but I don't want to lead him on if there's nothing there. I'll have to think about it, maybe talk about it with Bianca and Hollie. Instead of giving him any indication one way or the other, I give him my standard smile that I always plaster on when I don't know what to say.

Tyler edges closer to me, and I instinctively hold my breath. I think he's going to kiss me. I can feel my heart rate speed up, not in excitement but with nerves. He leans in and just as I'm steeling myself to be ready, he diverts his lips to my cheek giving me a gentle kiss. I let out a soft sigh, thankful that he hasn't tried to push things further. I guess Tyler really is a nice guy.

"I'll see you in class next week, Violet. Save me a seat for me, won't you?"

"No problem," I say before unlocking my car and sliding into the driver's seat.

Before I can close the door, he grabs ahold of it. "Text me when you get home, okay? I want to make sure you get there all right."

This time my smile is genuine as I nod my agreement and close the door between us. I start the engine and head out of the parking lot to the main street. The entire time Tyler is standing there in the dark, watching me, making sure that I'm okay.

It's about twenty minutes before I reach home, and as I'm putting my key in the door, my attention gets drawn to the house next door. A light is on in the living room and I think I see a curtain move. Our poor new neighbor is probably seeing if Bianca came home to block his driveway with her car again. That girl has balls going toe to toe with a cop. I just hope that she doesn't make an enemy of our new neighbor before Hollie and I even have a chance to meet him.

The house is silent as I set down my bag on the table in the entryway, leading me to believe that both Bianca and Hollie are out for the evening. I'm not ready to head to bed just yet and decide instead to dive into the latest Steven King novel that I bought this morning and hadn't had time to start.

I leave the lights off and settle into our comfy couch, drawing the throw that's hanging over the back around me. I pick up my eReader and dive into the rich fantasy world the master of horror has created.

I'm not sure how much time has passed before two beams of light cross over my face, pulling me out of the story. I wait a few minutes but the light remains steadily seeping in through the curtains. I don't know if it's my natural cowardice or the book I'm reading but I decide not to go check outside. The light is obviously the headlights of a vehicle and I don't know why anyone would be just sitting in their car this late at night.

I'm getting a little freaked out at this point but remind myself that there's a cop next door now. Sure, I don't know him but if I ran over there screaming because someone tried to break into the house, I'm sure he would help me. That's what they're like, sworn to do, right? God, I really wish that Bianca hadn't pissed him off. Just as I get up to go check that all the doors and windows are locked, I see the light move, going off into the distance, followed by the sound of a heavy engine fading away. I let out a sigh of relief. I've got to stop letting my imagination get away with me. This is a crowded neighborhood. There are plenty of reasons someone could be sitting in their car in the middle of a Friday night. Right?

NINE

DANTE

Me: Testing.

Yes, I just sent a text to myself to make sure my phone is working. You can never be too sure. Especially when you're waiting for a woman to let you know she needs rescuing from a bad date and you're prepared to be her knight in shining armor.

Too bad as the hours creep on, it's becoming more and more apparent that she doesn't need me at all. Am I jealous? Absolutely. I'm man enough to admit it to myself. I want to be the one taking her out on a date, laughing with her, telling her how beautiful she looks, kissing her . . . nope, not thinking about that or anything else that she might be doing on her date right now.

Instead of being where I really want to be, I'm sitting here on my couch, in sweatpants, with the TV on mute while I try to read. Normally, reading de-stresses me. I like to immerse myself into a world that doesn't contain my own problems. Instead, this Steven King thriller is just reminding me of all the horrible things that could happen to Violet out there all alone without protection. Yes, I'm jealous. But it's not only that. There's a feeling in my gut that something is wrong. A feeling that I can't seem to shake.

I am absolutely aware of how pathetic I am in this moment but I can't bring myself to care. I go back to my book, but after stopping to check my phone for a text from Violet another three times, I give up and put it aside. I'm filled with nervous energy and start pacing the expanse of my living room. It's a good thing I had sprung for the plush carpet or else I would be wearing a line in it.

Why didn't I ask her where her date was going to be? That way I could drive by and just take a peek, make sure she's okay. Creepy? Yes. An option I wish was on the table? Absolutely.

I briefly consider calling Bianca and seeing if I can fish for the information from her. I'm sure that Violet told her where she would be. My Violet is a smart girl, she would never take off with some guy without making sure she was safe. That's the only comfort I get as the large grandfather clock I inherited from my parents ticks away in the foyer.

I know I can't call Bianca. Her not calling me out when I asked about Violet's date the other day is a minor miracle. If I called her with some lame excuse now and tried to get the information from her, she would definitely know something was up. The last thing I want is for her to know I have a tiny insignificant little crush on her best friend.

Instead of bothering my daughter, I grab a beer from the fridge and settle back onto the couch, forgoing the book that's done nothing but ratchet up my anxiety, and unmute the television. Some mindless TV is just what I need to distract myself.

Unfortunately, the universe has some kind of sick, twisted sense of humor and immediately the sounds of Keith Morrison on Dateline streams through my surround sound speakers. They are focusing on a case involving the disappearance of a young woman. She was at a bar with her friends, left, and vanished without a trace. I mash down the power button on the remote with such force that, for a moment, I worry I broke it.

I can't just sit here; I feel like I have ants crawling under my skin. I've never felt such a need to do something, anything, in my life. I glance at the clock and see that it's just past midnight. She should definitely be home by now, right? Before I can put too much thought into my slightly unhinged actions, I toss a tee shirt on, grab my keys, and head out to my truck.

It only takes me a few minutes to drive over to the girls' house. When I was deciding which rental property to put Bianca and the girls in, I had several open options but decided on this one because it was closest to me. It's not that I'm much of a hovering parent—present actions excluded—but if something went wrong, I wanted to make sure that I was easily accessible.

As I approach the house, I slow down and pull over to the curb right in front of the neighboring house. It's with a sense of relief that I see Violet's car sitting in the driveway, safe and sound. That is until I realize that he may have picked her up. I let my head fall forward and hit the steering wheel, a loud groan escaping me. At this point I'm not sure what to do so I just sit there, staring, looking for any sign of life inside the small house. I don't see either Bianca's or Hollie's cars in the driveway or parked on the street, so I can only assume that if there's any signs of life inside that it will be Violet.

I don't know how long it is that I sit and stare at the house before there's a forceful knocking on my window. The sound startles me so much that I physically jump into the air. I turn and see a man about a decade younger than myself staring at me. He's dressed in what looks like pajama pants and a tee shirt. I'm about to tell him to go fuck off when he hits my window again, this time with a clinking noise that comes from his Seattle PD badge hitting the glass.

I roll down my window before asking, "Can I help you with anything officer?"

"It's detective. And yes, you can. You want to tell me what you're doing sitting out here in your truck at midnight staring at my neighbor's house?"

Well, shit. I guess the new neighbor moved in. "Actually, Detective, I own that house. My daughter lives there with her friends. I just wanted to check and make sure she got home all right." He's intently studying my face and I hope that the slight lie isn't enough for him to assume that I'm up to no good and . . . what? Take me downtown? Wouldn't that be just great? How would I explain something like that to Bianca?

His face is an impassive mask, giving away nothing. "Can I see some ID, sir?" I quickly pull out my wallet and extract the ID, handing it over. He studies it for a moment before handing it back. His posture relaxes the slightest bit and I get the feeling that while he thinks I'm probably telling the truth, he isn't letting is guard down. "Haven't you heard of a phone?"

I give a lame attempt at a chuckle and explain to him that Bianca wasn't answering. I don't think that I've ever lied to a police officer before and it's making me jumpy. One wrong move and I'll be in handcuffs.

"Look Mr. Moreno, it's late. Why don't you head on home. I'm sure your daughter will call you back when she's free." He hands the ID back to me and I toss it onto the passenger seat, not even bothering to shove it back into my wallet.

"Of course, you're right. I'll just head home. Thanks for keeping an eye out for the girls. I feel better knowing there's a police officer on the street looking out for them."

He merely nods his head and starts back toward his own house without a word. I release the breath that I'd been holding and put the truck in drive, heading back home.

I don't know what the fuck I was thinking driving over here in the middle of the night. There's absolutely no reason that anything should be wrong with Violet. People go out on dates every day and nothing happens. I know that my jealousy was making my imagination run wild, but I still can't help the pit that's formed in the bottom of my stomach saying that something just isn't right with this guy.

The rest of the weekend went by at a snail's pace. I tried reading, watching TV, working, and I even gave cleaning a shot. Nothing seemed to make the time go faster. I know it was my own pathetic need to see Violet. All that time spent doing nothing left me to the unfortunate realization that I may be developing feelings for the young woman who was not only my employee and daughter's best friend but also seventeen years younger than me.

I knew it was a mistake hiring her. I thought that maybe the proximity would help me see her in a more realistic light instead of some sexy nymph I was lusting after. Well, I saw her in a more realistic light all right. The problem is that I'm liking everything I'm seeing more and more. It's not like I could ever act on these feelings. Violet would be repulsed that her best friend's father was coming on to her.

And even if, by some great miracle, she wanted to give us a try, Bianca would absolutely lose her shit. It's not worth destroying both my own and Violet's relationship with her for whatever this might be. No, I'll just stay quiet, admiring her from afar.

When Monday morning finally rolled around and Violet came floating into my office, it felt like the first time I could take a breath of fresh air in days. Unfortunately, that air was lined with the scent of jasmine that has my pants immediately feeling a size too small. *Fuck.*

After our initial *good mornings* she made her way to her writing desk and got to work. I'd like to think that I wasn't going to ask. At the very least, I hoped I could hold out a few hours. Instead, seven minutes and thirty-seven seconds later was my breaking point.

"So, how was your date?"

She turned toward me, looking as surprised by the question as I was. "Uh, it was . . . fine actually."

I raise my eyebrow at her. "Just fine? No sparks?" I know I shouldn't be getting into this with her. This was absolutely none of my business but apparently my mouth didn't give a fuck.

"Yeah, fine. I don't know about any sparks. I'm not sure I'm a 'sparks' kind of person." She averts her eyes from me back to her computer screen, making it obvious that she doesn't want to talk about this with me. My enamored brain doesn't give a shit.

"Just promise me something."

"What?" She's looking at me skeptically.

"That you won't just settle. You deserve sparks, Violet." Her mouth drops open and her face turns red. Her eyes immediately avert from mine. I've embarrassed her. But she needs to hear that. If even a fraction of the vibe I got off her parents is true, I don't know if anyone's ever told her that before.

Before she says anything in response, the phone on her desk rings. "Moreno Construction. How can I help you? . . . Oh hey, Adrian. What can I do for you today?"

My eyes narrow as I focus on her face that's partially turned away from me. Adrian is the foreman of my second group of workers. They're out doing some renovations on a business park across town. What I'd like to know is how she seems to know Adrian already. How did I never notice how many single men work for me before? I'm adding a marital status question to all employment applications from now on.

I turn back to my keyboard, attempting to finish the email I was typing to some prospective clients. Instead, my focus is entirely on Violet's phone call.

"Oh no, let me just check." She rifles through some papers that are neatly stacked on her desk. "Yes, his timecard is right here . . . Either Dante or I will give the payroll company a call . . . No, it's not a problem at all. Please, let him know that I'll get this corrected as quickly as possible . . . Okay, thanks for calling, Adrian."

She hangs up the phone and before she says anything I'm already jumping in. "What was that all about?"

She frowns down at the timesheet in her hand. "I guess one of Adrian's guys didn't get his paycheck on Friday. I'm going to call the payroll company." She frowns down at the timesheet once again before reaching for her phone.

"What else is wrong?" I ask.

She just shakes her head. "It's nothing. Really. Don't worry, I'll take care of it."

"Something's wrong, Vi. You're looking at that timesheet like it just murdered your best friend, and since that person happens to be my daughter, I find it disturbing." She gives me that soft smile that makes my heart beat faster in my chest. "You know you can tell me anything, right?"

"Well, it's just that . . . these time sheets. They're a little archaic."

"Archaic?" I know my tone is coming out as a little offended but I can't help it. I don't want Violet associating me with anything old, let alone archaic.

Her pretty lips turn down into an even prettier pout. "See, I knew I shouldn't have said anything."

I want to smack myself in the head. "I said you could tell me anything and I mean it. What's wrong with the time sheets besides them being archaic." I shoot her a wink on that last word to let her know that I'm joking with her.

"If we just modernized the system a little it would be easy for your employees to self-serve some of these things. Plus, they wouldn't have to fill out a paper every day and then have Jake or Adrian come drop them off to you weekly. I know of services where they can enter their time into an app on their phone, they can view their pay and hours, they can even get direct deposits."

I look at her surprised. I thought this girl was a college student. Why does it seem like she's more confident and capable of running an office than I am? "How do you know all of this? You said that you listened to your dad do negotiations on the phone all the time but I highly doubt he was putting payroll systems into place for his company."

"You're not wrong. No, during my summers in high school my mother would drag me to every debutante event she could find. It was exhausting and just, not for me. The only way out of it was to spend my days at my dad's office. One of the women in the HR office took pity on me and let me hang out with her. Most days I spent either reading or helping her with minor tasks. I picked up a lot of things from her on how to run an office."

"I guess I have her to thank for all this." I point around me at the office that is a million times more orderly than before Violet joined the team.

"I really haven't done much," she says, going shy on me.

"Oh please, I wouldn't even have known where to look for that time sheet if Adrian would have called me. Plus, I would probably spend half the day on the phone with the payroll company trying to fix the problem that I know you'll handle in minutes." Her face is starting to glow with a pretty blush I rather like on her. "Why don't you get me some pricing on some of those apps you're talking about and we'll look into it. Anything that requires me to have less paper floating around here is a good thing."

She nervously fiddles with a lock of her hair. "No problem, I can have those numbers to you by end of week."

We spend the rest of the day companionably working side by side until it's time for her to leave for class. As she packs up to go and the only thing I can think of is that I don't want her to leave. It barely feels like work when I get to share it with her. Once she leaves with a gentle goodbye and a small wave, the office is dead silent. I turn on some music in a vain attempt to fill the void that Violet has left, but it doesn't help. I guess now is as good a time as any to drive over to Roxhill and check on Adrian and his crew. Maybe I can apologize to his guy about the payroll mix up in person.

I'm just shoving my keys into my pocket when I hear the sound of the front door downstairs. My heart soars for a moment hoping that Violet has come back. That hope is

MADE TO BE YOURS

quickly shattered when I hear a distinctive *clack, clack, clack* on the hardwood floor.

Some additional pieces of information I've collected about Violet Daniels: She always brushes her hair to the right side of her neck, never the left. She prefers knee length skits over pants. And even though she's short, she rarely wears high heels unless the occasion calls for it.

No, instead of the blue eyed, black-haired beauty walking through the office door I'm greeted by the visage of my ex-wife. "How the hell did you get in here, Amanda?"

She strides into my office, all tight jeans and boobs that does absolutely nothing for me. "Bianca told me where you keep the spare." *Looks like I'll be moving that and having a talk with my daughter.*

"What do you need? I was just about to head out to a job."

"I saw little Violet leaving here. It was so sweet of you to give the tiny thing a job." I clench my jaw. I don't appreciate the snide way she's talking about Violet but I can't let it show.

"Look, if you don't need anything I've got to take off."

"I just wanted to check again on the properties you have. I found a place that I think I'm going to take but I just want to make sure you don't have anything for me."

This woman gets on my nerves like no other. "Amanda. There's nothing. If I had something, I would have told you. What is this obsession with getting into one of my properties? And while we're at it, why are you moving here? You've never expressed any interest in moving to Seattle. Hell, you've only been here to visit Bianca a handful of times since she moved here four years ago. What's going on with you?"

She lets out a sigh and gives a little jump, sitting on top of my desk. I guess it would be rude to rip out the papers she's sitting on and dump her on the floor, but the urge is strong. "I lost my job, okay?"

"What? How? You've been working there for years? Did the doctor close his practice or something?"

She gives out a huff and shrug, turning her head away from me. I know from my years with her she's hiding something. "Amanda," I say in a warning tone.

"Fine. I was having an affair with him for the past year and his wife found out. After promising me for months that he was going to leave her, the second she found out, he dumped and fired me. That bitch wife of his didn't keep her mouth shut about it either. Now I'm the town pariah. I can't find a job at another practice and I feel like I'm one step away from people shunning me in the streets."

Something doesn't seem right. "How did his wife find out?"

"I told her, okay?" She raises her voice at me. "He said he was going to leave her! I was just giving him a little nudge."

I let my head fall back and rub the bridge of my nose. "Jesus Christ, Amanda. What the fuck were you thinking? Does Bianca know?"

"Of course not! And you better not tell her. She just knows that I broke up with my boyfriend. Besides, this is a good thing. It was time for me to get out of that town anyway. I didn't want to spend my entire life living in one place. Now I get to be here with you and Bianca."

"The keyword there is *Bianca*. We're not friends, Amanda. Hell, we're barely acquaintances. The last time we spent any time together at all when our daughter wasn't around was when she was two. I don't expect that to change anytime soon."

She pushes off my desk and crosses her arms over her chest. "Jesus, Dante, you don't have to be such an asshole all the time."

"I guess you just bring it out in me. Like I said, I gotta go." I stand and gesture toward the door so that she'll exit in front of me. She passes me while muttering under her breath and makes her way out. Not for the first time I wonder what the fuck seventeen-year-old me was thinking but brush it off. Without Amanda I wouldn't have Bianca, and I'll be eternally grateful to her for that.

TEN

VIOLET

By the time Thursday rolls around I feel like I've developed a pretty good routine between work and school. Working for Dante hasn't been nearly as boring as I thought it would be. I mean, sure, it's not the most thrilling thing in the world but I'm finding a sense of accomplishment in getting everything in order and making sure all the cogs are running smoothly. Dante is listening to me and my suggestions, he's even decided to implement the new time recording and payroll system I suggested. For one of the first times in my life, I feel like I'm making a difference.

In fact, I'm working on the installation of the new system when I receive a text. I quickly glance at it and see that it's my group text with Hollie and Bianca. I'm about to turn my phone back over and look at it later when I catch a preview of Hollie's message. *Hollie has a date with Archer? Holy hell.*

I almost drop the phone. I mean, we knew she had a crush on him; Bianca even suspected that he returned the sentiment. Not in my wildest dreams did I think she would actually get a date with her billionaire hotel mogul boss. I shouldn't be surprised, though. Hollie is one of the smartest, kindest, most beautiful human beings that I know, and it looks like she's calling an all-hands-on-deck meeting to help her get ready tonight. I quickly type out my response letting her know that I'll be there.

I really am happy for Hollie but I can't help but be a little jealous as I slide my gaze over to where Dante is on the phone. If there's hope for her and her boss, maybe there's hope for me and mine. I don't kid myself, though. I know our situations are far different. Archer may be older than Hollie but he's not *that* much older. Also, he isn't her best friend's dad. Not to mention the fact that her mother wouldn't have an aneurysm if she dated him. Nope, Hollie's luck is decidedly better than my own.

I pull my eyes away from the object of my affection and focus back on price comparing lumber. *Joy.*

"What the hell are adult Capri Suns?" Dante's voice startles me out of my thoughts.

"What are you talking about?" I ask.

"Bianca says she wants adult Capri Suns for her party. Here," he says, shoving the phone at me, "maybe you can tell me what the hell she's talking about."

I look at her text and smile. This is so Bianca. "I think she's going for the adult kid party vibe. She means she wants pre-made alcoholic drinks in pouches like those old Capri Sun drinks."

"Where does she think I'm going to find something like that?"

I hand him back his phone and pick up my own. "I can order some online." A few clicks later I have a hundred pouches being delivered to us via two-day express mail. "There you go, now you just have to get the stuff to fill them."

"I'm telling you, every time I turn around she has a new request. She's twenty-three, shouldn't she be throwing her own parties by now?" I'm pretty sure he's joking but just in case . . .

"You should feel good that she still wants you included. I think I'd rather crawl through broken glass than have my parents involved in anything social that I'm doing."

He rolls his eyes in my direction. "I'm sure they're not that bad."

"You'd be wrong. Once, in second grade I met a girl at our local park with my nanny. I wanted to invite her over to play so much that I begged and begged my mother for days to call her mom and invite her over. Finally, she gave in and said she would set something up. I was so excited I could hardly wait. When the day of our playdate finally arrived, I opened the door and some kid I had never met was standing there with her mom. Apparently, Mom thought she was a much more appropriate playmate than the kid I had met at the park." Even now, years later, I still feel disappointment at the memory. Not just the memory of not getting to play with the child of my choice but the disappointment of my mother's total disregard of what I wanted. I was too young to know it then, but it would be a reoccurring theme in my life up to this day.

"Yikes," he says in an attempt to lift some of the sadness that's seeped in from my pathetic story. I just shrug and turn back to my computer like it's no big deal. It really shouldn't be. Those are just the breaks. "You know what," he says interrupting my thoughts. "Why don't we get out of here?"

I look at him in surprise. "And go where?"

"I mean, we're obviously going to need a lot of stuff for this shindig my daughter is determined to throw. Let's go shopping."

"Shindig?" I raise my eyebrow.

"If you're going to make fun of my old-man vocabulary, I'm not inviting you to come with me." I can't help but laugh. If he's an old man, then I don't know what you'd call someone who was actually old.

"Sure, let's get out of here. I just processed some receivables; you should be able to afford the small fortune in booze Bianca is going to require."

He groans and grabs his keys. "You're killing me, Vi."

Once we make it out to his truck, he doesn't hesitate this time, he grips my hips, causing a small gasp to escape my lips at the contact and hoists me up. For just a second we're both frozen face to face, eye to eye, mere inches apart. The sensations from his hands being on me are running from my waist to the top of my head and back down to my toes. If I leaned in just the tiniest bit, I could kiss him. I bet that would give me those sparks that he was talking about. Abruptly, he drops me into the seat and makes sure my legs are tucked in before closing the door and ending any moment that my mind may have conjured.

It's not long before we're wandering the packed aisles of our local Costco. "So, what do you think we need *besides* a shipping container's worth of alcohol?" I take the lead and steer the cart toward the paper goods section.

"Unless you want half your plates and glasses broken, I'd suggest stocking up on this stuff."

"Well, it's not like they were expensive but lord knows I don't want anyone stepping on glass." He grabs paper plates and napkins and tosses them in the cart while I heft a package of the obligatory red Solo cups over my shoulder before dumping it into the cart to join the others.

"What do you plan on doing for food? It's probably a little too soon to get anything perishable," I say as we make our way through the store.

"I was going to order catering from the Mediterranean place down the street. Do you think that's okay?"

"That's fine, I wouldn't worry too much about ordering like, full meals or anything. It's going to be mostly Bianca's art friends and if I've learned anything from attending a plethora of art shows with her, it's that the art crowd loves good appetizers. Maybe we should just grab chips and things like that for today?"

"Good idea."

We're making our way through the store, chatting about nothing and everything when I spot something sitting on one of the produce displays. "Oh my god, look! They have rambutans!" I excitedly grab a package containing the tiny fruits that resemble sea urchins and show them to Dante.

"Rambu-whats?" He's suspiciously eyeing my find like he doesn't quite trust them. "What the hell are they?"

"They're rambutans. They're little fruits that are kind of like lychees." The explanation doesn't seem to make him any less leery.

"They look like hairy red and green golf balls sorely in need of a trim," he says making me laugh.

"I've read about them and seen them in pictures but I've actually never come across any. I can't believe that they have them here. I've always wanted to bake something with them."

"Sold." He grabs the package out of my hand and gently places it on top of the pile of items in our cart.

"Oh no, I didn't mean for you to get them. It's not worth me baking something with them." I go to reach into the cart to grab the package and he pushes my hand away.

"What are you talking about? You want to make something with them, let's get it."

"You don't understand," I say with a groan.

"What are you talking about, Violet?"

"I'm a bad baker, okay?" I know I've raised my voice but I'm annoyed that he's forced me to admit this flaw to him. "I love baking but I'm bad at it. Nothing ever comes out right."

"I'm sure that's not true."

"Oh, but it is. Just ask your daughter. I mean, one time I actually mixed up the salt and sugar. I think Hollie had to drink a gallon of water before her body was back to being balanced out. The sad thing is that I really love baking. I find it calming, following the step-by-step instructions. It gives me something to focus on and it helps to melt away any stress I have going on in my life. It's tragic really," I add admittedly rather dramatically.

Dante is giving me a frown of disapproval and the last thing I want to do is hear him tell me I shouldn't bake anymore. I move away from him but he gently grabs my arm, sending another tingle through my body. He's got to stop doing that.

"Look, Violet, mixing up salt and sugar isn't that big of a deal, I'm sure everyone has done it—"

"It wasn't just that, I—"

"But," he continues like I didn't just rudely interrupt him, "don't let that stop you from doing something you love. Just because you've made a few mistakes doesn't make you bad at it. If you really love it, just keep going. Besides, I bet they aren't half as bad as you're making them out to be."

"You'd be wrong," I grumble under my breath.

He stares at me for another beat before a smile forms on his face. "I'll tell you what. I suck at cooking, like, truly, I'm abhorrent. But there are a few things I can make. Why don't you bake me something with these tiny dust balls and

I'll make you dinner. Then we can both practice something that we may not be the best at?"

"You'd do that for me?"

"Hey, it's not just for you. I've got to eat too. Plus, I can't tell you the last time I got to eat something home baked. I'll do dinner and you can make dessert once we get back to the house. Deal?"

I'm pretty sure my jaw hits the floor but I do my best to slam my mouth closed before he notices. Having Dante cook me a dinner is something I didn't even know that I wanted but now that it's a possibility I can't think of any other way I'd rather spend tonight. Suddenly, realization hits me and I deflate. "I really wish I could, but Hollie has a date tonight with Archer and I promised her I would help her get ready."

I can see him physically rear back at that revelation. "What do you mean Hollie has a date with Archer? He's her boss and like, twelve years older than her."

"What's the problem with that?" I ask, my tone coming out more harshly than I mean it to. "They both really seem to like each other. It's just a date." I'm sure that my avid defense of Hollie and Archer has nothing to do with my desire to date my own much older boss. Nope, it has nothing to do with that at all.

"I mean, if it's what they both want, I guess it's okay. I'm just surprised is all," he says. He has that cute furrow in his brow that he gets when he's thinking deeply on something. Like always, I want to reach up and smooth it out.

"Her date is at seven," I say nervously. "I could bake at home and then bring it over then?"

"Sounds good, it's a date." My breath catches and Dante's face immediately turns a shade of red I've never seen. "I don't mean a *date* date. I mean, well you know what I mean."

Of course he doesn't mean it's an *actual* date. I get that. Even if for just the tiniest of seconds my heart had leapt in my chest. "Oh, course not." I laugh, hoping he doesn't see the pink that's surely spreading across my cheeks. "But I'm warning you, when you have to spit whatever I make out into the trash, I'm going to say I told you so." His only response is a smile and a wink that makes my knees a little weak.

ELEVEN

DANTE

What the fuck was I thinking? I really am a spectacular idiot. I'm supposed to be keeping my distance from Violet, not inviting her over for home-cooked meals. I just couldn't seem to stop myself.

After we left the store and got back to the house, I sent her home for the day. There was nothing pressing that needed to be done and I wanted to give her time to do her baking. When she talked about how bad she was at it, I felt horrible. I know Bianca told me it was bad, but I didn't expect to find that even Violet believed it.

I could see in her eyes how much she loved doing it. It doesn't matter what she brings over tonight, I'm going to find something good to say about it, even if it's the worst thing I've ever eaten. It's not like she's going to be getting a gourmet meal out of me.

I move around the kitchen checking the refrigerator and going through cabinets. Maybe Bianca is right. Maybe I should stop relying on takeout so much. Unless Violet is in the mood for some slightly moldy cheddar cheese with a side of ketchup packets, it doesn't look like I have much to offer. I know I promised her a home-cooked meal but she might have to settle for takeout.

I pull up the trusty delivery app on my phone and decide on Thai food. I know that I've seen her eating pad Thai before so that's a safe bet. I quickly add a variety of other dishes to my order and schedule the delivery before running upstairs to take a shower. Once I'm standing in my closet, trying to decide what to wear, I realize that I'm treating this like an actual date.

This is NOT a date. I just need to repeat that to myself several more times. When Violet shows up here in a few hours, I don't want her to think I'm some creep trying to take advantage of her. I look at the clothes hanging in my closet once again and let out a sigh. Besides, it's not like I have any date clothes. It's been years since I've put in any effort. I guess it doesn't hurt to put in some now, you know, for practice. I grab a pair of jeans that I rarely wear, meaning that they aren't worn out or splattered with paint, and a sweater that Bianca gave me for Christmas a few years ago and quickly get dressed.

Once I'm back downstairs, I look at the clock and realize I still have about forty-five minutes before Violet's going to show up. I decide to set the table to keep myself busy. I almost set everything up in the dining room but at the last second decide that's way too formal for a casual dinner between friends.

After I've finished putting down some of the only matching place mats, dishes, and flatware I own onto the kitchen table, I look it over with a critical eye. I feel like it's missing something. I almost grab the big candle that sits on the bookshelf in the living room but stop myself, realizing that definitely screams date. Why is this so difficult?

I decide to leave the table as is and grab a beer from the fridge before making my way to the living room and flipping on the TV. I just need to distract myself, so I throw on some comedy I've seen a hundred times, and it isn't long before I notice that my leg is bouncing up and down uncontrollably. I shouldn't be this nervous. This is just having dinner with a friend, an employee even!

Finally, the food arrives, and I take it into the kitchen. I'm about to dump everything from their takeout containers into other dishes when I realize that one, I'm being ridiculous and two, I don't think I have that many serving dishes. I've obviously been a bachelor for way too long.

After what feels like an eternity the doorbell rings and I open the door to find Violet standing there with a large, white, circular dish covered with a towel in her hand. I notice immediately that she's also changed her clothes. Earlier today she was wearing a pair of jeans and a simple blouse. Now, don't get me wrong, she looked beautiful, she always does. But tonight, she's blowing me away.

Now she's wearing a simple black skirt that hits a few inches above her knees and is made out of some kind of wispy material that swishes as she balances from foot to foot on the front porch. Her top is a soft pink, covered in the tiniest of hearts, that dips low in the front, giving me a view of what I shouldn't be looking at, and just skims the top of her skirt allowing me the tantalizing glimpse of the porcelain skin below.

"Um, hey." Her voice pulls me out of my daze and I quickly bring my eyes back up to her face.

"You look beautiful," I say before I can think better of it. A pretty blush covers her cheeks but she doesn't look freaked out, thank God.

"Thank you," she says softly before pushing the dish in her hands toward me. "I made clafoutis."

I quickly take it out of her hands and step out of the way so she can get past me into the house. "What's a clafoutis?"

I ask starting to lift the edge of the towel so that I can take a peek. Before I can see anything, she smacks my hand away and passes me on the way to the kitchen, inadvertently drawing my eyes to her swaying hips and ass.

"Not yet. You promised me dinner first. If I have to embarrass myself with my baking the least you can do is show me your cooking."

"Yeah, about that . . ." Before I can explain, she comes to a dead stop in front of me and I can't stop myself in time from crashing into her. I instinctively wrap my arm around her waist so that she doesn't fall forward, and before I know it, I have her back pulled tight up against my front, my fingers grazing the soft skin of her stomach and I'm instantly hard. Her hand comes up and rests on top of mine for just a moment before she pulls away. I can only hope she didn't feel my arousal at our contact.

"I thought you were going to cook," she says, gesturing to the table stacked with takeout containers without looking me in the eye. *Shit, I really hope she didn't notice how hard she makes my dick.*

"I guess I should have picked up something at the store," I say sheepishly. "It turns out there was nothing in the house that was actually edible. Plus, I can't really subject you to my cooking so I ordered us some Thai food. You like pad Thai, right?"

She looks at me with a surprised expression. "Yeah, how did you know?"

"I'm not completely oblivious." I laugh. "I've seen you get it before, and I ordered a bunch of other stuff as well. Why don't you serve us, and I'll grab us some beers."

It's not long before the previous awkwardness is forgotten and we're chatting while devouring our dinner. After a few minutes, I notice she hasn't taken a sip of her drink.

"Did you want something else?" I ask indicating her untouched beer.

"Um, actually, I don't really care for beer." There's another fact about Violet that I get to tuck away.

"You don't like beer? Why didn't you say something?" I get up, remove the untouched drink from in front of her, and head to the fridge.

"I didn't want to offend you, I'm easy. I like going with the flow," she says shrugging her shoulders and fiddling with her fork.

"That's crazy, Vi. What were you going to do? Not drink anything for the entire dinner? You like wine, right? I know I've seen you drinking that. What would you like?"

"Anything white would be great." I take a moment to give her a hard stare before she breaks out into a gentle chuckle. "I'm serious this time, I'll take any kind of white wine you have, I love it."

I pull a bottle of Pinot Grigio from the fridge, then grab two glasses along with an opener, bringing it all back to the table. "So, do you always just take whatever someone gives you even if you don't like it?" She gives me another shrug and looks away. Apparently, this is an uncomfortable topic for her but I want to understand her more than I've ever wanted to understand anyone I've ever met, so I continue to push. "Why?"

She finally turns to face me head on and takes a breath like she's about to spill state secrets. "You wouldn't understand. You didn't grow up with my parents, my mother really. She has very specific ideas of what I should do, what I should wear, how I should act. After a while, it just became easier to do whatever she wanted. Once, I was out of her house and away at school I could sometimes get away with just telling her I was doing what she wanted and then do my own thing but still, most of the time, it's just easier to let everyone else have their way. That probably sounds pathetic, but I don't mind putting my wants on the back burner. I've been doing it all my life."

I knew her parents were overbearing and a bit controlling but I honestly didn't know that this was how she lived her life. My heart hurts for her. I can't imagine never really getting what I want, always just doing what other people want to do. Even something as simple as what she's going to drink at dinner. How much of what I thought I knew about Violet was her just going along to get along?

In that moment I resolve to not be a person who just lets Violet go with the flow. I don't want her to feel like she has to twist herself into knots to please me because I'm her boss and, well, I'd like to think her friend as well at this point.

"I'll tell you what. You promise to always tell me what you want. What you *really* want, not what you think I want to hear, and I promise you I'll never get upset about it."

She eyes me skeptically. "Dante, you don't have to do that."

"Oh, I know I don't. But if we're going to be spending time together—as boss and employee," I quickly add, "then I think it's important that we're both honest with each other, right?"

She seems to consider what I'm saying for a moment and then nods her head at me and gives me that soft smile that more and more often is making my heart stagger in my chest. It's not something that I want to examine too closely right now so I quickly change the subject. "And now, since we have this newfound pact of honesty, why don't you tell me what you want to do with your life. You've mentioned several things you'd like to do with your degree but what do you really want. I promise not to tell your parents," I say with an exaggerated wink that just makes her roll her eyes.

She seems to consider my question for a minute, and I give her the space to decide what she's going to tell me. Finally, she says, "I have no idea what I'm going to do with my English degree. If I had to choose right now, I would probably teach. I enjoy school and can see myself being happy in the world of Academia. But there's only one thing I've always wanted to do with my life. God, I've never told anyone this before. Not even Bianca or Hollie." She pauses putting her face in her hands like she's about to admit something really difficult for her. I sit there, still as a statue, like any movement from me might send her skittering away. After a deep breath she continues, rushing the words like she's trying to get them out before she loses her courage, "I've just always wanted to be a mom. I know it's not a particularly modern thing to want to be, but it's all I've ever really wanted. I've always wanted to do things with my child that my parents never did with me. One of the reasons that I love baking is because our cook at home used to let me help sometimes and it was one of the few times I felt close to an adult. My mother just told me all the things we made were going to make me fat."

I'm honestly a bit taken aback. I thought for sure Violet would have some big plans with her degree. After all, she's seemed to fight her parents pretty hard to stay in school. She's looking at me and must see my surprised expression because she covers her face with her hands again. Her voice comes out slightly muffled as she continues, "God, I knew I shouldn't have said anything. It's so stupid. Who wants to be a parent because their own sucked so much?"

I reach across the table and gently place my hand on her arm, fully concentrating on her and trying to ignore the sensations I get from the contact of her bare skin with mine. "There's nothing wrong with that, Violet. It's great you want to be a mom. And wanting to be a better parent than your own is something you'll find that ninety-nine percent of parents out there strive for. It isn't selfish. You'll be an amazing mother."

"What about you? Do ever want any more kids."

I can't help but let out a laugh. "I'm way too old for that."

"No, you're not," she says rather vehemently. "A lot of men your age are just starting families. Just because you started early doesn't mean you have to be done."

"I won't lie and say that I haven't thought about having another child a few times over the years," I admit. "Raising Bianca has been the greatest joy of my life, I would have loved the opportunity to actually be there for every moment. Divorcing Amanda and moving here gave me a finite amount of time with her. But if it hasn't happened by now, it's not going to happen for me. I'm just too old and set in my ways to start over." Violet frowns at me but doesn't try to argue the point. "Anyway, it's time for what we've all been waiting for, why don't you grab that clawfoot thing you made."

"It's a clafoutis." She laughs while fetching it from the oven where it's been warming. "It's a French dessert that's traditionally like a flan with black cherries and powdered sugar." She sets the baking dish in front of me and takes off the towel. I hate to say it, but I'm a little surprised when the dessert is revealed. It looks, well, amazing. From everything I've heard, this should look nothing less than like it was set on fire. I figured she was going to make some cookies or brownies or something but she walks in here with some kind of French dessert I can barely pronounce let alone make myself.

"It looks great. But I thought you were going to make it with those little hairy things." I examine the dish closely and see no sign of those spindly golf balls I was worried about choking down in the store.

She rolls her eyes at me once again. "Dante, these *are* the rambutan. You peel them and they look kinda like lychees. See?" She points to the little pieces of fruit that look like peeled grapes and I'm relieved that I won't have to pick green hairs out of my teeth. She quickly cuts two slices of the dessert and plates them, frowning slightly and poking at the pieces. "It's a little runnier than it's supposed to be. See? I told you this was going to be a disaster."

"What are you talking about? This looks awesome." I grab a plate from her and before she can say anything else, I scoop up a bit of the thin flan and shovel it into my mouth. She's staring at me, her own plate untouched, nervously awaiting my reaction.

"This is delicious." I say, taking another bite.

"Shut up." Comes flying out of her mouth before she can stop it and I let out a laugh while she blushes and covers her mouth.

"Man, I must be rusty if I try to compliment a woman and all she tells me is to shut up." I thought I was going to have to lie and tell her it was great while slogging through whatever it was she made. Instead, I finish my plate and reach for another slice. "Anytime you bake, you go ahead and bring it over here to me where it will be appreciated."

Now her smile isn't the soft, rather shy one I'm used to. No, now it's beaming at me. "I hope you mean that because there are plenty of things that I make that nobody wants to eat."

"Good," I say, licking my fork. "There will be more for me then."

Her phone gives a gentle buzz where it's sitting on the table and she glances at it quickly before looking back at me. "You can check that if you want."

"I'm sorry, I don't want to be rude but I just want to make sure there isn't a problem with Hollie or anything." She picks it up quickly and the expression on her face turns to one of mild unease.

"What is it? What's wrong?"

"Nothing," she says, turning the phone upside down and placing it back on the table.

"It's obviously something, you're not very good at hiding your feelings. Is everything okay with Hollie?"

"Oh, I'm sure she's fine it wasn't that." She chews on her bottom lip a moment, giving me the urge to reach over and pull it away from the ministrations of her teeth. "It was actually Tyler. The guy I went on a date with last week?"

My body immediately goes rigid. The last thing I want to hear about is her date. "Have you decided to give him a second chance?" I ask through clenched teeth.

"I don't think so. I just don't know what to say to him. I don't want to hurt his feelings and we have class together once a week. I guess I'm not very good at this type of thing. It's been a week since we went out and I've just been dodging his questions about going out on a second date. I mean, he was nice, there really isn't a good reason I shouldn't go out with him again."

How about the fact that I'll punch him in the face?

Now, all I'm thinking about is her taking that beer she didn't want and I'm worried that she's going to go out with this guy again just because it would be easier than having a confrontation with him.

"Vi, you don't need a reason not to go out with him again. If you aren't feeling it, you can just let him know that you think you're better off as friends. Don't let him pressure you into anything."

"I'm not." Her tone is defensive, and I sense that I'm overstepping my bounds here so I decide to go the playful route. Well, I'm hoping it will come off as playful to her while I'm one hundred percent serious.

"If this guy gives you any trouble, you just let me know and I'll hunt him down and they'll never find his body." Luckily, she seems to think I'm joking and laughs. I decide to put this conversation to the side for now but I fully plan to follow up later and make sure she didn't have any trouble getting rid of this guy.

I notice that we've finished the wine I've brought out and grab us another bottle. Even though dessert is long gone, we're still talking about anything and everything under the sun. We're having a friendly argument about the best book-to-movie adaptations when she admits to me she's never seen *Strangers on a Train*.

"How is that even possible?" I ask. "It's a classic. One of Hitchcock's greatest films."

"I don't think I've ever even seen a Hitchcock film."

"What is this blasphemy you speak? His films are some of the best ever made."

"Hey, I'm a student of literature remember? Not a film student."

"Well, this is something we're going to have to rectify immediately." I stand and grab her hand, leading her into the living room. "It's just a good thing for you I'm cultured enough for both of us." It wasn't until I stood up that I realized how tipsy the two beers and two bottles of wine had really made me. I'm not drunk, I'm still steady on my feet, but I can tell that my inhibitions are lowering. Unfortunately for me, it's the part of me that knows I should keep my distance from Violet that seems to be diminishing. I've had more fun this evening than I've had in a long time and I don't want the night to end.

In a split-second decision I grab another bottle of wine from the fridge and collect both of our glasses, carrying them into the living room. I stop slightly behind the couch so that Violet can't see me yet and spend a few moments taking her in. She's sitting near the middle of my couch, fiddling with her skirt so that it's lying around her legs just right before slipping off her shoes and tucking her feet delicately underneath her. Standing behind her affords me a glimpse down the front of her shirt so that my eyes rest on her cleavage and I'm immediately back to being hard. I can see the lacy edges of her bra from where I'm standing and, for just a second, I let myself imagine slowly sliding my hands up the front of her shirt and cupping her beautiful breasts, feeling her nipples tightening underneath all that lace. I only feel the slightest bit of guilt as I drag my eyes away and up to her face. There's a redness on her cheeks and chest that indicate she's not immune from the effects of the evenings wine either. That, more than anything else, tells me that nothing could happen between Violet and me tonight. I would never take advantage of her in that way.

I move to the front of the couch and instead of sitting at the end, as far away from her as possible, I sit right in the middle next to her, our legs almost touching. I pour us each another glass and recognize the fact that our closeness is a definite indicator that I should *not* be having any more alcohol. Still . . .

"Here you go." I hand her a glass and she greedily takes another two gulps. "Whoa, slow down there. I've got plenty more in the fridge, I promise."

She gives me a smile, "Sorry, I'm just . . . having a really good time."

"Me too," I say softly. I've gotten the feeling all night that she's been enjoying my company but it's nice to have the confirmation. Though we've known each other for years, we rarely, if ever, spend any one-on-one time together. The unfortunate thing for me is that it's only making my crush quickly turn into a straight up obsession. Taking another sip of my wine, I decide that's a problem for tomorrow. Tonight, I'm going to enjoy my evening with a woman who I'm quickly developing feelings for.

I find the movie on one of the many streaming services I'm paying way too much money for and start the film. It isn't long before my eyes are wandering from the screen to the beautiful woman at my side. I can see her hardened nipples straining against the fabric of her shirt and I immediately offer her the blanket that's always draped on the back of the couch.

"Thanks," she says, pulling the soft fabric over her lap. "Here, we can share." Before I can say anything she's rearranged the blanket so that it's covering not only her legs but mine as well. While settling the blanket, her hand accidentally brushes across the raging erection that her nearness and familiarity brings. I have to use every bit of resolve that I have to suppress my groan. She tries to test my self-control further by scooting closer so now the tips of her knees are resting on my thigh.

I watch as her breath seems to quicken, causing her breasts to rise and fall in rapid succession and, for the first time ever, I'm wondering if this attraction isn't one sided.

She's studiously watching the screen but I can't seem to take my eyes off of her and her flushed cheeks as she takes another sip of wine.

It's just the alcohol you idiot, she doesn't want anything to do with your crotchety old ass. Just as I'm thinking that, her head slowly falls to my shoulder.

"Is this okay?" she asks. *Ummm, fuck yes, it's okay.*

"Of course." She scoots a little closer and, before I know it, her hand is also resting on my thigh. I feel like I'm living in a parallel universe. One where I get the woman of my dreams. Where she's not put off by my age or the fact that I'm her best friend's father. A universe where she's just a gorgeous, kind, wonderful woman and I'm the lonely man that wants her with everything in my being. I want to wrap my arm around her shoulder and pull her closer. Maybe lift her up and onto my lap so that I can cradle her in my arms. Instead, I sit here, stock still, watching as her eyes slowly close and her breathing evens out.

"Violet," I whisper after a few minutes. There's no response and I know that she's out like a light. The movie continues to play in the background, and I sit here in the exquisite torture of having Violet touch me, but without me being able to touch her.

I move my hand under the blanket draped over us both and quickly grab my dick, giving it a firm squeeze. I'd give anything to unzip these jeans right now and give it some breathing room but with Violet so close, peacefully sleeping, that's not going to happen. I keep my eyes on the sleeping angel draped along my side and resolve to sit in discomfort the rest of the night.

TWELVE

VIOLET

When I open my eyes it takes me a moment to place where I am. It isn't long before I realize that I'm lying on the sofa in Dante's living room. The film has been switched off and I'm spread out on the sofa with the soft throw blanket covering me. I sit up, just a little too quickly, and the room starts a lazy spinning.

Well, I haven't been asleep long enough to get hung over. I'm definitely still a little drunk.

I look out the window and see that it's still dark out, at least I haven't been sleeping here all night. The next thing I look for is Dante himself but he's nowhere to be found in the room. I feel around on the coffee table in the dark and my hand hits an empty wine glass, almost sending it to the floor, before I grab onto my phone. I look at the time and realize I've only been asleep for about an hour.

I think over the evenings activities and try to suppress the tinge of embarrassment I feel. After Bianca and I sent Hollie off on her date, I made my excuses to Bianca about having to meet with some people from class and quickly changed into an outfit that I thought would show off my best assets. I knew I was being ridiculous but I was finally, after all these years, spending some alone time with Dante that didn't involve work and I really wanted him to see me as more than just some kid.

It had been a great evening and I know I drank way more wine than I should have. By the time we made it to the living room to watch the movie I was feeling emboldened. I probably should have sat at the end of the couch, but instead, I plopped down right there in the middle, forcing him to cozy up to me. Being that close to Dante had been intoxicating. Or maybe that was just the wine. Either way, I was inclined to push the envelope.

Getting under the blanket with him? Putting my head on his shoulder? The smell of his cologne? This all left my heart beating faster and my body flushed with arousal. My nipples had become so hard it felt like they could cut glass. I'm not sure if it was my wine-soaked brain or maybe just wishful thinking but I could have sworn that Dante was sporting an impressive erection in his jeans. One that I might have *accidentally* brushed against when arranging the blanket over us both.

I wanted to savor every moment of the closeness we were sharing but once my head was laying against his shoulder, his steady and perpetual heartbeat lulled me into a dreamless sleep.

Since I haven't been asleep that long, I figure he must still be awake so I decide to go find him. I raise off the sofa and stumble a little, letting out a giggle, my head swimming.

I don't find Dante in the kitchen so checking his office is my next stop. I pad up the stairs on my bare feet and open the door leading to the office which is as empty as the kitchen. I let out a sigh and am about to head back downstairs when I hear a noise coming from down the hallway. I can't quite tell what it is, maybe Dante is talking to someone? A bolt of jealousy runs through me as I think of him on the phone with some woman. I just want to check. There's nothing wrong with that, right?

I make my way to his bedroom as quietly as I can and stop outside when I see that the door is closed. I'm considering whether I should knock or not when I hear the weird little sound again. No, it doesn't sound like he's talking. It's more like a groan, maybe? What if he's sick? I mean, we both drank an awful lot tonight.

I slowly turn the knob on his door, if he's sick I don't want to startle or embarrass him. I just want to make sure he's okay, that's all. I push the door open, inch by inch, trying to catch a glimpse inside. Once the space is wide enough for me to ease my head in, I can freely look around but still don't see Dante. I'm confused until I hear the same grunting again and see a door across the room that's cracked open with light streaming out of it.

I can only assume that's his bathroom and he's in there throwing up. I know I should turn around. I really do. Any other time I never would have even opened his bedroom door but I'm filled with a liquid courage tonight that seems to be encouraging me to do things I never would otherwise.

I'm still a little concerned that he's ill and needs assistance so I quietly move across the plush carpeting to where his bathroom door is cracked open. Inside is something that I never could have anticipated seeing.

There in the shining light of the bathroom stands the man of my dreams, shirt off, pants slid below his hips, hunched over, one hand bracing himself on the sink, while the other hand is stroking the long shaft of his cock.

"Ugh." There's that noise again. I was wrong. He's not sick. Not at all. If the expression on his face is any indication, he's deep into his own pleasure. His eyes are closed tight, jaw clenched, and his face is flushed as he glides his hands up and down his long shaft.

I've imagined Dante's cock a hundred times, hell, maybe even a thousand, but nothing my imagination could conjure can compete with the reality of what I'm seeing. His cock isn't the first one I've seen in person but it's the only one I've ever really craved seeing. Now that I have, how could I ever look at another man's?

It looks huge, even in his large and obviously capable hands. I can see the veins running down the sides as he picks up his pace. The head is so red that it almost looks angry. Every few strokes, he takes his hand up to the head and circles it, collecting drops of pre-cum and bringing it back down his solid length, causing it to glisten in the light. Whenever he circles the head, his body gives a little shiver, like the pleasure is almost too much for him to take.

My breathing has picked up and I open the door just a little wider so that I can get a better look. I know I shouldn't, but I can't seem to help myself. Whether it's the wine or the fact that this is my fantasy come to life, I don't know and I don't really care. My entire body feels both hot and cold at the same time. I know without putting my hands to my pussy that I'm already drenched.

His firm grip continues his up and down stroke and I can't help but bring my hand up to lightly caress my aching nipples. My own teasing touch sends a shot of lust straight between my legs and I rub my thighs together, looking for a little relief.

I should leave. I should get out of here before he catches me, but I can't. I'm transfixed by the rhythmic ministrations of his hand. I'm not even sure I've blinked since I've been standing in the doorway. I've never been so horny in my entire life. I would get on my knees right here and now and beg him to fuck me if I thought he would do it. Instead, I take my hand away from my breasts and move it slowly down my skirt, slipping my fingers underneath the band of my panties, until my fingers are buried in my soaking wet slit.

The pleasure of touching myself while watching Dante do the same thing is unbearable and a whimper escapes my lips before I can stop it.

Dante freezes mid-stroke, his head turning toward me. His expression lies somewhere between embarrassment and horror. Then his eyes travel to where my hand is shoved inside my skirt and his expression changes to one of pure desire. His brown eyes are so dark that they're almost black. Still, he just stands there and stares at me, his hand on his magnificent cock, waiting for . . . something, I don't know what.

"Don't stop," I whisper. He lets out a groan so deep I can feel it in my chest and before I know it, his hand has returned to slowly moving up and down his angry member. His movements restart my own and I rub my hand up and down my dripping pussy, making sure my fingers slide across my engorged clit. This is the most erotic thing I've ever taken part in, and I never want it to end.

His dark eyes are locked on me and neither of us can look away from the other. I move my other hand up to my top and slowly drag it down, revealing my bra-clad tits to him, before slipping my hand inside and gently squeeze my nipple, letting out another whimper.

"Fuck," he whispers softly, the pace of his hand picking up. His cock is almost constantly dripping pre-cum at this point, and I have the incredible urge to gather it onto my fingertips and taste it. Instead, I slide the tip of my index finger inside my dripping hole before bringing the moisture back up to encircle my clit. I'm breathing hard now, my chest heaving, almost panting.

"What were you thinking about?" I ask in an almost reverent whisper, not wanting to do anything to ruin this moment but also having to know.

"I can't tell you that, Violet," he says breathlessly, increasing his speed.

"Why not?"

"You know why." He looks deep into my eyes, and I do know. I know he was thinking about me. Is this the first time? Does he always think about me when he's rubbing his cock and giving himself pleasure? Does he always wish it was my hands on him?

My own fingers pick up the pace and I can't help but pull my breast out of my bra, giving me better access to the nipple that's begging me for attention and seems to have a direct line straight to my clit.

He gasps when he's sees my naked tit out for him. His hand is moving so fast now that it's almost a blur. His grunts and groans are coming more frequently and are feeding my own climbing arousal. I can feel my entire body tighten and I know that I'm close, I want him to realize that I'm right here with him, as turned on as he is so I let him know, "I'm going to come."

That seems to be all he needed to hear. His body stiffens and his hand tugs on his cock another two, then three times before his hips thrust forward and he lets out a moan, a moan that includes my name right before shooting his cum all over the countertop in several spurts.

The sight sends me over the edge and my entire body shakes with the force of my orgasm. Unable to keep my eyes open any longer I squeeze them shut tightly while my body rides wave after wave of pleasure. My knees feel weak and I use the hand that was once squeezing my nipple to grab onto the doorframe to keep me upright. When my orgasm finally subsides, I open my eyes and find Dante staring at me. His jeans are pulled up, hiding his cock from my view but they are neither buttoned nor zipped. His face is conveying to me he's both confused and sorry.

It's only in that moment that everything hits me. I snuck into Dante's room and spied on him when he was alone having an intimate moment. Not only did I intrude on that, but I also touched myself, made myself come while he did the same to himself. I've violated every piece of trust that he had in me and acted like nothing more than some kind of sex-crazed maniac.

Embarrassment and shame are both warring inside me to be the emotion at the forefront and still, Dante hasn't said a word. I do the only thing I can think to do at this point. I run.

As soon as I rush in the front door I spot Bianca in the living room working at her easel. I barely get out a greeting to her before I escape to my bedroom and lock myself inside. The thought of being in the same room as my best friend right now sends me into a minor panic, like maybe she can see what I did written all over my skin.

I furiously pace back and forth, trying to calm my breathing. *What the fuck just happened?*

I almost hope the entire thing was some kind of fever dream, that way I won't have to die from embarrassment. I must be out of my mind. Maybe I can plead temporary insanity. I'm definitely going to have to quit my job. I can never face him again.

I flop down on my bed and stare at the ceiling, letting the images of the scene in the bathroom wash over me. I feel flushed and I'm not sure if it's from mortification or arousal. If I'm honest with myself, it's probably both.

Not even my wildest fantasies could have prepared me for what I saw and what I *did* in that bathroom. I let out a groan and roll over onto my stomach, burying my face deep into my pillow. Maybe I could smother myself like this and put myself out of my misery. My eyes are closed, but it's like the image of Dante holding his hard, angry cock is burned into the back of my eyelids.

It takes a few very long minutes before I realize I wasn't the only one in that bathroom. Yes, I absolutely walked in on Dante having a private moment that I shouldn't have but he could have stopped. He could have kicked me out. He could have called me every name in the book for spying on him, but he didn't. No, he continued stroking his cock, watching me while I derived my own pleasure from his. Doesn't that mean something?

He doesn't seem like a man that has casual sexual encounters. In fact, I've never seen him with a woman. Hell, he's never even mentioned one. I know Bianca has been worried about him being lonely. Wouldn't he have stopped things if he wasn't at least attracted to me?

I start the scene over one more time in my head, watching the entire thing play out like a movie. I hear his groans, see him looking into my eyes, watching as I played with my nipples and had my hand down my skirt. When I asked him what he was thinking about, he told me I already knew. Then, when he came all over the counter, he called my name.

He was thinking about me. Dante *wants* me.

I almost let out a squeal of excitement at the realization but manage to control myself. The thought that this man that I've wanted for years might actually want me as well is dizzying. Or maybe that's just the residual effects of the wine. No, I'm pretty sure I sobered up the minute my orgasm was over and I realized what we had just done. I'm elated . . . and horny again. Stripping down to nothing, I pull my vibrator from my nightstand and come for the second time this evening in record time.

Once I'm done, I roll over and close my eyes, trying to get some sleep, but my mind is running a thousand miles a second. I feel like there is a world of possibilities open to me now that just an hour ago didn't exist. Does he just want to sleep with me? Does he want to date me? It's not like we don't enjoy each other's company. I mean, at least I *think* he has a good time when he's with me. He wouldn't have wanted to hang out tonight otherwise.

It takes hours for me to finally fall asleep and when I wake up the sun is high in the sky. Thank God I was planning on going to the library today instead of work or else I would be hopelessly late. I reach over and grab my phone from the nightstand only to find I've already received a text from Dante.

Dante: Good Morning. Do you think you can come over tonight so we can talk?

I clutch the phone to my chest, a smile overtaking my face. A good morning text from Dante. That has to be a good sign. Sure, he wants to talk, but that's understandable. There are things we need to work out. Are we going to tell Bianca? Are we dating? These all seem minor compared to the fact that Dante wants me. Me, Violet Daniels, the nerdy literature student with the hopeless crush on the older man.

Me: Good Morning to you too. It'll have to be after nine, I have a study group that I can't miss.

His response is almost immediate. Like he's been waiting to hear from me. The thought makes those butterflies that live in my stomach take flight.

Dante: Great. I'll see you then.

I trace his name with my fingertip like a schoolgirl before I notice the time. If I don't get a move on, I'll be behind schedule all day and will never make it over to Dante's on time.

It's a busy day between doing research, working on my thesis proposal, and spending a few hours with my study group. By the time it's all over I'm exhausted and just want to head home and crawl into bed. The only thing keeping me going is the fact that I'm going to get to see Dante.

I pull up outside his house, turn off the engine, and take a deep, steadying breath. While I'm nervous, I'm also more excited than I've ever been. I take a few minutes to study myself in the visor mirror. I was right; I do look tired, but still, there is a sparkle in my eyes that I'm not used to seeing and I know that's all him.

I dig through my purse and find the lip gloss that I don't often use, applying a light layer to my lips, making them look just a little fuller. The last thing I do before I leave the car is run a brush through my hair and try to fluff it up a little, but it's no use. It would take a mountain of product to give me some volume, and I didn't have time to go home before coming over. Besides, I don't want to look like I'm trying too hard. With one more deep breath, I make my way to his front porch and ring the doorbell before I can chicken out.

Before the sound of the bell even fades the door is swinging open, revealing the man of my dreams. I thought maybe he would look different to me after last night but he still looks like the same insanely attractive man that I'm used to. Well, besides the fact that I can now accurately picture what's underneath that plain white tee and pair of well-worn jeans.

"Hey," I say with a shaky breath.

"Hey. Come on in." He gives me his own nervous smile and steps to the side, letting me in before closing the door behind me. We're both silent, just staring at each other. He looks more nervous than I feel, if that's even possible.

We seem to be at a stalemate. Neither one of us wanting to make the first move so I decide for once in my life I'm going to be brave. Before I can think too much about it, I practically launch myself at him, my body slamming into his, my arms going around his neck. He obviously wasn't expecting my surprise attack and takes a half step back, steadying me against him. Before he can say anything, my mouth is on his. I press my lips against his and the feeling sends a shiver down my spine. He's still for a few seconds, letting me lead the kiss until the feeling of our bodies pressing together, my lips on his, causes me to let out a moan.

Suddenly, he's taken over the kiss. It's no longer the soft exploratory kiss I started but something hot and heavy. His lips slant over mine while one of his hands gets buried in my hair and the other is on my hip. I try to wiggle closer to him, feeling like it will never be enough.

He's hard again, just like last night. His cock is digging into the soft skin of my stomach and I gasp. Immediately his tongue enters my mouth, taking what little breath I had left away. I've kissed boys before but it's never been anything like this. His tongue seems to search my mouth, demanding that my own dance with his. My nipples are hard and I try to rub them against his chest but there are too many layers of clothing between us and I can't get any relief so I let out a whimper.

Suddenly, his mouth is ripped away from mine, and his hands are no longer encircling my body. He's holding my upper arms to steady me while he takes a step back, leaving me feeling cold and unsatisfied. I tilt my head back to look at him, not really understanding what's happening. My mind is clouded with a haze of lust but when I look into his eyes, I see sadness . . . and regret.

"Violet, we can't." Those three words send a sharp stab of disappointment into my body. "I'm so sorry."

"But I thought you liked me. I thought you were attracted to me."

"I am," he says hurriedly. He turns his head away, no longer able to look me in my eyes. "I'm too old for you, Violet. And then there's Bianca . . ."

Well, what can I say to that? I always knew that he saw me as a kid. It's one of the reasons I've tried to forget about him over the years. And Bianca would have always been an issue between us. Who can fault him for putting his daughter before me? I have the sudden realization that he didn't call me over here because he wants to be with me, he had me come over so he could let me down easy and I'm mortified.

"Does this mean I'm fired?"

He looks a little stunned by the question. "No! Of course not. We can just forget this ever happened."

If he thinks this whole thing is something I can just forget he's crazy. I've made a complete fool of myself and it's taking everything I have to not burst into tears in front of him. He may be older than me, think he's better than me, that I'm just some silly girl but I won't let him see me cry. I won't prove his point for him.

I'm trying to think of something to say that will show just how much I don't care when I feel a buzzing against my leg. Relieved by the interruption, I pull my phone out of my front pocket and see that Bianca's sent me a text. I give an involuntary flinch at the sight of her name but unlock my phone to read it, giving me precious moments to get my emotions in check.

Bianca: Something happened between Hollie and Archer. She just got home and she's having a total meltdown, I'm not sure what to do. Can you get here ASAP?

Say what you will about Bianca, the girl has impeccable timing. I try to push Dante to the back of my mind, to a place where I put things I don't want to deal with, and instead try to focus on my concern for Hollie. I don't know what could have happened. Last I knew, Archer was taking her to some fancy charity dinner tonight.

I shove my phone back in my pocket and turn toward the front door. "I've got to go, that was Bianca, there's a problem with Hollie."

"Vi, don't you think we should talk about this?" He puts his hand on my shoulder to stop me from leaving but I shake it off like his touch is poison.

"There's nothing to talk about. You've said everything that needs to be said. You don't have to worry about me, I get it."

"What are you going to tell Bianca? You know, about us?"

He's nervous. Afraid that I'm going to spill this secret and ruin his relationship with his daughter. I carefully school my features so that he can't see the pain that this entire conversation has caused me before turning to face him. "There's nothing to tell. There is no us." Before he can say anything else, I'm out the door without so much as a backward glance.

THIRTEEN

Dante

As I watch Violet walk away from me, I can't help but feel remorse along with a hefty helping of guilt. It's possible that was one of the most difficult things I've had to do in my adult life. The very last thing I wanted was to shoot Violet down.

After she fled and left me alone last night, I tossed and turned in bed, not getting a single moment of sleep. Violet had been my fantasy come to life. My heart about exploded when I saw her standing in my bathroom doorway but then I took in the entire picture. Her eyes were glassy with desire, cheeks pink, her hand down her skirt. It was obvious from her quick panting breaths that she was pleasuring herself while spying on me. I should have sent her away but I couldn't find the strength. Instead, I continued stroking my dick all while wishing that her skirt would disappear so I could get a better look at what she was doing. As soon as she pulled out her tit and I could see her dusty pink nipple, hard as a rock, I lost control. The sound of her voice telling me she was going to come made my every nerve ending come alive and I came harder than I have in recent memory.

On the one hand I was in awe of the fact that she seemed to be as into it as I was, if not more so with her stealthy actions. I never could have imagined that someone like

Violet could want me even a fraction of the amount that I want her. On the other hand, I was filled with guilt. I should have put a stop to it. We were both drinking, and I know that there was no way she would have been so bold without the alcohol loosening her inhibitions.

By the time the sun rose, I knew what I had to do. I needed to nip this in the bud before it got out of hand. There were so many reasons that we shouldn't be together, even if it was just for a night or two of passion. I'm so much older than her. People would see us together and immediately judge both of us. I would be the creepy old man preying on a young innocent girl and she would be classified as some Lolita. While I could handle the scrutiny, I would never put her through that. People would constantly be in her ear telling her how wrong it was. Her friends, her classmates, fuck, her parents would completely lose their shit.

Even if we could survive all the talk, the gossip, the dirty looks, the fact remains that she's young, she wants to start a family. Eventually, she would outgrow me. I've already admitted to myself that I have feelings for Violet, what would happen to me a month down the road, shit, six months, a year? I would be in too deep and when she inevitably moved on, I would be left all alone once again. But this time it would be worse, this time I would know what it would be like to be with someone that I truly cared for. No, it's better to end it now before either of us gets too invested.

Then, of course, there's Bianca. That text she received from my daughter right before she took off was another reminder that we both had relationships to protect. I know that neither of us wants to hurt Bianca and I know that she would feel betrayed. There is no way that she would understand. Hell, I barely understand myself.

Unfortunately, all of my reasonings and good intentions almost went right out the window when Violet kissed me. I had been shocked to say the least. Then my body gave into what it wanted and I kissed her back with everything I was feeling inside me. It wasn't until I heard her little moan that I was brought back to my senses and remembered why I asked her to come over in the first place and pushed her away. I could see both arousal and hurt in her eyes when I told her that we couldn't do this and it made a little tiny fissure in my heart but I know that I'm doing the right thing. For both of us.

I try to keep myself busy for the rest of the weekend. I've never wished I had a more active social life than I do right now. I could hang out with Jake, we've certainly done it before, but I know him. He'll either tease me about Violet or try to push me into hooking up with some stranger. Neither of those things sounds very appealing. Instead, I stay home and do housework. Things I haven't done in years—like clean the baseboards—are suddenly a priority. The house has never looked so good. I could try to lie to myself and say it's all for Bianca's party next week but I'm not very good at believing my own lies these days.

When Monday finally rolls around I head into my office. Waiting for Violet is some kind of sweet torture. I don't know how to act around her now, what to say to her, but that doesn't change the fact that I want to be near her. Is this how my life is going to be from now on? Even I think I'm pathetic. When the time reaches ten a.m., I finally give up on Violet coming in today. I mean, she doesn't have a set schedule so she's perfectly within her rights to not show up. One of the reasons she took this job that's completely beneath her is because she can come and go as she pleases.

But I know that she's avoiding me. I'm not happy about it but I understand it.

Tuesday, it's the same thing. No Violet in sight.

On Wednesday, instead of sitting at my desk, sulking and waiting to see if Violet comes in, I head out to the strip mall job site to check on the progress. There's really no need for me to be there. Adrian has the project well in hand and we're ahead of schedule but I've got to get out of here.

"Hey, boss-man, what brings you out here to our humble abode?" Adrian asks me as I approach. He shakes my hand, enveloping it in the drywall dust that's covering him from head to toe.

"I just thought I'd come out here and check and see how everything's going," I explain lamely.

He gives me a funny look, then just shrugs his shoulders. "We're about to demo that last unit on the end. Since you're here, you might as well lend us a hand." Good. Some punishing physical labor is just what I need today so I follow him to the unit in question and grab a well-worn sledgehammer.

A few hours later I'm covered in dust and sweat, my shirt clinging to my body like a second skin, my back and arm muscles aching, my chest heaving with exertion.

"Man, jefe, you've really got to get out to the site more you look like you're about to keel over." Adrian laughs at me. I smile and give him the finger before going in search of a water bottle. Just when I'm finishing chugging the entire thing down, my phone rings and I can see it's Bianca. I take a seat on my trucks tailgate and answer.

"Hey, pumpkin, what's up?"

"Hey, Daddy!" Here we go.

"What do you need?" I can hear her let out an exasperated sigh on the other end of the line.

"You know, you always assuming I need something is starting to get old."

"Well, when you stop calling me Daddy when you need something I'll stop asking."

"*Anyway*," she continues, sounding exasperated. "I was going to get drinks and dinner tonight with Mom, do you want to come?" I suppress a groan. The last thing I want to do tonight is hang out with Amanda. I'd much rather sit at home, drink a beer, and stare at the television like a zombie but it's hard for me to pass up an opportunity to hang out with my daughter. We make plans and I say goodbye to Adrian, heading home so that I can shower and change.

It's pouring rain when I arrive at Bianca's favorite restaurant so I make a mad dash to the door. You'd think that after I've lived in Seattle for so many years I'd be smart enough to keep an umbrella in my truck. Apparently I like to live dangerously.

Once I'm inside I shake myself off like a dog, dislodging as much of the rain as I can, and scan the room. I don't see Bianca anywhere but I spot Amanda sitting at the bar, a bright blue blended drink in her hand. I let out a sigh and walk over taking the stool next to her.

"No Bianca yet?"

"It looks like she's running a few minutes late," Amanda says. She takes a sip of her drink and gives me a smile. "I figured I'd get a head start."

"That sounds about right," I mutter.

"Jesus, Dante, do you have to be such an asshole all of the time?" I want to snap at her but she's not wrong. I really should be making more of an effort, especially if she's going to be living here now. With Bianca dictating our get togethers it seems like I'll be seeing a whole lot more of her from now on.

I decide to take her question as rhetorical and instead ask, "So when is it that you're making the move?"

"Not for a few more weeks. I'm just here this week to sign some paperwork for the rental, set up my storage unit, you know, take care of some odds and ends. Since Bianca's party is in a few days I figured I'd just stay in town."

"Are you staying with the girls?"

She lets out a laugh. "No way. I didn't want to live with a bunch of twenty-somethings when I *was* twenty-something."

"Well, you also had a kid then."

"Very true. No, I'm staying in an Airbnb this week. It's the cutest little place near the college."

"That's good. It's nice that you'll be here for her party."

"Are you kidding? Bianca basically insisted. You know how stubborn that girl is. She gets that from you, you know."

I let out a chuckle. "I'd say that's probably something inherited from the both of us."

"And what are we supposed to do at a party filled with a bunch of twenty-three-year olds? God, I'm going to feel ancient." She gulps down the rest of her drink and orders another. I glance at the door to see if Bianca has arrived yet but she's still MIA so I ask the bartender for a beer.

"It won't be so bad, I know a couple of her friends. They're nice and can be fun to be around."

"Are you kidding me?" Amanda's volume seems to have risen the with completion of her first drink. At least I think it's her first. "They're a bunch of children. What could we possibly have in common with those kids? It's going to be a long night."

"I don't know, her friend Violet and I have a lot in common, we both read, watch the same movies . . ." I trail off when Amanda's eyes narrow in on me.

"Yeah, Violet," she says with disdain. "That girl is a stuck-up bitch. She never even bothers to speak to me."

I feel my hackles rise and can't help but defend Violet against the unwarranted viciousness of my ex. "She's not a bitch. Violet's just shy. Plus, you've only met her, what? Four times? Of course she's not going to be comfortable around you."

"Whatever." She abruptly grabs her drink from the bartender's hand and proceeds to suck down at least another shot of alcohol. "Besides, she rich. What's she doing living with Bianca anyway? And on your dime no less! You should be making her pay through the nose. Her parents can afford it."

"Look, Violet lives there because I asked her to. I asked both her and Hollie to live there. I don't want Bianca living in that house alone and if I can afford to help all three of them start out their lives and not have to worry about paying rent then I'm going to do it. Why else have I been busting my ass all these years if I can't afford to help the people I care about."

"I'm just saying—" Before the two of us can get into a knock-down-drag-out fight right here in the middle of a busy restaurant I'm saved by the bell. Or rather, the buzz. I pull my phone out of my pocket and see Amanda sifting through her purse searching for her own. Because of that I'm not surprised by the message I've received.

Bianca: Sorry guys! Something came up and I can't make it. I'll make it up to you! Promise! <heart emoji>

"It looks like we've been stood up," I say just as Amanda is pulling out her own phone.

"You've got to be kidding me," she mutters. "Since we're already here should he just have dinner?"

I consider it for about a half of a second before deciding I'd rather eat the moldy cheese in my fridge. "Look, it's been a long day. I think I'm just going to call it a night."

I pull out my wallet to pay for my beer but before I can set the money down Amanda's already getting up from her own stool. "You've got me covered too? That's so sweet of you," she says in that artificially saccharine tone that grates on my nerves. Instead of responding, I just toss down another two bills. It's easier than arguing with her about it.

We make our way back outside where the rain is still coming down in sheets. "You can make it to your car okay?" I ask.

"I actually took an Uber from the Airbnb."

I want to leave her to order her own ride, I really do, but my mama, God rest her soul, would whoop my ass if I left the mother of my child out here standing in the rain. "Come on, I'll give you a ride."

She gives me a grin and follows me, sprinting over to my truck. Once we're both settled inside and I have the heat cranked up, I start to navigate through the slick streets as quickly as I can while still being safe. Amanda sits in the seat beside me jabbering away about Bianca's party, but I mostly block it out, only paying attention to the GPS directions to where she's staying.

It feels like an eternity but we finally pull up to her rental about twenty minutes later. I can't wait to get home and put this entire day behind me. I put the truck in park and turn to Amanda who has suddenly gone silent. Before I can get out the words that let her know we're here, her mouth descends on me, only catching the corner of my lips and my cheek in a slobbery kiss. I instantly push her away and use my hand to wipe the saliva she's left behind on my face.

"What the actual fuck, Amanda?" I practically shout.

"Come on, Dante. We're both single, I'm moving to the city. Don't you think we owe it to each other to give us another try?"

"What the hell are you talking about? We haven't been together in twenty years and that's not changing anytime soon. We were together once and you cheated on me."

She crosses her arms over her chest and starts pouting like the mature adult that she is. "C'mon Dante, can't you let that go? We were young back then, things are different now."

"You're right, we were young. Definitely too young to have a baby. But together we somehow managed to raise a strong, independent, and talented young woman. That's all that's between us now and all that ever will be between us."

She grabs her purse from the floorboard and exits the vehicle with a "fuck you" muttered under her breath before slamming the door, making me cringe. I wait until she runs to the front door and safely makes it inside the house.

I let my head fall forward, hitting the steering wheel, and take a deep breath. I don't know what the hell is going on. I haven't seen any action in years and now suddenly, in the span of a few days, I have two women throwing themselves at me. One of them I would give my right arm to kiss again, the other was like being facially attacked by a venomous snake. With the way things are going, it feels like I'm going to spend the rest of my life as a monk.

FOURTEEN

VIOLET

I'm an idiot. A moron. A complete and utter fool. The one time I decide to go after something that I really want and this is the result. This is why it's just easier to sit back and let life happen. I can't believe I thought that Dante wanted me back. I should have known better. How did I not think for a single second that he was calling me over there to let me down easy? Then when he made it very clear he didn't want me to tell Bianca it was like a stab through the heart. I can't believe he thought that I would say anything to her. Shit, I'm never going to tell anybody about this. I will take this mortification to the grave.

So I spend the next several days doing what any other sane person would do, I avoid Dante Moreno like the plague. I don't even bother going into the office on Monday or Tuesday. By Wednesday I've accepted that there are a few things that I really do need to get done. If suppliers don't get paid, there won't materials for the guys to work with. So before class I drive by his place several times until I see that his truck is gone. Like a chicken.

I know I can't avoid him forever but I sure as hell can avoid him right now. Maybe I should just quit, but I've never been much of a quitter. Hell, I'm still in college. Of course, that probably has more to do with avoiding my mother setting me up to marry some lawyer than it does my aversion to quitting. Maybe it's time I start rethinking letting my mom set me up. I'm obviously doing a pretty shit job of picking men for myself. Besides, just because my mom picks him doesn't necessarily mean that he's going to be a horrible person. Maybe I'll be pleasantly surprised. It's not like one date means I'm agreeing to marry the guy.

I finish everything I need to get done as quickly as possible and leave Dante a note letting him know that he needs to call Dimitri back regarding a slab of marble he was inquiring about and high tail it out of there.

I actually manage to arrive to class a few minutes ahead of schedule, so I take a seat and start reviewing my notes. Just as I'm about to get to the second page, someone flops down in the seat next to me.

"You wouldn't be avoiding me, now would you, Violet?" I look up and see Tyler sitting beside me with a wide smile on his face. He really is a good-looking guy, I'm not sure why he hasn't given up on me yet. I haven't been avoiding him necessarily. No, I'm saving that activity for Dante. I've just been skirting around the issue of a second date.

"Of course not, how's it going?"

"Pretty good. I went out on this awesome first date with a girl but I can't seem to nail her down for date number two. Any advice you can give me?" I can feel my cheeks start to heat from not just his compliment but from him calling me out as well.

"I'm really sorry, I've just been so busy. School has been nuts and now I've got a part-time job, so I honestly haven't had time to do much lately." At least it's not a lie. I haven't done anything but work and school for weeks. Unless you count getting drunk with Dante and coming together in his bathroom. I shake my head to dislodge the image that's been invading my thoughts all week.

The corners of his mouth turn down into a slight frown of disappointment. "Look, I really don't want to pursue someone who isn't into me so say the word and I'll let it go. I just thought we had fun and could try out a second date to see where it goes."

Before the incident with Dante, I probably would have told him that I wasn't interested but my fresh rejection has me rethinking things. I did have a good time with Tyler. Sure, it wasn't the best first date but that doesn't really mean anything. He was probably nervous. I know I was. What could it hurt going on a second date? Maybe we'll really hit it off, and if we don't, well, then we can both call it quits knowing we gave it a shot.

"I'd really like to go out again," I tell him.

"You would?" He seems surprised and I feel a bit bad for not getting back to him sooner. He really is a nice guy and we have a lot in common.

"Yeah, I would," I say with a genuine smile. Talking with Tyler is making me feel a little bit better about the whole Dante situation. He may not want me but at least someone does.

"What about this weekend? My friend's band is playing at a bar downtown. I could get us on the list, we wouldn't even have to wait in line." I try not to physically flinch at that. The thought of being squished into a crowded bar with music so loud I can't think doesn't sound appealing in the least. But maybe I can have my date with Tyler and at the same time save face with Dante. His rejection won't be nearly as embarrassing if he sees that I've moved on. He doesn't have to know that this is basically a last chance date.

"Actually, it's my roommate's birthday this weekend and she's having a party. Maybe you could come with me?"

"Sounds like fun. I can't wait." He leans forward and softly kisses my cheek. I resist the urge to rub the spot he just kissed, and I don't take that as a good sign. Oh well, if this doesn't work out there's always dear old mom to turn to. I shudder at the thought.

Before we can make any further plans Dr. Muzio walks in. "All right ladies and gentlemen, let's quiet down. We've got a lot of things to get through today and there's no time to waste." I turn away from Tyler to face the front of the room but not before I catch him giving me a wide smile. This is a good thing, I remind myself.

The secondhand desk in my bedroom at home is tiny and wobbles a little when I lean a little too far to the left. I'm sitting here, trying to work on a paper for my Thursday class but all I can hear is clanging and crashing outside my door. I know it can't be Hollie because she's not due back until tomorrow. There was an emergency with her mom and she had to go back to her hometown to handle it. Thank God Archer showed up to help her because I wouldn't have known what to do besides lend my moral support.

Since I've written about four words in the past ten minutes, I leave my cave and go in search of Bianca who I can only assume is following in her father's footsteps and starting her own construction company in our living room, by the sound of things. I find her in the kitchen, cleaning what looks like every paint brush she owns.

"Decide to do a little spring cleaning?" I ask. She jumps at the sound of my voice coming from behind her and grabs at her chest.

"Jesus, Vi, you scared the shit out of me. I didn't know you were home."

"With all that noise going on how would you be able to tell?"

"Noise?" she asks like she has no idea what I'm talking about.

"Yeah, you know, the banging . . ."

"Ohhh, right. Yeah, sorry about that. I was stretching a canvas and I couldn't find my staple gun so I decided to use tacks. But the only way to get them in there securely enough to hold the canvas is to hammer them. You haven't seen it have you?" She's talking a mile a minute while continuing to work on her paint brushes.

"Seen what? The canvas?"

"The staple gun," she says while unscrewing the cap on the paint thinner. The fumes rise up and enter my nose, coating my throat, and causing me to cough. "Sorry," she adds. "I'm trying to get together a bunch of stuff and I've gotta be out of here in a few minutes."

"No, I haven't seen the staple gun. Did you try outside on the patio? I think I saw it out there last time you were stretching canvas."

"Oh yeah!" She drops the handful of brushes she was holding into the sink and rushes to the backdoor. I let out another cough and start opening windows so we don't pass out from the fumes. Besides the tiny mountain of paintbrushes piled by the sink, she has tubes and pots of different paints scattered about. There is a stack of sketchbooks on the coffee table with graphite pencils and erasers sprinkled around it, including a nice little group of them on the floor. I go over and scoop them up, adding them back to the pile from where they came.

Now, I'm not saying that Bianca is the neatest person on the planet. Hell, she's an artist and sometimes her creative mind takes her places that my more analytical one can't follow. That means keeping a clean working or living space isn't always high on her list of priorities. But it's unlike her to have all of her supplies out at once and treat them so carelessly. I'm not upset about the mess, she'll get around to moving everything eventually, I just wonder what is going on.

"Found it!" she shouts as she comes back inside, holding the staple gun up in triumph before tossing it into a pile of canvas and wooden frames in a corner of the living room.

"Sooo, what's going on, roomie?" I ask, genuinely curious.

"Ugh, I'm trying to get some stuff together so that I can go babysit," she says casually, like it's no big deal. Like the craziest thing she ever said hasn't just come out of her mouth.

I know that my jaw has hit the floor, I can feel it hanging open but can't seem to close it. Bianca hates kids. Okay, I don't know if she *really* hates kids but she's certainly said she hates them enough. And it's not just lip service either. Bianca avoids children the way an alcoholic avoids AA meetings. She's said many times that she never wants them and whenever one is in the general vicinity, she heads the other way. I'm pretty sure she doesn't even know any kids.

"Who the hell are you babysitting?" I ask, genuinely concerned for whatever child is going to be in her care.

"Oliver." She doesn't even bother to look at me. Maybe she's joking.

"Who's Oliver?"

"You know, Detective Dickwad's nephew."

Who the hell . . . "Are you talking about our new neighbor?"

"Yeah, he's a total dick but his nephew is pretty cool." I must have fallen asleep at my desk and I'm having some kind of stress dream. The past few days have apparently been too much for me to handle.

"So let me get this straight. You're going to babysit this Oliver kid, who is the nephew of a cop and our new neighbor, who you hate?"

She finally stops and looks over at me. "Yeah, that's basically it."

"And all these art supplies?" I ask, trying to piece this all together.

"He saw one of my pieces and liked it so I thought that I'd bring over some stuff that he could use. I mean, you're supposed to entertain kids when you're babysitting them, right?" The look on her face is one of genuine curiosity and I can tell the question is legitimate, I'm not sure she's ever babysat a day in her life.

"Yeah, entertaining them is good. So, how old is Oliver?" I mean, I should probably make sure he's not going to eat the paint, right?

Her brow has that furrow in it that her father gets when he's deep in thought. "I'm not sure actually. I mean, he can walk and talk and stuff." Is it rude to facepalm your best friend?

"You do realize that means he can be any age from one to eighteen, right?"

"Well, I'll ask him and let you know."

"You're sure about this?" I ask. If this were any other activity, I wouldn't be questioning her but I'm not going to lie and say I'm not a little concerned.

"Yeah, it should be fine, it's just a couple of hours."

"Okay, well if there's a problem just call me. I'll be home tonight." She drops what she's holding and scoops me up in a hug. Bianca always gives the best hugs. With how small I am and how tall she is, I get completely enveloped. I hug her back tightly. Really needing the comfort from my best friend, even if she can't know why.

"You're the best, Vi. I mean, you probably can't tell but I'm a little nervous. I don't spend much time with kids." I choke back a laugh and try to keep a straight face because I can tell she's serious.

"Not a problem, I'm here if you need anything at all."

She abruptly releases me and starts patting down her pockets. "You don't know the time, do you?"

I reach into my own pocket, pulling out my phone. "It's a quarter after six."

"Shit!" She runs into her bedroom and comes back with her own phone. "Okay, nothing from either of them. I'm in the clear."

"What are you talking about?"

The biggest shit-eating grin I've ever seen overtakes her face. "Mom and Dad are out on a date right now, thanks to me."

My heart, my breath, time itself seems to stop for a moment at her words. I have to make a conscious effort to suck air back into my lungs and pray that restarts my heart.

"Are you okay, Vi? You look a little green."

"Yeah, I'm fine," I say rather weakly. "So you did it? Your mom and dad are finally getting back together?" Is this why he rejected me? He's just been waiting until the right moment to get back together with Amanda. I should have known. Bianca's been telling me for weeks that they were right for each other. I thought it was just the wild fantasies of a child who will always want her parents to be together. If they're out on a date then I guess those fantasies weren't so wild after all.

They're probably laughing together about me right now.

"Well, I wouldn't say they're back together yet. But I think this is a pretty good start. They'll both be at the party this weekend and maybe after a few drinks . . . well who knows, right?"

I silently nod my head at her while she turns back to the task of gathering her supplies. I desperately want to cry but won't allow myself. Not just because I'm standing here in front of Bianca but because I won't let him control me that much. We were never together. We had one sexually charged moment because we were both horny and drunk and one kiss that I forced on him. Crying would make something more out of the situation than it is. No, this doesn't warrant my tears.

"Well, I'm going to head back to my room and work on my paper. Good luck tonight."

Bianca glances over her shoulder at me, smiling. "Thanks, Vi. I'll see you when I get home." I don't bother responding and trudge down the hall back to the solitude of my bedroom.

FIFTEEN

DANTE

"A little help, please?" I rush over to where Archer Clarke, billionaire hotel mogul and friend, is currently carrying two twenty-five-pound bags of ice through my front door.

"I got it," I say, taking one of the bags from him so he can walk inside unimpeded. Behind him is Hollie, who is his girlfriend now, I guess, and her sister Paige, who doesn't look particularly thrilled to be here. "Thanks for helping out you guys."

"Of course," Hollie says with a smile, setting down a bag of decorations. "You know I'd do anything for Bianca, and I come with two helpers." She indicates to both Archer and Paige.

"Where should I put this?" Paige asks, holding out a bag of miscellaneous party supplies. I motion to the kitchen table with my head while I lug the bag of ice to the kitchen counter. The three of them start busily working away at unpacking what they've brought, and I can't help glancing past them to the front door, waiting for Violet to walk in. I move closer with the intention of shutting the door but give a quick scan of the front yard for any sign of Violet or her car. Finding nothing, I close the door and head back to my helpers.

I shouldn't be surprised that Violet isn't here, she's managed to avoid me all week. She's still coming in and working. I know because she leaves me notes about what she's done and things that I need to handle, but the girl must have some kind of sixth sense for when I'm going to be here and when I'm gone.

I want to ask Hollie where she is. I know that I shouldn't ask, I shouldn't care that she's not here yet. Apparently, a week without Violet has made me a weak man. Was it only a month ago when I was satisfied with only seeing her on random occasions?

"Uh, Hollie? Where's Violet? I thought she was going to help set up." That sounded calm and collected, right? Not like I desperately need to know if she's ditching the party in order to avoid me.

Hollie looks up from where she's mixing some kind of bright pink drink in a pitcher. "Violet's bringing a date tonight so I told her she should stay home so she could get ready. I think we can get everything done without her."

She has a fucking date? A week ago her tongue was in my mouth. A week ago I watched her come while I stroked my dick. And now she has a fucking date? I take a deep breath and try to look casual, but I must not be doing a very good job because Hollie is looking at me strangely.

"Uh yeah, of course. There's not that much to do and you brought Archer and Paige." Her eyes stay on me another moment before smiling and turning back to the drink she's concocting.

I know that I have no right to be angry she has a date. After all, I'm the one who said that nothing could happen between us, but she's moving on just a little fast, isn't she? I tamp down the urge to jump in my truck, drive over to her place, and demand an explanation that isn't owed to me.

I feel like I'm crawling out of my skin, that I'm covered in fire ants and there's nothing I can do about it. Instead, I carry a bag of ice outside to the patio where Archer is already packing drinks into my large cooler that I use for camping. When I slam the bag to the ground with just a little too much force he looks over at me with a shit-eating grin on his face.

"So, Violet, huh?" he says.

"What about her?" I snap unintentionally as I tear the bag of ice open, spilling half of its contents. "Fuck!"

"Are you finally going to admit that you're into her?" I pause in my fiddling with the ice to straighten up and look at him.

"I don't know what you're talking about."

"Please, Dante. We've been friends for a long time. You've wanted that girl for a while now. Seems to me, from the expression on your face when Hollie told you she was bringing a date tonight, that things might be coming to a head."

"Whatever. I'm too old for her," I grumble.

He just shrugs. "Plenty of people think that I'm too old for Hollie." Well, he's not wrong. He's a good twelve years older than Hollie is. I'd be pissed if she was my daughter, even though I know Archer is a good guy. Just another reason that Violet and I shouldn't be together. "Look, you can't base your decisions on what other people are going to say. I'm the happiest I've ever been in my life and that's all because of Hollie." The man is telling the truth, I'll give him that. Archer was a miserable bastard before she came into his life.

"But what about Bianca? She's Violet's best friend. She'd never forgive us."

"Your daughter is a spitfire, it's true. But anything worth doing is going to be tough."

"It may seem exciting to Violet now, but what if she decides she doesn't want to be with an old man? Aren't you worried that Hollie is going to change her mind?"

Archer shakes his head at me. "You're full of excuses, Dante. It wouldn't matter if Hollie was the same age as me or if I was fifty years older. There's always a chance that someone will change their mind in a relationship. That's the risk you take. But I'll tell you right now, if Hollie changes her mind tomorrow and decides she doesn't want to be with me, at least I've gotten to spend this time with her. Hollie is the love of my life and I'll cherish every second I get to spend with her."

I'm surprised with the vehemence in his voice. In all the years that I've known Archer, he's never spoken about anything the way he speaks about Hollie. And her being the love of his life? I don't know. Maybe it could be worth the risk of a broken heart.

"Look, Dante, since you're basically the one who introduced my future wife to me—" I can't help but choke on my own saliva at that. Archer Clarke getting married? I know they aren't engaged but it looks like he's already planning to lock her down. He just smiles and continues on. "Let me give you a piece of advice. When I went looking for her after I fucked up and almost lost her, Violet stood firm. She didn't want to let me near Hollie until I proved that I wasn't going to hurt her again. I'm a powerful man but your daughter and Violet put me in my place. Violet has the type of loyalty that is rare in this world and shouldn't be overlooked, no matter what her age is. Don't let the fact that you're scared of getting hurt stop you from what might just be the best thing to ever happen to you." With that he claps me hard on the shoulder and moves back inside to check on his girlfriend, leaving me alone outside with my thoughts and feeling just a little bit like a fool.

The party is in full swing. There are people everywhere and you can hardly move without getting jostled this way and that. The music is blaring and there are way more than fifty people here. I'm considering killing my daughter. That will have to wait because, at the moment, I'm leaned against a wall with the perfect line of sight to the front door. I'm trying to casually sip my beer and hope that nobody notices that I've been waiting for Violet to show up for the past thirty minutes.

I thought a lot about my conversation with Archer outside. Hell, I haven't done anything *but* think about our talk. I've come to the conclusion that he's right and I'm an idiot. It was an easy conclusion to get to. I don't know how this is going to work with Bianca or her parents, we can figure that out as we go, but Violet and I belong together. At the very least, we owe it to each other to give it a shot. I know that I hurt her by rejecting her last week and I'll do anything I can to make it up to her. I'm not going to throw away the first chance at happiness I've had in years because I'm scared.

It's another twenty minutes of anxious waiting before the door opens and the woman I've been waiting for walks in. I've always thought all those movies were bullshit. You know the ones where time seems to slow down around you when the woman of your dreams walks into the room. I'll never make fun of those movies again. She walks through the door in slow motion, her hair swishing against her shoulders, her gait causing her breasts to gently bounce, the skirt of her dress swaying against her thighs. Then, she smiles. It's that gentle smile that I've come to love. As I'm watching, my heart in my throat, she turns that smile to the person behind her. It's only then I notice the man that she's with, his hand resting gently on her hip like it belongs there.

I want to walk over there and rip his hand away from her. If I'm being honest, I'd like to take his entire arm off for daring to touch her. I don't have a right to have these feelings, I'm the one that pushed her into the arms of another man, but that doesn't mean I give a fuck. Soon Violet's going to know that she's mine.

I take another sip of my beer and push off the wall that's been propping me up for the better part of an hour while I've been waiting for her. I'm about to make my way toward her, not having a clue what I'm going to say when somebody grabs my forearm. I turn and see Amanda sidle up to me, a lascivious smile on her face.

"So this is where you've been hiding," she purrs at me. I don't know how I can make it any clearer to this woman that I have zero interest in getting back together with her but I'm growing tired of this game. I look away from her back to where I just saw Violet and her crystal-clear blue eyes meet mine. They narrow when they see Amanda's hand on me and before I can step away, she turns, whispers something in her dates ear and they both move in the opposite direction.

Fuck. This isn't going to be easy.

"Look, Amanda, I thought that I made myself pretty clear the other night that I wasn't interested. I don't know what game you're playing but count me out."

She doesn't even have the decency to look put off by what I'm saying to her. Instead, she stretches up so that she can whisper in my ear over the raucous sounds of the crowded house. "Maybe *I* haven't made *myself* clear, Dante, I want you. And I always get what I want."

Jesus Christ, what is she a child? She always gets what she wants? I shake off her hand and take a significant step away from her so that she can no longer touch me. "This isn't some fucking game, Amanda, and if you can't keep your hands to yourself, you're not going to be welcome in my house any longer."

"We'll see," she says with a smile and walks off toward the makeshift bar we have setup out on the patio. I turn back toward Violet but she's gone.

I'm about to go find her when Bianca comes over and envelopes me in a hug. "Thank you so much for my party, Dad. You're the best."

"You're right, I am." I squeeze her back, always happy to have affection from my girl.

"I know it's a little bigger than expected, the guest list got a little out of hand and it looks like some people brought friends."

"It's fine, pumpkin, as long as you have fun. Well, that and the cops don't get called." She averts her eyes from me, and I wonder what that's all about but quickly brush it aside. "But don't think I'm the one that's going to be cleaning up this mess." I remind her, gesturing to the piles of half-eaten plates and empty plastic cups and drink pouches that are littering every available surface.

"No worries. Hollie, Archer, and Paige said they would help."

"But not Violet?" I ask, knowing that I can't give too much away. Luckily for me, while my daughter is very smart and talented, she's not always the most perceptive when there are feelings involved.

"Oh, she offered. But I told her to forget it. This is her second date with Tyler, and I want her to be free to spend the evening with him, if you know what I mean." She laughs and winks at me like that statement hasn't just sent me into a blind panic. If Violet thinks she's spending the night with that boy, she's got another thing coming. "Oh, I forgot! Even Mom offered to stay and help so we should be covered." That brings my attention straight back to her.

"Do you know what's going on with your mom?" I ask.

"What are you talking about? Nothing's going on with her, well other than her moving and everything. Why?" I didn't really expect that Amanda would share with her the reason she's moving to Seattle and the details surrounding her leaving her last job. No matter how much I want to, I'm not going to hurt my daughter by telling her that her mother seems to be moving here out of a mixture of lack of options and the inexplicable decision to start perusing me instead of moving here to be closer to her own daughter.

"Look, I'm not trying to cause problems but if she mentions anything to you, maybe just gently let her know that I'm not looking to date right now."

"W-what? But I thought you two were getting along."

I narrow my eyes and study her obviously guilty expression closely. "Bianca, was you canceling on us the other night intentional?"

"No! I mean, the canceling wasn't intentional, something really did come up. I just thought that maybe you two could get to know each other again . . ."

I let out a groan and rub the bridge of my nose in frustration. "You're trying to parent trap us, aren't you?"

"Absolutely not! Why does everyone keep saying that? In order for it to be a parent trap I'd have to lock you in a room together. I'm just simply . . . facilitating get-togethers. That's all."

"Jesus Christ, Bianca. Aren't you old enough to know that your parents aren't getting back together? You're twenty-three years old. We haven't been together since you were two."

Her eyes narrow in on me with a glare and she crosses her arms over her chest in a defensive gesture. "Hey, you don't have to be an asshole about it. I just want you to be happy, Dad. You sit in this house all alone. You don't date. You're turning into a grumpy old man. In case you haven't noticed, Mom is pretty awesome and moving to a brand-new city. So, sue me if I just want two people that I love to be happy. And if they can be happy together, what the fuck is wrong with that?"

I shouldn't have brought this up here. I know that. There are too many people around and I don't want to ruin Bianca's birthday. At some point I'm going to have to sit her down and make it absolutely clear that I will never be getting back together with her mother but now isn't the time.

I pull her back into another hug and squeeze her tight. "I'm sorry, let's not talk about this right now. It's your birthday." She gives me a kiss on my cheek before pulling away and smiles. "Besides I haven't even given you your present yet."

"Present?" Her eyes light up and I can't help but laugh.

I pull the folded sheet of paper out of my back pocket and hand it over to her with an exaggerated flourish. "I hope you don't mind, you know I'm shit at wrapping."

"Of course not," she says, plucking the paper from my hand and unfolding it. She takes a moment to scan it and then looks back at me questioningly. "You got me something from Dark Arts and Crafts?"

"Actually, I opened an account for you at Dark Arts and Crafts that I will pay for—" She cuts me off with a squeal and throws her arms around my neck. "That I will pay for, as long as it's under three hundred dollars a month, for the next year."

"This is amazing, Dad! Thank you so much! I can't believe it."

"Yeah, well just remember that you don't have to spend the entire three hundred every month," I grumble good naturedly. "Now, go have fun with your friends. I'm going to grab another drink." I hold up my empty beer bottle to show that I'm indeed in need of a drink and not about to go hunt down her best friend. I watch her run off to tell her friends about her gift and smile to myself, happy that I can give her this.

Some people might think that I spoil Bianca, but I've worked hard since I was seventeen years old to give her a better life. I don't want her to have to struggle the way that I have always had to. My parents were far from rich and even though they wanted to, they couldn't do much to help Amanda and me with Bianca. Now I'm in a position where I can help launch her into adulthood and the artistic career of her dreams and that's exactly what I'm going to do. It doesn't hurt that Bianca asks for very little from her mother and me and really does seem to appreciate everything we do for her. No, she's not spoiled and I'm damn proud of her for chasing her dreams.

I was never much of a dreamer. I never had the chance. There was always too much responsibility on my shoulders.

But as I glance around the room looking for Violet, I start to wonder if maybe it's time for me to start dreaming.

I make my way from room to room, constantly scanning for my black-haired beauty. Why does it seem like my house has doubled in size? What I do spot is Archer about to pull Hollie into a darkened corner and I smile even if it does make me a little jealous. I truly am happy for them. Both Archer and Hollie have had a tough go at life and it's nice to see two people that I care about find joy in each other.

Just as I'm about to move on, Hollie catches my eye and pulls away from Archer, moving toward me. We're in the living room where the speakers are loudly pulsing away with some kind of techno beat that I don't understand nor care for, so when she reaches me she has to get up on her tiptoes and almost shout in order to be heard over the din.

"She's in the garage." I look at her and am about to pretend like I don't know who she's talking about when she gives me a look that says I shouldn't even bother to deny it. I glance past her to Archer who lifts one of his shoulders in a shrug, indicating that he didn't tell her anything about our earlier conversation. Damn, that girl has always been too perceptive for her own good. Or I guess in this case, my own good. But she's also always been good at minding her own business, so I don't think she'll say anything to Bianca. At least not unless she speaks to Violet first.

But I don't have time to get her assurance of silence right now. With the information of Violet's whereabouts fresh in my mind I'm anxious to get to her. "Thanks." She just gives me a small smile and makes her way back to her boyfriend leaving me to thread my way through the throngs of party goers to get to the garage.

Once the door closes behind me, I'm thankful that most of the sounds of the party are muffled out here. While there's still a few people milling around, there aren't nearly as many people here. I rarely use the garage since my truck is too large to fit inside. Instead, I have the space set up as a kind of game room for when people want to come over and hang out. There's a poker table in the corner that currently has four people sitting around it, drinking and playing cards. The center of the room is largely occupied by a pool table that I probably never should have bought since I've only used it a handful of times. There's a group of people that look deeply invested in a game of eight ball and I'm glad that someone is getting some use out of it.

In the corner of the room opposite the poker table I see that little blond-haired punk sitting on one of the chairs we have lining the walls. He has a drink in one hand and Violet's in his other. That's not the thing that's making me see red, though. What's about to send me over the edge is that he's tugging at her. It looks like he's trying to get her to sit in his lap and I can tell by the look on her face how uncomfortable she is. She's not pulling away from him exactly but she's certainly not making any moves to join him on the chair.

Violet is my sole focus as I move into the room, my sights set on her like a laser. I knock into a few of the people at the pool table and vaguely hear their protests behind me. I don't give a flying fuck. That's my girl he's making uncomfortable.

Once I'm within a few feet of them, Violet seems to finally notice me. Her eyes go wide and now she's actively trying to tug her hand out of that idiot's grasp. I don't know if it's because she wants to make an escape from me or if it's because she doesn't want me to see him touching her. Either way she's not going anywhere unless it's with me.

"Violet," I bark out, my voice coming out much more harshly than I mean it to. My anger isn't for her. "Who's this?" I nod my head toward her date but don't take my eyes off her face.

She doesn't look at him either when she responds. "This is Tyler." She straightens her shoulder and lifts her chin, challenging me. "My date."

Tyler gets out of his chair, still holding my girl's hand and sets down his drink before offering me his hand to shake. "Hey, nice to meet you, man." I ignore him.

"I need to speak to you," I tell her.

"I'm a little busy right now, Dante. Can't this wait?" Her date is smart enough to pull his hand back, realizing that I have no intention of shaking it and is swiveling his head back and forth between Violet and me.

"No, it can't," I say through gritted teeth. If he doesn't get his hand off her in the next few seconds, I'm going to lose it. She must see how close I am to going over the edge because her eyes widen slightly and she turns to her date.

"Can you give me a minute, Tyler? This is my boss."

"Oh, sure," he says, dropping her hand so that I can finally take a deep calming breath. "I'll just go grab another drink."

She shoots him a smile that doesn't quite reach her eyes and I motion for her to follow me out of the room. I want to lead her straight to my bedroom but it would be too tempting to rip her clothes off and bury myself deep inside her, claiming her as mine. Instead, she follows me up the stairs to the office. Once inside I close the door and flick the lock before turning to face a very pissed off Violet.

"What the hell are you doing, Dante? There's nothing that needs to be done that can't wait until Monday." Her cheeks are flushed with anger, arms crossed against her chest, her breasts heaving and her eyes blazing at me. I realize that I've never actually seen Violet mad before. She's never looked sexier.

"This can't wait." I move forward quickly, stalking my prey. She takes a step back, trying to put some space between us but before she can get away her ass bumps into my desk. Trapping her between it and me, I glare into her eyes and come to the realization that she looks turned on.

My intention was to bring her up here and talk to her, tell her that I want to give us a chance, but I can't seem to help myself when it comes to her. I bring my hand up and tangle it in her hair, pulling her head back so she's looking me in the eyes. Before she can ask what I'm doing, my mouth is crashing against hers in a savage, possessive kiss.

She lets out a gasp as soon as our lips meet and I take the opportunity to invade her mouth, claiming every inch of it with my tongue. I run my other hand over her hip, taking in the gentle swell there and let out a groan.

Before I know what's happening, she's ripped her mouth away from mine and is using the flat of her hand on my chest to push me back. I let her move me away, not wanting to invade her space like that asshole downstairs.

"What the hell, Dante?" Her eyes are glassy and she's practically panting from the intensity of our kiss. I want to draw her back to me but resist. Barely. I know that there are things that need to be said.

"Why would you bring that kid here? To punish me?" I ask, trying to catch my own breath.

"How would me having a date be punishing you? You've already made it very clear to me that you're not interested

in anything I have to offer, except maybe my office skills."
I look around the room pointedly, then back at her with a
raised eyebrow. "Not these kind of office skills. Can you be
serious for a second?"

"I'm sorry, Vi. I really am. I shouldn't have pushed you
away. I was an idiot."

"Well, I'm not going to debate that," she grumbles under
her breath. "What am I supposed to think? You tell me
nothing can happen between us, then the second that I'm
with someone else you throw all of that out the window?"

"I know it looks like that but it's not true, baby." The
endearment falls from my lips without any forethought and
it feels good. Her body gives a tremble and I reach up,
rubbing my knuckles down her cheek. "I already knew that
I made a mistake. I regretted it the second you walked out
the door last week. I know that anything between us would
be . . . complicated. But I want to try. That is. If you still
want to." It feels a little like begging, and honestly, right
now, with how hard my dick is, I'm not far off from it.

She bites her lip and turns her face away from me, causing me to frown. "What about Amanda?"

"What about her?" I ask, thoroughly confused by this
topic change.

"I thought that maybe you were going to get back together," she whispers and looks at the floor.

"Baby, I don't give a fuck about Amanda. I haven't wanted anyone but you for at least a year now."

That confession seems to have an impact. Her head jerks
up and her eyes search my face, trying to see if I'm telling
her the truth. She must like what she sees because she
pushes herself away from the desk and presses into me,
molding her body against mine, causing me to let out a
growl from deep inside my chest. I place my hands on her

hips to steady her, then stand perfectly still, allowing her to make her decision. She gets up on her tiptoes and tilts her face up at me. She's too short to reach me so I bend down and meet her halfway.

Our kiss isn't as savage this time but it's no less hot. It's a kiss of exploration. Our lips are seamed together and our bodies are molded to one another. I know she can feel the hardness of my cock against her soft belly just like I can feel her hardened nipples against my chest.

While still locked together in a passionate embrace, I slide my hand slowly over the globes of her ass and down to her naked thigh, taking slow so that she can stop me at any time. I move my fingers inch by tantalizing inch back up the front of her thighs until I'm cupping her panty clad pussy.

She lets out a whimper and pulls her mouth away from mine, her lips swollen from our kisses. "Is this okay?" I ask while slowly rubbing her mound. She nods her head and takes a deep breath before arching her back, pushing her pussy more firmly into my hand. Her panties are drenched, showing me just how much she wants this, when a thought occurs to me. "Baby you're soaked. Is this for me or for him?" I ask, holding my breath while waiting for her answer.

She looks taken aback by my question. "You, it's only ever been you." She whispers this like it's a confession and I can't wait any longer. My hand delves inside her panties where I find her soaking slit causing me to moan. My dick jerks in my pants and I know that my boxers are soaked in pre-cum. I easily find her swollen clit and take my time circling it.

She lets out another little mewling sound and thrusts her hips at me, wanting more. I know I have to make this fast before someone discovers we're missing so I delve farther, letting my finger enter her tight channel just long enough to gather more moisture and bring it back up to her clit where I proceed to alternate between flicking and fondling her engorged bud. Her fingers are clawing my shoulders, trying to get me closer to her while her breaths are coming out in little gasps. If she doesn't come soon, I just might.

All of a sudden her body stills, all of her muscles tensing up. She buries her head in my shoulder and starts to moan loudly as her body starts to tremble. I feel a sharp pain at my pec and realize that she's biting me to try to control the sound of her orgasm. My hips involuntarily thrust forward and I feel another spurt of pre-cum leave my dick, begging to be buried inside this woman in my arms.

I hold her tightly while she rides through her orgasm until her body stops shaking and she pulls her head away from my chest, looking up at me with what I can only describe as a little bit of awe. I know that her expression is just mirroring my own.

I thought what we did last week in my bathroom was the hottest thing that had ever happened to me but here we are, standing in the middle of my office, both fully clothed, and I can't remember ever being more turned on. I keep my eyes locked on hers as I pull my hand from her panties and out from under her skirt, slowly bringing my fingers up to my lips and sucking her juices off my fingers. She's both sweet and tangy at the same time and I can't wait for the day when I can bury my face in her pussy and feast on her. Her eyes have gone as big as saucers as she watches me clean her from my fingers.

By now I know we've been gone from the party for quite a while and people are going to start to notice that we're gone. We haven't even discussed how we're going to handle this yet so it's probably not a good idea for people to find us locked in a room together that reeks of sex.

I reach back down and smooth out her skirt, making sure there are no telltale signs that she was just fucked by my fingers. "Come over for dinner tomorrow." It's not a question but she nods and says okay anyway. I move to leave the room but stop and turn back to her. She's still standing there in a bit of a daze and I know she'll need a few minutes to get herself together. "And get rid of the date, Violet."

I don't even bother waiting for her answer before I slip out the door and make my way back downstairs with a smile on my face.

SIXTEEN

VIOLET

Life's felt slightly surreal since Dante pulled me into the office last night. When I finally collected myself enough to rejoin the party going on downstairs, the first thing I did was look for Bianca. I wasn't sure how long we were up there, so I said a little silent prayer that she hadn't noticed her father's or my absence. When I found her, she was playing an adult version of Red Light / Green Light, complete with a variety of shots. Judging by how she seemed to wobble every time someone yelled *red light*, I don't think there's a chance she noticed me missing.

Fortunately, or maybe unfortunately, depending upon how you look at it, Tyler was also taking part in the game, and he seemed to have had even more liquor than Bianca. To be honest, even if Dante hadn't walked into the garage and pulled me away from him, that was going to be my last date with Tyler. From the moment he picked me up last night he was acting fairly aggressively toward me. It was like the fact that I'd agreed to a second date somehow gave him permission to notch up his pursuit of me tenfold. The entire night he was handsy, arrogant, and pushy.

I quickly made my excuses to both Bianca and Tyler, saying I had a headache and I needed to go home. All I wanted to do was get out of that house and back home where I could think clearly. I didn't plan on letting Tyler drive me home. It was obvious he was past the point of driving, but when he didn't even offer to find me a ride all of my misgivings about him were confirmed.

When I'd invited Tyler to the party, I didn't expect the night to turn out how it did. I figured Dante would ignore me, maybe even roll his eyes a little at me bringing a date to his house so soon after our last encounter. All I wanted was for him to not think of me as some loser that was pining after him. The last thing I expected was for him to be jealous. Jealousy can make us all do stupid things, which is why I'm a little concerned about showing up at his house for dinner tonight. What if it's just like last time? He wanted me in the moment, but by the light of day, what if he's changed his mind? It's already happened once.

Now, here I am standing on Dante's porch once again, decidedly more nervous than I was the last time. I have a plate of cookies I made in one hand, and I can't stop nervously fiddling with the skirt of my silver floral dress. This time when he opens the front door, there's a huge smile on his face. He grabs my hand and pulls me inside, firmly shutting the door behind me before plucking the plate out of my hands and setting it on the side table. Just as I'm about to greet him, his mouth slams down onto mine, and every thought in my head gets wiped away.

His arms circle me and cradle my body gently while his lips play with mine, alternating between soft and hard kisses that seem to have a direct line to the ache between my legs. When he finally pulls back, my head is spinning a little and I feel dazed. Well, that's different from last time.

"Sorry," he says. "I just missed you."

"I missed you too," I say shyly. I'm completely out of my depth here and hope that he's going to be happy to lead the way, because I honestly have no idea what I'm doing.

He picks my plate of cookies back up and drags me into the kitchen behind him. I let out a little gasp of surprise when I see the table.

"This is actually what I wanted to do the last time you came over, but I didn't want freak you out."

I look over at him, and while he's still smiling, he also looks a little uncomfortable. For the first time, I realize he might be just as nervous as I am. I turn back to the table where there's what appears to be an honest-to-God home-cooked meal not from take-out containers. He set the table beautifully with not only a small bouquet of brightly colored daisies but lit candles as well.

"I love it." And I really do. Is it sad that nobody has ever put in this much effort for me before? He pulls out my chair, and I take a seat before he slides me in and then sits himself down across from me. "So you actually cooked something today?" I ask, keeping my tone light and teasing.

"Well, I may be a mediocre cook, but I'm pretty good at using the grill out there." He motions behind his back to the set of French doors leading to the patio. "I've made some grilled chicken, asparagus, and baked potatoes."

"It looks amazing," I tell him. "Thank you."

"Don't thank me yet. Let's just hope it tastes as good as it looks." He grabs the various platters and serves me while I take a sip of the glass of wine he already had sitting at my place, and it occurs to me how nice it is that he remembered.

We both start eating, and I'm surprised how delicious everything is since he only used an outdoor grill. We don't even have one at the house, but maybe we should look into it if it can produce chicken this juicy.

We idly chat about inconsequential things, and after we've made it through such riveting topics as my class schedule and the weather, we lapse into silence.

"Well, this is awkward," I blurt out. Eager to fill the empty space with something, anything.

He just laughs. "You're right, it is. I'm sitting here trying to think about how to bring up the topic of, well, us."

"Good job, mission accomplished." I smile and take another bite of my potato that's smothered in butter.

"True. I've thought about this a lot since last night. If I'm being honest, I haven't stopped thinking about it since last week. I really like spending time with you, Violet."

I can feel my cheeks pink. "I like spending time with you too."

"Thank God for that," he mumbles before continuing. "And it's rather obvious that we're both attracted to each other."

I thought I was blushing before, but as soon as he says that, my mind goes back to watching him stroke his thick, hard cock in the bathroom. I give him a slight nod of acknowledgment, urging him to continue.

"For me, I'd like to see where this goes. Honestly, this week without you has sucked, and I don't want to go through that again."

Everything he's saying is making sense and reflects what I'm feeling, but I have to ask, "What about Bianca?" I see him flinch a little at the question, and I can't say I blame him. It's obviously something that's been on both of our minds.

"Maybe we don't tell her? Just for now."

I can't help but feel relieved. While I'm excited about the prospect of being with Dante, the thought of losing Bianca over it has my stomach churning. "I think that's a good idea." I've spent the entire day thinking about this conversation, what I wanted to say, how I wanted to play this. Even though Dante and I seem to be on the same page, I'm still incredibly worried that I'm going to do something to mess this up. I'm young and inexperienced with relationships compared to him, and while he says he wants to spend time together, be together, I don't know what that means. And frankly, I haven't gathered up the courage to ask. It'll be best if I lay the ground rules down so that they're easy, something he can accept, and that way I'll know how to protect my heart.

I stare a little over his shoulder and not directly into his eyes because I have a feeling that Dante will be able to tell I'm lying if I'm looking straight at him. "I think we should probably keep this casual between us. There are too many other outside factors that need to be addressed if we're anything more. There's Bianca and my parents. Let's just call it what is, some fun between friends, and then we won't have to deal with any of that."

I take a deep breath and move my eyes back to him and see a frown on his face that he quickly covers up. He's probably annoyed that I beat him to the punch. "Yeah, sure. Casual sounds good. For now."

I nod my head and let that last part hang in the air between us. He really doesn't need to promise me anything he doesn't want to give. I know Bianca has never really seen him date. Why would he want to start now? He probably thinks he's appeasing me, but he really doesn't need to.

In an attempt to end this uncomfortable conversation, I pop out of my seat and grab the plate of cookies I made.

I'm really not sure about them. They didn't turn out how I wanted them to. They're way flatter than the ones I've bought at the bakery before, but I figured I would bring them over just the same. At least he could see that I made the effort.

"So, are you ready for dessert?" I ask, pulling off the foil covering. "They're lavender and honey macarons."

He gives me a smile and reaches for the plate, picking up one of the purple-and-white sandwich cookies.

"They didn't turn out the way I wanted them to," I admit. "They should be much fluffier than this." I poke a little at the cookies before picking up one of the thicker ones.

"They look pretty good to me," he says before popping the entire thing into his mouth. I study his face closely while taking a nibble of my own. I think the lavender flavor might be too strong. I probably should have gone for something a little more traditional.

He lets out a little moan that I feel right between my legs and shuts his eyes for just a second. "This is fucking delicious, Vi."

I narrow my eyes, looking for any sign that he's lying to me, but it seems like he might be telling the truth. "Are you serious?"

"Of course, I wouldn't lie to you." He reaches for the plate and grabs another of the flattened cookies and pops it in his mouth. "I mean, I've never had a macaron before, so don't know how fluffy they're supposed to be, but these taste amazing."

His genuine compliment warms my insides. While I wouldn't have been upset if he didn't like my treat, most people don't, the fact that he's enjoying something that I've made makes me feel special.

He abruptly pushes the plate away from him and stands up, slowly approaching me, making my heart rate pick up. "Honestly, they're great, Violet. But there's something else I want for dessert."

Before I can ask him what he wants, he's pulling me up out of my chair and pressing the length of his body against mine. I can already feel through his jeans that he's hard as his cock rubs against my belly, and I shudder at the touch. He leans down and kisses me softly, rubbing his hands along my body, gently caressing the sides of my breasts before moving down and sweeping his hands over the globes of my ass, then making his way back up again. A whimper escapes my lips.

"Is this okay?" he asks, putting his hand on the tie that's holding my wrap dress together, and I give him a nod. "Words, Violet. I need to hear the words."

"It's okay." My voice sounds breathless and needy even to my own ears. He oh so slowly unties the bow at my waist, then parts the silver and floral fabric that's covering me. He takes a tiny step backward, eyes roving over my body, which is covered in only my bra, panties, and the dress that's hanging off my shoulders. His pupils dilate and his breathing picks up as his eyes run over my breasts, down to between my legs, then up to my face, like he doesn't know where to look first. I can feel myself getting wetter under his stare and hope that there isn't a wet patch at the front of my panties.

"You're so fucking beautiful," he says before coming back to me and capturing my lips in a searing kiss. The contact of his fully clothed body against my own mostly naked one forces a gasp from me, and he takes advantage of that by slipping his tongue into my mouth, stroking mine with his, tempting it to play with him.

I'm clutching tightly to his biceps in an attempt to stay upright. I've never felt sensations like these running through my body, and I don't know what to do besides hold on to him for dear life. His hands move inside the hanging pieces of my dress and cup the underside of my ass. Before I know it, he's lifted me into the air and set me down on the edge of the dinner table.

Suddenly, I'm overtaken by nerves. I'm not sure what he's expecting of me or from tonight, and I don't want to disappoint him. "What are you doing?" I ask.

"Having my dessert." He resumes kissing me and slips his fingers inside the waistband of my panties, giving a tug. I manage to lift my ass just a little, so he's able to slide them off and down my legs, letting them fall to the floor. I'm overcome with embarrassment and lock my knees together when he tries to spread my legs open wide.

He looks up at me questioningly. There's no annoyance or impatience reflected in his eyes, just the question of whether I want to continue. I don't want to tell him, but I know I need to. It would be unfair of me not to.

"Dante . . . I'm a virgin." I turn my face away from him, not wanting to see his disappointment. I'm sure he was expecting to get someone experienced, instead he gets the shy girl who's only ever given a hand job before. My eyes water, but I hold back my tears while I'm sitting here half-naked on his kitchen table.

"Baby, look at me."

I give my head a little shake and keep staring out the window.

"Violet." His tone tells me he won't be happy until my eyes are on him, so I look back at his face, searching for some sign of his disapproval.

"You know there's no shame in being a virgin, right?"

I shrug my shoulders at him in silent response.

"You're fucking perfect. It doesn't matter if you're a virgin or not. In fact, I couldn't think of anything hotter than being the first man to be inside you. That is, if you're ever ready for that. But that's not what we're doing tonight."

"It's not?" I ask in surprise.

"Nope. Has anyone ever tasted this sweet pussy before?" He's stroking my knees in a gentle and soothing motion. Just the thought of him doing that to me causes a gush of wetness to fill my pussy.

"No, never."

He lets out a growl that sounds like it comes from deep in his chest, and his hand tightens slightly on my knee. "Would you like me to?"

I bite my lip, trying to get my nerves under control, and nod my head at him, not quite believing that this is really happening.

"Words, baby. Remember?"

"Yes, please."

"Please what?" Holy hell, is he really going to make me say it? The only other option would be to get off this table and tie my dress back around me, and there's not a chance in hell of that happening.

"Please taste my pussy," I whisper. He closes his eyes and takes a deep breath, and I know he can smell my arousal. When he opens them, I swear his eyes are pitch black. I've read in novels that can happen when people are aroused, but I never thought it was real. Well, it looks like I was wrong.

He pulls my legs apart, exposing me for the first time, then quickly sinks to his knees between my open legs. "You're so fucking beautiful," he whispers before diving into my drenched slit. He takes a moment to suck each one of my lips into his mouth, moving his tongue over them before releasing and giving them a gentle kiss.

It should embarrass me how wet my pussy is for him, but there's something in the way he's so enthusiastically running his tongue up and down my slit that doesn't let me feel any kind of embarrassment. It's almost as if he's enjoying this as much as I am.

His tongue and lips are everywhere. Everywhere, that is, except where I need them. It's like he's ignoring my clit on purpose, and I start to wiggle my ass, hoping to encourage him to touch my swollen nub that's screaming for attention. He pulls back, letting me see his face glistening, covered in my juices, and gives me a wicked smile. "Was there something that you needed, Vi?"

I let out a groan. "You know what I need."

"Did you need this?" His finger enters my aching channel, just up to the first knuckle, enough to tease me and cause my hips to buck off the table. Holy shit, I'm going to need more of that. Pulling out, he takes the moisture that he's gathered and runs it up to the apex of my sex, circling my engorged clit but purposefully missing it again.

"Dante." I can hear the whining in my voice but am too far gone to care.

"Or maybe it was this you needed." He covers my sex with his mouth and thrusts his tongue inside me. My hands move from gripping the table to clutching at his hair, trying to pull him farther into me. I've never felt anything like Dante's tongue inside me, and I'm desperate for more.

"I know, I bet it's this," he says before moving up and attacking the bundle of nerves that's only become more and more sensitive while waiting for him. He sucks it into his mouth, and I let out a cry I'm sure the neighbors can hear. At this point I'm practically humping Dante's face while

I hold him firmly in place by his hair, and I couldn't care less. If his enthusiastic performance is anything to go on, it seems my noises and movements are only spurring him on.

I'm so close to going over the edge but still want this to last. I want to enjoy this as long as possible in case I wake up and this was all just a dream. My orgasm's building, and I try to hold it back, to savor every second.

He stops batting my sensitive nub back and forth for just a moment and says, "Let go, Violet. Come on my face, baby."

It's his dirty words added to the fact that he immediately sucks my aching clit into his mouth that makes it so I can't hang on another second. My orgasm rolls through me in wave after wave as I undulate my hips and clasp his face into my pussy. I hope he can breathe down there because my muscles are so locked up in my orgasm that I don't think I could let go if I tried. I can hear some kind of high keening noise, and it takes me a moment to realize that I'm the one making it.

Finally, the crashing waves of my orgasm turn into lapping at the shore, and I'm able to let go of Dante even though there are still tremors going through my body. I've had plenty of orgasms in my life. I thought nobody could play my body better than I could. But I was wrong. Oh, so wrong. I thought his fingers inside me last night were magic, but I've never felt anything like this before.

Dante is back on his feet and kissing me. I can taste myself on his lips and hungrily stroke the inside of his mouth with my tongue, wanting more of him, of us mixed together. I bring my legs up to wrap around his waist and pull him in closer to me. The bulge in his pants is rubbing against my oversensitive sex, and all I can think about is getting him in my hand, my mouth. I reach down to unbutton his jeans, but his hand wraps around my wrist, stopping me.

"You don't have to do that, baby."

"I know. I want to."

He lets out a little groan before stepping back from the table. Finding my panties on the floor, he gently slides them back up my legs until they're firmly back in place. "Today was about you," he says, kissing me on the forehead. "We have plenty of time to do everything you want to, but tonight, let's just be together and enjoy each other's company, okay?"

I sigh in disappointment but jump down off the table and wrap my dress back around myself without complaint. I help him clean off the table and wash the dishes while we chat. It's comfortable and domestic in a way I wasn't expecting, and my mind wanders to a place where it could be like this with the two of us all the time. Cooking together, cleaning, making love. It would without a doubt be a dream come true, but I need to remind myself that we're taking things slow and keeping it casual.

When we're about done, I hear my phone buzzing on the table, and I go check it. For just a second, my heart speeds up in my chest, and I imagine it's Bianca wondering where I am. Instead, it's a text from Tyler. I haven't spoken to him since I left him drunk at the party last night.

"Who's that?" Dante's voice comes from right over my shoulder, making me jump.

"It's Tyler, the guy from last night."

Dante doesn't say anything for a long moment, and I don't bother responding to Tyler's text. I move to put the phone back into my bag when he stops me. His face is serious, and I know that whatever he's about to say is important, so I give him my full attention.

"We may be casual, Violet. But I don't share." The feeling that he's putting a claim on me is real and sends a jolt of yearning through my body. He doesn't want me seeing anyone else while we're together, figuring out what this is. My mind immediately turns to Amanda.

"Me either," I say forcefully.

He gives me a wide smile and leans down to plant a soft kiss on my lips. "I'm glad to hear it."

We wander into the living room and are about to scroll through the streaming service selection when my eye catches on his eReader sitting on the coffee table. "What are you reading?" I ask, pointing to the device.

"I just started the new Stephen King that came out a few weeks ago."

"Really? Me too. But I haven't made it very far yet. Between school, work, the party and well"—I glance at him sitting by my side and smile—"everything, I haven't had much time to read for fun."

"How far along are you?" He reaches for the eReader, then leans back into the couch.

"I think I've only just started chapter three."

"Well, I'm on chapter four. Come here." He stretches his body across the coach and pats the spot in front of him. I'm not sure what he's doing, but there's no way that I'll miss an opportunity to cuddle on a coach with Dante.

I gingerly sit and then slowly stretch out next to him, keeping as little contact between our two bodies as possible. Apparently, he's not having any of that, and he wraps his arm around my waist, then jerks me closer to him so that his front is pressed seamlessly to my back. I lay my head down on his shoulder and breathe in the spicy scent of his soap, closing my eyes and savoring this moment. Before I can open them again, Dante starts reading.

I know that there's a huge smile covering my face. I can remember all the way back to that first day when I met Dante, and the second I heard his voice I thought how amazing it would sound reading to me. Now here I am, in his arms, enjoying a book with him. My hand absentmindedly goes to the book charm lying on my chest.

As his voice drones on, entertaining while soothing me, I can't help but think that I'm totally and utterly screwed. How will any other man that comes after Dante live up to this? I know there's no way we can really and truly make this work in the long run. Not with Bianca, my parents, and our ages. Not to mention the fact that I want a family, and he's said he's not interested in starting all over again. There just seems to be too many things in the way. For now, I shove all those thoughts to the back of my mind and soak in this perfect moment with him that I never thought I would get.

SEVENTEEN

VIOLET

Being cocooned away with Dante Moreno is not a bad way to spend a few days. We passed our time with talking, laughing, reading, watching TV, and orgasms. So many orgasms. That man's fingers and tongue are magic. Honestly, they should be added as the eighth and ninth wonders of the world.

The only problem—if you could even call it one—is that all the orgasms are mine. He's never once pushed for sex. Hell, he's never even let me touch him. Frankly, it's making me feel a little insecure. Does he not want to sleep with me?

Even though we spent our days wrapped up in each other, I insisted on going home every night. If Bianca noticed I was gone and questioned me about it, I didn't want to have to lie. I figure a lie of omission has got to be better than an outright lie, right? I'm getting pretty good at justification. Sleeping alone left me longing for Dante, so as soon as the morning rolled around, I was right back at his side.

I've been spending so much time with him, I figure he must be sick of me by now and want some space, but every time I was gone he'd text me, checking in and asking when I'd be back, making my heart melt. The past few days have been an exquisite torture.

The only real thing causing me stress has been Tyler. His texts have been increasing in frequency and aggression. I haven't mentioned it to Dante because I know this is something I need to handle on my own. We have class together today, so I'm going to talk to him and make a clean break. I'm terrible at confrontation, in fact I avoid it at all costs, but I know I need to take care of this before it gets out of hand. And Tyler deserves for me to let him know it's not going to work out face-to-face.

I hurry down the hallway, clutching my messenger bag, and scurry into class just as Dr. Muzio is about to begin. I'm not ashamed to admit that I planned it this way. Talking to Tyler will be much easier after class. Speaking to him beforehand and then having to sit next to him for the entire class is a whole level of awkwardness that I'm not ready to handle. I look around the classroom and see that the only open chair is directly next to Tyler.

Great.

I shoot him a quick smile, not meeting his eyes, and slide into the seat. While I'm setting down my bag, the professor starts his lecture and I can feel Tyler's hard stare on me, sending a little chill of dread through my body. Why is breaking up with someone I've gone out with twice so hard? Oh right, because I'm a total wimp.

Even though I'm trying to concentrate on what Dr. Muzio is saying, Tyler's heavy stare stays on me, distracting me. Shouldn't he be taking notes too? Class seems to simultaneously drag on as well as fly by. When we're finally let go with a reminder about the paper we have due next week, I feel ready for this confrontation.

Everyone else packs up their things and starts heading out of the classroom, but Tyler and I seem to have a silent, mutual understanding that we're going to stay right here and talk. When everyone clears out, he jumps right in before I can get a word out.

"What's going on, Violet? Why haven't you been answering my calls or texts? I thought we had fun this weekend."

I take a deep breath and try to remember what I planned on saying. "We did. I had a good time with you, Tyler, but I just don't think it's going to work out between us."

"I don't understand. Just last week you said you wanted to see where things would go with us."

I really wasn't expecting him to push back, so I need to scramble for something to say. I'm definitely not telling him I started hooking up with my longtime, much-older crush and that there's no way he can compare.

"You're right. I wanted to see where it could go. You're a good friend, Tyler. But I'm just not feeling a romantic connection between us. I hope we can still be friends." I honestly thought that would be the end of it. If somebody told me they wanted to just be friends I would let it go and head off to lick my wounds in private.

Obviously, Tyler Crosson and I aren't built the same way. I watch his face as it heats and turns red. Not the soft red you get on your cheeks when you're embarrassed, but that deep crimson that signals a seething anger. He rises out of his chair so that he's hovering over me, and I have to lean my head back to look into his eyes that have suddenly turned a steel-cold slate.

"So you're fucking someone else, is that it?"

"Excuse me?" The shock and indignation I'm feeling can be clearly heard in my voice. I quickly grab my bag and scramble out of the chair, so that he'll no longer be looming above me.

"You heard me. I'm not good enough for you, is that it?"

"I didn't say that, Tyler. You're a nice guy. I just don't have those kinds of feelings for you." I clutch my bag tightly to my chest and take a small step backward, out of his reach.

"A nice guy." He lets out a humorless laugh. "You know, all you bitches say you want a nice guy, and then when one is standing right in front of you, you throw him away. Well, let me tell you something, sweetheart. You're the trash, not me."

Before I can respond to that, he grabs the back of his chair and flings it to the side. It crashes into the wall behind him and I nearly jump out of my skin at the sound. I'm ready to bolt for the exit, but before I can, he pushes past me and mutters, "Fucking bitch." He makes his way out of the door before I can move a muscle.

I stand still as a statue in the middle of the room, letting the shock run over me. My eyes water, but I'm not going to let myself cry over that asshole. It's not that what he said hurt my feelings. I know that none of it is true. It's just that I was so scared in that moment that I froze up. I should have run or screamed or *something*. Now, there's adrenaline coursing through my veins, and I have no way to let it out except through tears. Wiping at my eyes, I take a steadying breath. At least it's over now. I won't have to deal with him anymore.

Except in class. That thought really does have me almost releasing my tears. I could see if I still have time to withdraw, but I really don't want to give Tyler the satisfaction. I need this class, and I'm not going to mess up my academic track because he's a childish asshole. No, I'll just have to arrive late and get out of here the second class is over. I'll make sure I don't sit near him. Besides, this is probably just a little temper tantrum. I bet by next week he'll have realized what an ass he was and feel embarrassed.

I poke my head out of the classroom, relieved when I don't see Tyler lurking in the hallway. I make my way out to the parking lot, far more vigilant than I've ever been before.

When I get home, I find Hollie packing up her bedroom. She said that she was going to be taking Paige and moving in with Archer, but I suppose I didn't think it was going to happen so soon.

As I move over to her bed and take a seat, I'm struck by how stark the walls look without all the pictures of us from the past few years she had hanging there. She's buried deep in the back of her closet and is throwing things out toward a large open box in the middle of the room, completely missing it every time. When she hears me adjusting my legs underneath me, she pops her head out and smiles. "Hey, Vi. How was class?"

"Pretty shitty, actually," I say with a sigh. She tilts her head in question and then plops down next to me on the bed, which causes me to rise several inches in the air before landing rather ungracefully, sending us both into giggles.

"What happened?"

"Well, class was fine, but Tyler was decidedly not."

"Ah, so you let him down, and he didn't take it well," she says knowingly.

"That would be an understatement. I believe he called me trash and a bitch—twice."

She rears her head back in surprise. "That little prick! Do you want me to kick his ass for you? You know I will. Or let me tell Archer about it. He really likes you, and what's the point of being rich if you can't hire a hitman for your friends?"

I can't help laughing at that. God, I'm going to miss her.

I reach over and give her a hug. "Are you sure you want to move in with your super-hot, rich, and loving boyfriend? Wouldn't you rather stay here with me?" I swear there's only the littlest bit of a whine in my voice.

She just smiles and hugs me back. "As much as I'm going to miss you and Bianca, I'm going to have to pass. Besides the fact that I'm head over heels for the grumpy bastard, I've got to take care of Paige too, and there's no room for her here."

"I know, I know. Can't a girl just complain about it a little?" I pull back so that I can look her in the eyes, pushing all jokes aside. "You know that I'm super happy for you, right? I know that life hasn't always been easy for you, and I'm so happy that you found Archer. He really loves you, you know?"

"Yeah, he does," she says, getting a bit of a dreamy look on her face. I feel just the tiniest bit of jealousy. It must be nice knowing where you stand with the object of your affection. She seems to shake herself out of it before turning back to me. "So, are you going to tell me what's going on with you and Dante?"

I know I must look shocked, and that's because I am. How does she know? What does she know? I thought I had been doing so well with keeping things under wraps.

"Both you and Dante suck at hiding your feelings," she says with a grin.

"What are you talking about?"

"Please, girl, you two are so obvious. I mean, you've been in love with him since you met him, and he's been staring at you with hearts in his eyes for at least a year."

That has me taken aback. What is she talking about? Dante has never looked at me as anything but a kid until recently. "What? That can't possibly be true."

She just shrugs. "I only know what I see."

While I'm not sure if I believe that, I decide I can't lie to her. I'm already deep in this lie of omission with Bianca, and I'm not going to start outright lying to Hollie. Besides, I haven't had anybody to talk to about all of this, and it would be a relief to be able to confide in one of my best friends.

"It just started," I admit in a rush. "But we've agreed to keep it casual."

At that, she laughs. It's not even a chuckle but a big belly laugh. "Sweetie, I don't think either of you is capable of keeping it casual, but if that's what you want to tell yourselves for now, you go right ahead. So, you have to tell me. How is it?"

"How's what?" I ask in confusion.

"You know. *It.*" She wiggles her eyebrows at me suggestively, and I can't help but giggle.

"It's not like that. Well, it's a little like that, but we haven't had sex. I'm not sure he wants to. He won't make a move, and every sign I throw out that I'm ready, he just ignores."

"Oh, he wants to. Believe me. I bet he's just trying to take it slow. Dante's a good man. You might have to actually verbalize that you want him to pop that cherry instead of just dropping hints."

That's an interesting and embarrassing thought. Actually saying out loud that I'm ready to have sex with him seems cringeworthy, but then again, if I can't talk about it, maybe I'm not ready.

"So, is it just a sex thing for you? Are you just trying to lose your virginity?"

"How can you say that?" I'm a little indignant that she would even suggest such a thing. She should know me better than that. "If that's all I wanted, I could have slept with any number of guys years ago. It's just that Dante . . . well, he's amazing. Yeah, he's sexy, but he's also kind, and funny, and so smart. He makes me laugh. Can you believe that sometimes we actually lie on the couch together and he just reads to me? I never thought I could simultaneously feel so comfortable and so turned on by a man." I look back at Hollie and she has a grin a mile wide on her face. She knew this wasn't about sex for me. She was goading me.

"You love him." I can feel my cheeks turn pink, and I look away, staring at her empty bedroom walls.

"Yeah, I do," I say softly, admitting it for the first time. "I've always said it was just a crush, and I guess that it mostly was. But then I started spending time with him, and it became so much more than that. Now, I'm absolutely screwed because I told him we should keep things casual, but truthfully, I want so much more than that. I want everything with him."

"Violet, I don't think he wants this thing to be as casual as you think he does."

"No, he really does. He's told me how he doesn't want to be a dad again, and I want to have children, Hollie. I'm not sure that's something I can compromise on."

"You never know. He could change his mind about that."

"Maybe. But even if he did, what about my parents? They would lose their shit. And then there's Bianca. I've been justifying not telling her because this thing isn't anything serious. If it became something more, I'd have to let her know, and she would hate me. I can't lose her."

"I feel like you're underestimating Bianca. I don't think she'd have as big of a problem with it as you think she would."

"How can you say that? She's been pushing Amanda and Dante together for weeks. All she wants is for her parents to get back together. She'll absolutely hate me."

"All I know is that if she hears it from someone else, or if she finds out some other way, it's going to be much worse than if you tell her yourself."

I drop my head into my hands, exhausted from going around and around in my head about this. "I know. I know you're right, but if this is just going to be a fling between Dante and me, then I don't want to upset her. You won't tell her, will you?" I look up at her pleadingly.

"Look, you know I won't go running to her and telling her about you two. It's not my business. But if she figures out that something is up, asks me straight out if something is going on between you two, I can't lie."

I just nod my head. That's fair. It wouldn't be right to ask Hollie to lie for me, and I wouldn't want her to.

"But considering how wrapped up she seems to be with our new next-door neighbors, I don't think we have anything to worry about," she says with a smile.

"Oh man, did I tell you she actually babysat for him a few weeks ago?"

"What?!" Hollie exclaims in shock.

"Yeah, that's exactly what I said. He must have cast some kind of spell on her. She actually seemed excited to watch his nephew. She packed up a bunch of her art supplies and brought them over there and everything."

"And we're sure this kid is still alive?" she asks, only partly in jest.

"As far as I know." We're both grinning at each other and again a melancholy washes over me. "I'm going to miss this. Who am I going to talk to about Bianca's level of crazy?"

"Stop, you're going to make me cry," she says before wiping at her eyes. "I'm just a phone call or text away. Besides, how long do you think it's going to be before both Paige and Archer are driving me crazy and I need to escape? I mean, do you know what they're doing right now? He's taken my sister, who's never owned anything other than secondhand jeans and tee shirts, to his personal shopper at Nordstrom. He wanted to take her to Saks, but I had to draw the line somewhere. I know when I get back he's going to have spent a small fortune on her. She's going to be spoiled rotten in no time."

Even though Hollie is complaining, I know that she's thrilled Archer has taken such a liking to her little sister. She might complain about Paige being spoiled, but I can tell she's thrilled that she's going to have things and opportunities that Hollie herself never had.

"Well, whenever they drive you too crazy, you come over here and visit me."

"That's if you're actually here and not over at Dante's." She makes obscene kissing noises, and I can't help but laugh, grabbing a nearby pillow and throwing it at her. How this girl can manage the day-to-day life of one of the most powerful men in the city and still act like a thirteen-year-old I'll never know. I'm just happy she's my friend. And even though I hate to admit it, she's right. If things continue on with Dante much longer, I'm going to have to tell Bianca. I can only hope that she won't hate me after she finds out.

EIGHTEEN

DANTE

Over the past few weeks, I've been able to gather new little pieces of Violet to add to my collection. I now know her sweet pussy tastes like heaven, I've memorized the sounds she makes when she comes from my fingers and my tongue, and I know that if I nuzzle this certain spot on her neck, she practically unravels.

I thought being with Violet would be like a dream. I was wrong. It's so much more than that. I thought I was obsessed with her before. I was wrong again. How can I spend practically every moment of every day with someone and still feel like it's not enough? If she thinks she's getting rid of me, well, she's got another thing coming.

When she first told me she wanted to keep things casual between us, I could feel a pain take root in my chest. Unfortunately for her, I'm not a casual kind of guy. But if that's what she needs right now then that's what I'll take if it means I can have her. I know what's between us is more than something casual, but I also recognize the complexities of our relationship and the relationships attached to it. That's the reason why, even though I take every opportunity to make her orgasm, I haven't slept with her yet.

I can tell she's getting frustrated with me, but I know that if she lets me take her virginity, it's all going to be over for me. She'll feel like mine and only mine. Then when she eventually leaves me and moves on to someone more appropriate, who can give her the family she so desperately wants, it will crush me. Not letting her touch me has been an act of self-preservation that we're both paying for, but I'm trying to hold out, if not for when she realizes she has feelings for me at least for when I know she won't regret it.

I glance over to my right and watch her working away on the computer. I should concentrate on my own emails but can't help taking just a moment to drink her in and marvel that, at least for now, she's mine. The schedule has me at the site with Adrian today, checking on some work before a city inspector shows up tomorrow, but I'm finding it harder and harder to pull myself away from her. The time where I wanted an assistant so that I could spend more time out of the office seems like a distant memory now.

Instead, I'm held here by the girl of my dreams. Her raven-black hair flows over her shoulders while she bites her bottom lip in concentration. Today she's wearing a dress that's a deep purple color and brings out the porcelain quality of her skin that's so different from my own. Nestled between her breasts is the book charm necklace I gave her all those months ago. She wears it almost every single day, and I'd be lying if I said my heart rate didn't pick up every time I saw it on her. She's kicked her shoes off under her desk, and I can see her toenails painted a soft pink, tap on the floor beneath her.

As if she can feel my eyes on her, she twists her head and catches me staring, gifting me with one of her soft smiles. Her phone starts incessantly buzzing away on her desk, and she breaks our eye contact to pick it up. After a few swipes, she frowns and lets out a sigh before placing the phone back where it was.

"What's wrong?" I ask.

"It's nothing. Just my mother."

"Oh yeah? What does she want?" I try to hide the disdain in my voice, but I don't think I do a good job of it. I'm not Vivian Daniels's biggest fan. In fact, the more I learn about her from Violet, the less I like her. While I might not have been physically there for Bianca every single day that she was growing up, I was always available to her. I tried to encourage her, and I made sure that she knew I loved her every step of the way. That doesn't seem to have been the case with Vivian. In fact, I get the distinct feeling that she wanted a mini-me as a daughter, and Violet could never measure up in her eyes. Yeah, I have a thing or two I'd like to say to Mrs. Daniels. And I won't even start on her absentee father.

"She's set up a date for me with one of the junior partners at Dad's firm for Friday. She says if I insist on wasting time in school, the least I can do is work on finding a suitable husband while I'm doing it."

"A date?" I croak out. She'll go on a date with another man over my dead body.

She must read the murderous expression on my face because the next thing I know, she's trying to reassure me. "I'm not going, Dante," she says with a laugh. "I have zero interest in dating anyone from my father's firm. You know that's not the kind of life I want. The last thing I need is to date a man that's going to ignore me the way he does."

I notice right away that this isn't a blanket rejection of any and all dating in the future, so I have to reassure myself with the fact that we agreed to be exclusive even if what we have is casual. But I can't explain how desperately I need to hear her say she never wants to date anyone but me. Since I can't get that assurance from her right now without freaking her out, I need to feel her body against me, her lips on mine to give me some sort of physical reassurance.

"Come here," I demand, and she dutifully pops out of her chair and saunters over to me, purposefully adding a sway to her hips that makes me groan.

"What do you need, boss?" she asks before plopping down into my lap and wrapping her arms around my neck, drawing me down for a kiss. Who am I to deny my girl anything? This kiss is soft and unhurried. I try to put the tender emotions I feel for her but can't say into the kiss, and soon, we're both left panting.

"You keep looking at me like that every day, Violet, and we'll never get any work done."

"Can I help it if my boss is the sexiest man I've ever laid eyes on?"

I can feel my chest swell at her praise. I've always been told I was easy on the eyes, but it honestly never meant anything until Violet said it to me. As long as she wants me, I don't care what I look like to anyone else. "Keep saying things like that to distract me, and I'm going to have to give you a spanking."

"You promise?"

There's a rosy bloom to her cheeks and the round globes of her ass wiggle in my lap, instantly making my dick strain painfully against my zipper. I know that she's not used to dirty talk, but she's been hesitantly trying it out with me. She always seems to be so embarrassed, and I wonder when she'll realize that with me, she can do no wrong.

She throws her leg over me, so now she's straddling my lap and gently placing kisses down my jawline before reaching down to rub my hard cock through my pants. I instantly let out a spurt of pre-cum and rear my head back, giving her better access to my throat. Since I gave in and finally let myself be with Violet, I've gone through a small fortune in pants. Believe me, my dick is less than happy with my self-control, which rapidly seems to be slipping as she grasps me tightly through the denim fabric, making me gasp.

I'm about to say fuck it to waiting for the right time and take her right here on my desk when the front door slams, and we can hear heavy footsteps on the stairs. We both momentarily freeze, looking at each other with wide eyes, before jumping into action.

Violet scrambles off my lap, almost falling on her ass in the process, but I grab her arm to keep her upright. She smooths down the skirt of her dress and makes it to her chair just as Jake walks into the room. I scoot my chair more tightly into my desk, so he can't see my raging erection straining to rip a hole in my pants.

"Jake." The word comes out as more of a growl than I mean it to. He's silent a moment and looks at me curiously, but I do my best to keep my face passive, not giving anything away. The last thing I need is for him to find out about Violet and me. It would be all over the job site before the day was over.

He seems to finally notice Violet sitting in the corner. Thankfully, it looks like she was able to get herself together. In fact, you would never be able to tell that just moments ago she was straddling my cock and trying to seduce me. Her face is the very picture of innocence and serenity.

"This must be Violet," he says, making his way toward her, and I have to resist the urge to move between them and stop him from getting too close.

I know that she's aroused right now, and the thought of another man smelling her scent fills me with a type of jealousy I've never experienced before.

"It's nice to finally meet you face-to-face."

"Hey, Jake," she says shyly before shaking his hand. "It's nice to meet you too. Now you're not just a bodiless voice on the phone."

"Oh, I've got a body all right." He's got a charming smile plastered on his face, and I want to punch it right off.

"Jake!" I bark at him. "Don't you think that's a little inappropriate?"

He looks at me strangely. I know that he's just joking around. Inappropriate jokes are what Jake does. He doesn't necessarily mean anything by it, but he can find someone else to joke and flirt with, not my Violet.

"It's fine, Dante," Violet says. "I'm not incapable of taking a joke after all." Fuck. I can tell by the tone of her voice that she's annoyed with me, but she better get used to it. If any man other than Jake had been trying to flirt with her, he'd already be laid out flat on the floor.

Violet and I are staring at each other, and Jake's head is ping-ponging between the two of us, like he's trying to figure something out. Suddenly, there's a mischievous glint in his eye, and the corners of his mouth turn up in a smirk. This can't be good.

"I just wanted to drop off these bills of lading for the supplies that were delivered this morning," he says before handing Violet a few slips of papers. I notice his fingers don't touch hers, and I'm glad that I don't have to kill one of my best workers and friends.

"Thanks so much," she says, flipping through the receipts, making sure everything is in order.

"Listen, if you're not doing anything Friday night, I'd love to take you out. There's this little bar over on Fifth that has some great live music I think you'd enjoy." As Jake asks out my girlfriend, or whatever she is to me, he slides his eyes over in my direction, and I know he's doing this just to fuck with me. That's the only reason he's still alive right now.

It takes all my self-restraint to keep from kicking him out of my office, but I want to give Violet a chance to answer him. Not only am I interested in what she has to say, but I don't want to be one of those men who smothers his woman. She gets enough of that from her mother. If she wants to be with me, she needs to make that choice.

"That's really nice of you, Jake. Thank you for the offer." I take a deep breath. I don't expect her to accept, but there's always that lingering doubt in the back of my head. "But I'm actually seeing someone right now."

The tension that was flowing through my body immediately releases followed swiftly by something like satisfaction. She may not have said it was me she's seeing, but just the fact that she would acknowledge to him that there's someone in her life is more than enough for me. Well, at least for now. God, when did I become this pathetic? Oh right, the moment I started to see Violet Daniels.

"Well, if you change your mind, you have my number," he says with a wink, like he doesn't know that his life is in danger. Violet just smiles and thanks him but doesn't give any indication that she plans on taking him up on his offer.

Once Jake's left and gotten back to what he's actually supposed to be doing, which isn't hitting on my girl, the weight of both his flirting and her mother's efforts to take her away from me have become too much. I need to remind her she's mine. She doesn't even notice as I make my way to her desk and spin her chair so that she's facing me, her eyes blinking in owl-like surprise. I drop to my knees in front of her and spread her legs. Her sharp intake of breath makes me smile as I hike up her skirt, ready to pull down her panties, then my hands meet her bare skin.

Shocked, I look up at her. "Have you been sitting here all day with no panties on?"

She gives me that shy smile and a quick little shrug. "I figured why bother when you usually have them off of me by noon?"

I let out a growl from deep in my chest. "So you were just sitting here, talking to Jake, with nothing underneath you dress? That's unacceptable, baby."

Her expression clouds with confusion. "It's not like he could see anything."

"It doesn't matter. This is mine, you understand?" I ask while cupping her hot sex in my hand. She lets out a moan, and I can feel how slick she is already. I raise up off the floor and take her by the hand over to my desk. Placing a hand in the middle of her back, I gently push until she's bent over it, cheek pressed against the cool wood, ass in the air which she has the audacity to wiggle at me. Doesn't she realize I'm trying to hold on to what little control I have left?

I slowly lift her skirt, letting it caress the backs of her legs, then reveal the round curve of her bare, pantiless ass to me. "I'm the only one you don't wear panties around, Violet." I pull back my hand and give her a sharp swat on her right ass cheek. She lets out a little squeal and jumps, trying to lift herself off the desk, but I have my hand firmly holding her down.

"What are you doing, Dante?" Her voice is a husky whisper, and I can tell that this is turning her on, so I continue.

"Teaching you what happens when bad girls go around and don't protect what's mine." I deliver several more spanks, alternating between each of her glorious cheeks. It's not so hard as to really hurt her, just enough to provide a little sting. She lets out a low moan that causes my dick to twitch in my pants, and I take a minute to kick her legs apart, revealing her pink and swollen pussy. My hand slowly caresses and kneads her pink ass as I bend down and whisper in her ear, "You like this, don't you, baby?"

She doesn't answer but lets out a little whimper of desire. I run my fingers down her slit and realize that she's soaked. Taking my opportunity, I plunge my finger into her tight channel, causing her to shout out my name.

"I didn't hear you, Violet. Do you like this?"

"Oh, yes," she moans, wiggling her ass, trying to push her pussy farther into my hand. I lazily play with her wet pussy, only occasionally brushing against the swollen nub of her clit.

The sight of her bent over my desk, so clearly aroused, is too much for me and I unzip my pants, much to the relief of my restrained dick. Jesus, there must be an imprint of my zipper on it. I start to stroke my rock-hard shaft while I alternate between light slaps on her ass and dipping into her pussy to play with it.

"It's too much, please, Dante. Please. Please." Her begging is the last straw and I start mercilessly finger fucking her with two fingers while my thumb firmly rubs against her swollen bud. She's writhing against my hand, making those unintelligible sounds that I now know signal her imminent climax.

Suddenly, her body stiffens, and she lets out a scream, but I don't stop my ministrations. I continue to pump my fingers in and out of her while her orgasm racks her body, and when she turns her head to look at me, still in the throes of her pleasure, eyes hazy with lust, I'm done. I let out a shout and with one more hard stroke of my shaft, my seed spurts out, landing on her ass. If there's a more beautiful sight than my cum covering Violet's reddened ass cheeks, I've never seen it.

When we're both fully satiated and staring at each other, panting, I pull her up from the desk and hold her in my arms, murmuring soft reassurances in her ear. How beautiful she is, how much I want her, and a plethora of other things that are probably unintelligible. I grab some tissues off my desk and clean us both up before pulling back so that I can see her face. "I'm so sorry. That wasn't too much for you, was it?"

"Dante Moreno. Don't you ever be sorry for giving me the best orgasm of my life."

"But the spanking—"

"I liked it," she says, trying to hide her embarrassment at the admission.

Goddamn, she's perfect for me.

I smile and kiss her while her hands inch under my shirt and caress my stomach. I'm a little self-conscious that it's not the hard planes of muscles I had in my youth, but I'm still pretty solid, just a little squishy in the middle. And Violet doesn't seem to mind. In fact. As I look at her, I can see her eyes are darkening with desire once again.

"We can't, baby," I moan, and she reaches up to place a kiss against my lips.

"I don't know. It looks to me like we can." She raises her eyebrow at me and nods her head down to where my dick is straining against my pants once again. Damn, this girl has me as horny as a teenager.

"Violet, I think it would be best if we waited."

I can see irritation flash in her eyes, and I know that I'm in for it. "Wait for what, Dante? If you don't want me, just say so. I'm getting pretty sick of throwing myself at you and being rejected." She makes a move to pass me and leave the room, but I take hold of her wrist before she gets too far, spinning her back around to face me.

"That's not it. You know that's not it." I grab her hand and put it back on my engorged member, causing us both to groan. "I think it's pretty obvious by now that I want you."

"Then why won't you have sex with me? Is it because I'm a virgin? Is it . . . unattractive?"

I feel gobsmacked at that. She doesn't understand the absolute joy I felt when she told me her virginity status. Just the thought of being the first man to be inside her was enough to have me almost coming in my pants.

"Of course not! I don't have a problem with you being a virgin. Quite the opposite in fact. I . . . I just don't want you to do anything you might regret."

She still looks rather annoyed, and I know I'm doing a poor job of explaining this. But how do I tell her why I don't want to sleep with her without giving all my feelings away?

"Do you remember that dinner we had a few weeks ago? You told me I could always tell you what I want and that you wouldn't get upset about it—"

"I'm not upset." I try to explain.

"Everybody is always telling me what I should and shouldn't do. Making choices for me. Hell, even my mother is trying to tell me who to marry. So, I'm telling you right now, Dante, I want you to fuck me, and I want you to do it right now."

I'm not sure if it's her standing up for what she wants or her simply demanding that I fuck her, but all of that carefully maintained control I've been holding on to with an iron grip just snaps. I forcefully pull her into my body and crash my lips down to hers, her mouth yielding to me right away, accepting my tongue, tangling it with her own. My hands grip her ass tightly, and I lift her up, letting her wrap her legs around my waist. Her hot pussy is cradling my rock-hard dick, and I want to throw her on the floor right now and rut into her like a wild animal.

But this is her first time, and it's damn well going to be in a bed. I make my way down the hallway with Violet in my arms, our lips never leaving each other, and kick the door to my bedroom open. I set her down on her feet next to the bed and take in her glassy eyes, flushed skin, and heaving breaths, knowing that she's ready for me.

I reach for her dress and slowly drag it up her body, revealing inch after tantalizing inch of her to my hungry gaze. It's not long before she's standing in front of me in just her bra.

"Take it off, baby." I pull my shirt over my head and toss it to the floor, then discard my pants and shoes into the same pile.

She's standing in front of me now, every inch of her bare to me. I can see her working to keep her arms at her sides and project an air of confidence, but I know she's self-conscious about the smaller size of her breasts. The size doesn't matter to me. They're fucking gorgeous. I love that I can cover them completely with my hands, can feel the full weight of them. I love that when I suckle and bite at her nipples I can get half her breast into my mouth and how her back arches toward me, wanting more.

Those thoughts propel me to her, and I sink to my knees, nuzzling my face between those gorgeous tits. I gently lave one nipple with my tongue while playfully tweaking the other. My actions cause a shiver to run through her body, and she delves her fingers into my hair, holding me tightly to her as I switch breasts.

I move back up her body and then playfully toss her to the middle of my king-size bed, causing her to let out a giggle. She looks so gorgeous there, and all I can think about is burying my cock so deep in her we won't be able to tell where one of us ends and the other begins. I slowly crawl up her body, kissing and licking every spot I pass before making it to her lips. I kiss her until we're both breathless again while my hand makes its way down to her glistening and swollen pussy, still sensitive from our games in the office. My fingers wander down to the entrance of her channel, and I press a single digit inside her, working it in and out. I know that she's going to be a tight fit, and I want to make sure that it isn't too painful for her.

Her hands are roving all over my body like she doesn't know what to hold on to. She takes her nails and lightly scrapes down my chest and over my nipples.

"Fuck," I shout out as my cock leaks pre-cum onto her thighs. That shy smile is back on her face, but there's a mischievous look in her eyes. I can see that she's enjoying discovering that she can give me just as much pleasure as I give her. Fuck, if I can give her a fraction of the pleasure that she gives me, she would be in some kind of euphoric coma.

Another finger goes inside her, and I scissor them as I gently work them in and out of her, stretching her so that she can accommodate me.

She's making these little gasping sounds and thrusting her pelvis at me. "More. More. Please."

I don't have it in me to make either of us wait any longer, so I settle between her legs, hook my hand under her knee and pull it upward, opening her up to me. I kiss her softly but hungrily before I pull back and look into her eyes. What I see staring back at me tells me she wants me just as much as I want her. "You know that if we do this, Violet, there's no going back."

"I know," she says, thrusting her hips up, causing the tip of my dick to slide through her slick folds. I almost plunge into her right then and there, but I need to make sure she understands.

"I'm serious, baby. The second I get my cock inside you, that means you're mine."

She looks me straight in the eye, her gaze steady and unwavering. "I was made to be yours, Dante."

With that declaration, I can't hold back any longer and I start slowly pushing my way inside her. I'm being as gentle as I can so as not to hurt her more than necessary, but Violet is having none of it. She's arching her back, thrusting her hips up to meet mine. The sounds of her moaning and begging fill the room.

I'm gritting my teeth and my body is covered in sweat with my attempt to hold back from ramming my cock in her to the hilt. When I'm finally seated fully inside her, I have to close my eyes. She's so tight and the pleasure is almost too great. I can't come the second I make it inside her pussy like some inexperienced sixteen-year-old. I breathe through my nose and start to count backward from one hundred as I wait for her body to adjust. "How do you feel, baby?"

"Perfect." She gasps and wiggles beneath me. "Can you move?"

"I don't want to hurt you."

She circles her hips and lets out a little moan, not of pain but of pleasure. That's all I can take, and I pull almost all the way out before smoothly gliding back inside her tight sheath. Again and again I do this, all the while she urges me on, begging for me to go faster. It's not long before I'm slamming into her like the wild beast she's turned me into. I've never felt such pleasure in my life, and while I want to spill my load inside her, I need for her to come first. I vow to myself that her pleasure will always come before mine.

Over her cries of pleasure, the word *mine* keeps repeating over and over again in my head. With every thrust I make her more mine until it becomes this physical need that takes over. I have to be the first one to paint her insides with cum. I have to be the only one.

I reach between our heaving and undulating bodies and place my thumb directly on her clit, pressing down firmly. This seems to make her almost jump out of her skin. When she starts making a mewling noise, I know I can't hang on much longer. "Come for me, baby. I need to feel your pussy milking my cum out of me."

My words seem to push her over the edge, and she screams, my name bouncing around the bedroom as her entire body shakes. She's clutching at my shoulders, and her nails dig into my flesh. The sharp pain combined with her pulsing pussy shoves me over my own cliff, and I bury myself as far inside her as possible as I unload spurt after spurt of my seed deep inside her, flooding her until it's leaking out onto the sheets.

Eventually we both come down from our high. I don't know how long it is that we both lie there, me buried inside of her, her clutching on to me for dear life. When I start worrying I might be crushing her underneath my weight, I head to the bathroom, cleaning myself up and grabbing a warm, damp washcloth before returning to her.

She's lying on her side in the middle of my bed, and I swear that my heart skips a beat. I never thought in my wildest dreams that she would be here. That she would want me as much as I want her. I could have guessed that she would be the best sex of my life, but it's nice to have it confirmed.

I sit next to her and stroke her hair. "Open your legs, baby." She's too tired to question me and parts them so I can see where my cum is leaking out of her swollen pussy. I quickly clean her up and discard the rag before crawling back into bed and joining her.

I pull her tightly into my arms and watch as she drifts off into a sated sleep, her head on my shoulder. There's a sense of rightness, happiness, joy even, that's taken up residence in my body, and I know it's all because of the tiny woman in my arms.

I always thought that there were just some people that were never lucky enough to find real, true love in their life. I figured I was one of those unlucky people. But maybe the reason that I'd never found love was because my perfect person was busy growing up, finding her own place in the world, and I just needed to be patient. Lying here with Violet in my arms, staring at her sleeping face, I know that I'm not one of the unlucky ones anymore.

NINETEEN

VIOLET

I never imagined that cloud nine was an actual place, yet here I am, sitting on it. Since the night we finally slept together, I've barely left Dante's side. Sure, he's had to go to job sites or meet clients, and I've occasionally had to dash home for new clothes or to grab something I needed for school, but all in all, we've been joined at the hip. You'd think that would make this burning need I have for him diminish, but no, it's still just as strong, if not stronger. I certainly wasn't putting as much effort into hiding this from Bianca as I had been, but luckily for us, she seemed to be busy with things of her own.

That first night together, he woke me up several times throughout the night. It was like he was desperate, hungry for my body, and I wasn't much better. We came together again and again, each time building a stronger connection. I can feel him on my skin even when he's not with me. We were both so carried away that we never once worried about any kind of protection.

Luckily I trust him wholeheartedly and know that he would never let me near him if he would be putting my health at risk, but it wasn't until the next morning when he was holding me in his arms that I remembered to tell him I was on birth control, so he didn't have to worry. While the thought of having a little person who's a combination of both Dante and me sends my heart into overdrive, I know that's not what he wants, so I'm glad I could reassure him we were safe. But my reassurances were met with a strange look on his face that I didn't understand. Just as I was about to ask him what was wrong, he was back to his normal smiling self, and I shrugged it off.

A few days later, I was coming back after class, and I found him buried deep in the back of a cabinet in the kitchen. When I questioned him about what he was doing, his smile nearly blew me away. He presented me with a set of rather expensive baking pans, a stand mixer, and cabinets that were fully stocked with all the baking basics I could ever need.

He said it was because he wanted me to bake whenever I wanted, but he also wanted me there with him. I'd like to say that I accepted the gift gracefully, but instead I burst into tears. That seemed to really freak him out. He rushed over to me, promising that he could take it all back and we could pick out things together. He didn't understand that they were tears from an overwhelming sense of happiness. I'd never received such a thoughtful gift. Well, almost never, I thought while bring my hand up to play with my charm necklace. Once he understood I wasn't upset, he kissed away my tears, then fucked me senseless on the counter. That was a fun evening.

We've also managed to finish the Steven King book we were reading together. Somehow, the master of horror is a little less scary when Dante's deep and gravely voice is reading it to me. Now we've started a spy thriller that's been on the *New York Times* bestseller list that we've both been meaning to read.

It's been almost like a dream. Everything is going so well that I find myself holding my breath, waiting for the other shoe to drop. We've both been staunchly avoiding bringing up the topic of telling Bianca. I'm not sure which one of us wants to avoid it more.

In fact, the only dark spot on what I would call some of the best days of my life is Tyler. I thought that his little tantrum at school would be the end of things. I guess I was just being naïve because, a few days later, I started receiving texts from him. They ranged from mild, "Hey, I'm going to Chance's tonight, do you want to meet me?" to the extreme, "Sluts like you only want scumbag men. I can't believe I wasted my time on you."

The only good thing is that he's stopped showing up for class. I was so nervous to return the first time after our confrontation that I had to put my hands in my pockets to keep them from shaking. But I didn't want to drop the class and give Tyler the satisfaction of knowing he'd messed with my head so much.

When I entered the classroom and saw that he wasn't there, a wave of relief ran through me. Then, when the next week rolled around and he wasn't there again, I started to relax. The texts may be continuing, but at least he's not bold enough to confront me in person.

I've considered blocking his number, but the thought of not knowing what he's up to or what his mood is makes me nervous. I'd rather keep tabs on him, even if it's just by reading his vile texts and never responding. Telling Dante about the messages would be the next logical step, but I'm determined to handle this myself, and I don't want to worry him needlessly. They're just texts. I can deal with them on my own. Besides, I only get one every couple of days, and I have a feeling Dante would go absolutely ballistic and hunt down Tyler, which is something I definitely don't want.

I hear the ding of my timer and go to the oven to pull out my bran muffins. I thought they would be nice and healthy, and Dante could grab one for breakfast when he's on his way out to meet his guys tomorrow. When I set them on the counter, I notice they haven't quite risen like muffins are supposed to. I tilt my head from side to side, examining them, thinking about what I might have done wrong. I know I followed the recipe I found on Pinterest to the letter, but I always follow recipes and there always seems to be something wrong.

I poke one of the little brown muffins, and it seems squishy but not exactly soft like you would expect. In fact, they remind me of those fiber cakes you can get at Trader Joe's. Maybe I'll just tell him that's what they're supposed to be. Just as I'm considering my little white lie, I hear the front door slam behind me.

"Lucy, I'm home," he calls out with a rather impressive impersonation of Desi Arnaz. I turn to look at my man, and the butterflies take flight in my stomach once again. He's wearing his standard uniform of work boots, blue jeans, and a tee shirt, but today sweat is causing the thin fabric to cling to him. He's so fucking sexy. If I could, I would be waiting for him every day when he gets home for the rest of our lives. Add in a couple of kids and I honestly couldn't imagine a more idyllic life for myself. I know that's not what he wants, but that doesn't stop me from dreaming.

"I made you fiber cakes." I point to the little, condensed cakes and give him my sweetest smile. He doesn't have to know they were supposed to be muffins. "You can take a couple to work with you in the morning since you're always running late."

"Thanks, baby," he says while crossing the room, then bends down to give me a light kiss that quickly turns heated. When he pulls away, I can see the desire in his eyes, and I know it matches my own. "I wouldn't always be running late if you'd let me out of bed in the morning."

My cheeks heat. It's true that there have been a few times he was about out the door and I dragged him back to bed to give me a few more orgasms to start off my day. "Sorry."

He pinches my chin between his thumb and forefinger, tipping my face up to his. "You never have to be sorry for wanting me. Wanting us. Understand?"

I quickly give him a nod, and before I know it, he's got me up in his arms and held firmly there with his hands under my ass. I wrap my legs around him, holding on tight.

When I feel his rapidly hardening length press against my cotton-clad pussy, I give a little wiggle and let out a moan. This man makes me go from zero to sixty at a moment's notice. His sweaty shirt is pressing against my clean one, and I run my fingers through his slick hair. "You're all sweaty," I murmur before taking my tongue and running it down the length of his neck, getting the salty taste of him in my mouth.

"Fuck," he groans and lets his head fall back, giving my mouth better access to him. "Yeah, I was helping Adrian and his guys with some demo work on a couple of the last units." His hands tighten on my ass and pull me harder against him. It would be wrong to rub up on him like a cat in heat, right?

"Come on," he says, carrying me up the stairs.

"Where are we going?"

"Right now, I'm going to take a shower. Then we're going to get dressed up, and I'm taking you out on a proper date."

"A date?" I squeak out. We've spent so much time together the past month, but never on an official date. Now we're finally going on a real, honest-to-God date. Most of our time is spent at his house, and I've truly been okay with it. I'm pretty much a homebody at heart, and really, all I need is to be with him. But a girl can only go so long before she worries that the man she's seeing might be ashamed of her. However, I also recognize that, though it's been unspoken, we've been trying to lie low. Not just so we don't run into Bianca, but also so we don't see anybody that could say something to her and blow our secret.

"Yeah, I want to take my girl out and spoil her, so I'm going to need to get cleaned up."

"Mmm, would my man like some company while he's getting cleaned up?" There's a glint in his eye, and I know that showering won't be the only thing we do in the bathroom.

Showering takes twice as long as it should. First we get clean, then he fucks me up against the smooth tile wall, so we have to get clean all over again. I don't mind. I love using my hands to soap up his body and rigid cock with the shower gel that gives him that spicy scent I love.

When we finally make it out, I quickly blow dry my hair while he gets dressed. Once he's done, he comes back to the bathroom and starts playfully pulling at the towel I have wrapped around me.

"Cut it out, mister. If you don't stop, we'll never get out of here."

He gives me an exaggerated pout. "Maybe we should skip the date and just go to bed," he teases.

"Oh, no you don't. You've promised me a date, and that's what we're doing. Now go to the office and go through the messages I left you, so I can get dressed in peace."

"Of course, dear," he says mockingly before bending down, planting a quick kiss on my lips, and heading to the office, leaving me to get ready. Once my hair is dry, I realize I don't have any product to put in it, so decide to put it up in a sleek high ponytail on top of my head. It's cute and sophisticated, so it should work for wherever we're going. Which I probably should have asked about, but I know he likes to surprise me, whether it's coming home with my favorite Italian takeout or a bouquet of hydrangeas he bought when he saw them and thought of me. To be honest, he's given me more attention in the past six weeks than my parents have my entire life.

That thought is a little depressing, especially because I keep getting texts from my mother about setting me up with someone from my dad's office. She doesn't even say hi or ask how I've been. I don't understand what I've ever done to be such a tiny blip on the radar in her life.

Instead of sinking into the morose thoughts that my family brings up, I shake it off and start going through the small collection of clothes that I've gathered at Dante's. It's been rather cold and rainy out lately, so I decide on a deep blue sweater dress with a scoop neck. Normally, I pair it with a knee-high boots, but since those are back at my house, I dig out a pair of little black ankle booties and put those on. I top the outfit off with my book necklace nestled between my breasts. I almost never take it off, and I'm not going to start now.

I make my best attempt at putting on some light makeup. Just a little concealer, eyeliner, and a tinted lip balm. Even though it's not fancy, I think it looks pretty good. The liner is making my blue eyes pop, and they really shine out against my dress. I think even Bianca would be proud of the job I did . . . as long as she didn't know it was to seduce her dad into bed later. Not that I'll really have to seduce him. Dante can never keep his hands off me for long.

Just as I'm double-checking everything in the mirror, I notice Dante standing behind me, staring. I nervously shift from one foot to the other when he remains silent, his eyes on me.

"Is this okay?" I ask. "You didn't say where we're going, but I figured this outfit would work most anywhere."

"You're so fucking gorgeous," he says with genuine conviction in his voice. "How did I end up this lucky? It shouldn't be possible."

His words fill me with joy and a deep sense of belonging. He always has the nicest things to say to me, but I've never been one for taking compliments well, probably because I've never really received any.

"You're joking, right?" I indicate him in his well-cut black slacks and light blue button-down shirt. "You're the sexiest man I've ever seen." I chew on my lip for just a second, quickly weighing the pros and cons of what I'm about to tell him. In the end, I just say fuck it and go for it. "You realize that I've wanted you since the very first time I laid eyes on you, right?"

A look of confusion comes over his face. "But that was over four years ago. You were just a kid."

I can't help a self-deprecating laugh at that. "Oh, I'm very aware of when it was and how you saw me. You helped me carry all my boxes up from my car to our dorm room because my parents didn't bother to make the time to drop me off at school. Then you literally called me a kid."

He takes a step toward me and gives a playful tug to my ponytail. "I wish I had known how you felt. Maybe if I did, it wouldn't have taken me three whole years to figure out what an amazing woman you are."

Now it's my turn to be confused. "But we haven't even been together for two whole months. What do you mean, three years? We've known each other for four."

"I've wanted you since Bianca's twenty-second birthday." His confession makes my heart skip a beat. "I don't know what happened. It's like a switch flipped, and I stopped seeing you as a kid that was my daughter's friend and instead saw the smart and sexy woman you'd become. I felt like a lech, but that didn't stop me from trying to see you every chance that I got."

I'm blown away by this revelation. He's wanted me for a year? How is that possible? If only I had known—

"And by that time I was avoiding you like the plague," I mutter, but he still manages to hear me.

"I noticed you weren't around as much. Why were you trying to avoid me, baby?" He takes a step closer and wraps his arms around my waist, pulling me into him so that our bodies are pressed seamlessly together in that way I love. Almost as much as I love him. Though that's something I can never say out loud. He may have felt an attraction for me a year ago, but that doesn't mean that he loves me the way I love him. I have to remind myself that this is going to end and when it does . . . it's going to be devastating.

"Well, I had a crush on this guy that was a lot older and super inappropriate for me that didn't know I existed," I say teasingly, trying to cover up my deep feelings for this man. "I was trying to avoid him every chance I got so that I could move on from him."

I can hear a little growl from the back of his throat before his lips capture mine, giving me a hungry kiss filled with yearning. I can almost taste how much he wants me. He has to force himself to pull away and leave me breathless, panting after him. "There's no moving on, Violet. You're mine now, remember?"

I nod my head, still a little dazed from that intense kiss.

"The words, Violet. I need the words."

"No moving on. Got it."

"Good," he says, running a slightly shaky hand through his short hair, mussing it. I know he calls me his, however I'm also smart enough to know that there's an unspoken *for now* at the end of it. But I'm determined to enjoy being his for as long as he'll have me.

"Fuck, I was joking before about skipping out on our date, but now I really do just want to take you to bed."

"No way," I say, playfully slapping him on the chest. "I'm starving. You're taking me to dinner."

"Yes, dear," he says in that joking way, like that of a whipped husband, that makes me laugh. That's another thing that's happened since I've been with Dante. He's brought out a playful side of me that I didn't even know existed.

After reapplying the lip balm that Dante kissed off, I toss it into my purse just as I hear my phone buzz. I pull it out to see who it is and frown.

Tyler: How about dinner tonight, beautiful?

So apparently Tyler's having a good day. Even though these kinds of texts from him are tone deaf and I never respond, they're still infinitely better than the other ones I get from him.

"What's wrong? Who's that?" Dante asks. He must have noticed my face when I read the text. For just a second I consider lying to him, but then decide that there's no point.

Besides, this is a pretty mild text. I can just downplay it a little so that he doesn't worry too much.

"It's Tyler."

"Tyler? That little douchebag you went out with?"

I roll my eyes, but don't bother defending him. He doesn't deserve it. "Yeah, he's been texting me occasionally. I broke it off with him weeks ago, you know that, but he doesn't seem to have gotten it. He just asked me out for dinner tonight."

"You're kidding. Do you want me to talk to him?"

I shake my head. "While I appreciate the offer, it's nothing I can't handle. I haven't been responding to him, and he's actually stopped showing up for class. I should probably just block him. It's honestly nothing for you to worry about." And it really isn't. Tyler has turned out to be nothing more than one of the thousands of keyboard warriors out there, brave behind their computer or phone screens but otherwise relatively harmless.

"Well, I don't like it. If he doesn't stop, let me know and I'll take care of it."

"I appreciate that, but it'll be fine. Now, let's get out of here before my stomach starts growling." He seems to shake off the Tyler conversation and grabs my hand, pulling me along behind him.

TWENTY

VIOLET

It didn't escape my notice that we drove a good thirty minutes before arriving at the small Italian restaurant he made reservations at. There was no need to tell me it was so that we could avoid bumping into anyone we knew. While I understand the caution and wouldn't have made a different choice myself, I still wish there was a way that we could just hold hands and walk down the street to our local café. But we can't always get what we want.

After Dante lifts me out of the truck, we make a run for the door since it's sprinkling out. I've lived in Seattle my whole life, and I've found that unless the rain is really coming down, it's more of a hassle to carry an umbrella than it is a help. Especially if you're just going to the car and back.

The inside of the restaurant is warm, the walls covered with dark wooden paneling giving it an old-school feel. Every table is covered with a white linen cloth and topped with a flickering votive candle. It reminds me of those old-school Italian restaurants you see in movies. When we're greeted at the host stand by an exuberant older man with graying hair, a thick mustache, and a heavy Italian accent, the picture is complete.

After seating us at a small table against the front windows, he makes sure we know tonight's specials and then leaves us to review the menu.

"This place is so charming. Have you been here before?" I ask.

"Nope. Actually, Jake gave me the recommendation. He said if I was going out for Italian food and didn't go here that it would be a crime."

"Jake? He doesn't seem like the type to frequent a place like this. He strikes me as a burger and beer in front of a big screen playing the latest game type to me."

Dante lets out a laugh. "You wouldn't be wrong in that assumption. I can't tell you how many nights I've spent at a sports bar doing just that with him. But he does go on a lot of dates, so I figure he's probably visited most of the restaurants in the city at one time or another."

"I can definitely see that. Jake seems like the consummate ladies' man."

"He sure seemed eager enough to meet you when you were first hired." There's a hint of jealousy in his voice that sends a tiny thrill through me. I love it when Dante gets jealous. He doesn't turn into a complete asshole, but just the thought that he wants me all to himself does something to warm my heart.

"Well, you can let him know I'm already interested in somebody else," I tease.

He lifts his brow at me. "Oh really? Anybody I know?"

"Hmmm, maybe." He reaches across the table, takes my hand and flips it before lacing his fingers through my own. It feels so natural being here with him in this beautiful restaurant holding hands, and I think, not for the first time, that I could do this for the rest of my life. I just wish that was possible.

"What was that?" he asks.

"What was what?"

"You looked sad for a second. Is something wrong?" He looks concerned, and I love him even more for it. *Damn it.*

I play it off, not wanting him to know the depths of my feelings. "You must be seeing things. I mean, you are getting older. Should I take you to get your eyes checked?"

"Ouch." He grabs his chest in mock pain. "That hurts, baby." Then, before I know what's happening, the teasing goes out of his eyes and they turn into molten chocolate instead. "You better be careful, or I'll take you home and show you just how much you love my age and experience."

My heart rate picks up, and I can immediately feel a dampness between my legs. The thought of Dante doing things to my body sends a wave of lust through me. "I think that you probably should. I mean, I could use a reminder."

"Baby, you have no idea." He squeezes my hand and starts caressing the inside of my wrist with his thumb, making my body want to combust right here on the spot.

Before our teasing can go any further, our waiter comes over and takes our order, effectively cooling off our heated exchange. Regardless, I can still feel my pussy tingling at the prospect of what Dante is going to do to me when we get home.

We spend dinner chatting pleasantly. We talk a little about work, and I remind him that Jake needs him to visit the site tomorrow and sign off on the completed project, so they can present to the homeowners. I have to be honest that I'm pretty excited about this one being done. Not because it's been any trouble, but because this is the first real project I've been a part of completing since working for Moreno Construction. It's given me a genuine sense of pride that I wasn't expecting to feel.

The conversation then drifts to the spy novel we've been reading. The author is famous for his plot twists, and we have a good time giving our best guesses on what it will be.

Just as the meal is winding down, I excuse myself to go to the restroom. I follow the long, dimly lit hallway to the back of the dining area, where the waiter indicated the ladies' room was located. When I'm done, I check reflection in the mirror. My eyes are lit up, and my cheeks have a healthy pink to them that's not from any blush—mostly because I didn't have any. I tighten my ponytail and apply another layer of lip balm before leaving.

I'm just exiting and starting to make the trip back down the long hallway when there's a voice behind me, close to my ear.

"So that's who you left me for? Do old men get you wet, Violet?"

I let out a little gasp and spin around to find Tyler standing there. I haven't seen him since our confrontation after class weeks ago, and while he's still the same guy, he looks different somehow. His clothes are slightly disheveled, and his hair is sticking up like he's been running his fingers through it. The biggest difference is his eyes. They always had a friendly look to them, but now there's a gleam of anger and malice I haven't seen before.

I don't know what the hell he's doing here, but I won't cower away from him.

"I didn't leave you for anybody, Tyler. We went on two dates. It didn't work out. It happens. You need to stop texting me. I'm just not interested."

He takes a step closer to me, getting into my personal space and forcing me to move backward until my back hits the wall. "You wouldn't even kiss me, but I bet you spread your legs for him like the slut you are. I bet he likes it rough, doesn't he? I would have been so gentle with you and treated you like the lady that I thought you were." He spits the words out at me with a level of vitriol I'm surprised at, though I probably shouldn't be considering the texts he's been sending.

Before he can say or do anything else, I put my hands on his chest and put all my strength into shoving him away from me. He must not have been expecting the move because it sends him reeling back into the opposite wall and I take that moment to make my escape. I hightail it out of the hallway, and once I'm back in the dining room, I glance behind me and am surprised to see no trace of Tyler.

I take a few moments standing at the back of the restaurant to steady myself and get my breathing back under control. What the hell is he doing here? Did he follow me? No, that can't be right. We left from Dante's house and took his truck. He wouldn't know how to find me. I convince myself that this was all just a big coincidence and won't happen again. We live in a city with approximately a quarter of a million people, not to mention the Seattle metropolitan area has about four million residents in total. What are the odds that I'll run into him again, especially if he's dropped his classes as it seems? No, this was a one time thing. I can handle this. They're just words, and even though I love literature and know the importance of words, they can't hurt me.

By the time I get back to the table, Dante's already paid our tab and is ready to go. "Are you okay, Vi? You were gone awhile and you look a little upset."

I force a smile that I'm not really feeling and brush off the earlier encounter. I just want to forget it ever happened and don't want to ruin our date. "Yeah, I'm fine. I just ran into somebody I know from school. No big deal."

He studies me but must not see anything that worries him too much. He wraps his arm around my waist and we head outside.

The problem with my practice of never taking an umbrella unless it's pouring does have one downfall. Though the rain was just a sprinkle earlier, while we were inside, it's become a torrential downpour.

"Stay here and I'll go get the truck and bring it around so you can stay dry," he says.

"Nah, let's make a run for it. I'll race you. On the count of three. One, two—" I take off like a shot.

"Hey!" he shouts from behind me. I can hear his heavy footsteps pounding the pavement, and I pick up my pace. The rain is coming down in sheets, and I'm soaked in an instant. I see the lights flash on the truck and smile because I know he's opened it, so I can get inside as soon as I get there. Instead, when I hit the truck, I turn around. He's only a few steps behind me, and I thrust my hands in the air.

"I win!"

"You're a cheat!" he yells before gathering me into his also soaked arms and kissing me deeply. When he pulls away, he says, "Now get in the truck before you catch your death," and gives me a smack on the ass that has the desire I felt earlier springing back to life.

He lifts me into the truck and then runs around to the driver's side, hauling himself in as well. Once we're both safely ensconced inside, I laugh. Not a tiny giggle but a real genuine laugh from deep inside me. I've never felt so free to be myself as I do when I'm with Dante. It's like he accepts every part of me—the serious, the scared, the silly—and he always seems to want more.

"I didn't know my girlfriend was such a little cheat."

My breath catches in my throat as he shakes the rain out of his hair, but water is still streaming from his body, making his clothes cling to every muscle.

"Girlfriend?" I ask softly, almost scared to hear what he has to say.

He turns slightly in his seat so that he's facing me. "Well, you're not seeing anybody else, are you?" His voice is as soft as mine, like he's almost as nervous as I am, but that can't be possible.

"Of course not," I rush out. I don't want him to think for a second that there's anybody else.

"Do you *want* to date anyone else?"

"No." The word comes out as almost a shout. The thought of seeing anybody else is so repugnant to me, I don't even want to think about it. When this man eventually breaks my heart, there's going to be no way I'll ever find a man that can measure up to him. He always has been and always will be the man I measure all other men against. That's going to suck for them.

"Then I'm pretty sure that makes you my girlfriend."

His eyes bore into mine, waiting for some kind of response, and I say the only thing I can think of in that moment. "Yeah, it does."

"Come here." His voice is stern and brokers no argument. I grab his outstretched hand, and he pulls me over the console to the driver's seat. I'm on my knees, straddling his lap, and I wrap my arms around his neck to hold myself steady. He reaches down and moves the seat all the way back, giving me a comfortable space to fit between him and the steering wheel.

I can feel his hard length underneath his slacks and am both impressed and flattered at how much this man always seems to want me. It's almost as much as I want him.

"I think my gorgeous girlfriend needs to be punished for cheating, don't you?"

The exhilaration of him calling me his girlfriend again clouds the last part of his sentence for a second. That is, until I feel the smack on my right ass cheek through the material of my dress and panties, causing me to jump in his lap.

"Hey!" I exclaim loudly. In answer, he gives me another swat on my left cheek. There's too much material to cause any real sting, but the surprise makes me jump again, and my pussy immediately floods, soaking through my panties.

I let out a soft moan. "What are you doing?" I ask in a daze of growing lust.

"Don't you think bad girls should get punished?" he asks, his voice somehow both stern and playful at the same time. He pops my behind again, and this time I grind down onto him, making us both moan.

"Yes," I gasp. "But here?" We both look around, and I realize the truck is shrouded in darkness and rain. There are so many raindrops covering the windows that I can't see out, which means nobody can see in. Of course, there's always the chance that we could still get caught. We're in a parking lot for God's sake, but that seems to just be heightening my arousal. Now that I know nobody can see us, I'm all in for this punishment.

The first time Dante spanked me, the feelings it flooded me with surprised me, and while it stung, it was never hard enough to cause me any actual pain, just enough to heighten my arousal and make me want him that much more. He's spanked me several times since, and I've only grown to love it more.

Instead of answering my concerns, he goes back to kissing me. Teasing my mouth with his and tracing my lips with his tongue, causing me to gasp. While I'm focused on what he's doing with my mouth, in the background there's the sensation of his hands slipping under my dress to my ass as he slowly raises my dress to around my waist, leaving me in the black thong I slipped on after our shower.

As our tongues play together, I unbutton his soaking wet shirt and spread it wide, exposing his chest to me. I run my hands over it and feel the hard panes of his body, shaped by hours of hard labor. These aren't some muscles for show that you get by spending hours in the gym every day. No, these are the kind of muscles you get doing hard work to provide for your family.

His hands are massaging each of my ass cheeks, and I'm torn between thrusting back into his hands so that he'll knead them harder or arching forward to rub my pussy against his thick cock. Before I can make my choice, there's another smacking sound followed by a sharp sting on my right cheek. Oh, shit.

"Do good girls cheat?"

"No," I moan.

Smack.

"No, they don't."

Smack. I let out a sharp cry.

"Do you want to be a good girl?"

Smack. He's alternating between cheeks now, and I can't stop my body from wiggling on top of him. I want more, but I don't know of what. More spanking? More of his cock?

"Yes."

Smack.

"Yes what, Violet?"

Smack.

"I want to be a good girl." I feel like I'm yelling as my voice reverberates through the cab of the truck.

Smack.

"Don't," I gasp. He stops the spanking and instead grabs my ass cheeks in both hands, gently massaging the stinging globes.

"Don't spank you anymore or don't stop?" he whispers in my ear. I feel like a cat in heat, wanting everything all at once.

"I don't know," I admit in a whining voice. I press down hard against his trapped cock, and I wouldn't be surprised if there was a wet spot on his pants from my juices escaping my panties.

"Pull out my cock, baby."

I instantly move to follow his command, fiddling with his belt before finally getting it unbuckled. I make quick work of his pants and reach in to wrestle his cock free from its confines. It's hard and hot in my hand, the tip covered in pre-cum. It looks absolutely divine, and if there was any room, I would bend down and take it in my mouth so I could taste him. Instead, I get a firm grip and slowly stroke him up and down, paying close attention to that spot just under the head that seems to drive him crazy.

While I'm concentrating on the hard cock in my hands, he's shoved aside my panties exposing my wet pussy to him. He drags his middle finger through my moisture, letting it just glance off my clit, causing me to whimper.

"Good girls don't get wet pussies from their spankings, baby." He brings his finger up, and I can see it's slick with moisture. He pops it into his mouth, sucking on it, seeming to savor my taste. The thought drives me out of my mind, and as soon as he pulls his finger from his mouth, my lips are against his. My tongue delves into his mouth, seeking every hint of my flavor that's now mixed with his own.

"You're definitely naughty," he says before giving my ass another pop.

All the sensations, all the foreplay out here in the open, is too much for me. I need him inside me. Right. Now.

"Up," he commands and I move up, balancing myself off of his lap and onto my knees. He leans back, allowing me to still keep hold of his cock. "Slide that sweet pussy down on my baby. Let me fill you up."

I've never been on top before. Just the thought makes me nervous. I have no idea how to move, how to give him pleasure in that position, but I do know that he won't let me fail at it. He knows my body, maybe better than I do, and he'll make it good for both of us.

Grasping the base of his cock firmly, I take a second to drag the tip of his cock through my drenched folds. Dante's closed his eyes, and it looks like he's doing everything he can not to rush me. His hands grip my hips, and he carefully guides me down. Once his tip is notched inside of me, his eyes pop open and go to where our two bodies are joined together.

"That's it baby, take this dick." His words embolden me, and I sink down a little more, causing us to moan in unison. Pleasure is radiating through my body as I hold on to his shoulders to steady myself and slowly sink down, inch by excruciating inch, until he's finally seated all the way inside me. Every time we fuck, I always feel so unbelievably full. I thought after the first time that it would eventually stop being so intense, but that hasn't happened yet.

I worry my lip, suddenly nervous again as I say softly, "I don't know what to do."

He gives me a kiss before saying, "Your body knows what to do, baby. Just move and do whatever feels good."

"I want to make sure you feel good too."

"Believe me when I say that no matter what you do, it's going to feel good for me." His eyes are shining with the truth of his words, so I do a little experimental tilting of my hips. The movement makes him sink farther inside me, which I didn't think was possible, and causes me to gasp. There's a growl emanating from deep in his chest, and I know that he's barely holding on. Emboldened, I circle my hips before tilting back and forth and raising up just a little on my knees before dropping back down. I let out a cry when I feel his cock rub that spot deep inside me that drives me crazy.

"You found it, didn't you, baby?" I nod my head and make the same movement again, feeling every nerve ending in my body light up.

Dante grabs at the neckline of my dress and jerks it down, revealing my black lace bra which he quickly shoves down as well. His hands completely cover my tits, and he pinches and squeezes my nipples while I work myself over on his pulsing member. His hands on my tits feel so good that I inadvertently thrust them into his face, begging for more. He takes my hint and covers one nipple with his mouth, sucking it in and swirling it with his tongue.

The new sensations only drive me on, and I move faster, panting in my exertion. I can feel myself approaching my orgasm. It's like I'm running toward the cliff but can't quite get there.

As if sensing what I need, he grabs my ponytail tightly and pulls my head back, exposing my neck to him. He nuzzles me in the spot he knows drives me wild. Someone is chanting Dante's name over and over again, and it takes a moment before I realize that someone is me.

Almost simultaneously, his hand moves to where our bodies are joined together, and he presses down on my clit, hard, while his teeth nip at the delicate skin of my neck. "Come all over my cock, you dirty girl."

Apparently, that's all that I need to finally reach the finish line. I scream, letting it echo throughout the cab. My body tries to curl in on itself as my orgasm rips through me. I hold on to Dante's shoulders for dear life as I ride it out. The entire time he's firmly rubbing my clit with his thumb, prolonging the sensations that are causing me to collapse in on myself.

When I finally come down, Dante grips my hips and holds them steady. He starts thrusting up into me. His pace is rapid, harsh, and exhilarating. I knew he was holding back, letting me explore, so I'm happy to let him have this time to be in control of my body and use it for his own pleasure.

He's jackhammering into me from below, and I'm doing what I can to stay upright, my tits bouncing relentlessly in his face. He catches a nipple in his mouth once again and gives it a sharp bite. The dual sensations are working their magic on me, and I can feel another orgasm building from deep inside.

I bury my hands in his hair and hold him against my chest, encouraging him to continue playing with my aching nipples. I'm so lost in my haze of desire I don't even think twice as I whisper in his ear, "Come inside me, Dante. Fill me up with your cum."

That seems to do it for him, and he slams me down on top of him. I can feel his cock pulsate inside me, his cum coating my walls, which sends me into a second orgasm. The walls of my pussy milk his cock, eking out every last drop of him inside me.

By the time we've both come down from our highs, we're each panting and damp. I'm not sure if the wetness is sweat or from the rain we ran through. He's pulled me into his chest while leaving his cock planted deep inside me, even as I can feel it softening. He's stroking my hair and nuzzling my neck, making me feel cherished.

"Violet, I . . ." He trails off and I pull back so I can look at him. I wait patiently for what he's about to say. He shakes his head, clearing it. "You're amazing. You know that, right? These past few months have been like a dream."

I give him a soft kiss before pulling back and looking into his eyes again. "For me too." I wish I could say so much more.

TWENTY-ONE

DANTE

I almost told her I loved her last night.

The evening had been so perfect, and when it was topped off by that amazing sex in my truck, all I could think was that I could do this forever. I wanted to tell her I loved her so badly, but at the last second, self-preservation kicked in, thank fuck. Besides, I'd made enough admissions for one night. Between calling her my girlfriend, admitting that I've wanted her for the past year, and sharing how happy our time together has made me, I already felt exposed and vulnerable. It's not a feeling I'm used to or comfortable with yet.

But there was one thing that I did realize last night. I can't go on like this. I want Violet in my life. Permanently. I'm going to have to figure out a way to make that happen. How am I going to convince this young, vibrant woman with her whole life ahead of her to hitch her wagon to a man who's already lived a full life, already had a family? I don't know the answer, but I'm sure as fuck going to find out. The only thing I know is that I'm not letting her go.

Why would I? So she can date idiots her age like that Tyler kid that doesn't seem to have a clue she's not interested? Or maybe she'll finally go out with some of the men her mother has lined up for her, so they can get married and have their own family? That thought makes me feel physically ill. No, there's nothing left to do but to convince her to stay with me. I just have to come up with a plan.

You would think that her admitting to me she's had a crush on me all these years would make me feel better, and to a certain extent it does, but it also makes me worry that this thing between us might be her just living out a schoolgirl fantasy while I'm playing for keeps.

I know she wants children. She told me once that being a mother was the thing she wanted to be with above all others. I thought I was done with that phase of my life. The dirty diapers, midnight feedings, all the crying, none of it appealed to me. But when I think about doing all of that with Violet, well, it doesn't seem so bad. In fact, it feels almost right. Like maybe I'm the man that's supposed to make her a mother. It sounds crazy, even to me, but the thought of having a baby with Violet stirs something inside of my chest that I can't describe. If that's what she wants, then I'm willing to give it to her.

I know that one of the major obstacles is going to be my own daughter. She's been pushing me hard toward getting back together with her mother, and it just isn't going to happen. Even if I wasn't in love with Violet, I would never get back together with Amanda. Even if she hadn't cheated on me, we were never right for each other. I'm just going to have to find a way to ease Bianca into the idea that Amanda's not the one for me. Then after a while I can tell her I've started seeing someone and can eventually introduce her to her own best friend? Fuck, that doesn't sound like a good idea either.

I know that even though it will be tough, Bianca and my relationship will bounce back. Even if it's not exactly as it was before. We have a deep bond, and I don't think there's

MADE TO BE YOURS

anything that could sever it completely. She may be pissed at me for a while, but she would get over it. Probably.

I'm more concerned about her relationship with Violet. She told me once that she couldn't lose Bianca, and I believe her. Violet doesn't have much of a support system. Her parents are useless, so she's basically created her own family with Bianca and Hollie. I'm more worried that Bianca might never forgive Violet for what we've done. To save her familial relationship with me, she may shift all the blame to Violet. I know I can be an emotional support for Violet, but I'm not so out of touch to believe that I'm all she'll need. She'll need her family, the one she created for herself.

I'm not sure the best route to take, but I know that even if I can convince Violet we belong together, we'll have to tread lightly when it comes to both of our families. I decide to just give myself some time to think over how to handle both Violet's parents and Bianca.

Sure, there will be other people out there that frown upon our relationship. They'll say shitty things about me and even worse about Violet, but they don't matter. What do I care about what a bunch of strangers on the street think? I'll do my best to shield her from it, but I won't let them be the reason that we aren't together. But a little voice in my head reminds me that while I can handle it, Violet might not be able to. She's so shy and nonconfrontational. Maybe the things people say will slowly wear her down until she's ready to be rid of me.

It was hard leaving Violet this morning. I'm finding that every morning I wake up with her curled against me in *my* bed that I want it to be *our* bed. She was curled up on her side with her fist tucked firmly underneath her chin and her long black hair spread out across her pillow. I wanted to wake her up and fuck her for the next hour, but I knew my crew was waiting on me and that she would have to wake up to get to class soon.

I'm doing my last walk-through on the Kamber Street project before we bring in the homeowners. I'm not surprised when everything looks on point. Jake and his team have done an excellent job.

The house is almost unrecognizable from the run-down, dreary place we first walked into. Now, practically every inch of the interior has been gutted and redone. The house is full of light and modern touches. I know my clients are going to love it. I give them a call and arrange to meet them at the house tomorrow to walk them through everything that we've done.

The project was on schedule, and we finished just in time because I already have another job lined up for this crew. I've been lucky that business has always been pretty steady for me. I have great word of mouth from previous clients, and anytime Archer has a smaller job at one of his boutique hotel's he throws it over to us, not because we're friends but because he knows that we consistently do great work that comes in on time and on budget.

It's especially a relief that everything is going well with work now that I'm thinking of a future with Violet. I want to make sure I can provide for her in every way. If she wants to use her degree and work, I'm all for it. If she'd rather be a stay-at-home mom, I know I can make that happen. I've worked hard over the years, and between the business and my personal rental properties, we can have a comfortable life together without having to worry too much about money.

My phone rings in my pocket, pulling me out of my thoughts of the future. I see it's Bianca, and I answer with a smile. "Hey, pumpkin. How are you doing today?"

"Hi, Dad. You haven't seen Violet, have you?" My entire body tenses up and I can hear blood rushing through my ears. How could she possibly know? Did someone see us together last night and tell her?

"No. Why would you think I've seen Violet?" I rush out, my brain quickly scrambling for something, anything, that will smooth this situation over.

"Uh, because you're her boss. Duh, Dad." All the tension in my body releases, and I lean against the wall. I'm Violet's boss. Duh, is right.

"Right, sorry. I can hardly hear you. I'm at a job site. But I think that she has a class this morning, so she won't be at the office."

"Damn, I wanted to talk to her about something."

"Is it anything I can help you out with?"

"No, no, it's fine. I just wanted to talk to her about some stuff. No big deal."

I've known my daughter for twenty-three years, and I know when she's hiding something from me. I decide not to push. Apparently, we both have secrets we're not ready to share.

"So, Mom and I are going out tonight to celebrate her first day at her new job. Do you want to join us?" she asks innocently, but I know better.

"Bianca, I'm still pissed about the stunt you pulled last time the three of us were supposed to have dinner."

"It wasn't a stunt, I swear. I had to babysit at the last minute—"

"Babysit?" I ask incredulously, interrupting her. Now I know she's lying.

"Yeah, babysit. Why does everybody seem so surprised by that?"

"Well, you've never exactly hidden your dislike of children, honey." I pace the large, empty living room of the house.

"Yeah, well, Oliver is different. He's a pretty cool kid."

I'm stunned. She's done everything she could to avoid children since she was a teen and got her diagnosis, but she actually sounds fond of whoever this kid is. Maybe, as she's growing older, she's deciding that she really does want a family.

I say my next words hesitantly. I don't want to upset her, but I want her to remember that she has options. "You know, it's been a long time since we spoke to that doctor. There's a lot of new—"

"Stop!" she snaps at me. "This is not a discussion we are having right now. Or ever. I told you I don't want kids. Just because I babysat one kid a few times and didn't hate it doesn't change that. So just leave it."

"You're right, I'm sorry." I know why she's being defensive, and it's clear this is a subject she's not willing to talk about right now. That's fine. At least she knows I'm here if she ever wants to talk about it. So, instead of pushing, I bring the topic back around to Amanda. It's time to make it very clear to my daughter what my intentions are with my ex-wife. "I don't think I can make dinner tonight. I'm going to have to work late in the office, since I'm going to be out most of the day and it's Violet's day off." I don't mention that I have every intention of spreading Violet out on my desk and eating her pussy until she screams my name instead. For obvious reasons.

"That's too bad. Maybe we can stop by afterward and say hi. Make sure you aren't working too hard."

"That's not a good idea, honey." I take a step outside to the newly poured patio, complete with built-in barbecue and fire pit for a little added privacy. "Listen Bianca, I really need you to hear me on this, okay?"

"Yeah, Dad. What's going on?"

"You need to cut this shit out with me and your mom. I know you're trying to fulfill some wild fantasy where the two of us get back together, but I already told you it's not going to happen. The only connection I have with Amanda is because of you. The truth is, if you hadn't come along I would probably have broken up with her while we were still in high school and been happy to never see her again. I don't need you or anyone else interfering with my love life. Whether I'm with somebody or not, your mother and I have absolutely zero chance of getting back together. You need to get rid of this crazy idea of yours once and for all. Do you understand?" I stop my rant and wait for her response. Even though I know what I said came off harshly, it felt good to finally get it off my chest, especially if it means that Bianca will stop pushing Amanda and me together.

Her voice is ice cold when she speaks next. "You won't even give her a chance, Dad. She's changed since back then. You're just being a stubborn asshole, and it's going to keep you alone for the rest of your life."

"Bianca? Bianca!" I pull the phone away from my ear and see that she's disconnected the call. I should have realized that I was pushing her hard enough to bring her fiery temper out. She doesn't normally direct it at me, but when she does, it stings. The good thing about my daughter is that she gets over things like this pretty quickly. I just hope that she's really gotten the point that Amanda is not the one for me. I just worry she might be less forgiving when she finds out her best friend is.

"Everything all right out here, boss?" Jake's poked his head outside and is watching me pace the length of the patio. "You know, we didn't account for that amount of wear and tear when we poured that concrete. Careful you don't wear a hole in it."

"Don't be a smart ass," I tell him and take a seat on the edge of the newly installed fire pit. "Bianca and I were just having a . . . disagreement."

"Oh. So, she's found out about you and Violet, huh?"

I jerk my head up in surprise. I never told Jake about Violet. How could he possibly know? Archer, Hollie, and now Jake? I must be really horrible at keeping my feels on lockdown. It's a wonder Bianca hasn't figured it out yet.

"There is no me and Violet," I say, trying to deflect.

He lets out a genuine laugh from deep down inside and shakes his head like I'm being ridiculous. "I knew the second I walked into your office and saw you two together that something was going on. I don't think you're as good at hiding it as you think you are."

"Fuck." I run my fingers through my hair, trying to bring down my anxiety. If Jake figured it out from just seeing us together once, what hope do we have of hiding it from anyone else?

"I assumed when you asked me for a restaurant recommendation a few days ago that it was for the both of you."

"It was," I admit. "If you knew that there was something going on with Violet and me, then why did you continue to flirt with her?"

"Because I could tell it was getting under your skin." He crosses his arms across his chest and gives me a crooked smile.

"You're such a dick, Jake. Don't you have, like, five other women you could be chasing around?"

"Nah." He drops his arms back to his side and leans his hip against the wall. "I'm getting tired of all that. The chase is getting old. The catching is getting even older. I've been thinking about finding someone to maybe settle down with."

"Holy shit, words I never thought I would hear come out of your mouth."

"What can I say? Maybe you're rubbing off on me."

"Well, I haven't settled down just yet. First, I have to convince Violet, then I have to deal with our families."

"Are you shitting me? You think you need to convince Violet? That girl was looking at you like you hung the moon."

I want to flat out tell him he's wrong, but I can't for two reasons. The first is that I have noticed her looking at me with something in her eyes that I haven't quite been able to define yet. Second, I just straight up want it to be true. I want her to have feelings for me, love me.

"Well, let's hope you're right."

"Believe me, boss-man." He pushes off the wall and comes over to slap me on the back. "I know women, and I know when I see one that's in love."

"Okay, now you've gone right back to making me worried. If you've ever been in love, I would be shocked."

He gives me a sad smile and starts to walk off. "Maybe you don't know me as well as you think."

I can tell there's a story there, but I don't want to push him. Jake knows that if there's anything he wants to talk about, I'm here to listen.

My thoughts turn back to Violet, as they often do, and I try to think about what I can do to convince her to stay with me. I know that not all women, and Violet in particular, can be swayed by flowers and expensive gifts. But it's not a terrible place to start. I want to prove to her I know her, that I pay attention. I want to show her what every day with me would be like. Somebody who pays attention to her and takes care of her. Someone who cherishes her.

An idea for the perfect gift comes to me, but I worry it may take me a while to find. I call around to different dealers in the city and am relieved to find one that might have what I'm looking for, so I make an appointment for later this afternoon. I can head over there after I finish my consultation with some potential clients I have lined up. Excited by the prospect of getting Violet something I think she'll truly love and getting to spend the evening with her, all thoughts of my earlier conversation with Bianca have been washed away. I love my daughter, but right now I have to concentrate on getting the love of my life to fall for me.

TWENTY-TWO

VIOLET

Well, these were certainly going to be . . . different. Dante's house had become a place where I felt I could safely experiment with my baking. The man either truly liked everything that I made or else he was a human garbage disposal. It could quite possibly be both.

I've always loved baking, but now I realize I love watching someone else enjoy what I've made even more.

Tonight's experiment was brownies. I added some beer to them because I know how much Dante loves it. Then I found an old package of Red Hots in the cabinet. I tasted one first to make sure there was nothing wrong with the hot cinnamon lumps of sugar. After all, they could've been in there six months or six years, but they seemed to be fine, so I tossed them in as well. I'm hoping the results will be something he'll like.

I have the brownies cooling in the tray, and I'm just finishing up the salad to go with the lasagna I made for dinner. I check the clock again out of the corner of my eye. Dante is late. I don't bother texting him because I know he had a meeting with a potential client after he was done with the walk-through of the Kamber property. I'm hoping that it going long is a good sign, and that they're going to give Moreno Construction the job.

I've just finished setting the table when I hear the front door. "Hey baby, you made dinner?" He comes up behind me and wraps his arms around my middle, placing a kiss to that spot on my neck that drives me crazy. I turn in his arms and pull him down for a proper kiss.

"I sure did. Missed you." I still feel oddly vulnerable making even that much of an admission of my feelings to Dante, but every time I put myself out there he never lets me down.

"I'm pretty sure I missed you more."

See what I'm talking about? I can feel myself grinning like a fool.

"I'm going to run upstairs and clean up real quick, and when I come back down, I'll give you your present."

It's only then that I notice he's holding a plain white shopping bag in his hand. "You didn't have to get me a present."

"Of course I didn't have to. I wanted to." He gives me a quick peck on the cheek and heads upstairs to take his shower, bag in hand, presumably so I don't peek. Smart man.

I wonder what he could've gotten me. He has a tendency to pick out the best presents. I think about what it could be while absentmindedly fiddling with my beloved necklace. Abruptly, I realize that he always looks at the necklace when I'm wearing it and stares at me pretty intently when I play with it, but he never seems to bring it up and I wonder why. I hope it doesn't make him uncomfortable that it's obviously my favorite.

I cut the now-cool brownies in the pan and transfer them to a large plate. They're strangely thicker than brownies are normally. They're almost on the cakey side. Hopefully, he'll still like them. I guess these are now my official thank you for whatever he's gotten me.

I've just finished serving us each a helping of dinner and placed the plate of brownies into the middle of the table when Dante is back, freshly showered, in clean clothes, and with the mysterious white shopping bag in hand.

"Did you make these?" he asks, reaching for a brownie. I laugh and slap his hand away.

"Those are for dessert, mister. And possibly a thank you for whatever present you got me. We'll just have to see."

He sits down and motions for me to come to him. I don't even hesitate as I join him and he pulls me into his lap. "You smell amazing," he says. His nose is buried in my hair, and I'm happy that I washed it earlier with the jasmine shampoo I brought to keep here.

"Does that mean I get my gift?" I ask playfully. I think he knows I don't need presents, but now I'm curious. He hauls the bag over from where he set it on the table and places it in my lap before wrapping his arms around my middle, holding me to him.

"Open it, gorgeous." I blush slightly at his complement and reach into the bag, pulling out a heavy rectangular object wrapped in soft lavender paper and tied with a purple bow.

"You and your on the nose wrapping choices."

"What can I say? Violet's my favorite color."

That's it. I've melted. I'm a pile of goo on the floor. How am I supposed to concentrate on anything else when he says something like that to me and just turns my world upside down? I turn my head and capture his lips in a sweet kiss. I do everything I can to put all the emotions that I feel toward him but can't say into it. His intensity matches my own and leaves my eyes misty before he pulls away.

"Present." His voice is low and growly. I don't need to feel his hard cock poking into my thigh to know that he's aroused.

When I lift out the package, I immediately know it's some kind of book, so I unwrap it with care. First sliding off the purple ribbon, then carefully unfolding the wrapping paper.

What's left in my lap leaves me a little stunned. I reverently reach my hand out and stroke the leather binding with gold lettering. It's *Persuasion*. How does he know it's my favorite book?

"It's not a first edition," he says. "They didn't have any of those, and by the looks of Austen's other first editions, I'd have to sell one of my houses to buy one, but this was printed in 1865."

Carefully, I turn the cover back to reveal the title page and see that it was indeed printed then. I'm finding it hard to catch my breath. I know that even though something like this doesn't cost nearly as much as a first edition, a book in this condition and of this age still costs a pretty penny.

"How did you know?" I whisper.

"Know what?" His face looks puzzled, like I'm asking him some off-the-wall question.

"That *Persuasion* is my favorite book?" I continue to caress the pages lightly. I never thought I would own something like this and to be given it by Dante? Well, I don't know which of the gifts he's given me I treasure more.

"You told me silly." He laughs.

"No, I never told you that," I say resolutely.

"It was a little over two years ago. The night you moved into the house. We were talking about our favorite books and I guessed yours would be *Pride and Prejudice*. You told me you thought *Persuasion* was more romantic."

I'm stunned. I search my memory and can pull scraps of that conversation. He's right. I was reading *Count of Monte Cristo* and he told me it was one of his favorites, so I shared mine. How could he have remembered that? Hell, I was practically in love with him even back then and held every conversation, every interaction, with him close to my heart. How could I possibly have forgotten? And he remembered. Could he care about me more than I thought he did? Only someone with actual feelings for me would remember a five-minute conversation from two years ago, right?

I carefully place the book onto the table, far away from the plates holding our food, and turn in his lap so that I'm straddling him.

"You don't like it," he says. There's a worried look on his face, and he reaches up to my cheek. It's only then that I realize there are silent tears streaming down my cheeks. I'm so overwhelmed with emotions right now. I guess they needed somewhere to escape.

I shake my head. "No, I love it. It's amazing. I just can't believe you remembered that conversation. It was so long ago."

"I remember everything when it comes to you."

I move quickly and capture his lips with my own. I may have been the one to initiate the kiss, but he quickly takes over, ravaging my mouth. Somehow, both of our shirts are no longer on our bodies, discarded to the floor. My pussy is wet, and my breasts feel heavy and achy. I only get some relief when he unclasps my bra and then quickly latches his mouth on to one of my hardened nipples.

"Oh. Oh. Oh." The pleasure he's giving me doesn't allow me to stay quiet in his arms, and it isn't long before I'm grinding my pussy down onto his hardened length. I know my fingernails are digging into his shoulders while I hold him close as he alternates from one nipple in his mouth to the other, but neither of us seems to care.

I'm so lost in the mind-blowing pleasure he's giving me I don't really register the sound of the front door. Not until I hear, "Hey, Dad, I— What the fuck are you doing?!"

The sound of Bianca's voice has me trying to jump away from Dante, but instead of allowing me to move, he holds me close, rises up from the chair and then shoves me behind his back. It's only then that I realize I'm completely topless. I hide behind him and search frantically for my top, but then I see the green fabric across the room.

I peek past Dante and see not only Bianca but Amanda as well, standing in the entryway, mouths agape. I thought Bianca walking in was bad, but this is a million times worse. Of all the ways I thought Bianca might find out about us, her walking in on us having sex hadn't even crossed my mind. And Amanda being here? This is the stuff of nightmares.

"Well?" Bianca demands, her hands clenched angrily into fists at her side. I can tell by the look in her eyes that she's furious, and I want to break down into tears. This time they won't be happy ones.

"Don't take that tone with me, Bianca," Dante says, firmly holding his ground. He leans to the side and scoops up his tee shirt, then thrusts it behind his back for me to take, which I gladly do.

I slip the shirt over my head, and it comes down to my knees, making it look like I'm not wearing anything underneath it. Shit, does this make it even worse?

"You are in my house and I expect you to be respectful."

I can't stand here cowering and hiding behind Dante the entire time. This is something we did together, and I need to stand by him and try to explain. Maybe Bianca will be okay. She just needs time to get over it. Once Dante and I explain that we care for each other, she'll have to understand, right?

I have a flash of Hollie warning me that I better tell Bianca before she finds out on her own because it will be so much worse, and I realize I should've taken that advice weeks ago. Even if she eventually accepts the relationship, will she ever forgive the fact that I lied to her?

I step out from behind Dante's back and stand by his side, noting the fact that he hasn't looked at or acknowledged me except for handing me his shirt.

"I'm pretty sure I can talk to you any way I want when I walk in here and you're *fucking my best friend!*" She's practically screeching, and her eyes are boring into Dante. But Amanda, well, her eyes are on me and they're filled with unconcealed disdain.

"Language, Bianca," he says coolly. How can he be so calm right now?

I attempt to enter the heated conversation. "Bianca, I—"

"I don't think anyone wants to hear what you have to say right now, you little tramp."

I gasp at Amanda's words. How dare she? I wait for Dante to say something to defend me. Hell, I would expect even Bianca to shut that shit down. She's always been a women-supporting-women type of girl and doesn't let people get away with saying things like that in general, let alone to people she cares about.

But neither one of them says a word to Amanda. They're both too caught up in their battle with each other.

"So, this is why you weren't interested in giving Mom a chance. You already had easy access to Violet."

I have never felt so small as I do in this moment. Even my mother never made me feel this badly about myself for something I'd done. Mostly because I don't love her the way that I love these two people who won't even acknowledge my existence right now.

"Bianca, I already told you I wasn't interested in getting back together with your mother, and that has nothing to do with Violet. Even if she wasn't part of the equation, I would never be with her again."

Amanda lets out a little gasp, then narrows her eyes back on me. I don't know why she's concentrating so hard on me when nobody else is. "That's not what you said when we kissed in your truck after our date." She's speaking to Dante, but her eyes never leave mine.

I try to hide the hurt her words inflict on my fragile heart, but judging by the triumphant look on her face, I didn't do it well. I've never particularly cared for Bianca's mother, but seeing what I am right now, the woman is a straight up bitch. How could she derive so much pleasure from hurting somebody she barely knows?

"Amanda," Dante snaps. "You know that's not what happened. Stop trying to rewrite history like you always do."

Before Amanda has a chance to respond to that, Bianca has jumped back into the fray. "How long has this been going on?" she demands in a hard voice.

Come on Dante, tell her how long we've wanted each other. Explain to her we have feelings for each other.

"Since your birthday party."

"What?!" Her voice booms through the room and she looks at us with incredulity, but I also see some hurt there as well. I want to go hug her, but I know that I'm the cause of her hurt. "You've been lying to me. You've both been lying to me. How could you?"

"We didn't want to lie," I manage to interject.

She turns her angry eyes to me, and I almost wish I hadn't said anything so she would go back to ignoring me. "It doesn't look like you tried very hard to tell me the truth." She purposefully makes a show of eyeing her father's shirt that I'm wearing and I want to curl up into a ball. I can feel myself losing her.

She turns back to Dante. "So what is this? You just getting your rocks off? Is this a midlife crisis or something and she was convenient?" She lets out a laugh that's hollow and hateful. "And to think, I was the one that told you to hire her. So tell me, what is it?"

Now I know Dante is going to say something. He knows that we're not just some fling. We may have started as casual, and we haven't really spoken about the future, but he has to admit that we mean something to each other. Except, he doesn't say that. He doesn't say anything.

"I— I'm— I can explain—"

"Oh, this ought to be good," Amanda says with a sneer.

Tell them I'm your girlfriend! I'm screaming in my head for him to stand up for me, for us, but all I see is his mouth opening and closing like some kind of fish gasping for air.

In that moment, I think about all the times in my life I didn't matter. Every single time I was ignored, considered less than. Each time I had to put my wants aside for somebody else. And in that moment, I'm done with it all.

I may love Dante, but I finally realize that I love myself more. I snatch my purse off the chair, sling it over my shoulder, and walk to the middle of the room. All eyes are on me but I'm only looking at Dante, whose eyes are filled with some mixture of fear and remorse, which just tells me I'm making the right decision.

"You know what, Dante Moreno? You're not good enough for me."

He puts his hand on his chest, covering his heart like I've somehow wounded him, but I know that's not true. I turn on my heel, push past both Amanda and Bianca, and make it out the front door without shedding a tear.

No one chased after me when I left the house, and I haven't decided if I'm happy or sad about it. Once I made it home, I went directly to my room and locked the door. If Bianca storms in, demanding a confrontation, I'm just not up for it right now.

I know that I'll have to speak to her about it eventually, but it can at least wait until I stop crying. It's not long before I fall asleep, and when I wake up, I look at the clock, seeing that it's only just after eleven p.m.

The house is still eerily quiet, so I know that Bianca isn't home. Maybe she's so angry she stayed somewhere else tonight. It's been a long time since I've felt this alone. Normally, at a time like this, I'd talk things out with Bianca or Hollie. I can't talk to Bianca about it for obvious reasons, and Hollie doesn't live here anymore.

I pick up my phone and look at the time again, wondering if it's too late to call my other best friend. In a split-second decision, I make the call. If she can't talk, she just won't answer.

After three long rings, I hear a sleepy, "Violet?" on the other end of the line. Her tone is full of worry and concern and sends me into another wave of tears.

Holy hell, I'm not sure I've ever cried as much as I have the past few days.

"Honey, what's wrong?" Her voice sounds more alert, and I can tell she's awake now. In the background I can hear Archer's sleepy voice ask who it is and Hollie telling him that it's me.

"Hold on, Vi, let me go to another room." I try to stop my tears while she finds somewhere private where she can talk. "Okay, tell me what happened."

"She knows."

"Oh, shit. And let me guess, you weren't the one who told her."

I hiccup as I answer. "No, she walked in on us. Amanda was with her."

"Oh my God, I'm so sorry, honey. Do you need me to come over?" And that's Hollie for you. She could've said "I told you so," but instead she's willing to drop everything for me. At least I still have her.

"No, please, just stay home. I just had to ask you; do you think she'll ever forgive me?"

Hollie lets out a sigh. "I do, but it may take some time. Especially because of what she probably saw when she walked in on the two of you. Just give her some space. Let her come to you. Do you want me to call her?"

"That might be helpful. You don't have to make excuses for me just . . . just tell her how very sorry I am and that I love her."

"I will," she says in a soft voice. "And hey, at least you have Dante."

I don't have the mental bandwidth right now to explain to her that no, I don't have Dante. Not only did I lose my best friend, but I lost the love of my life as well. I'm not ready to admit it out loud yet.

"Yeah," I choke out. "Look, I'm sorry for calling so late. Why don't you get back to sleep?"

"Don't forget, you can call me anytime, Violet. Day or night, I'm here for you, and remember, you will get through this."

After we say our goodbyes and hang up, I venture out of my room to the kitchen, needing a glass of water. No one ever mentions how much crying can dehydrate you.

Suddenly, Bianca is at my side, and I nearly spew out all the water in my mouth. Instead, I swallow but it goes down the wrong pipe, and I end up coughing and gasping for air. I'm mildly surprised when Bianca starts pounded on my back so I don't choke. Well, it's that or she's getting her aggression out on me. She's not exactly being gentle.

After I manage to get myself together and am standing upright again, we stare at each other awkwardly.

"Do you want to talk?" she asks. I bite my lip. I know we need to, but frankly, I'm a little surprised she's ready to talk so soon after what happened.

"Are you sure? It's kind of late."

"Yeah, I'd rather get this out of the way." She exits the kitchen and heads to the living room, leaving me to follow behind her. Instead of sitting on the couch together like we always do, she takes the lone, extremely uncomfortable armchair which we've nicknamed Satan's Torture Device since after you sit in it for about thirty seconds, both your back and ass are in excruciating pain. That right there tells me everything I need to know about how she's feeling about me right now. I head across the room and sit on the sofa alone, facing her.

"No wonder pushing my parents together wasn't working. Why would it when Dad has a hot little piece on the side waiting at home for him?" Her words are rather harsh, but somehow her voice is verging on playful, which I find confusing. Regardless, I want to correct her of that assumption immediately.

"No! It wasn't like that, B."

"Then why don't you tell me what it was like? Were you just working out your crush?"

My mouth drops open in surprise. First Hollie knew, and now Bianca? Am I really that horrible at hiding my feelings? "How do you know about my crush?"

"Please, I'm your best friend, I knew. But I wasn't going to be a dick and call you out when you obviously didn't want to talk about it."

I choose not to point out that she called me her best friend in the present tense and just nod my head. "It started out as a crush, that's true. But it became so much more."

"He didn't take advantage of you, did he? Tell me the truth, Violet."

This conversation is just one shock after another. Not only does she think her father could be capable of taking advantage of someone, but it almost feels like she's taking my side.

"No, I swear. He didn't take advantage of me. In fact, I basically threw myself at him, and he turned me down. But we just couldn't seem to stay away from each other. We really care about each other. Or at least I care about him." I mutter the last part almost to myself.

"You're in love with him." It's not a question but a statement, one I can't deny. Bianca lifts herself up out of her chair and moves over to sit on the couch with me, wrapping her arm tightly around my shoulders. And there go the waterworks again.

"Do you hate me?"

"Of course not. You'd have to do a lot worse than sleeping with my dad to make me hate you. Though, now that I've said it out loud, it does sound pretty gross. Besides, Hollie called me and reminded me you would never do anything to hurt me on purpose."

Hollie is a goddamned saint. "I wouldn't, I promise. I love you so much. You and Hollie are the closest things I have to a proper family. I can't lose you."

"I love you too," she says, rocking me comfortingly. "You're my family just as much as I'm yours. I think that's why I was so shocked when I found out."

"Well, you don't have to worry about it anymore. We're over. Honestly, we were never supposed to be anything more than casual. We want different things out of life. I want to be a mom, and he doesn't want any more kids. He has you and his business, and he's happy with that. It was me that was stupid and fell in love. We always had an expiration date. It's one reason we didn't bother telling you. I think we both figured it would be over before there was the need to."

"He doesn't love you?" she asks, looking perplexed.

"Of course not. I think he made it pretty clear this afternoon, by not saying a single word in defense of me or our relationship, that his feelings don't mirror mine. He didn't even bother to fight for me, B."

"Well, all I can tell you is that he looked absolutely devastated when you left, then he read Mom the riot act and kicked us out about thirty seconds later." It should surprise me he that didn't take the time to try to explain everything away to Bianca, but nothing he does surprises me anymore.

"Are we okay?" I ask.

"Yeah, we're okay." She gives me another comforting squeeze. "But don't you ever hide something like that from me again."

"I won't," I promise her, and I mean it. "Does that mean you're going to tell me what's going on with you and the hot detective next door?"

Her eyes widen to the size of saucers, and she looks slightly panicked. "There's nothing going on between us. He's still a douchebag, but his nephew is cool. That's it. End of story."

"Okay, sure," I say, holding up my hands in surrender. "Just know that if you want to talk about it, I'm here."

Even though I'm not going to end up with Dante, at least I'll always have Bianca. She'll help me find a way to survive without him. Who knows, maybe someday in the far, far distant future, I'll find another man I could love. If I just keep repeating that to myself, maybe someday I'll believe it.

TWENTY-THREE

DANTE

She's right, I'm not good enough for her.

Her words played over and over in my mind last night, and I knew she was right.

Of all the ways I thought Violet and I might get found out, I never expected for my daughter and ex-wife to walk in on us when we were half-naked and going at it. If they had waited just a few more minutes before walking in, they would have seen a whole lot more, so I guess I can be thankful for that.

When Bianca started questioning me about what was going on, I was so dumbstruck at the situation that I didn't know what to say. My mind ran over every scenario I could think of, trying to find something to say that would damage Violet's relationship with Bianca the least, and I had come up with nothing. Maybe if she'd shown up alone, we could've all sat down and talked over what was going on, but with Amanda there it was impossible. She was calling names and antagonizing the situation. I was trying to find a way to get them out of the house as soon as possible.

While my mind was struggling to find a way to fix the situation, it looks like I ended up hurting the one person I never wanted to.

So yeah, she's too good for me. It's not news to me. I've always known it. It was one reason I tried to protect my heart from her, but I failed at that too. All my good intentions of showing her we belonged together, that we could be permanent, were thrown out the window. I was only fooling myself that we could ever be anything more than casual. She's already made her mind up, and I don't blame her one bit. Who wants to go through this kind of drama just to be with a used-up old man? I only hope that she can repair her relationship with Bianca someday. Violet needs her.

I don't blame her for walking out on me. I just wish she would've given me a chance to explain how I felt. But what's done is done, and I know it's probably for the best. She was going to leave me eventually. It's better to get it over with now, rip it off like a Band-Aid before I become even more invested than I already am.

Who am I kidding? I'm irrevocably in love with Violet Daniels. I waited my whole life to find love, and when I finally did, it was with someone who would have to be crazy to settle for me.

I can tell you one thing, with all the yelling, name calling, and accusations that were flying around the room, I was so proud of her for standing up for herself. I just wish she'd chosen something other than us, than me, to finally take a stand on.

I know without a doubt that I'll never fall in love again. I waited almost forty years to find my first love. There won't be another.

After Violet was gone, I ripped Amanda a new one. If she ever spoke to or about Violet like that again, I would make her unbelievably sorry. I knew she had her own secrets she was trying to keep, and unless she wanted them out, she better keep her mouth shut. I could practically see Bianca's ears perk up at the mention of her mother's secrets and felt a perverse glee that she'd get questioned all the way home. I then promptly threw them both out of my house.

I didn't sleep last night. At all. I wandered the halls of my empty house. I've lived here by myself for the past ten years, and the house has never felt as empty as it does now. I picked up my phone again and again, hoping to see a text from Violet but never finding one. I thought about texting her myself a hundred times, but every time I just ended up setting it back down, leaving everything unsaid.

I thought about reading, but when I saw the eReader sitting on the nightstand, I knew that as soon as I turned it on it would be on the last page of the book we were reading together. Try as I might, I'm just not ready to close it yet.

I ended up sitting on the coach, staring absentmindedly at the television, and I couldn't tell you a single thing I watched last night if my life depended on it.

When the sun starts rising in the sky, I decide I've had enough moping around the house. I make myself a cup of coffee, shower, and get dressed. I take a moment to study my reflection in the mirror and realize I look like shit. There are dark circles under my bloodshot eyes, and I have an overall air of misery hanging over me. Well, at least it's appropriate.

The very last thing I want to do today is go out and show my clients around their new house. If it wasn't for the fact that I have a few dozen guys counting on me for jobs, I probably would've said fuck it and blown the whole thing off. Instead, I call Jake to go with me. He's ready to handle clients. I'll just be there because it's expected.

MADE TO BE YOURS

When Jake picks me up an hour later, I get into his truck and close the door without saying a word. "Holy shit, boss-man, you look like crap warmed over."

"Thanks, that's basically what I thought too. You can handle these clients, right? I'm only going to be there for moral support or if they have any questions outside your expertise."

"Haven't you learned by now that there's nothing outside my expertise?" He laughs. After riding a few minutes in silence he continues, "So what happened?"

"Violet dumped me." When I say it out loud, it hurts more. The words make me feel ill. I want to double over and hold my stomach but force myself to stay upright. I don't need Jake knowing that I'm losing my mind.

"You're shitting me."

I just turn and stare at him unwaveringly.

"Okay, so you're not shitting me. In all the years I've known you, I've never seen you so happy. What the fuck did you do?"

"Gee, thanks. Look, we don't need to talk about this. Let's just get this done so I can go home."

Everything goes extremely well with the clients. They're happy with the work, and Jake handled everything without a problem. It looks like it's time to give him some more responsibilities. Good, because I think I might need to take a break for a while.

Once he drops me back at home, I grab a beer and head back to the couch, reclaiming the spot I sat in all last night. I don't know how long I sit there before I hear a loud knocking on the door. I've just decided to ignore whoever is out there when I hear the click of the lock and the door start to slowly creak open.

"Hello? Anyone in here?" It's my daughter's voice, and I'm a little surprised she's ventured back over so soon after yesterday's disaster. I thought she would stay mad way longer than this. Then again, she could be here to rake me over the coals. Yeah, that definitely sounds more like Bianca.

"If there's anyone in here and you're naked, I suggest you put some clothes on right now!" she calls out.

I can't help but chuckle a little at that.

"I am walking through the kitchen, and I am approaching the living room. I repeat, I am approaching the living room."

I roll my eyes. She is such a drama queen. She definitely gets that from her mother. "Shut up and get in here." I say in an airy tone so that she knows I'm only teasing. She walks into the room with her hands covering her eyes.

"Are you sure it's safe?"

"Oh my God, who raised you like this?"

"I ask myself that question all the time." She laughs before taking a seat on the couch next to me.

"You want something to drink?"

"A beer would be nice." We both head into the kitchen, and I fetch her drink before we sit down at the kitchen table. I flinch when I see the copy of *Persuasion* I bought Violet, still sitting there looking as dejected as I feel.

I take another sip of my beer and wait for Bianca to begin. I know she has things she wants to say, and it's best to just let her get them out.

"So, Violet, huh?"

"Yup," I answer, draining the last of my beer from the bottle and grabbing another one.

"I spoke to her last night, you know."

"You did?" I stop myself short of asking how she's doing. If she's fine, I don't want to hear about it. If she's upset, I don't know if there would be anything I could do to fix it anyway.

"Yeah. I asked her if you took advantage of her."

"What?" I practically shout. How could Bianca think such a thing of me? "I would never take advantage of Violet or anyone else."

"Yeah, that's what she said too." She doesn't look at me and instead starts picking at the label of her beer bottle. "But you've got to admit, an older man, a younger woman, that's how a lot of people are going to see it. Especially her parents."

"I know. That's one reason I didn't want to go public at first."

"Well, that's stupid," she says, surprising me. "You can't live your life based on what other people are going to think or say about you."

"Even what you would think?"

"If you'd bothered to ask me instead of having me walk in on it, I might've told you that I didn't mind as long as you were both happy."

What? That can't possibly be true. "But what about your mom?"

She lets out a long sigh, like she's explaining something to somebody that's on the low end of the IQ scale. Maybe she is. "How many times do I have to tell you I just want you to be happy? I don't want to see you alone. That's the only reason I was pushing you two together. Well, that and Mom seemed pretty gung-ho about it. But if you'd just told me you were seeing someone, I would've left it alone."

I guess her assessment of my IQ was correct. I was an idiot for not trusting in my daughter. She's smarter and more caring than I'll ever be. "Well, it doesn't matter now." I reach to the middle of the table and grab another of these brownie things that Violet made yesterday. The plate's sitting there half-empty now after I stress ate them most of the night. "You want one?" I ask.

"Sure." She grabs one off the plate and takes a big bite. She chews it for just a second before a look of disgust comes over her face and she rushes to the trash can to spit it out. What's her problem?

"Where did those come from?" she asks suspiciously.

"Violet made them yesterday before, well, you know."

"And you're actually eating them?"

"Why not? They're good. I mean, they're not traditional brownies, but I like them. I've practically eaten the whole batch already."

Several looks cross Bianca's face all at once, ranging from disgust, to surprise, to joy. "Holy fuck, you love her."

"I don't know what you're talking about." I'm not ready to admit my feelings out loud for Violet right now. It'll hurt too much.

"You have to love her if you can eat this shit. Damn, I've always heard that love is blind, but I never realize it doesn't have any taste buds either."

"You know, you really shouldn't talk about her baking like that. It's not bad. Some of the stuff she's made me has been unusual, but it's never bad."

"She's made you more stuff than just this, and you ate it all?"

"Of course. I mean, we did all sorts of things together. Of course she baked for me. What did you think we did all day?" I see Bianca open her mouth, but cut her off quickly. "Never mind, don't answer that."

"Dad, it's a universally known fact that she can't bake. This isn't just my opinion. She single-handedly gave food poisoning to the entire English department her senior year."

I just shrug. I don't know what to say to that, and I'm not sure I believe my daughter, who is prone to theatrics.

"But you *do* love her, don't you?"

I let out a sigh. "Of course I love her. Do you think I would mess around with one of your friends for the fun of it? Do you think I would risk not only our relationship but the relationship you two have as well if I didn't love her?"

"If you love her, why aren't you out there getting her?"

That's the question I've been asking myself all night. "She said it herself yesterday. She's too good for me. And she's right."

"Well, of course she's right." My daughter, always the first to raise my self-esteem. "Nobody is good enough for Violet. But you didn't even fight for her."

"What's the point? She's made her feelings very clear. Besides, she's young and smart and beautiful. She has her whole life ahead of her. She doesn't want to tie herself down to a man who's almost twice her age. She's going to want to go out and party, meet guys her own age, start a family."

"Now I really am wondering what the hell it was that you two did together, because it certainly wasn't talking. Violet hates parties. I always had to drag her along with me, and she always wanted to leave early. That girl dances like a drunken flamingo. It's not her scene, never has been and never will be. And meeting guys her own age? She's been trying that for four fucking years, Dad. And do you know why it's never worked out? It's because she's compared every guy she's met to you, and nobody can measure up. And as for starting a family, well, I don't know how you feel about that. All I can tell you is that you've always been an amazing father to me, and any kid would be lucky to have you as a dad."

I feel my eyes misting up. "Come here, pumpkin." She comes around the table and I wrap her in a tight bear hug. I always knew my daughter was amazing, but this is on another level. Not only is she not angry about my relationship with her best friend, but she seems to be all for it. "I'm the luckiest man alive to have you for a daughter."

"You're damn right about that." She pulls out of my arms. "Look, I won't betray Violet's confidence by telling you anything she said to me last night, but if you really love her, which your taste buds indicate you do, I suggest you go and actually talk to her."

Could Bianca be right? Could Violet feel about me the same way I feel about her? All I know is that I have to try. If I don't, I'll regret it for the rest of my life. "I think you might be right. I think the two of us need to talk and straighten a few things out."

"Good. But I'm going to tell you the same thing I told Archer when he came around looking for Hollie after making her cry. It doesn't matter that you're my father, I'll have no qualms about killing you and burying you in the foundation of one of your own buildings, never to be found, if you hurt her."

Jesus Christ, she threatened to murder one of the most powerful men in Seattle without blinking an eye, just because he hurt her friend. I'm simultaneously in awe of and terrified by her.

Bianca heads for the door and just before it closes, she turns back to me, offering me one last word of advice. "Fight for her, Dad."

"I will." That's a promise I intend to keep.

I spend the next few hours trying to come up with a plan. I need something that will show Violet how I feel about her and let her know how sorry I am for not speaking up yesterday, that I'm serious about us. There's only one thing I can think of, and the more the idea takes root in my mind, the more I realize that I actually want to do it. I'll really be putting myself out there, but this situation calls for one of those big romantic gestures you see in the movies, doesn't it?

I pour myself a shot of my rarely touched whiskey to settle my nerves and work up the courage to send her a text. The amber liquid burns my throat on its way down, and then I pick up my phone.

Me: I'm so sorry about everything that happened yesterday. There are things I need to say to you if you'll just give me the chance. All I'm asking is for you to listen to what I have to say. That's it. Can I come over to your place tonight around 8?

I set the phone down on the table, then take a seat and stare at it. I know it won't make her reply any faster, if she bothers to reply at all, but I don't have anything else to do.

Five minutes pass. Then ten. Soon it's been a half hour, and I consider taking another swig of whiskey, maybe straight from the bottle this time, when my phone buzzes.

Violet: Okay.

Well, it's not exactly an enthusiastic yes, but I'll take what I can get. I would have run over there right away, but there's something I need to pick up first. Once I'm back, I have just an hour to shower and get ready to head over there. My hands won't stop shaking when I try to shave, so I decide to just leave the few day's growth. She's never seemed to mind it.

I gather up my things, including her discarded book, and I'm about to leave the house when my phone rings.

Bianca Calling . . .

TWENTY-FOUR

VIOLET

I cried uncontrollably last night and woke up this morning, determined not to shed another tear over Dante. My heart may be torn to shreds inside my chest, but that doesn't mean I have to show it on the outside.

Instead, I take my time getting ready for class, doing everything I can to look my best on the outside. I even attempt a heavier makeup look than I usually sport, though I'm not sure of the results. It's a little thick and feels almost like a mask, but maybe that will keep the world from seeing the broken shards of my heart that have been left inside me.

In the back of my closet I find a bright green dress that Hollie once convinced me to buy, but I've never been bold enough to wear out. It's a cute cap-sleeved, A-line dress, but I've always found the vee at the neck a little too low and the skirt a little too short. If I did wear it out, it certainly wouldn't have been to school, but I'm feeling bold today. I slip the dress over my head and immediately rethink my decision when I'm reminded of just how short it is. Instead of taking it off, I dig through my dresser for a pair of thick black tights and pull them on. There we go, colorful and sexy but not showing anything I don't want to be seen. After finishing my outfit with some knee-high boots, my peacoat, and a matching green scarf, I'm ready to face the day. That's what I'll keep telling myself.

I take one last look in the entryway mirror, and my eyes fall to the book pendant that's hanging between my breasts. My eyes well with tears, but I sternly remind myself that I'm not crying any longer and blink them away. I gingerly touch the necklace. I've only taken it off a few times since Dante gave it to me months ago. I reach behind my neck to undo the clasp but then lower my hands back down to my sides. I can't. I'm not ready to take it off yet. *Baby steps.*

As I'm walking through campus, I stop off at one of the job boards. There's no way I can work for Dante any longer, so I'm going to have to find something new to supplement my income. The money I made at Moreno Construction was more than generous, so I have enough to carry me through until I secure another part-time gig.

I'm surprised to find that I'll actually miss working for the company. It wasn't just Dante that made me enjoy the job. I really liked the other guys that I got to deal with, like Jake and Adrian. I also enjoyed feeling like an integral part of the company. Being relied on to keep things running smoothly gave me a sense of purpose I was lacking in my life. I love literature, but with no real end goal in mind for what I was going to do with my degree, it feels a lot like I'm just treading water. At Moreno Construction I served a purpose. It was exciting when we finished the Kamber Street project on time, and I'm sad that I won't be able to feel that sense of satisfaction again.

I guess it's time to really think about what I'm going to do with my life. Wanting to be a mom is great, but I have no real prospective husbands on the horizon, and I need to be able to support myself. Plus, I would never be comfortable depending solely on a man for my income. I've seen too many women in my mother's circle lose their husbands to other women, then be left with nothing.

I pull out my phone and take pictures of a few of the job flyers that seem like they might be tolerable and decide that I'll start calling around tomorrow. I don't think I have the bandwidth to handle it today. The next thing I do is call the English department and make an appointment with my adviser. Maybe he can help me figure out what I should do with this literature degree I'm sitting on and the master's degree that's coming.

I *almost* text my mother and ask her to set me up with one of Dad's associates but come to my senses just in time. I'm not that desperate yet.

I recognize that I'm probably doing all these things at once to keep my mind off the loss of Dante, but all I can do is move forward, one foot in front of the other, and hope that eventually I'll come through the other side.

When I finally make it to my class and take a seat, the professor is just starting his lecture. I take out my laptop, my hands poised and ready to take notes.

Two hours later, I look down and realize class is over and I haven't written a single thing. My head is in the clouds. I probably should've called this day a wash. I've checked my phone at least a hundred times, telling myself it's definitely not to see if Dante's reached out, yet every time there's nothing from him a little part of me dies.

He made it pretty clear, by not sticking up for me or our relationship, how he felt about us, and when I ran out, telling him I was too good for him, well, I'm sure that was the final nail in the coffin.

At least I still have Bianca. I'm unbelievably lucky that she's forgiven me so easily and so quickly. I feel bad for ever doubting that she would be anything less than understanding and supportive.

On the way home, I debate picking up some things so I can bake but decide against it. I don't feel like I have the energy for it today. Besides, who would eat it anyway? The only person who ever seemed to enjoy what I made was Dante. Though I kind of hope he chokes on the brownies I left there last night. Maybe he gave some to Amanda and she'll get food poisoning. A girl can dream.

Once I get home, I call out for Bianca and get no response. I look at the clock on the wall and remember that her work schedule should have her home in a few hours. I should have stalled on campus until I knew she would be here. Being alone with my thoughts is not something I'm looking forward to.

Grabbing a glass of wine from the kitchen, I settle onto the couch and start surfing the many streaming platforms we have, to find something to watch. After rejecting the first few dozen things that have come across the screen, my phone buzzes from its place on the coffee table, and I absentmindedly pick it up, assuming it's Bianca asking if I want her to bring home takeout or something.

Dante: I'm so sorry about everything that happened yesterday. There are things I need to say to you if you'll just give me the chance. All I'm asking is for you to listen to what I have to say. That's it. Can I come over to your place tonight around 8?

I realize I've stopped breathing only when I gasp for air. My heart is audibly pounding in my chest. It's a text I both hoped for and feared all day. My entire being is shouting at me to respond to him and tell him to come over now, that we can work this out. The only thing holding me back is my fear of getting hurt again.

The text doesn't mention what he wants to say. Of course, I hope he apologizes, falls to his knees, and begs me to stay with him forever, but what's the likelihood of that happening? Maybe he just wants to end things cleanly so that there's no awkwardness between us. Maybe he wants to say, "Hey, it's been fun, but it's time to move on." My fear and anxiety of the unknown keeps me immobile for a good long while.

Finally, I realize I can't hide from him. This isn't some guy I can blow off and never see again. This is Bianca's father, and since I plan on having her in my life forever, that means he'll be there too, at least on the periphery. Besides that, he's the only man I've ever loved, and if I want to move on, closure is probably the best thing. That's the adult in me talking. The scared little kid wants to smash the phone with a hammer and hide under the bed for the next three or four years.

I don't really understand why he wants to come over at eight. Shouldn't he just come here now and get this entire thing over with, good or bad? I guess it doesn't matter, it just means I'll be sitting here in my anxiety for hours to come. At least it's only another hour or so before Bianca gets home. Maybe she'll know what Dante wants to talk about and I can pump her for information, so I'll know what to expect.

I'm not sure how to respond, so I eventually just send him an "Okay" to confirm our meeting. I don't get any other texts from him after that, so there's nothing to do but wait. I go back to searching for something to watch and eventually settle on *The Office* reruns, the US version and not the UK one. David Brent is just too mean for me.

I'll take a clueless but earnest Michael Scott any day of the week.

After binging three episodes, there's a knock on the door. I guess Dante couldn't wait for our chat either. My hands are sweating, and I wipe them down the skirt of my dress. My legs are surprisingly shaky as I make my way through the living room and to the door. With a deep breath, I open the door, hoping for the best but preparing for the worst.

What I wasn't prepared for was who was standing on the other side of the door.

"Tyler," I gasp. I thought he looked a little disheveled the last time I saw him. Now, he looks absolutely unhinged. His hair is dirty and unkempt. There are stains covering the front of his shirt that's been misbuttoned. If I'm not mistaken, he's wearing the outfit I saw him in days ago. It doesn't look like he's shaved since then either. But what's really scary is the look in his eyes. I've never seen that look before. It's cold and hard and sends a shiver running through my body. I immediately sense that I'm in danger and swiftly swing the door closed right in his face.

Except, that's not what happens. Instead of latching, the door busts out back toward me and bounces off the center of my face. Pain shoots through my entire head, and I'm momentarily stunned as Tyler pushes his way inside.

"What? You weren't going to invite me in?" His tone is dark, and for the first time in my life I really feel true fear. There's moisture on my chin, and I run my fingers through it, then pull them away to see that I'm bleeding.

"What do you want, Tyler?" I try to sound brave, like I'm not scared of him, but I know that I'm failing miserably.

"What do you mean? I'm just over here seeing how my girlfriend is. You're bleeding, sweetheart." He's moved in close to me, and I can smell the stale sweat and body odor that's wafting off him. He reaches a hand up to touch my face, and I flinch away.

"I'm not your girlfriend, Tyler. You know that. We went on two dates." That's apparently not what he wanted to hear because he slaps me across the face. Hard. I let out a cry and cradle my cheek. I'm cowering now, afraid of what he might do next.

"The only reason you're not my girlfriend is because you're a whore."

"You better get out of here before my roommate comes out of her room and calls the cops."

Instead of making him leave, my statement just makes me laugh. He runs his hand over my shoulder, and I try to move away but realize that he's backed me up against the wall. "You think I don't watch everything you do, honey? I know you're here all alone waiting for me."

I let out a whimper and frantically search the room for something, anything, I can use to defend myself. I spot my cell phone sitting on the coffee table across the room. Maybe if I can get to it, I can manage to call 9-1-1. I take a tiny step to the side, trying to inch closer.

"Aren't you going to apologize to me?" He grabs my arm and twists it hard. There's a popping in my shoulder, and I let out a pained yell, worried that he's going to dislocate it.

"Apologize for what?" I gasp, trying not to think about the pain as he continues his crushing hold on my arm.

"For cheating on me, of course."

"I didn't cheat on you, Tyler."

That seems to make him angrier. He threads his fingers through my hair at the roots. He's pulling so tightly that there are spots in my vision. "Yes. You. Did." Each word is punctuated by him slamming the back of my head into the wall. My vision is blurry, and if he wasn't holding me up by my hair, I would've staggered to my knees. "I saw you with him in his truck. You were acting like the little slut you are. You could have been mine, but instead you had to whore around like all the rest of them. I don't even know why I'm wasting my time on you."

He's screaming in my face, and I can taste his rancid breath. I'm dazed and weakened by his attack, but I hope that he's being loud enough for someone to hear us and get help. I realize that he's completely lost it at this point, and there's no reasoning with him, so I try begging instead. "Please, Tyler. I'm so sorry. Please, just don't hurt me."

Dropping my combative response seems to be the way to go because his features soften just slightly, and his grip on my hair loosens. "I know you're sorry, honey, but I have to correct you so you won't do it again." A burst of agony shoots through my entire right side and realize that he's punched me in the ribs. I can't seem catch my breath. Every time I try to breathe there's a sharp stabbing pain.

That pain seems to clear my head and gives me the sudden realization that I'm going to die. There's no one here to help me and I'm going to die right here on the living room floor if I don't do something. Since he had to let go of my arm to punch me, he's only got a loose hold of my hair now. I can barely see out of my right eye, since it's swelling shut from where the door hit it, but I can still see my phone on the coffee table. It's my only chance.

I dart to the right past him, surprising him. I can feel hair being ripped from my scalp, but don't have time to register the pain. I'm almost to the coffee table when his heavy body plows into me from behind, causing us both to crash down onto the glass coffee table. It shatters into a thousand pieces beneath us and I can feel glass shards embedding themselves into my skin. There's a dampness all over my body and I know that rivulets of blood are pouring out of me. I just hope none of my major arteries were nicked.

"You stupid fucking bitch," he screams at me before punching me in the face. My body is exhausted and broken, my mind cloudy. I can't do anything but lie here for a minute and try to catch my breath. The taste of copper fills my mouth, and I wonder how much of my body is actually bleeding.

I see Tyler push himself up off me, and besides a few cuts on his hands and arms, he looks relatively unscathed, confirming my hunch that I took the brunt of our fall.

"You know, if you wanted cock so bad you didn't have to go to an old man to give it to you. I've got a perfectly good one right here." He grabs the crotch of his pants and makes a lewd gesture at me. A new rush of fear floods my body. Is this asshole going to rape me? I don't care if I die fighting. There's no way that's going to happen.

I scream, "Help! Somebody help me! Please!"

Tyler rushes toward the open front door, and I sigh in relief, sure he's going to leave now that I'm calling for help. Instead, he returns with a roll of duct tape in his hand. I scream louder, but he quickly covers my mouth with the tape, wrapping it around my head before tearing the piece off, rendering my screams ineffective. I'm freaking out in earnest now, afraid of what he's going to do to me. Why didn't I tell someone about his texts, about him showing up at the restaurant? I thought he was harmless. I was obviously wrong.

He bends down and places a kiss on where my lips would be if they weren't covered by the tape. "Don't worry, honey, I'll make it good for you."

I try to struggle up to my feet, but the room is swirling and tilting around me. Before I can make it upright, he's got me by the hair again and starts dragging me across the floor. I scream and kick out with both my legs, trying to dislodge his hold on me, but it's no use. So instead I grab for anything I can get my hands on. I feel my fingers close around something large and hard, and I feel a stinging down the center of my palm. I realize it's a piece of glass from the coffee table, and though my first instinct is to immediately release this thing that's hurting my hand, I desperately hang on.

All of my struggles have slowed his progress toward the bedrooms, so I take the opportunity to use all the strength I have left and twist my body around so that I'm facing him. I bring my hand up and plunge the piece of glass into his calf. He lets out a howl and tries to pull his leg away without letting go of me, but I manage to keep my grip. I twist the glass so that it goes in farther and opens up the gash. Hot blood spills over my hand and I pull down hard, dragging the glass shard through muscle and flesh before it's finally too slick with our combined blood and slips from my hand.

Tyler's face is purple with rage, and the last thing I see is the bottom of his shoe coming toward my face before everything goes dark.

TWENTY-FIVE

BIANCA

These stupid fucking shoes.

I won't lie. I love high heels. They make me feel sexy and powerful. I wear them every day to work even if I'm only working the front desk of the studio. But today, these shoes can suck it. Just as I was walking to my car after work my heel caught in a crack in the sidewalk, and I went crashing to the ground, skinning my knee. What was worse was the heel had broken off my favorite pair of Betsey Johnsons.

As I'm scanning the street for a parking space, I see Violet's car parked at the curb and smile. I can't believe that she and my dad thought I would be angry that they were dating. Is it a little weird? Of course. But it's not like I have any reason to be mad about it.

Sure, I was trying to push my parents back together, and maybe for a fleeting moment I thought it would be cool if my parents were together again, but I just wanted them both to be happy. I know my mom has dated quite a bit in the twenty years since they divorced, but I've never once seen my dad date. I was honestly a little worried he was still hung up on her. Well, it looks like Violet took care of that.

I'm not much of a romantic by any stretch of the imagination, but I do have spectacular taste in friends, and if Dad can find happiness with one of them, then more power to him. He honestly couldn't do better than Violet.

I finally find a spot several houses down and grab my destroyed shoes from where they've been sitting in the passenger seat.

I carefully navigate the sidewalk barefoot, keeping my eyes down so I can avoid any rocks, twigs, or in one case a line of ants on the way to do whatever ants do.

It's because I'm so focused on where I'm stepping that I don't notice the door to the house is wide open until I've almost reached it. I call out "hello" and stick my head inside, then let out a gasp. The living room looks like it was hit by the Tasmanian Devil. The chairs and end tables have been knocked over, their contents strewn across the room. But what really draws my eye is the coffee table that's shattered into pieces and is covered in blood.

Now that I've spotted it, I also see blood in other places, a small patch against the far wall, a few drops in the entryway, and most terrifying, a long trail to the hallway leading to the bedrooms. I can hear a man's voice coming from deep in the house, but I can't make out what he's saying.

If this was a few months ago, I would've rushed in and probably gotten myself killed. But Carson's been telling me I've been taking too many liberties with my safety, and I know he's right. There's a fine line between being brave and being stupid. What I'm looking at right now is something that I have no way of handling.

Suddenly, I remember Violet's car parked at the curb. Unless she went somewhere with someone else, she's in there. My heart catches in my throat and I freeze, not knowing what to do.

Crash.

The sound of glass breaking from deep in the house seems to snap me out of my indecision. I immediately drop the heels in my hand, along with my purse, and take off at a sprint across the lawn. I don't stop running until I make it to the door of the house next door.

It sounds like Oliver's got that obnoxious kids' station turned up to eleven, so I pound frantically on the door. "Carson! Carson, please open up! Carson!"

It feels like it's years before the door opens, but logically it was probably more like fifteen seconds. The door swings in and I'm filled with relief at the sight of his concerned face.

"Bianca, what's wrong? Are you hurt?" He starts moving his hands over my arms, presumably looking for injuries, but I shake him off.

I don't have time to catch my breath but manage to gasp out, "The door was open. Everything's broken. There's blood. So much blood. Please."

His face morphs from concern back to his serious cop face, and it starts to calm me. He pulls me inside.

"Please, you have to hurry," I beg. "I think Violet's in there."

"Fuck." He turns to the small safe he keeps by the door and punches in a code before pulling out his badge and a heavy looking black gun. I can't take my eyes off it. What if something goes wrong, and he accidentally hits Violet? What if the guy in there has a gun and Carson gets shot? I feel like I'm going to throw up.

He bends over slightly so that we're eye to eye, forcing me to look away from the gun in his hand. "Bianca, listen to me. I need you to stay here with Oliver. Lock all the doors and windows and take Oliver to the den in the middle of the house. Lock the front door behind me and don't open it for anyone but me, understand?"

I just nod my head and look out his window back toward my house. This is taking too long.

"Bianca, do not leave this house. I'll go get Violet."

"Please. You have to make sure she's okay. She has to be okay." I clutch his sleeve, but he just nods his head at me, then walks out the front door, moving towards my house as quickly as possible with his head swiveling back and forth, gun held low. I do as he's instructed and make sure all the doors and windows are secure. I'm tempted to sit and stare out the window to find out what's happening, but I know that if there's shooting, a window is a dangerous place to be. If something is wrong with Violet, Carson is the best chance I have of saving her, and he doesn't need to be worried about me doing something stupid. Plus, I need to find Oliver and make sure he's safe, away from the windows, and if possible, oblivious to the chaos that's happening next door.

I head toward his playroom and say a little prayer that maybe Violet isn't in the house after all.

TWENTY-SIX

DANTE

"Where is she?" I demand as Bianca paces back and forth in front of the intake station in the emergency room.

"She's somewhere back there." She waves her hand in the air to indicate all the rooms with doctors and nurses rushing around. "They won't tell me anything because I'm not family. Carson's back there somewhere too, but he hasn't bothered to come tell me what's going on," she says, obviously distressed.

"Who's Carson?"

"The police officer that lives next door." She stops her pacing and grabs my arm. "He saved her, Dad. At least I hope he saved her. No one will tell me if she's all right. But I caught a glimpse of her when they were loading her into the ambulance and she . . . it didn't look great." There are tears streaming down her face, and I realize I can't place the last time I saw Bianca cry. I thought I was worried before. Now I feel completely frantic.

From the second I got the phone call from Bianca telling me that Violet had been attacked and was headed to the hospital, it's felt like the floor was pulled out from under me. I just found her. I can't lose her. We haven't had enough time together. Forever wouldn't be long enough.

I move toward the nurse sitting behind the tall partition. "I need to see Violet Daniels, now!"

This doesn't seem to impress the nurse at all. "Like I told your friend there, I can't release any information or let you back there unless you're a family member."

I don't even have to think. "I'm her fiancé."

"Yeah, he totally is. They're getting married any day now."

I want to snap at Bianca that she's not helping, but I know her heart is in the right place.

The nurse eyes me like she's not sure I'm telling the truth, but in the end it looks like she figures letting me through is easier than arguing with me. She's not wrong.

"I'll buzz you in. Go all the way down the hallway and make a right at the end. She's in room 147. You can sit in the waiting area outside until the doctor comes to give you her status."

Without hesitation, I push through the door and can vaguely hear Bianca go right back to arguing with the stern gatekeeper. "You know that means she's about to be my stepmom. I should be able to see my stepmom." I don't have the capacity to think about *that* at the moment, so I just follow the instructions given to me until I'm standing outside Violet's room. The door is closed, and though I want to barge in, I take a seat like I was told so that the doctor can find me.

If I'm being completely honest with myself, I'm scared at what I'm going to find behind that door. I sit in the uncomfortable plastic chair, put my hands together and pray. I'm not sure I've prayed since I was a child, but if ever there was a time to start back up, it's now.

"Dante Moreno?" I look up expecting to find the doctor but instead, there's a man who looks vaguely familiar in front of me in slacks and a polo shirt, the front of which is covered in blood. "You'll have to excuse the appearance. I haven't had time to change."

I just nod my head and wonder who he is. "Sorry, I'm Detective Carson Turner. I live next door to Bianca and Violet."

I stand and shake his hand. So that's where I recognize him from. I decide not to remind him he caught me sitting in my truck outside the girls' house that one night if he doesn't already remember. "Bianca said you saved Violet. I can't thank you enough."

"I'm just glad that I was there, and Bianca had the where-withal to come get me instead of going in on her own." If the situation wasn't so serious, I would have laughed at that. It's something that Bianca absolutely would do.

I sit back down and he follows me, sitting in the chair across from my own. "Can you tell me what happened? I didn't get much out of Bianca. I only know that Violet got attacked at home."

He pulls out a little notepad from his back pocket and reads over what are presumably his notes. "It looks like the assailant was a Tyler Crosson. Do either you or Violet know him?"

It takes a second, but the name clicks. "Yeah, he is, well was, in one of her classes at school. She's known him for years. They went out on a couple dates a few months ago, but she ended it. She told me he was still texting her, but it was stupid stuff like asking her out to dinner when she'd already told him she wasn't interested."

"Actually, it looks like it was a bit more than that." He pulls out a plastic evidence bag holding Violet's phone and shows me a couple of texts. At first, all I can see are the specs of blood on the casing of the phone, but it isn't long before I'm concentrating on the words on the screen. Sure, there are the harmless texts that Violet was talking about, but they're interspersed with other, far more aggressive texts. They're calling her names, telling her she's a whore and a slut. Saying that she'll be sorry for leading him on.

"She never told me." My voice sounds strange to my own ears. Why wouldn't she tell me this?

"Don't beat yourself up. She probably thought it wasn't a big deal, that he would just go away. Most of the time, they do."

"But not this time," I whisper.

"No, not this time. We ran his name, and it turns out Violet isn't the only female that's caught his eye over the past few years. He already has two restraining orders taken out on him for stalking, and at least three other women have complained directly to the university. That's what I've found out in only the past hour. I wouldn't be surprised if we find out more. But it looks like Violet is the first one that he's actually attacked."

I don't want to ask the next question because I'm afraid of the answer, but I need to. "Did—did he rape her?"

Carson shakes his head. "No, I don't believe so. When I found them, she was passed out on the floor of her bedroom still fully clothed, and it looked like he was trying to wake her up. He wanted her to see what he was going to do."

I'm both relieved and sickened at how close she came to being violated by that monster. I put my head in my hands and take a deep breath.

"I have to tell you, Mr. Moreno, you've got a strong girl there. It looks like she took a piece of glass and slashed the hell out of his calf and Achilles tendon even though it tore up her hand pretty good. She really slowed him down with that. It gave her enough time for Bianca to come home and run to get me."

I thank him again, and he rises out of his chair, about to leave, when I stop him with one last question. "What happened to him?"

He shakes his head and gives a little shrug. "Once he saw me enter the room, he came running at me with a knife he'd brought with him, so I had to take the shot. He died on the way to the hospital. An officer will be by later to take a statement from Violet, but the whole thing's pretty cut and dry. And since the assailant is deceased, she won't have to go through a trial."

I let out a sigh of relief, and before I can thank him again, he's already headed back down the hallway.

I can't stop myself from imagining what happened in that house over and over again. What if we never had that fight? I could have been with her. What if I'd gone over there earlier? He wouldn't have had a chance to get at her. All the what-ifs won't leave me alone.

I don't know how long it is before I see a doctor go into Violet's room. I literally sit on the edge of my seat, waiting for him to come out and speak to me. Just when I'm about to say fuck it and barge in there, he exits and calls out "Violet Daniels?" I look around, and there's nobody else sitting in the hall, so I don't know why he's calling her name out like there's a bunch of us here.

I get up from the chair and rush over to him. "I'm Dante Moreno, her fiancé." Every time I say it, it feels right, and I swear that if she's okay, I'm going to make it true.

"I'm Dr. Prinz, the head of emergency medicine here." I shake his hand.

"Not that I'm not grateful, but doesn't the head of the ER not normally deal with many patients?"

"You're correct. However, I got a call from Archer Clarke who told me that if I didn't personally oversee this case, we could kiss his donation goodbye this year."

Bianca must have called Hollie and told her what happened, and Archer went into crisis mode. I've never been more thankful to have such a rich and powerful friend. I look at the doctor in front of me. He's about my age, which means he must be amazing at what he does if he's head of his department. But most notably, he doesn't look angry or annoyed at being bossed around by Archer, and I'm thankful for that. I need this man to do everything he can for Violet.

"Can you tell me what's happening? Is she going to be all right?"

"She's going to be fine, Mr. Moreno. In fact, despite a laundry list of injuries, there's surprisingly nothing too serious. When you see her, I want you to keep in mind that she looks much worse than she actually is." My heart seizes a little in my chest as he lists off her various injuries. "She's had some staples for a gash in the back of her head as well as a concussion we want to monitor. She has multiple cuts and abrasions on most of her body from what I understand was a glass coffee table, there are a few bruised ribs which we can't do much for but manage the pain, then there's the laceration across her palm . . ."

The list seems to go on and on. With each injury he lists off, I start to feel more and more physically ill. I can't believe he said there was nothing major wrong. She could have died. I'm wondering how bad it would be if I lost my lunch all over the scuffed linoleum floor when I hear, "—we're going to want to keep her another night or two to monitor the concussion and make sure the baby's all right."

My ears ring and I swear that my heart stops beating for just a moment. I bring my hand up to my chest, ready to punch myself to restart it when it kicks in at triple time. "Did you just say *baby*?"

He opens up Violet's chart and scans the pages again. He's taking his time like he doesn't realize my entire world is in his hands. "Yes, it looks like she's only a few weeks along. Four at the most. I've ordered an ultrasound to see if she's far enough along for us to get a gestational age."

"We didn't know." My voice comes out as a whisper. I don't even question if Violet knew or not. Even if she knew and didn't tell me, I would have been able to read it all over her face.

"I'm not surprised this early in the pregnancy."

"Did you tell her?" I ask, gesturing toward the door.

"No, we didn't talk about the baby. She was only awake for a minute or so before falling back asleep. The pain is taking a lot out of her, and we can only use minimal drugs to keep the fetus safe."

The fetus. We're going to have a baby. A baby that's half me and half Violet. I should be terrified. I didn't want another child, and even though I had resigned myself to opening up the possibility again if I wanted to be with Violet, I guess it hadn't really sunk in. I don't feel any of that trepidation anymore. All I feel is unadulterated joy. How I could be so happy standing alone in the middle of a hospital? It feels like my life is starting all over again, and I can't wait. But first, I need to see for myself that Violet is all right, and then I need to get her back.

"Will you let me tell her about the baby, Doc?"

He gives me a smile and pats me on the back. "Sure thing. Why don't you go in and see her? The nurses will be in to record her vitals soon, and I'll be back to check in with you in a few hours."

"I can't thank you enough for taking care of her."

"There's no need to thank me. Helping people is what I do. But if you wanted to do something, tell Archer Clarke to double that check he's planning on writing." He gives me a wink, and I make a mental note to tell Archer to triple it. "Just remember, it looks much worse than it is."

I slowly push the door open, being as quiet as possible. It's eerily still in the room except for the gentle hum and lights of machines.

Violet's always been small, but she looks downright tiny in the hospital bed. When I get close enough to see her clearly in the dim light, I almost fall to my knees. "She looks worse than she actually is," I repeat to myself. And thank fuck for that.

Her entire face is swollen and bruised with what looks like a split lip before it was closed up with stitches. Her right eye is so swollen I have no doubt that when she wakes up, she won't be able to see out of it, and her head is wrapped in gauze, presumably from the staples the doctor mentioned. This is only what's peeking out from the top of her hospital gown. I don't even want to think about what the rest of her looks like underneath. I sit down hard in the chair next to the bed.

"What did he do to you, baby?" I don't expect a reply and I don't receive one. I reach for her hand, but see that the one closest to me is bandaged heavily, so instead I move the chair around to the other side of the bed and gently take her free hand. My other hand gently rests on her flat abdomen and I wonder what she'll look like once she's round with our child. "I'm so, so sorry, baby. I love you both so much." Then I do something I haven't done in twenty years. I cry.

"Dante?" A small scratchy voice calls out my name, and I lift my head from where it had been lying on the bed next to her. My back cries out in protest, indicating that I've been here for quite some time. I was correct about her right eye. It's completely swollen shut. Her left eye is about half open, and what I can see of it is filled with tears.

"I'm right here, baby. I'm not going anywhere."

"I'm so sorry," she whispers.

"What are you talking about? I'm the one that should be sorry."

"No, I should have told you about Tyler. I didn't tell you how nasty he was getting. I didn't tell you that he confronted me when I was going to the bathroom when we went out for dinner. If I had just told you, none of this would've happened."

"No one could have foreseen this, Vi. There's no reason for you to be sorry. I'm just so happy you're okay."

"What happened?" she asks. I tell her the story I've pieced together between Bianca and Detective Turner. How Bianca showed up, knew something was wrong, and went and got him, so he rushed over to the house and saved her.

"What happened to him?" she asks. There's fear in her eye and in her voice. I don't know how she's going to react to the fact that he's dead, but she's going to find out eventually.

"He didn't make it. He attacked Detective Turner with a knife and was shot. He died in the ambulance on the way to the hospital." She's quiet after that, turning her head and closing her eyes. I let her have a few minutes to absorb the information before I ask, "Violet?"

"Does it make me a bad person that I don't feel sad that he's dead? I mean, shouldn't I not want him to die? He attacked me, but we used to be friends. I should feel bad, but I just feel happy instead. I'm glad I'll never have to see him again, and I'll never have to worry about him coming after me."

"There is nothing wrong with that, Violet." There's conviction in my voice. I need for her to believe me. "Of course you're happy he's gone. I'm only not happy because I want to kill him myself for laying a finger on you. I'm the one that's sorry. I should have been there."

She looks away from me again and it breaks my heart. "Thank you for coming to see me, but you really don't have to stay."

That sends me reeling. How could she think I would leave her here? I tighten my hold on her hand. "Why would you say that? Why would I leave?"

"You made it pretty clear the other night that we didn't mean anything to each other. In private you call me your girlfriend, but in the light of day, when I was getting called a side piece and your intentions were being questioned, you had nothing to say. That tells me how much you valued what we had."

"What we *have*, Violet. This isn't over between us. I'm so sorry things happened the way they did. I was taken by surprise with Bianca and Amanda showing up, and the truth is, I was scared. Scared about what would happen to your relationship with Bianca. Scared to let you know how much I need you. Scared that once our relationship was out in the open, people would make you realize that you're just wasting your life with an old man like me. You could do so much better.

"You were one hundred percent right when you said that I don't deserve you. I don't. But the problem is, now, I don't know how to do this without you. I was fine until you came along. I had my daughter and my company, then out of nowhere you came crashing into my life, and there's no way I can ever go back.

"You've filled up every hole in my life that I didn't even know existed. Just the thought that I might've lost you showed me I have to be brave and risk the pain I'll feel if you leave. None of that matters because you, Violet Daniels, are the love of my life. You're my first and last love and my best friend all rolled into one. I patiently waited thirty-nine years for you, and now that I have you, I'm not letting you go."

Tears are silently streaming down her face. "Is all of that true?"

"It's the truest thing I know, baby." I dig deep into the bottom of my pocket where the tiny jewelry box has been since I pulled it out of my safe deposit box earlier today. "In fact, the reason I didn't come over earlier today—" I choke on the words because I know if it wasn't for this, I would've been with her.

She gives me a small grimace that I take for a smile and nods her head at me, sensing I need her reassurance right now.

I clear my throat and continue, "It was because I was getting this out of my safe deposit box." I open the velvet jewelry box and show her the ring nestled inside. "I was coming over tonight to ask you to be my wife. This ring was my mother's. She left it to me when she passed away. If you don't like it, I'll get you a new one. If it's too soon for you, that's okay too. I'll wait until you're ready. The only thing I won't do is live without you."

She squeezes my hand three times, just like in that Taylor Swift song she loves. "I thought for years I was in love with you, but I was wrong."

My stomach clenches, and I hold my breath. She can't possibly be telling me she doesn't love me after I poured my heart out to her.

"How I felt for you then is nothing compared to what I feel for you now. I love you so much. I love you more than I thought it was possible to love another person. Hell, you've taught me what love truly is. I didn't learn that from my parents like I should have. I learned it from you. How you treat me, how you make me feel. I want to be with you."

I breathe out a sigh of relief.

"But I also want you to put that away for right now." She pulls her hand from mine and reaches out, closing the box I've been holding in my hand. "I'm not saying no. In fact, if anything, I'm saying soon. Just . . . not right now when I'm in the hospital and we're just making up from our first real fight."

Am I disappointed? Sure. Am I willing to wait until she's ready? I'd wait until the day I die for her. Plus, she said soon. I'll take it for now. I put the ring back in my pocket and retake her hand in mine. I need to tell her about the baby before some doctor or nurse slips up and tells her before I can, but right now doesn't seem like the best time.

I get up out of my chair and lean over her, barely brushing my lips against her bruised and battered ones so I don't hurt her. Patient. I can be patient.

TWENTY-SEVEN

VIOLET

You'd think that I'd be used to being overlooked by my parents by now, but I'm still a little surprised when, hours later, they still haven't come to see me in the hospital. They live twenty minutes away. It's not exactly a long trek. I can tell that Dante's fuming, but he won't talk to me about it. I know he's been trying to get ahold of both my mom and my dad all day and night, but the furthest he's gotten is leaving a message with my dad's secretary.

My body is radiating a constant, aching pain that's making me a little sick to my stomach. Whatever meds they're giving me don't seem to help a whole lot. Dante told me I was going to need to stay overnight as a precaution because of my head injury, which is just fine with me. I'm not particularly fond of hospitals, but the thought of pulling myself up and walking around holds no appeal, especially with the deep pain emanating from my ribs with every breath.

It's not long before we're moved to a private room upstairs that looks more like a hotel suite than a hospital room. I mean, my parents are wealthy, but I've never seen something like this. I look at Dante questioningly, and he just gives me a smile.

"Archer," he says.

Ah, I should've known. I'll have to thank him.

Bianca arrives with overnight bags for both Dante and me. The second she sets eyes on me, she bursts into tears, which honestly freaks me the hell out. I've never seen Bianca cry. Not once in the four years I've known her. She rushes to the bed and grabs my left hand, since the right is bandaged tightly.

"I'm so sorry, Violet. I should've gotten there sooner."

"What are you talking about? You saved my life, B. If you hadn't come home and gotten Detective Turner . . ." I trail off not wanting to think about all the things Tyler would've done to me. Dante gets up from the chair he's been sitting in and places a gentle kiss on the very top of my head.

"I just keep thinking that if I left work earlier or something, I could've prevented this."

"If you'd left work early, he would've attacked you too. You can't think like that."

"I just love you so much. I don't know what I'd do if something happened to you."

I'm being told an awful lot how much people love me today and it's . . . nice. Especially considering I never heard it growing up.

We chat for a little while, but when my eyes start to droop, Dante ushers her out of the room with promises that she can come back and visit tomorrow.

He sifts through the bags and pulls out the copy of *Persuasion* he gave me—could that have been only yesterday?—and I left at his house when I fled.

"Rest, baby." He gingerly smooths my tangled hair away from my face.

"You won't leave me, will you?" My voice is small and tired to my ears.

"Never." He settles into the chair next to my bed and reads to me. It's not long before his voice, combined with the familiar story, lulls me to sleep.

I wake up several times during the night to find Dante passed out with his head lying on the edge of my bed, one of his hands grasping mine, and the book lying open next to him.

The morning is a blur of people constantly entering and exiting the room. There are doctors and nurses rushing around. Bianca, Hollie, and Archer come to visit, which gives me a chance to thank him for pulling strings at the hospital, which he just shrugs off. Underneath that grumpy exterior, he really is a kind man, and I'm happy that he has Hollie. I'm even visited by a police officer that needed to take my statement.

Reliving yesterday's events is the last thing I want to do, but I know it's better to get it over with so that I can put this whole thing behind me and start living my life again. A life that's now going to include Dante, decidedly *not* on a casual basis. I keep it together through the interview and manage not to cry. Dante holding my hand and stroking my wrist with his thumb to distract me from my feelings seems to help.

Between all the visitors and my constant drifting in and out of sleep, it's not long before the day has faded into early evening and Dr. Prinz stops by to look at my chart.

"How are you feeling tonight, Violet?" he asks while shining a penlight in my eyes that makes me want to punch him in the face. The bright light causes a searing pain to shoot through my head.

"Honestly, I was better before you shined that bright light directly into my brain."

"I'm sure." He chuckles, jotting down a note. "Anything else?"

"The pain has gone down some, but my ribs and the back of my head still hurt quite a bit. Oh, and this morning I was feeling pretty nauseous, but it seems to have gone away now. I figure it was probably from whatever pain medication I'm on."

"I see," he says with an odd inflection in his voice. "Mr. Moreno, could I have a word with you in private?" If I was feeling like myself, I would've objected to this wholeheartedly. I don't like to be left out of things, especially when they are obviously going to be talking about me. But since I won't be jumping out of bed and following them out into the hallway, I lie here and wait patiently for their return.

About five minutes later, the door opens and Dante comes in, sans Dr. Prinz. He looks nervous, which in turn makes me nervous.

"What was all that about? What's wrong?" I ask, feeling a mild panic rise inside me. What if there's something else wrong that they didn't see at first? I could be internally bleeding or something. My mind starts to spin out with the possibilities.

He comes over to the bed and takes my hand. "Sweetheart, I need to tell you—"

"Oh my God, Violet! You look awful!" My mother's shrill voice bounces off the walls as she comes bursting in dressed like she's going to a cocktail party instead of visiting her daughter in the hospital.

"I'm all right, Mother," I say softly, trying to bring the general volume of the room down to tolerable levels.

"Have they called the plastic surgeon about your face?" she asks while leaning over to get a better look at me. "This simply won't do."

Should it surprise me that my mother is more worried about how my face looks than my actual well-being? Probably. But it doesn't. Vivian Daniels has always been consistent in her priorities.

"Where's Dad?" I ask, looking behind her.

"Oh, he's on a business trip, but he sends his love." Sure he does. He cares so much he couldn't even pick up the phone to call me himself.

Up until this point, Dante has stood off to the side, letting me take the lead with my mother. Now, as if sensing my distress, he moves back over to my bed and places a hand on my shoulder.

My mother clocks his movement and familiarity instantly. "And you would be?" she asks with a sneer.

"Dante Moreno, ma'am. I'm Bianca's dad. We met at the graduation party." He stretches his hand out to her, but instead of taking it, she merely turns from him back to me.

"What is he doing here?" For a woman who runs in the upper-crust circles of Seattle society, you'd think she'd have some manners.

I reach up to where Dante's hand rests on my shoulder and grip it. I want to present a united front while also drawing from his incredible strength.

"Actually, Mother, Dante is my boyfriend."

She's quiet, staring back and forth between the two of us, then settles on our clasped hands. "Boyfriend?!" she finally shrieks. "How can he be your boyfriend? He is very obviously a man."

"Actually, he's my soon-to-be fiancé."

Dante silently squeezes my hand three times, letting me know he loves me and supports me. That he's ready to step in if he needs to, but for once, I don't need anyone to tell me how to stand up for myself. He's already taught me how to do that.

"Violet Daniels, you will cut out this nonsense right now. I knew it was a mistake to let you remain at that school. I told your father we should have cut you off and forced you to take your place in society where you belong."

"No, Mother. I won't cut it out. Dante and I are in love, and we're going to be getting married." I realize that I sound very much like a petulant child but it's all true.

"But he's twice your age and . . . *a laborer*." She stage whispers that last part with disgust in her voice.

"Mother, you will not be rude to the man that I love. I neither want nor need your support. While, I would like it if you and Dad could spend some time getting to know him, if you don't want to do that, well then it's your loss. I was never going to be the perfect little copy of you that you always wanted. I never wanted to marry a rich man and float from party to party. That's you, but it's not me. I'd like for you to be in my life because you're my mother and I really do love you. But don't mistake my wanting you to be in my life for me needing you to be."

She looks absolutely aghast. I wish I had my phone on me so I could take a picture of the expression on her face. Her eyes are as wide as saucers, and her mouth is hanging open. The pale skin of her face, that she's always so careful to keep out of the sun, is slowly turning an angry shade of red.

"You think you can do everything on your own, Violet? Fine. Then that's it. No more paying for your school, no more car. And don't you dare come crawling to me when that one"—she points a bony finger at Dante, who just raises his eyebrow at her—"decides to leave you high and dry. You'll be nothing."

"No, Mom. I'll be something. I just won't be what you want," I say softly, sadness filling me that things have to be this way.

She turns on her heel and stomps out of the room. She tries to slam the door behind her, but it's one of those slow close doors, and I know that *really* pisses her off. Slamming doors is probably her second favorite pastime, only after drinking martinis.

"Are you okay?"

I look over at Dante and can see the concern written all over his face. "I will be. Those were things that needed to be said a long time ago." I let out a sigh. "When I get out of here, I'm having so much wine. I mean seriously, like bottles of the stuff."

"Um, about that . . ." He trails off. He looks like he's searching for something to say and is rubbing the back of his neck nervously.

"What did the doctor want, anyway? Did he say I can't have alcohol or something? Is it something with my liver?" My analytical mind has kicked in and I'm trying to figure out what the doctor could have told him.

"Well, you can't have wine for a while at least." He sits back down in the chair next to me and gently strokes my hair. I know I look like something out of a horror film with my face bloody, swollen, and bruised, but he keeps his eyes steadily on mine. "There's a reason you were feeling nauseous this morning, and they didn't just want to keep you overnight to watch for your head injury."

"Just tell me what, wrong. Please!" I'm panicking now. What have they been hiding from me?

"You're pregnant, sweetheart. We're going to have a baby."

My mind instantly goes blank, and my hands unconsciously move to my abdomen as I wrap my arms around myself.

"They told me yesterday when you were admitted, and I wanted to be the one to tell you." I'm pregnant? How is that possible? Then I have a thought that terrifies me.

"Oh my God, is it okay? Did Tyler hurt my baby?"

"Shhh, no, no. The baby's fine. They just wanted to keep an eye on the both of you for an extra day or two. It seems the one thing we can be grateful for is that Tyler somehow didn't hit the baby."

I think I'm in shock. "How far along?"

"Just a couple of weeks, maybe a month at the most. They want to do an ultrasound before you leave to see if they can get a gestational age."

I feel like I'm having an out-of-body experience. I'm pregnant. With Dante's baby. I'm going to be a mom. I don't know how this is possible.

"Dante, I swear to you I wasn't lying. I was on birth control. I took it every day. I promise I didn't lie."

"I know you didn't lie, baby. You're not the type of woman who would do something like that. No birth control is one hundred percent effective."

"But you didn't want this," I say miserably. Then a thought hits me. "You knew I was pregnant. That's why you came in here telling me how much you love me. That's why you proposed, isn't it? You're trying to do the right thing, just like you did with Amanda."

I watch as the emotions play on his face, concern, surprise, offense, and finally sadness. "I know it's my fault you think that. If I'd just come clean to you about my feelings earlier, you wouldn't think that of me."

"But you told me you didn't want any more kids. You said you were done building a family. I don't want you to be with me out of obligation."

"I told you that before we were together, when I didn't think I wanted to start all over again with a baby. If I'd known I could have a child that was made of the two of us, I never would've said that, but back then, it didn't seem possible."

All those declarations of love, then that surprise proposal. It has to be because he knew I was pregnant, right? Then again, he was coming over to talk before everything went to hell yesterday. I just don't know what to believe. I'm tired, sore, and overwhelmed.

"Do you still have the necklace?" I don't need to ask him what necklace he's talking about.

"Check the clothes I had on yesterday. I know I was wearing it." I motion to the bag of my belongings that the EMTs brought in with me. He sifts through my torn and blooded dress and tights before pulling the shiny silver necklace out from the bottom of the bag. I heave a sigh of relief. I wasn't sure what had happened to it in the melee.

He places the necklace in the palm of my hand, but I'm not sure what he wants me to do with it.

"You never figured out that the book opens, did you?"

I frown at him. What's he talking about? I've worn this necklace almost every day for months and months. I touch it. I fiddle with it. If it opened, I would know.

"Yeah, I didn't think so," he says with a soft smile.

He comes around and gently sets himself on the edge of the bed, careful not to jostle me and cause me pain. "The second I gave it to you, I thought I'd made a terrible mistake. It was impulsive, but I thought it could be a little secret that just I knew about, and it would make me feel the tiniest bit closer to you when you could never be mine."

I'm so confused. I don't know what secret he's talking about, so I just let him continue.

"Every time I saw you after that, I worried you were going to call me out. That my feelings had been revealed and you were disgusted by me, but you never did. I watched you wear it day in and day out, the symbol of my love for you, and it twisted me up inside that it was the closest I'd ever get to sharing my true feelings with you."

"Dante, I don't know what you're talking about," I whisper.

He reaches for the necklace in my hand, taking the charm between his fingers, and shows me the metal fore edge. "There's a little secret latch right here."

He hands me back the charm, and I scrutinize it with my good eye. There is the tiniest slit between the silver cover and pages. If I had noticed it, I would've just thought it was a flaw in the pouring process of the metal. The slit is so small I can barely press my fingernail into it. As I slide it along the seam, I can feel it bump against something that almost immediately gives way and the cover of the book pops open, causing me to gasp.

Etched in miniature print on the inside cover and on the first page is a quote I immediately recognize.

"You pierce my soul. I am half agony, half hope."

I look up at him, speechless. How could this have been here the entire time, and I never knew?

"When you told me *Persuasion* was your favorite book all those years ago, what you didn't know is that I went out and bought it the next day. I've read it again and again to be close to you.

MADE TO BE YOURS

"When you think that me telling you I'm in love with you and want to marry you is too fast and only because of the baby, you're wrong. I've loved you for a long, long time. Probably longer than I've even admitted to myself yet. I can't wait to start this new life and family with you."

He really loves me. He's loved me for a long time. He admitted to me yesterday that he was scared. Well, I was scared too. I thought this was too sudden on his part. There was no way he could've fallen in love with me and wanted to marry me so quickly. I didn't trust his feelings, but I should have.

"Ask me again," I say confidently.

"What?" He looks confused at my sudden change of subject.

I look him straight in the eye, nod my head and say, "Ask me again."

Realization dawns on his face, and he reaches into his overnight bag, pulling out the jewelry box again. He gets down on one knee, making me laugh, which sets off the pain in my ribs but I couldn't care less right now.

"Violet Daniels, my one true love. You're everything I ever wanted and didn't know I needed. You bring a light to my life that never existed before. Will you please let me spend every day for the rest of my life showing you just how amazing you are by becoming my wife?"

"Absolutely."

He lets out a little whoop and jumps up. Or rather, pulls himself up. He's not as young as he used to be, I think to myself with a smile. He takes my hand and gently slides the ring onto my ring finger. His mother had great taste. There's a large marquise-cut diamond surrounded on both sides by clusters of three smaller round-cut diamonds all set into a gold band.

"I know it's old-fashioned, but I can get you something different."

"Don't you dare, Dante Moreno," I say, clutching the ring to my chest. "I love it, and because it was your mom's, it makes it even more special. We can give it to our daughter someday." I gently stroke my stomach. It's relatively flat now and I'm trying to imagine how it will look in several months when I'll be showing.

"Oh God, we can't have a daughter. Do you really want another Bianca?" he teases. I love Bianca, but the girl is wild and stubborn as a mule.

"Well, maybe a boy wouldn't be so bad," I say with a laugh.

Lying here in this hospital bed, my body battered and broken, I've never felt so overjoyed. I didn't fall in love with Dante Moreno in an instant. It was a series of moments over the years. With each one, he collected little pieces of my heart until he was the holder of all of it, and I know he'll keep those pieces safe for the rest of my life.

EPILOGUE

VIOLET

We're not getting our wish for a baby boy. We're also not getting a baby girl. No, we're getting both. Let me just say, when birth control fails, it fails spectacularly.

Thank God I'm doing this with Dante, who's as cool as a cucumber, because I am freaking the hell out. Every time the hormones overtake me and I cry about how I'm not going to be able to do it, that I'm going to be a horrible mother, he just holds me and lets me cry while whispering encouragements in my ear.

While I'm thrilled, he seems even more excited about the prospect of twins than I am. As soon as the doctor gave us the news, Dante went out and started buying two of everything. Cribs, car seats, strollers, highchairs. Everything. They're starting to overtake the house. He's been working on the nursery nonstop the past two weeks, and he hasn't let me in to look at it yet. It's taken all my willpower not to peek when he isn't around.

I spend most of my days working in our home office for Moreno Construction. With everything that happened with Tyler coming to light, especially the fact that three separate girls had complained to the University and they'd done nothing, the school was more than happy to let me withdraw without penalty. They said when I was ready to come back, they'd have a place for me.

I'm not sure that will ever happen with the twins coming. Besides, I'm quite happy working with my husband. School had always been a placeholder for me until I found something that I wanted to do, and I know I've found it.

Dante and I were married three months to the day from when I was released from the hospital. He told me I could have any type of wedding that I wanted. He was even willing to hold off until after the twins were born, but the frown on his face when he said that just made me laugh. In the end, I opted for a small, intimate ceremony with just our closest family and friends in our backyard.

It was like a fairy tale with all the lights strung up and lanterns hanging everywhere. Bianca made sure flowers were overflowing from every surface. Even Jake, Adrian, and a few of the other guys pitched in and built a gazebo for us to use as a kind of altar. And no, my parents weren't there. Dante encouraged me to reach out to them, so I sent them an invitation, but when we received no response I wasn't surprised.

I've resigned myself that they aren't going to be a part of my life, and somehow finally accepting that has made me feel freer than I've been in years.

I squirm in our large king-size bed, trying to get comfortable, but the eight-month twin baby belly is no joke.

"You okay, baby?" a sleepy voice says behind me.

"Yeah, I just can't get comfortable, as usual." I feel him scooch closer behind me until the front of his body presses against my back. I immediately feel his hard cock poking my buttocks, which causes my legs to clench together and my pussy to flood in anticipation.

I thought I was hot for Dante before. It's nothing compared to what the pregnancy hormones have done to me.

"Good morning," he says while nuzzling that spot on my neck that he knows drives me crazy.

"It'll be a much better morning if you put that thing inside me."

He lets out a chuckle and doesn't stop rubbing his day-old beard growth against the sensitive skin of my neck. "Is my girl feeling needy this morning?" He cups my breast with his hand and I cry out. Not only have my breasts grown the past few months, much to my delight, but they're also incredibly sensitive. One night he played with them for so long I had an orgasm with no other kind of stimulation. I didn't even know that was possible.

"Yes, I need you." I gasp.

His other hand glides over my belly, and he stops to give it a little affectionate rub. That's one more thing to add to the long list of things I love about Dante. He always takes the time to show the babies affection, even before they're born.

Once he's done with my stomach, his hand continues down until it reaches the apex of my thighs. I let out a moan and lift my right leg, sliding it back over his own, to allow him better access.

"You're drenched. Is all this for me?"

"Always," I groan.

"That's right, this belongs to me." I can feel his hips shift behind me and suddenly the head of his cock is at my entrance. I try to move my hips back to take him in, but he holds me steady. "Be a good girl and let me take care of you."

He slowly enters me from behind, inch my agonizing inch. By the time he's fully seated inside me, I'm desperate for him to move.

"Please. I need you," I beg.

"Your wish is my command." He retreats slowly out of my tight pussy until just the head of his cock is left inside me before gliding back in. His slow, purposeful strokes continue, heating me from the inside out. I beg him for more, and when he finally starts moving faster, he releases my hip so that I can join him in his movements.

I can feel his cock start to swell inside me, and I know he's close, but never one to let me finish second, his hand goes to my clit, sweeping from side to side. I'm moaning uncontrollably now, my hips moving in a wild motion without any rhyme or reason. I can't think of anything except his hard, hot cock inside me and my need to come. At last, he pinches my clit tightly between his thumb and forefinger, and I'm catapulted into my orgasm.

My pulsing pussy is enough to milk out his own orgasm. He shouts my name and buries himself deep inside me as he fills me with his cum.

We're both gasping for air by the time it's over and I relish the afterglow, lying in his arms.

"I love you," he whispers in my ear, and I smile.

It's the same thing he tells me every morning and every night. He says it's because he wants to be the last thing I think of when I fall asleep and the first thing I think about when I wake up. I don't bother telling him he would be those things even without the constant declarations of love.

"I love you, too, more than anything."

THANK YOU FOR READING MADE TO BE YOURS!

Do you want to see what else Violet and Dante are up to? Download the Extended Epilogue by visiting www.eveste rlingbooks.com

Check out Bianca and Carson's story, *Protecting What's Yours*, available on Amazon.

Interested in Hollie and Archer's romance? You can find *Unprofessionally Yours* on Amazon today.

Thank You!

I hope you enjoyed reading Violet and Dante's story as much as I enjoyed writing it. If you enjoyed this book, please take a moment to leave a review. As an independent author, nothing helps us more than your reviews. I can't tell you how much I would appreciate it.

Sign-up for my newsletter at evesterlingbooks.com to be the first to know about new releases and bobus content!

ALL ABOUT EVE

Eve Sterling was born and raised in the Los Angeles area where she now resides after a brief detour to the San Francisco Bay Area. After climbing the corporate ladder for many years, she decided to take a break and pursue her lifelong passion for writing. When Eve is not coming up with more book ideas than she could possibly ever write she enjoys reading, binge watching shows with friends, and hanging out with her two dogs.

Contact me on social media!
Facebook: www.facebook.com/evesterlingbooks
Instagram: www.instagram.com/evesterlingbooks
TikTok: @Evesterlingbooks
Twitter: twitter.com/evesterlingbook
Website: www.evesterlingbooks.com
Email: evesterlingauthor@gmail.com

Printed in Great Britain
by Amazon

24451239R00199